Finally a Family

For two young women, keeping their babies a secret meant becoming single mothers. But when they were suddenly confronted with their past loves, was it time to reveal the truth?

We're proud to present

SILHOUETTE SPOTLIGHT

a second chance to enjoy two bestselling novels by favourite authors every month— they're back by popular demand!

September 2004
Finally a Family
featuring
A Dad for Billie by Susan Mallery
Finally a Father by Marilyn Pappano

October 2004
The Millionaire Affair
featuring
Mystery Man by Diana Palmer
Mandy Meets a Millionaire by Tracy Sinclair

November 2004
A Passionate Pursuit
featuring
The Girl Next Door by Trisha Alexander
Hesitant Husband by Jackie Merritt

Finally a Family

Susan Mallery
Marilyn Pappano

> **DID YOU PURCHASE THIS BOOK WITHOUT A COVER?**
> If you did, you should be aware it is **stolen property** as it was
> reported *unsold and destroyed* by a retailer. Neither the author nor
> the publisher has received any payment for this book.

All the characters in this book have no existence outside the imagination of the author, and have no relation whatsoever to anyone bearing the same name or names. They are not even distantly inspired by any individual known or unknown to the author, and all the incidents are pure invention.

All Rights Reserved including the right of reproduction in whole or in part in any form. This edition is published by arrangement with Harlequin Enterprises II B.V. The text of this publication or any part thereof may not be reproduced or transmitted in any form or by any means, electronic or mechanical, including photocopying, recording, storage in an information retrieval system, or otherwise, without the written permission of the publisher.

This book is sold subject to the condition that it shall not, by way of trade or otherwise, be lent, resold, hired out or otherwise circulated without the prior consent of the publisher in any form of binding or cover other than that in which it is published and without a similar condition including this condition being imposed on the subsequent purchaser.

Silhouette and Colophon are registered trademarks of Harlequin Books S.A., used under licence.

*First published in Great Britain 2004
Silhouette Books, Eton House, 18-24 Paradise Road,
Richmond, Surrey TW9 1SR*

FINALLY A FAMILY © Harlequin Books S.A. 2004

The publisher acknowledges the copyright holders of the individual works as follows:

A Dad for Billie © Susan W Macias 1993
Finally a Father © Marilyn Pappano 1994

ISBN 0 373 04967 6

64-0904

*Printed and bound in Spain
by Litografia Rosés S.A., Barcelona*

A Dad for Billie
SUSAN MALLERY

SUSAN MALLERY

has always been an incurable romantic. Growing up, she spent long hours weaving complicated fantasies about dashing heroes and witty heroines. She was shocked to discover not everyone carried around this sort of magical world. Taking a chance, she gave up a promising career in accounting to devote herself to writing romances full-time. She lives in Southern California with her husband—'the most wonderful man in the world. You can ask my critique group.'

To Terry, with love and thanks. Your accepting nature has taught me to be more understanding of those around me—including myself. Your self-belief has convinced me that in addition to being my strongest critic, I must also be my own best fan. Your determination to succeed reminds me to keep striving for my own goals. They say that while we can't choose our family, we can choose our friends. This time, dear friend, I chose well.

Chapter One

Crash!

Adam Barrington glanced up as a softball flew through his window, arced in a perfect half circle across the room, then *thunked* onto the center of his desk. As it rolled over the loose papers and spread sheets, he put out his left hand. The ball dropped off the side of the desk and directly into his palm.

Except for the tinkle of falling shards of glass, the room was silent. Adam leaned back in his chair and waited.

It didn't take long. About thirty seconds later a small face appeared at the broken window. A red baseball cap hid the child's hair and shadowed the eyes.

"You caught my ball."

"You broke my window." He rose to his feet and approached the mess.

"Yeah. I see." The kid glanced at the remaining bits of glass and the other intact panes. "What if I tell you it wasn't my fault?"

"Was it?"

There was a heavy sigh. "Probably. I mean I'm not playing catch with anyone, so I can't say someone else threw it. This window costs a lot. More than my allowance for a month, I bet." Another sigh. "My mom's gonna kill me for sure."

Adam fought back a grin. "Wait there. I'll be right out and we can discuss reimbursement."

The child slumped visibly. "It's never good when adults say *discuss,* then a big word you can't understand."

He chuckled as he walked through the hall and out the front door. The kid stood on the wide expanse of lawn beside the window and stared glumly at the shattered pane. At first Adam had assumed he was a boy, but as the child turned and pulled off the baseball cap, he saw "he" was a "she."

Short dark hair clung to her head; bangs, mangled by the cap, stuck out in uneven spikes. Wide and somber brown eyes watched him like a prisoner waiting for execution. Shorts and a grubby T-shirt covered a sturdy tanned body. She was somewhere between six and ten, he guessed. He'd never had much experience estimating children's ages.

"It looks bad," the girl said. "I'll pay for it, I swear. And even if you don't believe me, my mom will make sure. She's big on me assuming the 'proper responsibility.'" The last two words came out in a stern falsetto.

"I can't say I blame her, if you go around breaking people's windows."

"Well, I don't." The girl planted her hands on her hips.

"You broke mine."

"It was an accident."

"Somehow you strike me as the kind of child who has a lot of accidents."

Her lower lip thrust out mutinously. "I do not!" The lip curled up. "Okay. Some. A few. But not *lots.*"

For the second time in as many minutes, Adam had to fight the urge to grin. "What's your name?"

"Billie."

"I'm Adam." He thrust out his hand. They shook solemnly. He gave her the softball. "I haven't seen you before, Billie. Are you from the neighborhood?"

"No. San Francisco. We just moved here. It's a long drive. How come you don't talk funny? I mean, you kinda do, but not like that lady in the store. But she was nice. She gave me candy."

Billie pulled a half-eaten sugar stick out of her shorts pocket. After picking off a loose thread, she stuck it into her mouth.

"Well?" she asked, after a moment.

"This is South Carolina, Billie. As far as we're concerned, you're the one who talks funny."

"I do not!" She gave the candy a last lick, then thrust it back into her pocket. "Can we play catch until my mom comes out? She'll want to apologize for my reptile behavior. Are you mad? We'll be neighbors. I don't want you to hate me or anything. I'm basically a good kid." She grinned, an impish light dancing in her wide brown eyes. "At least that's what my mom says when she doesn't know I'm listening. Do you have any kids? Mom didn't know if there were any on the street. I prefer boys. Mom says she's glad I'm a girl, but I don't know if it's so great. Have you ever had to wear a dress and then keep *clean?* Yuk." She pulled the baseball cap over her head.

Adam blinked several times. He didn't know where to begin. Reptile behavior? It seemed easier to focus on the obvious. "Neighbors?"

She pointed to the house next door. The Southwick place. "We're moving in. The furniture's not here yet, so we might have to camp out—on the floor."

He glanced over his shoulder at the house in question. The two-story structure, a smaller version of his own home, stood where it had for eighty years. In the last couple of months the old tenants had moved out and a string of workmen had taken over. The outside had been painted, the inside as well. Carpeting had been replaced and an electrician had fixed several old circuits. It hadn't been sold, that he knew. The only real estate office in town used his bank, as did the local escrow company. New tenants, he told himself. Another family. He didn't mind. It's not as if he'd for a moment thought Jane might move back. Her parents had retired to Galveston and she had—

He frowned as he realized he didn't know what she'd done. But it didn't matter. They'd been old news for a long time.

"Are you ready?" Billie asked.

"Ready for what?"

"To play catch. Mom'll be right out. She's trying to figure out what furniture goes where. If it ever gets here. I won't throw hard."

She tossed the ball with an easy underhand.

He caught it instinctively and threw it back. "Young lady, you do not have to worry about throwing too hard for me."

"I don't know. I'm the pitcher on my softball team. I have a mean curve ball."

Adam glanced at the broken window. "That I believe. How many wild pitches last year?"

She wrinkled her nose. "We won our division."

"How many?"

"I don't remember."

"Let me guess. Not some or a few, but a lot?"

She laughed. The sound reminded him of something, but before he could place it, she threw the ball, harder this time. "Yeah, a lot. Coach says I'll develop more accuracy as I mature."

"I hope that's soon. I have a lot of windows."

Billie tugged the cap over her eyes, and bent in a crouch.

"Here she is, ladies and gentlemen, the National League's first female pitcher. Not only has she pitched a record six shutouts in a row, but her batting average is close to five hundred." She cupped her hands over her mouth and breathed heavily to sound like background crowd noise. "She's pitching to her favorite catcher, a champion in his own right, Mr. Adam—" She paused and looked expectant.

"Barrington. Adam Barrington."

"Adam Barrington, one of the old-timers. He can still catch a mean curve ball."

"I'm honored," he said dryly.

She wound up and threw. The curve ball started out steadily enough, then lost its speed and direction. He lunged to the right, but it rolled past him and into the bushes.

"I gotta work on that curve," she said.

"Try the backyard."

"Why?"

With a flick of his wrist, he sent the ball toward her. "There's a screen of bushes and trees between you and my windows."

She wrinkled her nose. "I don't usually—"

"Bil-lie."

The woman's call came from the house next door. Adam stiffened. That voice. It couldn't be. He glanced at Billie.

"Moms." She shrugged. "They always know when you're having fun. Over here," she yelled. "Next door."

"Billie, there you are. We need to go into town and use the phone."

He turned slowly. The woman came around the hedge and stopped dead when she saw him. Her gaze darted between him and the child. Twilight had fallen upon the steamy South Carolina day, turning bright sky dark, softening the light. Sweat beaded on his brow and coated his back, but she looked as fresh and inviting as a Carolina sunrise. A loose flowing skirt and pale blouse hid all but the general outline of her body. Hair, true brown without a hint of red, had been pulled away from her face into a braid. Her bangs hung low, almost to her lashes.

From this distance he couldn't see her eyes, but he knew the color—hazel. Brown and green and gold. Wide and slightly tipped at the corners. He glanced back at Billie, still holding the softball. A band squeezed his chest, making it tough to breathe.

"Hello, Adam," the woman said quietly, slowly moving past the hedge and onto the lawn. "I see you've met my daughter."

Her daughter? The band tightened. He dropped his gaze to her left hand. No ring. So she'd married and divorced. He wasn't surprised.

Billie frowned at her. "How'd you know his name?"

"I grew up in this house, honey. I told you that."

Billie looked at him. "You lived next door to my mom?"

He couldn't speak. Slowly his gaze was drawn back to the woman. A longing swept over him. Hard and powerful, it crashed through his body, the need like an undertow pulling him down. But on its heels burned a rage so hot, the longing evaporated into mist and blew away. His hands tightened into fists at his sides. How dare she come back?

The depth of feeling startled him. He forced himself to take a deep breath, then release it slowly. It had been over for years, he reminded himself. His body relaxed; the fists uncurled. He felt nothing. That had been his choice then; it still was.

Emotions flickered across Adam's face. They passed so quickly, Jane didn't have time to label them. No doubt he was as stunned as she. Despite her expectations—*she* had known she was moving back to Orchard—this wasn't the meeting she'd planned.

"Hello, Jane."

How calmly he spoke, she thought, wondering if he could hear the pounding of her heart. His momentary loss of control had been squashed; she stared at the handsome but unreadable face of Orchard, South Carolina's leading citizen. Adam Barrington, bank president, favored son and brother.

He hadn't changed much. Still a hair over six feet, still lean yet strong, still sophisticated. Even in twill shorts and a T-shirt, he looked like an ad for a men's magazine. The caption would read something along the lines of "The Executive at Home." But in this picture there was no happy family. She'd asked. He hadn't married.

He continued to look at her, seeing she could only guess what. But she couldn't read *him*. Was he angry? He had every right to be. Her mind screamed at her to turn and run back to the safety of her house. It would only be a temporary solution; they were neighbors. The truth would come out eventually. Small Southern towns were notoriously bad at keeping secrets. For now she was safe. If he'd known, if he'd suspected—even Adam Barrington wouldn't have been able to stay that controlled.

On the long drive from San Francisco to South Carolina via southern Texas, she'd had many opportunities to plan the right thing to say when they met for the first time in years. Perhaps a casual conversation at the bank when she opened her account or an accidental meeting picking up the Saturday morning papers on fresh-cut green lawns. In every scenario, she'd imagined herself as detached, distant but friendly and well-groomed. Hot, wrinkled and frazzled didn't fit the picture at all!

"It's been a long time," she said, forcing herself to smile and walk those last few feet until she stood directly in front of him. She thought about offering her hand, but that seemed too strange. And as for a welcoming hug—he didn't look all that welcoming.

"How many years?" he asked.

"Nine," she said immediately, then cursed herself for her rapid response. He would probably think she'd counted the days. That she'd missed him and regretted her impulsiveness. She had, dammit, but he didn't need to know.

"So you guys were friends?" Billie asked, her head moving back and forth as she watched them intently. "Like you played baseball together?"

Jane forced herself to look away from Adam's mesmerizing gaze. Those brown eyes had always had a power over her, she thought as she brushed her damp palms against her skirt. Tall oak trees shielded them from the main road and the curious stares of neighbors. Word of her return had already begun to spread. At least no one would witness this awkward reunion.

"We dated," she admitted.

Billie paused, then continued to toss the ball in the air and catch it. "Oh." Her disappointment was obvious. At eight, her daughter had yet to find boys interesting for anything other than beating in sports.

"Briefly," Adam added.

He called two years brief?

"What happened?" Billie asked.

"Your mother went away."

Again the words were spoken with no emotion. He was telling a story that didn't matter to him anymore. If it ever had. The abridged version of life with Jane and Adam. Short, sweet, and while missing the point completely, it did convey the basic facts if not the mood of the whole event. A finality. It had been over for a long time.

"You're moving back?" he asked.

"That's the plan." She smiled brightly, not daring to meet his eyes. God knows what he would read there. The pocket on his T-shirt became fascinating. "My parents have settled down in Galveston, and the tenants living in the house here decided not to renew their lease. I, ah, there was a job opening at the junior high, so here we are."

"You're a teacher?"

"English!" Billie made a gagging noise. "The worst.

You should see the books she's always trying to get me to read."

"You only like stories with blood and killing. That's not literature or even suited for children. There are lots of classics that—" She stopped and shrugged. "It's an old argument."

"Who's winning?" Adam asked.

Jane smiled at her daughter and pulled on the bill of her cap. "She is, but I'm determined to hang in there."

"You never told me you wanted to be a teacher."

She searched his face. The familiar lines, high cheekbones, strong, square jaw, hadn't changed much. He'd been a man when she'd left. He would find differences in her though: the last time he'd seen her, she'd only been a girl. Legally a woman, but at heart, emotionally, still very young. Time had changed her, both inside and out.

"I did. Several times. You didn't listen."

The lines of the jaw she'd been admiring tightened with her words. Fire flashed in his brown eyes. A wavy lock of hair fell over his forehead, the only wayward thing about him. "I listened. You were the one who—"

He stopped and looked at Billie. Her daughter stood openmouthed.

"Who what?" Billie asked.

He shook his head, withdrawing from the heated conversation. "It doesn't matter. The repairmen have been fixing up the house for weeks. I'm sure you'll be pleased with their work."

Who what? Jane asked silently, repeating her daughter's question. Left? She'd admit to that. Left badly? Ditto. To understand why, he might do well to look to himself.

"Everything looks terrific," she said. Billie tossed her the softball. She caught it, then threw it back. "The upstairs bathrooms have been remodeled."

"That was a couple of years ago," he said.

Part of her marveled at the surface calm of their conversation. She wanted him to say something, do something, not just stand there like a polite acquaintance. He would have gone on with his life, might even have forgiven her, but forgotten—no way. Neither of them had. So he would pretend it didn't matter, and she would pretend not to feel guilty. A fair exchange, she thought. Except for one small eight-year-old problem.

"It's been great to see you, Adam," she said, ready to make her escape. "Billie and I have to get to town. It's late and the furniture company swore they'd be delivering today. If they're not, we have to make other arrangements."

He glanced at his watch. "The office will be closed."

"The headquarters are on the West Coast. They'll still be open."

"Uhh, Mom?" Billie stared at the ground and shuffled her feet. That didn't signal good news.

"What have you lost, forgotten or broken now?"

"A window."

Jane thought about the small amount of money they had to last them the summer. She wouldn't start teaching until September and her first paycheck wasn't due until almost the end of that month. Please, God, let the window be a small one, she thought as she turned to face her house. Maybe they could board it up for a few months. If it was on the side that faced Adam's yard, all the better.

"Where?"

"There."

But Billie wasn't pointing in their yard. Instead her small tanned arm thrust up toward the front of Adam's house.

"No," Jane said. "Not—"

"Yup. I was playing ball and it got away from me."

She glanced at Adam. He was studying her with that damned inscrutable expression of his. "All those times I ignored my mother when she told me to act like a lady are being paid back in spades. Sorry."

"No harm done," he said. "Except for the glass, of course."

"Of course." Was he making a joke? The great Adam Barrington risking humor? That wasn't fair, she reminded herself. He'd always been witty and charming. She'd been the one out of her element.

"It's over here." Billie walked ahead of them, past the front porch and stepped close to the bed of flowers in front of the freshly painted white mansion.

"Don't step on the...roses," she called as her daughter planted a tennis shoe squarely on a peach-colored blossom.

"Tell me those aren't still Charlene's favorites," she murmured half to herself.

"They are." Adam kept pace with her, stopping at her side when they reached the scene of the crime.

"See," Billie said, almost proudly. "It would have been a perfect pitch."

"Yeah. All that's missing is the batter, the catcher, a few other players and the umpire." Jane glanced up at Adam. He looked down at her. If she hadn't been so tired and out of sorts, she might have thought there was a smile tugging at the corner of his mouth, that the straight line didn't look quite as straight as it had a minute ago.

"It's just this one pane." Billie jumped up and pointed. Her landing crushed the rest of the rosebush. "Ow. It scratched me."

"Self-defense on the part of the plant. Let me see." Jane bent down and brushed the skin. "You'll live."

"I'm bleeding," Billie said with a whine in her voice.

"One drop. You won't miss it. Besides, you killed that rose."

Billie stepped onto the grass and stared at the squashed bush. "Oh. Sorry." She grabbed a stem, careful to hold it between thorns, and tried to straighten the broken plant. The stalk drooped to the ground. Crushed petals littered the soil. "It's a goner."

Jane rose and looked at Adam. "I mean this in the nicest possible way, but tell me that Charlene is dead. Because if she isn't, I'm about to be."

This time he did smile. The slow curve revealed perfect white teeth. Her heart fluttered madly against her ribs. She'd forgotten about his smile and how it made her feel that swooning was a lost art form.

"Charlene is alive and well," he said, his eyes crinkling in the corners. "She'll be out for blood when she finds out about this. You know how she feels about her roses."

"There's already been blood." Billie marched up to them and pointed at her leg. "You guys are adults. I'm a kid. You're supposed to get worried when kids bleed. And what about infection? You're always making me wash my hands."

A single drop rolled down and stained her sock.

"All right, let's deal with the medical emergency." Adam crouched down and pulled a handkerchief out of his pocket. He moistened the corner and blotted the tiny puncture. "It's stopped bleeding. You should be able to keep the leg."

"Good." Billie held on to his shoulder for balance. "It's going to be hard enough making the major leagues as a girl. With only one leg, I'd never have a chance." She glanced at the sky. "It's getting dark, Mom. Where are we spending the night?"

"In town. Come on, honey, I've got to go call the furniture company. Adam, I—"

His smile had faded and in its place was the distant coolness of a stranger. For a minute or two he'd forgotten, as she had. It had been like the old days, before she'd left town. Before she'd done the unforgivable.

She would apologize. Not now. It was too soon and she didn't want an audience, not even her daughter. Later, perhaps after he'd had time to digest the fact that they were going to be neighbors. In his present mood he'd deny there was anything to discuss, maybe even refuse to listen to her. If only he'd admit he felt something. Anger, hurt, regret. She'd carried her burden of guilt around for so long, she felt weary and overwhelmed by the weight. Even if he hated her, it would be a start.

"I'll get you the money for the window and the rosebush. My purse is in the house. I really do have to make that phone call. May I bring it by tomorrow?"

"Use mine," he said, staring at something over her head. He'd stuffed his hands into his pockets, as if to keep her from seeing the tight fists. But the outline of his knuckles pressed against the twill material of his shorts. Below, the muscles of his tanned thighs bulged against the skin. He still jogged; she could tell from the lean, powerful silhouette of his legs.

"Your what?"

"Phone, Mom. Geez." Billie stuffed her softball into her oversize pocket.

"I couldn't. It's long-distance."

"Of course you could," he said. "It'll save you the drive into town."

"It's only a mile."

She didn't want to go into that house. Too many memories waited there. It had been bad enough next door, but at least all the old furniture was gone and the walls had been painted and repapered. In Adam's house, things would be the same. Already the sun was setting and the scent of night-blooming jasmine filled the air. If she closed her eyes, she would be able to remember everything. She kept her eyes open.

"You're very kind," she said at last, because there was nothing else to say without admitting the truth. She'd come home for a number of reasons. The fact that the past stood in the way of most of them was something she'd have to get over. "After I make my call, we'll talk about the window."

"I picked out a bedroom that overlooks your house, Adam," Billie said, fishing her ball out of her pocket and starting toward the front door. "Maybe we could set up walkie-talkies, you know, like a secret club." She glanced at her mother. "No girls allowed."

When Billie threw the ball to him, he half turned as if he was going to toss it to Jane next. He caught himself and returned the pitch to Billie.

Jane thought about pointing out to Billie that she *was* a girl, but knew better. "Honey, I don't think Adam is interested in your 'boys only' club. He has a business to run and a life that doesn't have room for your wild ideas. And you're a little young to be calling him by his first name."

"He said I could."

"I said she could."

They spoke together.

Jane stared at the tall man and the short little girl. Their feet braced against the thick grass. Fists pressed into hips in identical stances of defiance. Billie had turned her cap backward so that the bill stuck out behind her and the band mashed her bangs against her forehead. Wide brown eyes, the color of thick mud—the color of Adam's—stared back at her.

Like father, like daughter.

He hadn't guessed. She'd have to tell him...eventually. But what was she going to say? It had been almost nine years since she'd left Orchard and Adam. Nine years in which they'd never spoken or corresponded. The control she'd always hated had been polished to perfection. He'd barely shown a flicker of emotion when she'd walked up to him. But that was about to change. She was done hiding. As soon as they were settled and she was sure the time was right, she'd share her guilty secret: he was Billie's father.

Chapter Two

"Fine." Jane raised her hands in defeat. "If Adam doesn't mind, then call him what you want." She glanced at him. "I'm giving you fair warning, when Billie decides she likes someone, his life ceases to be his own."

Adam looked down at the young girl standing next to him. He shouldn't indulge her on general principle; she was her mother's daughter. But he couldn't find it in himself to turn away from her engaging grin.

"All right!" Billie said, holding up her free hand. "Gimme five."

He hit her palm with his own, then walked up the stairs onto the porch. "The phone is this way."

"Wow! A swing! I've never seen one like that." Billie dashed across the porch to the old-fashioned swing hanging from the rafters. The worn chains groaned in protest when she threw herself on the seat. One forceful push against the wooden floor set the seat in motion. "This is totally cool. Mom, can we get one?"

"Maybe in a few months."

"Come try it."

"I've been on a swing before." Jane stared at the ground, looking at neither Billie nor Adam.

He understood her reluctance. The anger threatened again, slicing and hacking at his wall of self-control. That swing. That damn swing. He should have taken it down years ago. From the corner of his eye, he saw Jane glance at him. The quick darting look, the worry darkening her eyes and drawing the color from her skin, pleased him. If she hadn't—

But she had. And he'd stopped caring a long time ago.

"This way," he said, holding open the front door. Jane walked past him. A subtle fragrance licked against him. Elegant, yet welcoming, it left the taste of longing on his tongue. He wasn't as immune as he'd like to be, but he would never let on.

Billie slid off the swing and followed. "Can I come over and use it?"

"Sure. Anytime."

"Great." She stepped into the foyer and whistled. "This is some place. Wow! Stairs! Can I slide down the banister?"

She darted across the hall. Jane moved after her. By the time she reached Billie, the girl had one foot on the first stair.

"No you don't," she said, holding her firmly by the arm. "No playing on banisters, no softballs in the house. You know the rules." She plucked the ball from her daughter's hand and tossed him an apologetic smile. "We grow them wild out West."

"I think I can handle it." He stuffed his hands into his pockets. "How about lemonade and chocolate cake?"

Billie shrugged out of her mother's grasp and walked sedately to his side. "I'm always hungry."

"Why doesn't that surprise me?" He motioned to the

study. "The phone's in there. On the desk. We'll be in the kitchen. You still remember where that is, don't you?"

"Yes." She glanced at her daughter. "Don't get into trouble."

"Who me?" Billie looked up at him. "She's always doing that. Telling me to stay out of trouble."

Jane moved into his office. The last rays of sun filtered through the lace curtains on the windows beside the front door and caught the thick braid hanging down her back. The tail, tied in a peach-colored ribbon, ended several inches below her shoulder blades. He knew from experience that her hair, when loosed and brushed smooth, would tumble clear to her waist. Satin, he remembered. Living satin, all warm and sweet smelling. It could drive a man out of his mind.

The hand still in his pocket clenched tighter. The iron control he prided himself on kept him from groaning aloud or following her to touch the thick braid to see if it was as he remembered.

"So how long have you lived in this house?" Billie asked.

"What?" He forced himself to turn away from Jane and glance down at her daughter. "Oh, all my life." He led the way through the foyer and down a long wide hallway toward the kitchen.

"We've moved a lot. Mom says the first year I was born, we lived in a house, but I don't remember that. It's always been apartments. I like having other kids to play with, but I really need a yard. The landlord used to get mad when I practiced pitching in the hallway. It rains a lot in San Francisco. Does it rain here? Is it always this hot? Hey, you've got some old pictures here. Do you know people this old?"

She stopped in front of a display of antique photographs hanging over a narrow writing desk. Adam retraced his steps until he stood behind her. "They're of my family. We've lived in Orchard since the early 1800s."

"Who's he?" She pointed at a small grainy photo of a man in uniform.

"My great-great—I can never remember exactly how many greats—grandfather. He was a major during the war."

"The war?"

He touched the frame, then took her hand and led her down the rest of the hall and into the kitchen. "The War of Northern Aggression."

"I never heard of it." She paused in the middle of the room. "This is big. You've got two stoves. Is one broken?"

"No. My parents used to do a lot of entertaining. Why don't you sit here." He pulled out a stool next to the long center island, then lifted her up.

"Where are your parents now?"

He took a glass from the cupboard beside the double sink and set it in front of her. "They died."

"I'm sorry." Billie removed her cap and brushed her bangs flat. "Does it make you sad?"

"It was a long time ago."

"I had a friend at school. His mom died and he cried a lot. I told him he could share mine, but it didn't help. At least he still has his dad."

"I was a little older than your friend when I lost my parents," he said as he uncovered the cake and reached for a knife. "Nineteen. And I have a brother and sister."

"Older or younger?"

"Both younger."

"I wanted a brother, but Mom said it wasn't a good time." She turned on the stool and grinned when it spun. "Do you have kids?"

"No."

"A wife?"

He sliced off a generous piece of chocolate cake and slid it onto a plate. "No. Eat your cake."

She wrinkled her nose. "That's a grown-up way to say stop asking questions, huh?"

"Yes." He winked.

She giggled and dug in. "Mmm. This is great." A crumb fell off her fork and onto her chest. She tried to brush it away and succeeded in smearing a dark streak down her T-shirt.

He poured them each a drink, then pulled up another stool and watched her eat. There were flashes of Jane in her. The shape of her eyes, the gift of humor. But the rest of her personality had to come from her father. Jane had been sweet as a child, but never outgoing.

What had happened? he wondered. Billie hadn't mentioned anything about her father, although he knew it usually took two to produce a baby. It seemed odd that there wasn't a man around to take care of this little girl.

"Did you stop and visit with your grandparents on the way out?" he asked.

"Uh-huh. Texas. They live next to the water." She took a drink of lemonade. "It's nice there. I like the beach. Where are your brother and sister?"

"Dani lives in Atlanta. She's married and has a little girl about four years younger than you. Ty has a construction company in the next town."

"Dani's a girl, right? Short for Daniella?"

He nodded.

Billie licked a dab of icing off the corner of her mouth. "Mom knows her. I think they were friends a long time ago. Is there a tree house in the backyard? She talked about that on the drive out. My mom went to school here and everything."

"I know." So Jane had mentioned his sister but not him? No surprise in that. After the last time he saw her—

He forced away the memory, refused to acknowledge the coldness that had swept over him or the overpowering scent of flowers and burning candles.

"There's icing." She pointed to the chocolate ribbon left on her plate. "Want to split it?"

"You go ahead."

"Okay." She swept her finger across the gooey confection, then stuck it in her mouth. "Yummy."

It seemed easier to concentrate on Billie and ignore the past. He didn't believe in thinking about things that couldn't be changed. Choices had been made a long time ago. It didn't matter anymore.

"What are those for?" She pointed to the copper pots hanging on the far wall.

"Cooking."

"I've never seen pans that color before."

"Adam, who are you entertaining in the kitchen? I declare, you'll give our family a bad name."

Charlene Belle Standing, of *the* Carolina Standings as she referred to her family, swept into the kitchen. A bright purple caftan fell in soft folds to the floor. Several bracelets jingled on each wrist. Her hair, still a bright shade of red, had been twisted into an old-fashioned chignon. She was close to sixty, looked forty and acted like she was twenty-five. Or fifteen.

"My, my. And you are?"

Adam rose to his feet. "Charlene, this is Billie. Billie, my favorite aunt, Miss Charlene Standing."

Her blue eyes snapped at him. "I'm your only aunt, Adam. If I'm not your favorite, then I've been doing something terribly wrong." She moved closer to Billie and stopped on the far side of the island. Diamond rings on three fingers of each hand gleamed in the overhead light. "Child, you look so familiar, but we haven't met. I would have remembered."

For the first time since he'd met her, Billie was tongue-tied. She stared at the older woman.

"She's Jane's daughter. You remember Jane Southwick? She lived next door."

Charlene raised one arched brow. "I see. That explains it. You have your mother's eyes. A different color perhaps, but the shape's the same. Pretty eyes, I always thought."

He waited for her to make a comment on his introduction, to call him on his choice of descriptions for Jane. He could have said she was his old girlfriend, or at least a friend of the family.

"Is your hair really that color?" Billie blurted out at last.

"Obviously your tact must come from the other side of the family. Jane was always the most well-mannered child."

Billie grinned, undaunted. "I'm more trouble than I'm worth, but she loves me, anyway."

Charlene moved around the island until she was standing next to Billie's stool. She leaned close and took the girl's face in her hands.

"I was raised by wolves, you know," Charlene said.

"Really?" Billie's eyes widened to the size of saucers.

"When I was three, they stole me and kept me in the woods."

"Charlene," Adam said, his voice heavy with warning.

"Hush. I'm bonding with the child. That's what people do these days." She smiled. "You understand, don't you, Billie?"

"Sure."

Charlene kissed her cheek. "We are going to be great friends."

"Okay. Do you play baseball?"

"No, but I love the young men in their uniforms, and I bet heavily on our local team."

He fought the beginnings of a headache. "Charlene, don't start anything here. Remember what happened the last time Dani brought her kids? You taught her six-year-old to play poker. Dani was unamused and I suspect Jane will feel the same way."

"He's a sweet boy," Charlene said to Billie as she sat

on Adam's vacant stool. "But a worrier. It comes from raising his younger siblings."

"What are siblings?"

"Brothers and sisters. Adam went to Harvard."

"I've been to Texas."

"There are Standings in Dallas, I believe. They run cattle or oil. I can't keep them straight." She slipped off several of her bracelets and spread them on the island. "Do you like any of these, Billie? They're pretty, don't you think?"

"I guess."

Billie cast him a worried glance. He knew she wouldn't want to offend her new friend, but was less enthused about the jewelry than she wanted to let on. Now if Charlene had opened a box of baseball trading cards he was sure that would have been another story.

"Adam, I got through to the moving company. They won't be able—" Jane walked into the kitchen. Her gaze moved past him to the gaudily dressed woman next to her daughter. "Charlene?"

"Jane!"

His aunt stood up and held open her arms. Jane flew into her embrace. "Charlene, I've missed you so much."

"It's your own fault for leaving, child." The tears in her eyes and the catch in her voice took away the sting of the words.

Adam stood awkwardly on the fringe of the reunion. Charlene and Jane had always been close; of course they'd be happy to see each other. It didn't matter to *him*. He didn't feel anything, not even regret.

"Have you met Billie?" Jane brushed her cheeks.

"I have met your daughter. There's a lot of her father in her, isn't there?"

Jane stiffened slightly. "Some," she said cautiously.

Adam wondered if that meant she didn't like her ex-husband. Stupid question, he told himself. If she still liked the guy, they'd be together. Unless he'd left her. He wanted to ask what had happened, why she was alone. But he couldn't. Questions like that might make her think he was interested.

"Charlene told me she was raised by wolves," Billie announced.

Jane stared at her friend. "You didn't."

"It's the truth. As God is my witness."

Jane looked over her shoulder at Adam and rolled her eyes. "I can't believe she's still using that old line. You'd think after all this time she could be more creative."

Adam was tempted to smile back at her, to share the memory. His control instinct wouldn't let him. They had nothing left to share. Her grin quivered, then faded altogether. She turned back, hunching her shoulders against an invisible weight.

"What did the furniture company have to say?" he asked.

"The truck broke down in Nevada and won't be here until Monday."

"Monday," Charlene said. "You mean you're in that big house next door without a stick of furniture?"

"We brought a few things with us," Jane said.

"Not beds. Not food." Billie swiveled on her stool. "Can we stay in a hotel with cable this time, Mom? I hate these channels with nothing good on. Do you know that in one place they didn't have the sports channel?"

"You're not going to a hotel," Charlene said. "There are plenty of extra rooms right here."

Adam glared at his aunt. "I'm sure they'd be more comfortable in a place of their own."

"He's right. We wouldn't want to impose." Jane spoke without facing him.

"Why?" Billie asked. "I like Adam and he likes us. Charlene can teach me to play poker."

"Poker?" Jane stared at Charlene who was suddenly interested in slipping her bracelets back on. "Charlene, you can't teach a child—"

"I never said that. It was Adam. He's always accusing me of things that aren't true. I might be a little unconventional—"

"A little," Adam growled. "The town eccentric is more like it."

"That's not fair. Orchard is a backwater town. It's not my fault if I've had more experiences than the average local citizen."

"Experiences? Is that what you call it when you get on the CB and invite truckers to stop by and sample your—"

"Adam!" Charlene stood and straightened to her full height. She was barely over five feet. He wasn't the least bit intimidated. "There are children present."

"Just me," Billie said.

"Why don't you wait on the lawn?" Jane handed her daughter the softball.

"But I wanna listen. You *always* send me out when it gets good."

"When you're a grown-up, you can send your children from the room. It's one of the privileges of adulthood. Now scoot."

Billie pulled on her cap, then left the room. Her footsteps dragged audibly on the bare wood floor.

"I'm leaving," she yelled from the foyer. "I'll be outside. Alone. In the dark."

"Have fun," Jane called. "And stay away from the windows."

"Don't tell me," Charlene said.

"Yup. We're here five minutes and she's already broken one."

"Definitely takes after her father." Charlene smiled.

"What does that mean?" Jane asked quickly.

She put her arm around Jane's shoulders. "Only that you

never broke windows when you were a girl. You were always too much of a lady.''

Jane opened her mouth, as if she was going to protest, then shook her head. "I give up. It's late, we drove almost five hundred miles today. I adore you." She kissed Charlene's cheek. "But I can't make heads or tails of anything right now. Do not, under any circumstances, teach my daughter to play poker. Adam." She gave him a weary smile. "Thanks for the use of your phone. I'll get you the money for the window and the—" she glanced at Charlene "—the other thing tomorrow."

The overhead light cast shadows on her face and darkened the rings under her eyes. Lines of fatigue deepened the hollows of her cheeks. A few strands of hair had escaped from the braid. One wisp drifted near the corner of her mouth. He fought the urge to brush it away, to reach out and feel the silky smoothness of her skin. The anger was well under control, but the want— He'd always known it was the most dangerous emotion.

"I insist you stay here," Charlene said. "And Adam agrees with me."

Jane was looking at him. The need to punish her—hurt her as he had been hurt—boiled up inside. His silence would be telling enough. She would know he didn't want her here. But he wouldn't risk letting her think she still mattered. Better to let her stay.

"That's what neighbors do here," he said. "You'll have a whole wing to yourselves."

"I don't want to impose." Two bright spots of color stained her cheeks.

"No imposition." Even to his own ears his voice sounded strained. "Sally comes in five days a week. She always keeps the guest rooms ready."

"But—"

"No buts." Charlene linked her arm through Jane's. "It's all arranged. Let's go get that darling daughter of yours and collect your suitcases. I see you've kept your hair long. I like it. Maybe we can go to the salon together and you can get a trim. I hate to criticize, dear, but Billie's hair is quite atrocious. You might want to have a little talk with her about the merits of acting like a lady…''

Their voices faded as they walked toward the front door. Adam forced himself to relax. Jane and Billie would only be here for a couple of nights. It was a big house; they could easily avoid each other. And if they didn't—

He shrugged. *He* didn't have a problem with Jane Southwick now or ever. Nine years ago she'd shown him the truth about relationships in general and theirs in particular. Loving someone meant being left. He'd learned his lesson well. He'd offered his heart to a young woman once and she'd returned it broken and bleeding. That part of him was safely locked away, and no ghost from the past was going to find the key.

"You haven't told him, have you?"

Jane glanced around the cheerful guest room, but there was nowhere to hide. She finished putting out Billie's nightgown, then checked to make sure the door to the bathroom was tightly closed. The sounds of her daughter's off-key singing and the splashing of water against the side of the tub continued uninterrupted. All the activity was supposed to give her time to compose herself. It wasn't working.

"You know," Jane said, glancing up at her friend.

"How could I not?" Charlene stepped over to the bed and sat on the corner. "The eyes, her personality, the way she stands. A blind man could see it."

The hard lump in her stomach doubled in size. Jane felt herself grow pale.

"I meant that as an expression, dear," the older woman said hastily. "Nothing more."

"Good. Because Adam—"

"Men don't look for things like that." Charlene took her

hand and tugged, forcing Jane to sit on the bedspread, next to her. "Start from the beginning."

Jane folded her hands in her lap. "I've made a mess of everything."

"That sounds the tiniest bit exaggerated."

"I left here nine years ago, had Adam's baby and never told him." She paused and drew in a breath. "Now I'm back and I've brought home his child. What would you call it?"

"Fine Southern drama." Charlene's blue eyes glittered with suppressed laughter. She sobered quickly. "Sorry, dear. I understand your concern, but you are back, and you're going to tell him about Billie, and everything will be fine."

Jane twisted her fingers together. "I'm not going to tell him."

"What?"

"I mean, I am, but not just yet."

The lump grew again, pressing against her ribs and making it difficult to breathe. Dear God, she prayed, then paused. What to ask for? Forgiveness? She could use a strong dose of that. Common sense? That went without saying. Show me the right thing for my daughter, she thought. But would God listen? Would anyone? After what she'd done?

No one had told her guilt tasted so empty. That the hollowness would linger on her tongue, as though the emptiness was too much for her heart to bear, and the excess would seep out into her body, stealing joy and promise.

Charlene touched her arm. "Then why are you here if not to tell Adam about his daughter?"

"I am. I will. I thought—" She squeezed her eyes shut, but that didn't block out the past. "I thought it would be so easy. I'd show up, tell Adam I was sorry and he'd forgive me. Then I'd introduce Billie and we'd live as neighbors. Like a TV sitcom." She paused, feeling overwhelmed.

"I've been a fool. It's not going to be like that. It can't be. I should never have come."

"If your furniture is being delivered Monday, then it's a little late for second thoughts."

Despite herself, Jane smiled. "Always practical. And this from a woman who still claims to be raised by wolves."

Charlene straightened. "I *was* raised by wolves."

"You got lost in the woods for a day. The family dog was with you. That's hardly being raised by wolves."

A smile twitched at one corner of Charlene's mouth. "Dogs are related to wolves. And you're avoiding the real issue."

"I know."

Jane rose and walked to the window of the guest room. The sultry night air drifted past the curtains, carried lazily by a sleepy breeze. Familiar fragrances brought back memories. Jasmine for evenings, flower blossoms for day. The scents clung to her skin, a sticky residue from the humidity. So different from the life she had built, yet so right.

"I'm proud of what I've accomplished," she said, leaning on the window frame. "It was tough at first, financially, I mean. Billie was a good baby, but any infant is expensive."

The evening noises began, the screeching and chirps sounding like an orchestra being tuned.

"I couldn't go back to college until Billie started school three years ago," she continued. "But I never gave up the dream of teaching. I got my credential a couple of months ago. My parents offered me their house here, then I got the job at Orchard Junior High. It seemed like a sign. And a chance."

"To let Billie meet her father?"

Jane touched the lace curtains. Behind her, Charlene waited silently.

"Yes," she admitted at last. "It's what Billie wants more than anything. A father. But I hadn't counted on what it would be like coming here, seeing him, the house, knowing that I'd never escape. I owe her, I owe them both. And all I want to do is turn around and run back to San Francisco."

"What does this have to do with telling or not telling Adam?"

She released the curtain and turned to face the older woman. "I don't want to compound my mistakes. If I tell him and he's not interested in being a father, she'll be hurt worse than before."

Charlene frowned. "You can't hide the truth forever. This is Orchard, dear. Small Southern towns are notoriously bad at keeping secrets."

"I know, and I'll tell him. In my own time. But first, I want to know he wants her. I want to be sure that he won't punish *her* for the mistakes I've made."

"We don't always have the luxury of time."

"I know. I'm so afraid."

"Because you've kept him from his daughter for eight years?"

The dart hit home. She crossed her arms over her chest. "I didn't feel like I had any other choice at the time."

"You could have come home. Adam would have taken care of you."

"I didn't want that. I'd always been the quiet one, the obedient child." She tucked her hands in her pocket. "Adam was always ready to guide me. To tell me what was right for me, whether I wanted the information or not. I was afraid of him—of us." She shrugged. "I ran. Foolishly. And when I couldn't run anymore, I stopped. Only to find out I was pregnant."

"You could have come back then."

Jane remembered the cool fog of her first San Francisco morning. It had taken her almost a month to make her way across the country. As her stomach had churned with the lingering effects of nausea, and the tears left cold trails down her cheeks, she'd imagined going home. She'd humiliated Adam in the most devastating way possible, but if she told him about the baby, he would have taken her back.

For several hours, she'd stood staring out at the ocean. Her fear of going home, of giving up like her mother, had been greater than her fear of going forward. She'd left Orchard to prove to herself she had the strength to make it on her own. Returning at the first sign of trouble would have meant losing forever.

"My pride wouldn't let me come back," she said.

"Pride makes a cold bedfellow."

So Charlene wasn't going to accept the half truth. "I wasn't sure I mattered to him," she said softly, confessing the most painful secret of all. "I didn't want to be an obligation."

"He loved you."

"Did he?" She stared over her friend's head at a landscape hanging above the bed. The warm colors—the reds and yellows of the flowers, the mossy green of the trees—blended perfectly with the wallpaper. "Or did he know I'd be easily trained? A perfect banker's wife. Quiet, malleable, well mannered. Sometimes I thought he had a list that he checked whenever he met a woman. I was the most suitable."

"It wasn't that way." The older woman frowned. "You make him sound unfeeling. Adam is a passionate man."

Jane dropped her gaze to the hardwood floor. "I suppose with Billie as proof, I'd be silly to deny that." But her memories blurred about that night and the others like it. She'd been so young—too young. And too much in love. "I would have given him my soul. He was more interested in a hostess."

Charlene shook her head. "You're remembering him with the eyes of a child. Perhaps Adam had offered you *his* soul and you didn't notice."

"I loved him. I would have noticed."

Charlene watched her closely. The wrinkles around her

eyes and mouth had been formed by smiles rather than displeasure. Heavy makeup and the brightly colored hair couldn't disguise her softhearted nature. "Tell me about Billie."

Jane chuckled. "I'd like to tell you I've done a fine job with her, but I can't take the credit. Billie is...Billie."

"Her father's daughter?"

"Sometimes," she admitted, remembering the first time her child had looked at her with Adam's defiant gaze. The pain had been unexpected but she welcomed the connection with the man she had once loved. "I see him in her eyes." She moved to the bed and resumed her seat. "But Billie is so full of life and Adam—he's not *anything*. It's as if I'm an old acquaintance who has shown up for a weekend visit."

"What did you expect?"

Jane glanced down at Charlene's hands clasped in her lap. A few more age spots marred the pale skin, some wrinkles bunched at the knuckles, but other than that, these were the hands she remembered from her youth. The shiny rings glittered, the bracelets tinkled and rattled.

"I thought he'd hate me," she said at last, voicing the fear that had dogged her since leaving the West Coast.

"For nine years? Everyone has to let go sometime. Change. You did. Perhaps he did as well."

"He never married."

"That's true." Charlene glanced at her. "But he has been involved with several women. Adam is many things, but not a saint. Or a martyr. He didn't wait for you, Jane. That I am sure of."

"I know."

The lie sat heavily on her tongue. Logically, she *knew* he hadn't, but there had been a tiny piece inside her heart, the spot where dreams hid. Every year Charlene had sent a letter in her Christmas card to Jane's mother. Every year there had been no mention of Adam marrying. It didn't mean anything, she told herself, even as she dared to wonder if it did.

"You'll want me to keep quiet for now?" Charlene asked, smoothing a hand over her hair.

"I just need a little time."

"Don't take too long. He'll figure it out on his own, and if he doesn't, someone from town will. Better for him and Billie if he hears it from you."

Jane again fought the guilt that filled her with empty sadness. "There's a lot at stake. I could lose Billie."

"Never that." The older woman smiled. "She'll always be your daughter. And there's so much you could gain. Adam—"

"Mo-om, I'm shriveling up in here," Billie called from the bathroom.

"I'm coming." She picked up the nightgown and walked into the bathroom. "All clean?"

"I'm a prune."

Billie stepped out of the tub and into the fluffy towel Jane held for her. She wrapped the terry cloth around her child's body and began to rub. The scent of soap and freshly cleaned little girl tickled her nose.

"I love you, honey," she said, giving her a squeeze.

Billie eyed her suspiciously. "I heard you talking to someone. You aren't planning anything awful, are you? Not like those singing lessons?"

"No singing lessons," she promised.

"Good. Then I love you, too."

"Little girls shouldn't barter their affection. May I come in?" Charlene hovered outside the door.

"Sure." Billie brushed her bangs out of her eyes. "I wasn't bartering, I was checking. She always wants me to do girl stuff. Yuk."

"Perhaps because you are a girl," Charlene said.

"It's not my fault." Jane handed Billie the nightgown. She pulled it over her head and wiggled until it dropped past her knees. "Look at this. There's a kitten on it!" She pointed at the offending appliqué. "I've told her a thousand times I want pajamas."

"This was a gift from your grandmother," Jane said, reaching for a comb.

"Let me." Charlene took the comb and settled on the lid of the toilet. After positioning Billie between her knees, she began to tame her short cut. "I am so looking forward to you discovering boys."

"Why?" Billie sounded suspicious.

Jane turned away to hide her grin.

"One day you'll look up and the boy you thought was a terrific—" She glanced at Jane.

"Catcher," she supplied helpfully.

"Catcher...will be a charming, handsome young man."

"Not to me." Billie cocked her head. "You're not married. Mom told me."

"I am not like most women. I prefer my men—"

"Charlene," Jane warned.

"I was just going to say that I prefer them appreciative."

"I don't understand," Billie said. She yawned and rubbed her eyes.

"You will," Charlene said. "One day." She leaned forward and kissed her cheek. "I'm so pleased you're here. Both of you."

"We can still be friends, even if you don't know much about baseball." Billie wrapped her arms around Charlene's neck. Jane saw her friend hug her back.

"Thank you," Charlene whispered, her voice hoarse with emotion. "Now, off to sleep."

Jane settled her daughter in the big bed, handed her her worn teddy bear and plugged in the night-light she'd carted clear across the country. She and Charlene kissed her, then moved quietly into the hall.

"She's darling," Charlene said as Jane closed the door.

"And you look as tired as she did. It's late. We'll talk tomorrow."

Jane thanked her, walked to her door and pushed it open.

"Jane?"

"Yes?"

"I will keep quiet about—" she motioned toward Billie's room "—everything. At least until you figure out the real reason you came back."

Chapter Three

"Hi. You're up. I thought I'd be the only one. Mom's still in the shower. What's for breakfast?"

Adam bent the corner of his paper and stared at Billie as she bounced around the kitchen. Today's outfit was an exact duplicate of yesterday's except her T-shirt and shorts hadn't had time to get dirty. Yet. The red baseball cap covered most of her hair, the bill had been tugged down to her brows. A softball bulged from the oversize pocket of her denim shorts.

"You wanna play catch later? Mom says we have errands in town. Shopping, that kind of stuff. Oh, and to see about glass for the window. Did I tell you I was sorry about that?"

He shook his head. "No."

"I am. Really." She stopped in front of the table. "Whatcha reading?"

"The paper."

"Did the Giants win?"

"Who?"

"The San Francisco Giants. They're my favorite team."

He set down the financial section and flipped through until he found the sports page. "Here."

Billie sat next to him at the bleached oak table. "Thanks." She peered at his cup. "Do I get coffee?"

"No."

"Toast?"

He pushed his plate toward her and picked up the paper.

"Milk?"

"It's in the refrigerator." He scanned the columns until he found the article he'd been reading. Lack of sleep made his eyes burn. The house had been still. Jane and Billie's rooms were far enough away that he couldn't hear them, but he'd known they were there. Despite reading the most boring financial newsletter he could find, despite the shot of Scotch and the cold shower close to midnight, he'd been awake until dawn. That was the hell of it. He could force his mind to forget, but his body was less willing to cooperate.

There was a dragging noise behind him. He tried to ignore it. It was the "whoops" followed by mad scrambling and "I got it, don't worry" that caused him to look up.

Billie stood on top of a stool. One foot rested on the seat, the other on the counter. A glass balanced precariously in her grasp.

"What the— What are you doing?"

"Getting a glass. Mom told me not to bother you. She said we have to be quiet and stay out of the way." She climbed down. "I'm pretty sure I can stay out of the way, but the quiet part is gonna be tough."

"No kidding." He gave up and tossed the paper onto the table. "What do you normally eat for breakfast?"

She grinned. "Donuts?" she asked hopefully.

"Not a chance. How about cereal?"

"What kind you got?"

He opened the cupboard and scanned the contents. All the boxes contained sensible multigrain products. He glanced at Billie. "Somehow I don't think you'll approve of the selection."

"Then toast is fine."

She picked up a slice and nibbled on the corner. Her mouth twisted into a grimace as she tasted the marmalade.

He chuckled out loud, surprising her and himself. "I'll make you fresh. There's peanut butter in the fridge. Or honey."

"Great." She crossed to the fridge.

"Oh, and grab that bowl of fruit salad and the milk. Are we hitting all the major food groups here?"

"All of 'em except donuts."

"That isn't a major food group."

"Okay, a minor food group. But it's still my favorite."

Billie held the bowl of fruit and the milk in her arms, then bent over and reached for the peanut butter. Milk sloshed onto the floor and three grapes slipped from the bowl to land in the puddle. She straightened, the peanut butter jar clutched in her free hand, then used her hip to shut the door. He waited, but she remained oblivious to the mess on the floor.

They assembled breakfast together. Billie spread a thick layer of peanut butter on her toast, then looked around. "You got any bananas?"

"I think so. Why?"

"To put on the bread. It's yummy."

His stomach lurched. "I'll pass. You go ahead."

She handed him the fruit to cut, then she mashed the slices onto the flattened toast. While he poured the milk, she dished out two bowls of fruit. They each got a serving, as did the table. Only a couple of chunks hit the floor. He stepped around them and resumed his seat.

"Good, huh?" A milk moustache outlined the top of her mouth. Crumbs stuck to the peanut butter on her cheek.

Ignoring her engaging grin would require a man stronger than himself. "Yeah, it's good." He folded the newspaper and set it on the extra chair.

They chatted through their meal. Billie discussed the school she'd left behind and her friends. Although she must miss them, her outgoing nature would make it easy to settle in.

"There's a couple of softball leagues in town," he said. "Perhaps I could have a word with the coaches and see if there's any room for another player."

The last bit of her toast fell back to the plate untasted. Big brown eyes got bigger. "You'd do that? For me? After I broke your window?"

Adam cleared his throat. "It's no trouble. Besides, I have a lot more glass to worry about. If you're off playing on a team, I'll rest easier."

"You're the best."

She flew out of her seat and around the table, then flung herself against him. Thin arms, small but surprisingly strong, tightened around his neck. She smelled of soap and milk and peanut butter. The kiss on his cheek was sticky and wet, but he didn't pull back. Little girls and their dreams were out of the realm of his expertise but there was something about Billie that would be easy to get used to.

"I promise I'll never break a window again," she said.

"That's some promise."

She giggled. "Okay. I'll *try* never to break a window again."

"Better." He laughed.

"You're up early."

Adam stiffened at the sound of a new voice and glanced up. Jane hesitated in the doorway to the kitchen. Her eyes flickered from Billie, still standing next to him, to the table and back.

"We had breakfast together," her daughter said. "Adam helped. And he's going to see if I can play softball this summer. Isn't that cool? I'm gonna go tell Charlene." She turned to run out the back door. With her hand on the knob, she paused. "Is this the way?"

"Her house is down the path about two minutes. There's only one. You can't miss it," he said.

"Bye. Oh, morning, Mom." The door slammed shut behind her.

"All that energy first thing in the morning." Jane offered a tentative smile. "I'll just grab a cup of coffee, then leave you in peace."

"There's no need to rush off on my account." Even to his own ears, the words sounded stiff. He wanted her out of his sight—out of his life—as soon as possible, but he'd be damned if he'd allow her to figure that out. "Help yourself to breakfast."

"I'm not hungry." Jane walked over to the coffeepot and poured herself a cup. "You've made a friend for life."

The sundress she wore fit tightly across her back, then flared out to fall in soft folds just at her knees. The bright magenta fabric added a glow to the light tan on her shoulders and arms. Once again, her hair had been pulled back in a thick braid. The slightly damp rope gleamed in the light.

He hated the way his fingers curled, as if to encircle the braid. His gaze drifted down past the curve of her calves to bare feet with painted toenails. With a suddenness that surprised him, his mind filled with a picture from another time, so long ago. She'd been getting ready for a date with him. He'd dropped by unexpectedly and had caught her in the middle of her preparations. Fat pink curlers had covered her head. A ratty shirt, stolen from her father's closet, concealed her body to mid-thigh. She sat on the floor, her long legs bent, a tissue woven between her toes. Even now he could inhale the acrid scent of nail polish, see the tongue sticking out of the corner of her mouth as she concentrated, hear the shriek when she'd looked up and seen him watching her.

Her blush had climbed clear to her hairline, then dipped to the cleavage showing in the V of the white shirt. She tried to run from him, but he caught her easily. His body heated at the memory. Her protest had died amid roving hands and joined mouths. Later that night she'd been beautiful. A woman. But what he remembered was the teenager in curlers, shy but eager, trying desperately to please. He'd wanted more, he'd realized that day. Had wanted it all. So that had been the night he'd made his decision. It had changed everything.

The hiss from the coffeemaker as she replaced the pot recalled him to the present.

"My desire to get Billie on a softball team is purely selfish," he said. "Just looking out for my property."

"I'll take care of that window today. I know you're working, so I'll go to the hardware store."

"Working?" He frowned. "It's Saturday."

"I know. But you usually worked... I thought you'd still." She turned to face him, her eyes averted. "My mistake."

"One of many." He tried to call the words back, but it was too late. The first crack in the armor, he thought. There wouldn't be another. She couldn't get to him anymore. "When we were—" He paused and searched for the correct phrase. He didn't like the one that came to mind, so he tried another tack. "It was never my intention to continue that schedule. I did what I had to in order to get the bank healthy. While I don't keep what people refer to as 'banker's hours', I do only put in the usual forty or so." Another crack. There, in the sharpness of his voice. Jane set her coffee on the counter and walked toward him.

"Adam, I'm sorry."

"There's no need to apologize."

"You must feel—"

"Nothing." He cut her off before she could voice what he was doing his damnedest to ignore. "Not a thing. I don't want your apologies. I don't want—" A burst of anger struck the side of his soul. The blow caught him off guard. He took a deep breath. "Let it go. I did."

"I don't believe you." Her hazel eyes searched his face.

He made himself sit quietly, forced the lid down on his anger and secured the lock. "That's your problem." He glanced at his watch. "I've got a couple of appointments in town. Feel free to use the phone and call whomever you need."

"The phone?"

"To let people know you arrived safely. Or if Billie needs to speak to anyone."

"I spoke to my parents yesterday. Who would Billie call?"

She was making it difficult. He rose. "Your ex-husband. Billie has a father, does she not?"

"Oh." Jane twisted her fingers together. "Oh, that. I...there's no one to call."

"You have sole custody?"

Jane paled visibly and backed up a step. "Yes," she whispered. "I think so."

"Think? What do the divorce papers say?"

"Why are you asking this?"

"I want to know if a strange man is going to show up on my doorstep."

"There's no one. Billie and I are alone." She took another step away and bumped into the counter.

"I see." Her statement didn't please him, he told himself. Jane could have married six times since she'd left and it wouldn't matter to him. Why would he care that she'd probably left some other man the way she'd left him?

"We'll be fine," Jane said, crossing her arms over her chest. "There's the car to unpack and the house to clean. Don't worry about us. Billie and I have lots to do."

"She's a great kid."

For the first time since entering the kitchen, Jane looked at ease. "Really? You think so?" She smiled. "I know she thinks the world of you."

"She's just happy I didn't take off a layer of her hide for breaking the window."

"Billie knows you'd never hit her."

"How would she know a thing like that?"

"She's very wise about people."

"That's a good skill for someone her age."

Her arms dropped to her sides. "I wish I'd had it. I always saw what was on the surface. I never thought to look for more."

She was trying to tell him something, but what? "And now?"

Her eyes darkened as the gold fled. She moistened her lips. "I'm getting better. It comes with age."

"You don't look much older." He took a step toward her. The involuntary movement sent alarms ringing through his head. Being attracted to Jane would make his bid to forget the past that much harder. He didn't want to remember what he'd lost; it had taken too long to let go.

Feel nothing. It was the only thing that worked. But his feet continued to move closer, until he stood in front of her. The need to punish was lost as the rise and fall of her breasts, the bare feet inches from his own, again reminded him of that afternoon. She'd only worn panties under her father's shirt. Did the sundress allow much more? She'd filled out in her time away, not much, but enough. He smiled as he remembered her shyness the first time he'd touched her breasts. Her reluctance had been explained when she'd finally confessed that they were much smaller than Bobbi Sue's, with whom she shared a locker in gym class.

Adam had murmured he didn't care about seeing Bobbi Sue, dressed or naked. That Jane was the one driving him crazy. She'd allowed him to release the catch on her bra and had arched in pleasure when he touched her pale virgin skin.

He raised one hand toward her face. There weren't any lines to show the passage of time. Her cheek looked as smooth and soft as he remembered. She watched him fearlessly, until her eyes drifted closed.

No! He tightened his hand into a fist, then turned away. No more remembering. The past held nothing for him. It couldn't. He didn't want her.

"I'm late," he said, and left the room without once looking back.

Jane measured out the correct length and cut the shelf paper. One cupboard down, three to go. She brushed her bangs off her forehead. The muggy afternoon heat sapped most of her energy. After a morning in town, during which the replacement window for Adam's house had been ordered, Charlene had offered to take Billie for a swim at the club's pool. Jane had been invited to tag along, but thought she'd better start getting the house ready. It was Saturday, the furniture would arrive Monday. There wasn't a lot of time. Besides, with Billie gone, she'd work faster.

Unfortunately she also had time to think. About Adam. About that morning. One more mark against her, one more measure of guilt.

She'd lied. Not outright, of course. But a lie by omission remained a lie. He thought she was divorced. That she'd met and loved and married another. That Billie had a father somewhere out there. What would he say when he found out the truth?

There couldn't have been another man. Despite the miles and years between them, she hadn't been able to forget. Her daughter—his daughter—was a daily reminder. She couldn't move on until she'd let go of the past. So why did doing the right thing have to be so tough? The answer was easy: Adam.

He'd been so unaffected. Except for that brief moment, when he'd almost touched her face, he'd acted like a stranger. A well-mannered host offering refuge to distant, but unknown relatives. Not by a flicker of a lash did he let on that they'd once meant something to each other. How she wanted to blast him from his damn, cool self-possession. And she could do it. But for Billie's sake, she needed to bide her time.

Jane smoothed the paper onto the shelf. Charlene had warned her that he hadn't waited. But he also hadn't married. It was probably because she'd taught him not to trust anyone.

The back door slammed and Billie bounced into the room.

"We're back."

"How was it?"

"Great. I met tons of kids at the pool. The girls are kinda dopey, but I talked to some boys about the softball team." Billie dropped her towel onto the counter and raised up on tiptoes to offer a kiss. "They didn't believe me when I told them I was a pitcher."

"So she threatened to beat one of them up." Charlene entered the room. "I declare, we'll have our hands full trying to tame this one."

"I don't need taming." Billie thrust out her lower lip. "He said he didn't fight girls, but I knew he was scared." She assumed a fighter's stance, feet spread, fists raised. One strap of her bathing suit slipped down her shoulder.

Charlene ruffled her hair. "She's a tiger. And she dove off the high board."

"I'm impressed." Jane measured the next shelf. "Anything broken or lost?"

"Nah." Billie climbed onto the counter and wiggled to get comfortable. "Besides, Charlene told me that lots of kids break things. Adam kicked a football into his mom's chandelier when he was in high school."

Jane smiled. "I'd forgotten that, but now that you mention it, we could hear the screaming all the way over here."

Charlene inspected her work. "Sometimes it's easy to forget Adam wasn't always the responsible man he's become." The older woman lifted Billie down from the counter. "You need a bath, young lady."

"But I just went swimming. I can't be dirty."

"The pool isn't clean, it's wet."

"Mo-om."

Jane raised her hands in the air. "I'm staying out of this one, kid. You're on your own."

Charlene led her to the back door. "Let's go out to dinner tonight. They serve fried chicken at Millie's diner on Saturday, and Billie told me you rarely make it at home."

"I hate cleaning up afterward. I'd love to go to Millie's. Is the food still terrific?"

"This is Orchard. We don't take kindly to change."

Billie tugged on Charlene's hand. "Can Adam go with us?"

"No, dear. He's going out tonight with...a friend." She glanced at Jane, her shrug apologetic. "It seemed to be a sudden decision."

"Okay," Billie said. "But we can bring some back, in case Adam doesn't like his dinner."

They left together, with Billie still complaining about the bath. Jane cut the shelf paper, then slipped it into the space. She didn't care that Adam was going out on a date; it wasn't her business. If his cool response was to be believed, her return to Orchard hadn't affected him at all.

That couldn't be true, she thought, sagging against the shelf. But it was. If he'd come after her all those years ago, if he'd forced her to listen to him, given her a sign he cared, that she was more to him than a convenience, she might have been convinced to stay. He had let her go without a word.

Like it or not, they were going to be neighbors. He couldn't avoid her forever. Even if he didn't care about her, he had to be angry about the past, about what had happened. When he learned the truth about his daughter, the daughter that had been kept from him—

Jane bit her lower lip. She'd only seen Adam truly enraged once. The collections manager at the bank had tried to intimidate a delinquent widow by using physical force. When Adam found out, he'd been a man possessed. The rage in his eyes, the barely controlled violence in his stance, the deadly quiet voice he'd used to fire the employee, had frightened her and had made her wonder if she knew him at all.

Looking back through the eyes of an adult, she realized he had kept himself from her. The essence of what he was—the promising oldest son forced to grow up before his time—had remained hidden. She'd been no match for him. Even his carefully reined-in passion had frightened her virgin body. No wonder he'd let her go without a word. What had there been to say?

She opened another package of shelf paper and unrolled it along the counter. The easiest thing would be for her to go along with him and play her own game of pretending nothing had happened. But that wasn't an option for her. She had to think of Billie and protect her. Until they had put the past behind them, they couldn't face the present. Until he had dealt with his anger, she couldn't trust him with his daughter.

Jane sat at the window seat in the guest room. In the trees, morning birds called to one another and their young. It wasn't yet seven, but already the humid heat threatened. Another Southern Sunday, she thought, pulling her light, cotton robe closer around her body.

Last night Adam had stayed out late. She'd waited up as long as she could, but exhaustion had forced her to bed. This morning she'd rushed to the window and had caught a glimpse of him jogging off. He had to come back sometime, and she'd be waiting. They still had a lot to discuss, and avoiding each other wasn't going to make it go away.

After washing up in the bathroom, she pulled on shorts and a blouse. She would dress for church after her talk with Adam. She checked to make sure Billie was still asleep. Her child lay curled up like a possum. The light sheet covered everything but the tip of her head. Jane silently shut the door and made her way down the stairs.

The house echoed with morning stillness. Underfoot, the hardwood floors felt cool and smooth. Adam had pulled up the old wool carpets and replaced them with scatter rugs. Most of the furnishings remained the same, but yesterday she'd caught sight of a complex entertainment unit in the game room. While he'd kept the family portraits and photographs, the darker paintings had been exchanged for bright moderns and a few lithographs. An original cartoon cell hung in the hallway outside her bedroom. The changes in the house were minor, but no less important for their subtlety.

Reaching the bottom stair, she sat down and waited. It had been almost an hour. He *had* to return soon. So what was she going to say? How far was she willing to push him? Telling herself that dealing with his anger herself was better than risking it spilling over to Billie was one thing. Facing Adam in a rage was quite another.

The girl he'd known before would never have defied him. If he'd told her he didn't want to talk about something, she would have never mentioned it again. That girl had been lost somewhere between Billie's birth and the present.

The back door slammed and jerked her out of her reverie. Here goes nothing, she thought grimly as she rose and brushed her damp palms against her shorts. She walked through the dining room and into the kitchen. And stopped.

Adam stood with his back to her. His bare back. Since he'd last jogged out of sight, he'd removed his T-shirt. Sweat glistened on his skin, the sheen defining the rippling muscles clenching and releasing like thick ropes. One hand held the refrigerator door open. He reached in and pulled out a bottle of juice. He shook the container, then raised it to his lips. As he drank, her throat tightened and swallowed. A bead of moisture dripped from the bottle onto his chest and was lost from view. Her gaze drifted down, past the flat midsection rising and lowering with each deep breath, past the bulge indicating his gender, to long, powerful legs. She knew the exact moment he became aware of her presence. The sudden tension of his body forced her to look up.

He hadn't shaved. Stubble darkened his jaw and outlined the firm line of his mouth. A smattering of hair, damp and matted from the run, arrowed toward his waist. Her breathing grew ragged. Not from exertion, but from apprehension. She had initiated this meeting, it was up to her to tell him what she wanted. But her tight throat wouldn't allow speech.

Adam closed the refrigerator and set the bottle on the counter. After grabbing his T-shirt off the chair, he wiped his face and chest.

"What do you want?"

He stood with his hands on his hips. The elastic of his shorts dipped scandalously low; he looked every inch a dangerous man. Billie had the same way of standing, of looking defiant and angry. But Billie was only eight, still a child. Adam was—Adam was the girl's father.

"I ordered a replacement for the window," she blurted out.

His mouth twisted with irritation, but he didn't speak.

"I wanted you to know. It should be here Monday. They'll install it and everything."

"Fine."

He stood there, perhaps sensing there was more, or waiting for her to leave. Those eyes, she thought, at last letting her gaze meet his. Those damn eyes. He still made her feel young and foolish. At seventeen, the six years difference in their ages had loomed between them like an uncrossable bridge. He'd been forced into adulthood by the death of his parents and the responsibility of his siblings. She'd been forced into adulthood by her own actions.

"I'm sorry," she said at last.

"Did Billie break something else?"

"No. I'm sorry for—" She clasped her hands together to stop their trembling. "Dammit, Adam, say something."

"Such as?"

"Why are you so calm about this? I waltz in here after being gone almost nine years and it's like nothing happened."

He shook his head impatiently. "I don't have time for reminiscing. I'm not interested in the past. It's done with. Let it go. I have."

"You're lying."

"And you're beating a dead horse."

He moved to walk past her. She touched his arm to stop him. Her fingers brushed against hot, damp skin. A current leapt between them and she jerked back, half expecting to see smoke. He froze in mid-stride, caught between her and the counter.

"What do you want?" he asked, shifting until one hip braced against the cupboard. The T-shirt hung over one shoulder.

She stared at the hem of the garment, studying the tiny stitches as if the answer lay hidden in the weave or the design.

"I'm moving in next door."

"So?"

"There's no way to avoid—"

"The hell there isn't. I don't want to be friends. I don't, as a rule, socialize with my neighbors. So your living there doesn't matter to me."

She told herself his disinterest came from pain, but a part of her wondered if she was wrong. Was Charlene speaking the truth? Had Adam recovered from what had happened? Did she not matter anymore?

"Billie likes you."

"And I like her. I'll be friends with the kid. I don't need to deal with you for that."

If only it were that simple.

"So the past means nothing?" she asked. She knew she was really asking if *she* meant nothing.

He shifted. Again she risked raising her gaze to his. The brown irises had darkened to black. The lines bracketing his mouth deepened.

"What do you want from me, Jane? You want me to tell you I still think about you? I can't, because I don't. It's over. I've moved on."

"I'm not asking if you think about—" this was harder than she'd thought "—me. I understand that we've both moved on. But I won't believe you've forgotten what happened. How it made you feel. Or what I did."

He looked away then, staring past her to something she couldn't see. The curse he mumbled made her flinch.

"It doesn't matter," he said. "I don't care."

"I don't believe that."

He shrugged. "Believe what you want."

What was the old saying? In for a penny, in for a pound. "You once asked me to marry you."

He laughed harshly, the sound carrying more irritation than humor. "Hell of a coincidence. You once said yes." His arms folded over his chest. "Don't push me. I still don't understand what you're looking for, but I'm the wrong man. You don't want to get me angry, and that's about five seconds from happening."

"At last," she said, stepping closer, feeling her own temper rise. "The fine, upstanding Adam Barrington. Banker, model citizen. You mean there's someone inside? Someone real, with feelings? Is that a crack in the old wall there? I'm not completely at fault, you know. You let me go, damn you. Why? Why didn't you come after me?"

Jane covered her mouth. That wasn't what she'd planned to say at all. But it was too late.

"Let you go?" He spoke quietly, with a barely controlled rage. The muscles in his arms bulged with the effort of his restraint. His eyes burned with a hot fire that had nothing to do with passion and everything to do with rage. "You walked out on me. Not a word or a note. Just a church full of people and a bride who didn't bother to show up."

Chapter Four

Adam straightened his arms at his sides and balled his hands into fists. His muscles trembled at the effort to restrain himself. His angry words, so filled with frustration and hurt, hung between them, echoing silently against the kitchen walls.

Damn her for forcing him to give it all away. Control, he told himself. Get control. But it was useless. Hot emotion tumbled through his body, swept on by heated blood. It bubbled and rolled within him, building with speed and pressure until the explosion became inevitable.

"It wasn't like that," she said, speaking so softly he had to strain to hear her. "I never meant it to happen that way. I thought—"

He swore loudly, the vulgar word cutting off her apology. "You thought?" he asked sarcastically, his rage burning the last of his civility. "What did you think? That no one would notice? That I'd get over being publicly humiliated?

That your running away wouldn't be the topic of conversation around town for months?"

She lowered her head. She'd pulled her long hair back in a loose braid. Bangs hung down her forehead, but her neck and ears were exposed. A dull red flush climbed from the neck of her T-shirt to her hairline.

"I'm sorry," she whispered.

"Sorry? Is that the best you can do? There was nothing, Jane. Not one damn word. I'd seen you drive up with your mother. You were in the church. Then you disappeared. What the hell happened?"

She opened her mouth to answer. He cut her off. "Don't bother." He turned away and faced the cupboards. If he continued to look at her, he wasn't sure what might happen. "We all waited for almost an hour. I heard the people talking. I told myself there was a problem with the dress, or that you'd broken a heel."

He didn't have to try to remember that afternoon. The sounds and smells enveloped him like the clammy mist of summer fog. She'd insisted that the church be filled with roses. White roses. That scent had haunted his sleep for months.

He pressed his palms against the counter, as if the tile could cool his heated blood. He'd thought he'd forgotten it all, but the past broke through the wall of his control, swept across his emotions, unleashing the potential for destruction. Again his fingers curled toward his palms as if he could squeeze out the memories. Or the person who had caused them.

"Adam, I'm sorry," she said, interrupting his struggle to maintain a semblance of composure. "So very sorry. It was never about you. You've got to believe that. It was about me."

"You've got that right." He spun to face her. "You ran away. It was a childish thing to do. I'm the one who had to deal with the aftermath of your behavior and make up some story about what had happened when I didn't have a clue. I'm the one who sent the notes of apology, returned the gifts and paid the bill for a reception that didn't happen."

She raised her head. Unshed tears glistened in her hazel eyes. She blinked frantically, but it didn't help. A single drop rolled down her cheek. At one time her distress would have moved him. He would have gathered her in his arms and murmured words of comfort. Not anymore.

"Typical," he said, shaking his head. "The going gets tough and you cry. You haven't grown up at all."

"That's not fair."

"Don't talk to me about fair. What do you know about it? Did you ever give any thought to what you left behind? You squawk about my not coming after you. Lady, even if I'd wanted to, I didn't have the time. Someone had to handle damage control. I know all you were interested in was seeing how easily you could wrap me around your little finger, but I had—and, no thanks to you—still have a position to think of in this community. I do business with most of the town. I was putting my sister and brother through college. Did you ever stop to think that the fine people of Orchard might not want to trust their money to a bank president who'd been stood up at the altar? That they might begin to wonder if there was some flaw only you knew about?"

Despite the embarrassment staining her cheeks, she paled. "They wouldn't have."

"Think again."

She raised her arm as if offering an apology. "I didn't know."

He glared at her and she dropped her arm to her side. "You didn't bother to find out," he said. "All you could think of was yourself."

"It wasn't like that. I tried to tell you—"

"When? I was standing there in the front of the church.

Like a fool. When I figured out something was wrong, I was pretty much a captive audience. If you were trying to get my attention, you got it. But you didn't have the guts to stay and talk. That's what gets me the most. Not one word of warning."

"I did try to talk to you. Before the wedding. You wouldn't listen."

He reached for the T-shirt hanging over his shoulder and pulled it down. She jerked her head at the movement, as if she'd suspected he would hit her. Her reaction inflamed him. Despite her actions, he'd never given her reason to fear him.

"I listened but all we talked about was the wedding," he said, his jaw tight with suppressed emotion. "Do you want pale pink or blush for the napkins?" He raised his voice mockingly. "Wild rice or steamed potatoes?"

"If you disliked my conversation so much, why did you want to marry me?"

He folded his arms over his chest. "Everybody's entitled to one mistake."

She closed her eyes and swallowed. Another tear rolled down her cheek. "And I'm yours?"

"You said it, lady, not me."

She looked at him. "I didn't do it on purpose."

"Is that supposed to make it better? That you acted out of ignorance?"

She shook her head. "Of course not. I'm just saying that I was very young."

"I guess that works as well as any excuse." He fingered the shirt in his hands. "It's my fault, I suppose. I'm the one who tried to make you more than you could be."

She flinched as if he'd slapped her. "I knew you'd be angry, but I never really expected you'd hate me so much."

"You're not worth hating." He looked over her head. "I don't care anymore."

She reached out her hand again and this time touched his

bare forearm. The physical side of him—that masculine self that had never been able to get enough of her—reacted to the slight touch. Awareness quivered as the imprint of each finger burned into his skin. It wouldn't take much, he acknowledged, despising the weakness inside and her for causing it.

With a slow gesture, too deliberate to be ignored, he pulled away from the contact. Jane bit her lower lip and stepped back. It wasn't even close to a draw, he thought. He'd hurt her, but nothing like what she'd done to him, all those years ago.

"If you could just let me explain," she said, twisting her fingers together. "I never meant to—"

"I don't give a damn about your explanations. Or you."

Her hazel eyes studied him. Tears threatened again, but she brushed them away impatiently. "You're too angry to not care, Adam. Your temper gives you away."

One point for her, he thought grimly. "All right. I care enough not to want you in my life. How's that?"

She turned and walked toward the hallway. When she reached the door, she looked back over her shoulder. "Be careful what you throw away, Adam. You may find you need it after all."

After she fled into the quiet morning, he stood alone in the kitchen, drawing deep breaths into his body. Once lost, the control was difficult to recapture. Random thoughts raced through his mind. Memories from the past—lost dreams, half-forgotten moments. He'd offered her all he had and she'd turned him down flat. Publicly. Now she expected exoneration for her behavior. Hell would freeze over before he'd ever—

"Was that a discussion you'd want her daughter to hear?"

"What?" He spun toward the back door.

Charlene stood in the pantry. "I could hear you clear outside. Now I've sent the child off to find the berry patch.

If you two are going to quarrel, please find a more suitable location."

"We weren't arguing."

"It sounded like an argument." Interest sparkled in her blue eyes. "Do you want to talk about it?"

"No," he said curtly, then instantly regretted his sharp tone. "It doesn't matter, Charlene. Jane just wanted me to get in touch with my feelings, and I did."

Stupid, Jane thought as she pulled the brush through her long hair. Just plain stupid. She'd been stupid to think about coming back to Orchard, stupid to think she and Adam might be able to resolve anything by discussing the past, and stupid to plan to let him know about his daughter.

"Not my finest hour," she muttered, as she dropped the brush, then reached back and began braiding her hair. Her fingers moved efficiently, weaving the long strands into a French braid. The mirror over the dresser reflected her image. She averted her eyes, not wanting to see the guilty flush on her own face. Morning light filtered through the lace curtains and onto the carpeted floor. Like the room Billie slept in, this guest room had been decorated with warm colors and cozy prints. A handmade quilt covered the bed she sat on. The bright yellows and peaches blended in a star-shaped pattern. It should have been soothing. Despite the room, the cool shower and the stern talking-to she'd given herself, her heart still thundered in her chest. Her hands shook from the recent exchange with her former fiancé, and a strand of hair slipped out of her grasp, causing her to release the half-finished braid.

"Stupid." She picked up the brush and began vigorously stroking.

"You're gonna pull it all out," Billie said as she walked into the room.

"What?"

"Your hair. You're brushing too hard. Are you mad at me?"

"No, honey." Jane set the brush on the bed and held open her arms. "Come here." Her daughter stepped into her embrace and they hugged. "I'm not angry at all."

Billie had managed to stay reasonably clean, despite a quick trip to the berry patch. Jane held her at arm's length and studied her. The peach-and-cream floral print sundress brought out the tan on her face and arms. Her hair showed signs of recent contact with a comb. Brown eyes, so much like Adam's that it hurt to look at them, glared back mutinously.

"I'm not wearing that hat," Billie said. "And you can't make me."

"Your grandmother went to a lot of trouble to find one that matched that dress."

"I know, but it's dumb looking." Billie planted her hands on her hips. "I don't think God cares if I wear a dress to church or not."

"We dress nicely to show respect," Jane answered, trying not to smile at the familiar argument.

"Maybe." Her daughter brushed her bangs out of her face. "But I *know* he doesn't need me to wear a hat." She wrinkled her nose. "It's got ribbons and flowers. People will laugh at me."

"You'd look very pretty."

Billie opened her mouth wide and made a gagging noise, showing exactly what she thought of looking pretty.

Jane sighed. Compromise. It was the first rule of parenting. "You don't have to wear the hat."

"Whew. Thanks, Mom." Billie spun in a circle. The hem of her dress flared out exposing the denim shorts she wore underneath. "I'll even leave my softball at home."

"Thank you." Her gaze drifted past her daughter's bare legs down to sneaker-clad feet. "But you have to change your shoes."

"I'm not wearing those patent leather things. Yuk."

"Sandals are fine."

"Okay." Billie dashed from the room.

Jane picked up the brush. She'd given up trying to get Billie not to run in the house. As long as nothing terribly expensive was in danger of being broken, it wasn't worth the fight. Besides, the kid had way too much energy.

She smiled fondly as she remembered her own childhood. Being a tomboy had never been a question, let alone a problem. No, she had been a typical girl. Dolls and books, quiet games with two or three friends and little time outdoors. She hadn't even learned to swim until she was almost twelve.

Her fingers nimbly worked with her hair as her eyes drifted half-closed and she remembered the muggy heat of that summer, when the temperature alone had driven her to the local swimming hole. The big kids—the teenagers—had taken over one side, but the rest belonged to everyone else. Jane had stayed in the shallow part, dangling her feet while she sat on a fallen log. The combination of sun and friends and laughter had wooed her into relaxing. Then she'd seen him.

Goose bumps erupted on her skin as she remembered looking up and seeing a boy—a young man really—poised at the top of a platform one of the fathers had constructed. With the sun in her eyes, she hadn't been able to see his face, but she'd watched him dive cleanly into the water, barely making any splash at all. He'd surfaced close to where she sat.

When he'd gotten out, water streaming off his developed and tanned body, and laughed, she'd found herself giggling with him. Their eyes had met. Adam, she'd thought with some surprise. The boy who lived next door. But he wasn't a boy anymore. He'd shaken himself then, spraying her with water, and had invited her to jump off the platform with him.

She refused. She couldn't swim. Instead of mocking her like the other boys had, he'd held out his hand and led her to a quiet cove. He'd taught her to swim that summer, Jane remembered, finishing the braid and clipping a silk rose at the bottom. Slowly, patiently. He'd been a football player in the fall, a swimmer in the spring at high school. He'd been to the state championships once. A jock. Nothing like her. At eighteen, he'd been a prize catch in a small town like Orchard. She smoothed down her dress and allowed herself a bittersweet smile. He would have been a prize catch anywhere. And despite the other teenage girls ready and willing to spend their days with him, he'd taken the time to teach his twelve-year-old neighbor to swim.

A scholar, an athlete and a gentleman. Her heart never had a chance. He was her first crush. It had been as inevitable as the coastal tide. Her desires had been unfocused, just vague longings that had made her heart beat faster whenever she saw him. It wasn't until high school that she'd recognized the feelings for what they were. Love had quickly followed.

And she'd thrown it all away.

Jane rose from the bed and walked to the doorway of the guest room. The thick carpet muffled her footsteps. It seemed another lifetime ago that she'd been engaged to Adam. They were both so different now. Coming home had been—stupid.

"I just want you to know that I *hate* these," Billie said, joining her in the hall. She flexed one foot and glared at her sandals. "When I'm grown up, I'm never going to wear a dress again."

The shaft of pain caught her unaware and ripped through her heart. Billie was, if nothing else, her father's daughter. Adam had rebelled at dressing up. He'd been active in sports. He'd been—

She drew in a breath. He'd been the one she'd left standing at the altar. Oh, why on earth had she thought returning to Orchard would be a good idea? And if that wasn't bad enough, why had she insisted on pushing him to reveal his feelings about her walking out on him? It accomplished nothing except to bring those awful memories to the surface. If being in the same room with him before had been difficult, now it would be impossible. She'd have to think of an excuse to leave or move or—

"Jane! Billie! It's time to go. What are you two doing up there?" Charlene's voice sailed up the stairs.

"We're coming," Billie called down. "You ready, Mom?"

"Sure," she said, trying not to clench her teeth. If she was uncomfortable now, it was her own fault. Bearding the lion in his own den had been foolish. Maybe Adam would chicken out. Maybe he'd stay home from church. Maybe—

Maybe it was her fate to be punished for the rest of her days. She took Billie's hand and together they descended the stairs. Waiting at the foot stood Charlene in one of her bright voluminous dresses, and Adam. His dark suit emphasized the lean strength of his body. Damp dark brown hair gleamed. The slight waves had been tamed with water and a brush, but soon one or two locks would tumble over his forehead.

She felt heat climb her cheeks and prayed he wouldn't notice. He didn't. He wasn't looking at her, but at some spot over her head and to the left.

"Are you ready?" he asked quietly. Nothing in his voice hinted at the conversation they'd had not two hours before. Only the slightly clenched fists and the stern set of his mouth showed that emotions lurked below the calm facade.

"My tummy hurts," Billie said.

Jane glanced down at her and raised one eyebrow.

The little girl rubbed the top of her right foot against the calf of her left leg. "Okay. It doesn't."

"Billie isn't too fond of church," she explained to Charlene, careful to avoid looking at Adam again.

"I don't mind it too much, but they make you sit still so long." Billie drew in a deep breath and let it go in a sigh. "I like God and everything. The songs are okay. But there's always some old lady telling me to sit still."

"Charm school," Charlene said, taking Billie's other hand, and ushering her toward the front door.

"I don't think that's such a good idea," Jane said. "She's awfully young."

"This is Orchard, dear. We strive to turn girls into ladies, at any age."

"What's charm school?" Billie asked suspiciously.

"You don't want to know," her mother told her, keeping step with them. Adam brought up the rear.

As they walked outside, toward the dark sedan parked in front, she tried not to think about him. It was only for one more night. Her furniture would be arriving sometime tomorrow. If she worked at it, she'd never have to see him again.

Yeah, right, she thought as he held the rear door of the car open. What about her plans for an eventual father-daughter reunion? She still owed them both. Before Jane could make her move, Billie had ducked inside the car, with Charlene quickly on her heels.

"You sit in front," the older woman told her.

Jane swallowed uncomfortably. Adam closed the rear door and opened the front. She murmured her thanks as she slipped in past him. The scent of his body—soap, shaving cream, and some essence of male—taunted her. She wanted to breathe deeply and savor the fragrance. It made her think of sultry Southern nights and velvet-on-silk passion.

The door slamming shut with a bang caused her to jump slightly. In the back seat, Charlene and Billie chatted. Charlene spoke glowingly about charm school, but Jane could tell that her daughter was becoming more and more disenchanted by the second.

"Do I have to?" she asked, leaning over the front seat.

"I don't want to learn how to drink tea and dance. And I already know how to walk."

"Not like a lady," Charlene said. "You'll like it."

"I won't!"

Adam slid into his seat. She half expected him to take part in the conversation, but he just started the car and shifted into gear.

"Mo-om!"

Jane drew in a deep breath. "Billie, you don't have to go to charm school if you don't want to. Charlene, she *is* only eight."

"It's never too early to learn how to be a lady."

"I'm going to be a pitcher."

Jane bit back a smile and tried to relax in her seat. The conversation between Billie and Charlene continued as they debated the merits of their positions. She didn't glance to her left, but she was aware of him sitting so close. Except for asking if she were ready, he hadn't said a word. Not that any of this was his fault. It had all been a big mistake and she only had herself to blame.

The drive to church took about six minutes. As they pulled into the parking lot, Jane tensed and waited for the rush of memories to envelop her.

"Did you used to go to this church?" Billie asked.

"Yes, until I—" She cleared her throat.

"Moved away," Adam offered helpfully. She knew she was the only one to hear the sarcasm in his voice. She didn't dare look at him.

"That's right," she said softly. "Until I moved away."

A large crowd mingled on the edge of the lawn. One woman glanced at Adam's car as he parked it. She did a double take and nudged her neighbor. Jane couldn't hear what was being said but she watched as the news rippled through the group. The prodigal daughter had returned.

Oh, no! She'd never given a moment's thought to what it would look like if she arrived at church with Adam and

Charlene. And Billie. What would people think? Say? She was doing it again! Acting without thinking and leaving Adam to deal with the consequences.

Darting a quick glance to her left, she waited for him to comment on the interest they'd generated. Instead he opened the car door and stepped out. She fumbled with the handle, anxious to exit before he made his way around to help her. Nervous fingers slipped. He reached her door. When it opened, he held out his hand. Politeness demanded that she accept the gracious gesture. Her fingers brushed his palm. Sparks flew in all directions, landing on her skin and midsection, creating a warmth that threatened to make her tremble. His touch had always affected her. The flash of familiar electricity comforted as it excited. Was there still something between them?

She slowly raised her gaze, past the dark suit jacket, past the white shirt and faintly patterned blue tie. Past the squared jaw and straight lips to his eyes. The anger there, deadly and barely controlled, made her drop her hand and turn away.

While she struggled with her composure, several people came over and said hello. Some of the faces looked familiar, some did not. But they all stared. A few of the people she knew glanced from her to Adam, then back. The speculative look in their eyes made her blush. The rumors would sprout faster than kudzu. This had all the earmarks of turning out to be a crummy day.

Billie bounced beside her. "Oh, look. There's Matt. I met him at the pool. He's a catcher. I'm going to go say hi." She darted off without waiting for permission.

"Charm school," Charlene murmured quietly, before she, too, walked away to greet some friends. Adam also disappeared into the crowd to speak with someone.

Alone, Jane moved toward the front steps of the church. The old-fashioned white building had been recently painted. Green grass stretched out on either side of the path leading from the parking lot to the stairs. Lofty chestnut trees provided shade. They'd grown taller in her absence, she thought, glancing up at them. And the dogwoods had grown wider. Small changes really, not enough to keep her from remembering.

As she climbed the steps, she reminded herself it was all in the past. But it wasn't. As she stepped through the open double doors, time shifted. It bent until that day and this one touched, and she once again stood in the back of the church, her long, white wedding gown dragging at her with each step.

The church had been full, the townspeople eager to see Adam Barrington wed his bride. White roses, always her favorite, filled every urn. Wide ribbons curved along the center aisle, holding small white bouquets at the end of each pew. Even now, the scent of roses swept over her. Someone jostled her gently and she stepped into a corner of the foyer. The shadows blurred, the sounds faded, until all she could hear was her mother telling her it was too late to change her mind.

"You can't back out now," her mother had said, an edge of hysteria in her voice. "The wedding, the reception. It's all planned. What will your father say?"

A familiar theme growing up, Jane recalled. Her father had been the undisputed master of his castle. Her mother the eager subject. It was her mother's willingness to be what her husband demanded that had first given Jane a glimpse of what life with Adam might be like. Adam also made politely worded requests. As she stared at the people waiting to watch her marry, she had wondered if he loved her. Confusion, as real today as it had been nine years ago, filled her. Was she the most convenient bride? Young and easily influenced? Did he want *her* or had she simply fulfilled his list? They were so different. Six years had loomed large between them. He'd been a man.

More than anything, that had frightened her. In those

moments when her blood had run cold and her heart had thundered in her throat, she had seen that she wasn't enough. She might love him with all of her being, but she wasn't ready to marry him. It had been her first mature realization. Unfortunately, she had acted like a child. Even as her mother had begged her to reconsider, Jane pulled off the wedding gown and veil. She'd slipped on her jeans and shirt.

"What are you going to tell him?" her mother had asked.

"Nothing."

With that, she had run. Pausing only to peek into the church one more time, stopping long enough to catch Adam's eye and see him smile at her, warmly, trustingly, as any man would smile at the unexpected glimpse of his bride. He hadn't seen she wasn't wearing her gown. In that moment, she'd stopped to question her actions. Had his expression contained affection? Even love?

No, she'd thought as the tears had begun. Not love. Convenience. Suitability. She would never inspire the same kind of soul-stealing emotion that he created in her. Better to find that out now, rather than later. She'd escaped out a side door and had never looked back.

One cowardly, selfish act. Her life had never been the same. She'd lived with that mistake from that moment until this. Adam had been right, Jane thought, pushing away the past and looking around at the church. She hadn't allowed herself to think about the consequences of her actions. Oh, she'd acknowledged that he might be hurt or a little embarrassed, but she'd never considered in detail what he must have gone through.

Her Adam, so strong and proud, handsome. She remembered how her heart had fluttered whenever he'd smiled at her from across a room. She'd publicly humiliated him, had rejected him in the worst way possible. He'd worked hard for all he'd achieved. To think that she might have destroyed that. She shuddered.

She had hoped that by getting him to admit his anger now, she might lessen her own guilt. Another selfish act. She had forced Adam to relive those horrible days. And now, they both felt worse. As she'd said earlier. Stupid.

A soft hand touched her arm. Jane blinked, then tried to smile at Charlene.

"Are you all right?" the older woman asked. In the church the shadows muted the bright color of her hair, but the other woman was still a robin in a flock of sparrows.

"Fine."

Those wise eyes studied her. "There's no way to escape the past, my dear. You must make peace with it."

"Am I that obvious?"

"Only because I care about you."

"I'm just beginning to understand all the trouble I've caused," she said, averting her face from the probing glances of curious neighbors. "It's not flattering."

"You were young, child. You made the best decision you could at the time."

"Everyone paid a high price for that."

"Including yourself."

"I don't care about me. It's Billie that I'm worried about."

"And Adam?"

"Yes," she admitted.

It was as if Charlene's words conjured him out of the morning. He and Billie walked in together, the child's small hand held securely in his. They were speaking about something. Both their heads tilted toward each other.

The best decision possible at the time, Charlene had said. That wasn't true. All she'd accomplished by running was to keep father and daughter apart.

Adam said something and they both laughed. Their smiles were mirror images. How long before everyone guessed the truth? He glanced up at her, then turned away. Inside, a cold lump formed and pressed against her heart.

She'd been hiding, she realized in that moment of rejection. Hiding from the truth. The list of reasons she'd used for coming home—a good job, a small and friendly town in which to raise her daughter—had all been a smoke screen. She hadn't come home for a teaching position, or even for Billie. She'd come home looking for forgiveness and a way to set the past right.

Chapter Five

Despite the board covering the broken window, night noises drifted into Adam's office. He stared at the folders spread open in front of him and struggled to concentrate. The loan committee would meet Monday morning, as it had for decades. He could imagine the looks on his employees' faces if *he* wasn't ready.

Normally he could shut out any distractions. Whether it was neighborhood kids or grunts from Charlene's favorite Sunday night wrestling. But tonight— He closed the top file and sighed. Jane had called Billie in for her bath about fifteen minutes before. The eight-year-old's arguments as to why she didn't need washing had taken the better part of ten minutes. At the end, he'd been grinning broadly at her imagination and inventiveness. What a kid.

But it wasn't Billie's chatter that kept him from working. Nor was it Charlene's television shows or the crickets. It was Jane. He'd gone to church in that same building for the past nine years. Except for an occasional service missed because of illness or vacation, he'd been faithful in his attendance, and his attention. This morning, as now, his mind had wandered. The past, so easily disposed of when there was no reminder, slipped around the walls of his control. It weighed on him, made him lose track of the sermon or his notes on a loan.

When she had left, all those years ago, he'd been able to occupy his mind with the details of picking up the pieces. All the things he'd complained about to Jane that she'd left him to handle had filled his time and his thoughts. The act itself had been pushed aside, first for a few days, then indefinitely, until he'd lost track of it all. Occasionally, something would happen to remind him. He would recall a conversation, a moment, then shove it back where it belonged and get on with his life.

It wasn't going to be so easy this time, he thought as he dropped his pen onto the desk and leaned back in his leather chair. Violent anger had been his persistent companion most of the day. He hated her for making him remember, and himself for being sucked into something that should have ended a long time ago. He'd avoided the family dinner table, instead grabbing a snack in the kitchen and ducking out before Charlene could shanghai him. How long could he avoid Jane?

Damn her for coming back, he thought, staring out into the darkness. And for being the one who still got to him.

After taking a deep breath, he ordered his body to relax. She would be gone in the morning. He wouldn't have to see her again if he didn't want to. There had been weeks, even months between contact with the previous neighbors. Surely Jane was smart enough to want the same thing. If they both took a little time to plan this, they might never have to meet again. Would that be enough to shut her out? Not seeing her, not talking to her? He closed his eyes, but that didn't help.

Memories from years ago filled him. He'd just gotten his

Master's degree in Money and Banking and had been putting in a lot of extra hours at the bank to make up for his time gone. Financially it had been touch and go for a couple of years. The town of Orchard had been amazingly tolerant and trusting of a bank president in his twenties. Dani and Ty had needed money for college, not to mention his attention when they were home. And there had been Jane.

Time with her was something he had put on his calendar, scheduled like any appointment. Perhaps, he thought now, he could have wooed her more, but he'd had responsibilities. She'd understood that. All that was to have changed after the wedding. But she'd never given him the chance.

She had been young. Maybe too young, he thought with a flash of insight. She'd wanted him to demonstrate his affection by playing those silly romantic high school games. He hadn't had time to loll around on her porch and sip lemonade while gossiping about the prom. He hadn't had time—

Upstairs, footsteps thumped. Billie, he thought with a slight smile. If things had been different, he and Jane could have been married for nine years. They would have had a child of their own by now. A daughter who looked like—

He sat up straight in his chair. Billie? He started to do some rapid calculations. They were cut short when he realized he didn't know how old Billie was. Even as excitement and expectation flared inside him, he firmly squashed them. Billie couldn't be his. He and Jane hadn't made love often, and when they had, they'd used protection. She'd been embarrassed as hell about the diaphragm, he recalled with a grin. Her mother had refused to discuss any kind of birth control, so he'd been the one to take her to the doctor and wait during her appointment.

His smile faded. Sex. Another place he'd screwed up, he saw now with the twenty-twenty vision of hindsight.

"Adam?"

He glanced up, startled. He hadn't heard her knock, let

alone enter. Had his thoughts conjured her from the past? Was the woman standing in front of him real?

He studied her dark hair and the fringe of bangs that ended just above her delicately arched eyebrows. Hazel eyes held his gaze for a second, before flickering nervously toward the floor. One corner of her mouth quivered slightly, as if not sure whether to curve up or down. She still looked too damn young, he thought irritably. But she was real enough. The dress she wore—pale blue and loose fitting with a white blouse underneath—was the same one from this morning. He wouldn't have imagined her in that. In his mind, he liked to think of her teetering on unaccustomed high heels, her upswept hair adding height and attempting to make her look older. Or sitting on his porch, watching the sunset, a sleeveless blouse exposing her tanned arms, while the gauzy full skirt she wore outlined the curvy lines of her legs.

"I'm busy," he said curtly, as much to disconnect himself from his thoughts as to send her away.

"This won't take but a moment."

He made a show of closing the top folder, then glancing impatiently at his watch. "Yes?"

She took a step into the office. The room was large, and he'd taken advantage of the space. Bookcases lined two walls. The big walnut desk that had been his father's was the centerpiece of the room. A comfortable chair with its own table and reading lamp stood in one corner. The couch sat between the desk and door. About five years ago he'd pulled up the heavy rug and had refinished the hardwood floors. It was a comfortable room; a place he could work in.

Her hands fluttered nervously around her waist. She linked her fingers together, as if to still the movement, then rubbed her palms back and forth against each other.

"Sit down and stop fidgeting," he said, pointing to the couch.

"Sorry." Jane walked the three steps, then perched on the edge of the sofa. The black leather provided a perfect backdrop for her delicate features. The harsh color outlined the shape of her head, the curve of her cheek and the graceful sweep of her neck. She wore her hair pulled back.

"A nuisance," she'd said, when, years before, he pulled at the ribbons and freed the silky tresses.

"Beautiful," he'd replied.

Her innocent blush had thrilled him, as he had then taken what no man had seen or touched.

He shook his head impatiently. "What do you want?"

"To apologize."

He raised one eyebrow and waited.

"Not about Billie. She hasn't done anything."

"Yet," he said.

The corner of her mouth raised slightly. "Yet. It is one of the hazards of raising a tomboy."

"But worth the trouble."

She looked surprised. "I wouldn't have thought—"

"I'd never hold your behavior against your child, Jane. If you'd taken the time to know the man you were running from, you would be aware of that."

Hazel eyes flashed anger, as their color darkened to green. "If *I'd* taken the time? You're the one who couldn't bear to be away from your precious bank. I always came tenth on a list of five items. Don't talk to me about—" She stopped, her mouth still open to form more words. She clamped her lips together and sighed. "I didn't come here to fight."

"Why did you?"

"At church this morning... I'm sorry about all that. I should have thought..." She hunched her shoulders as if waiting for him to berate her for not thinking—again. When he didn't, she went on. "Those people, they all stared at us. I'd forgotten what a small town can be like. There will be rumors. I didn't want to cause you any more trouble."

He rose from his desk and walked around it until he stood in front of her. After moving a couple of folders, he perched on the corner nearest her. "I can handle it, if you can."

She nodded. "People will talk, though."

He shrugged. "I've been through it before."

"I know. I'm sorry about that, too."

"Forget it."

"I can't."

"Then it's your problem."

"You dismiss me so easily, Adam, but then you always did. I was too young and foolish. I was never like those other women you dated."

His temper threatened to flare but was put out by her words from the past. "I'm not like those other women." The phrase echoed over and over again. It had been winter. January, maybe, and cold for South Carolina. He'd started a fire and had spread a blanket for the two of them. They'd been kissing for hours, petting. He'd touched her breasts under the wool of her sweater, but when he tried to take off her bra, she'd resisted.

"I'm not like those other women," she said, her hazel eyes wide and afraid. "I've never done this before."

He'd taken her further than she'd wanted to go. He folded his arms over his chest and tried to ignore the flicker of shame. Further and faster. She'd never resisted, or said no, but he'd been aware that Jane would have been happy to keep their physical relationship less physical. Lovemaking had been—he frowned—awkward at best.

The memories made him uncomfortable and he pushed them away. But this time the thoughts refused to return to their small box at the back of his consciousness. They intruded with images that made him wonder if he'd crossed the line from ardent suitor to horny jerk with her. She'd been a young nineteen, he admitted to himself. He looked at her, sitting on the edge of his sofa, her fingers twisting together. She still looked young.

But nine years had passed. She had grown up. She was a teacher and a mother. That reminded him. Billie.

"How old is Billie?" he asked.

Jane swallowed as her stomach flipped over. Why did he want to know? "Eight."

He drew his eyebrows together as if doing the math. "And her father?"

"What?"

"Billie told me she's never met him. You and he want it that way?"

Oh, God forgive her, she didn't have the strength to say it. Not now. Not today. "It seemed like the best decision at the time."

"A kid needs a dad."

"Billie and I are getting by."

"She deserves more than just getting by."

"That's why I brought her home."

"Home?" His mouth curled into a cruel twist. "I'm surprised you'd still think of Orchard as home."

"I grew up here."

"And left."

And left. It always came back to that. "I'm sorry," she said, wondering how many times she would speak those exact words. "I never meant to hurt you. And you were right, this morning. I never did think about what my leaving would mean to the bank. You had all those responsibilities. I should have handled the situation differently."

"Yeah, a note would have been a nice touch. Maybe you could have left it on the church steps, weighed down by your bouquet and the engagement ring."

However well deserved, his sarcasm hurt. She didn't flinch, but had a bad feeling her pain showed in her eyes. She looked away. "I meant that I should have told you about my doubts when they first occurred to me. I should have talked to you. I apologize for that."

"I don't care enough to be angry or enough to forgive you, so seek your absolution elsewhere, little girl."

She stood up and planted her hands on her hips. "I am not a child."

His gaze raked her from the top of her head down to her sandal-clad feet. "You might not look like one, but you're still acting like one. Saying 'I'm sorry' doesn't mean a damn thing to me, Jane. What are you really here for?"

"I'm going to be living next door. We have to—"

"We don't have to do anything."

He straightened and glared down at her. Fire burned in his brown eyes—flames born of pain and suffering and a desire to exact revenge. She wanted to run—it had always been her way of facing problems—but the time for running was long past. She'd returned to Orchard because she needed Adam to forgive her, and because her daughter and her daughter's father deserved to know each other. But to get to that, she and Adam had to lay the past to rest. A high price for a family, she saw now.

"You used to frighten me," she said, fighting the urge to retreat and holding her ground. "But not anymore. Not your temper or your demands or your—" Her gaze dropped to his mouth, then back to his eyes. "You can't tell me what to do."

"Is that what this is about?" he asked, taking a step closer to her.

Back up, her mind screamed. Her muscles tensed to respond to the message, but she stiffened and remained in place. "What do you mean?"

"Don't play games, Jane." His gaze traveled over her face, then stopped at her mouth. "Years ago you wanted pretend passion. A boy, not a man. Is that why you've come home? To see if the woman likes me any better than the girl did?"

"No. I never—"

He reached out and grabbed her arms. Before she could

catch her breath, he pulled her up against him. Her breasts flattened against his chest as he clutched her upper arms and trapped her hands between them.

She braced herself for the fury, fully expecting to pay a high price for her defiance. She waited for rage and violence. Instead it was the impact of coming up against her past that caused her to sag against him.

Her sharp intake of air was silenced when his lips touched hers. He kissed her hard, punishing her with the pressure, moving back and forth quickly, without consideration for her pleasure, or even comfort. Before she could protest or even begin to pull away, the kiss softened. Slowly he withdrew, until they barely touched. Familiar, she thought, as his lips brushed hers. Familiar and welcome and wonderful.

The soft contact enticed her. He teased, allowing their lips to join, then withdrawing until only the air whispered against her sensitized mouth. Instead of holding her trapped, his hands began to rub her arms, moving from shoulder to elbow. Against her palm, his heart beat steady, the pace gradually increasing to match the rhythm of her own.

Men had kissed her, she thought as he swept his tongue across her bottom lip, but those memories paled by comparison with the reality of Adam's touch. He had been her first, her only lover. It had been his kisses that had given rise to young passion. But that girl had grown up, she realized as she opened for him. He no longer frightened her that way.

Despite her parted lips, he continued to trace a wet line around her mouth. First the outside, then the inside, teasing, tempting, but never entering. A low moan escaped her. She shifted back far enough to free her hands, then slid them up his arms, across his shoulders and around him until she could hold him close. Her fingers reached the coffee-colored silk of his hair. Sensibly short strands tickled her fingers.

She knew this man. The scent of him. And the feel of him. Those tiny hairs on the back of his neck, the strong line of his jaw, the sensation of a day's worth of stubble rasping against her fingertips. The taste of him. He grew tired of his game and slipped into her mouth.

"Yes," she whispered.

At last. His tongue moved delicately past her teeth to meet and embrace hers. They touched, tip to tip, then circled, rough to smooth. Long strokes imitated the act of love, whirlpool-like plunges dueled. He tasted exactly as she remembered. Sultry sweetness with a hint of the forbidden. His hands dropped from her arms to her waist, then lower and behind to her derriere. He cupped her curves.

Yes, she cried in her mind. She wanted him. He'd aroused her before, but always there had been the fear. Her body wasn't curvy enough. She didn't know how to please a man. She felt embarrassed by his looking and touching her.

She hadn't been taught by anyone but him, and now the fear was gone. She was a woman, ready to be taken by this man. When he pulled her hips close, she felt the length and breadth of his arousal. An answering heat rose between her thighs. He had readied her with a kiss.

"Adam," she breathed against his mouth.

It was as if his name had broken the spell that held him next to her. He stiffened in her embrace; his arms fell to his sides.

Don't, she thought frantically, as the haze of passion lifted and allowed her to recall the difficulty of their situation. He still hated her for what she'd done to him. She continued to withhold the truth of his daughter from him. An impossible circumstance.

She stepped back before he could completely reject her. Her eyes searched his, hoping for a lingering sign of arousal, a hint that his wall of control had been bridged. He stood tall, with his arms at his sides and his hands balled up in fists. There was nothing soft about him. Nothing forgiving. If it were not for the memory of his body next to hers, the sweet taste his tongue had left inside her mouth, she would have wondered if she'd imagined the moment.

Coldness invaded his eyes, stealing away whatever desire might have stayed. He stared directly at her. "That should never have happened."

Of course it should have, Jane thought touching her fingertips to her still-trembling lips. Didn't he get it? She wasn't afraid of him. A liberating thought, heady even. No fear. For months, years after she'd left Orchard, she'd carried around the weight of that fear. Her uncertainty, her knowledge that she wasn't woman enough to please Adam or strong enough to tell him what she was feeling had convinced her that she was so much less than everyone else. As she had survived and raised a child on her own, her confidence had grown, but she'd still shied away from men.

Her gaze dropped to his mouth. They should do it again, she decided, wondering if the passion and fire had been real. Had he felt it? Her stomach and thighs tingled with the memory of him pressing hard against her. He *had* felt something; she'd been touched by the proof of that.

She thought about stepping closer, of trying to tempt him. Even as she took one step toward him, he spun and walked to the window.

"I don't have an explanation," he said, staring out into the darkness. "I don't usually lose control like that. It won't happen again."

He sounded so angry and final. His words battered at her newly discovered passion until she was ashamed. He'd wanted to punish her, make her suffer as he had. The kiss had been about retribution, not affection or desire. The thrill and excitement began to die within her. She tried to hang on to the feelings. The moment had been important to her. Don't let it go, she told herself.

It was too late.

Defeat hunched her shoulders and she folded her arms over her chest. "See that it doesn't," she said, in a flash of self-preservation, then wondered if he knew she lied.

He stood so proudly, she thought as she stared at his back. Strong and broad. A man. He wore his power easily. The athletic prowess from his youth had stayed with him, adding grace to his movements. Tonight, however, he stood stiffly. The past weighed on him.

"Once your furniture arrives and you move into your own house, I don't want to see you again."

It hurt, she thought with a flash of surprise. It hurt that he could dismiss her so easily. Not seeing her wasn't an option. Not if he wanted to get to know his daughter. But then Adam didn't know he had a daughter. She'd have to tell him.

Not yet. She again touched her fingers to her lips. The sensitive skin quivered from his kiss. In a few days. When she was stronger. When the bridge between them didn't seem so long and dangerous.

"Good night, Adam."

"Good night."

She turned to leave. Before she could open the door to the hallway, he spoke.

"Jane?"

"Yes?" Oh stop, she told herself, hating how hopeful she sounded.

"It won't happen again."

The kiss. Of course not. Why would he have thought she'd think otherwise?

"I know." That was the hell of it really. She did know.

Chapter Six

He was as good as his word, Jane thought. He and the moving company.

The large van containing all of her worldly possessions had shown up promptly at ten Monday morning. Adam had disappeared from her life a couple of hours earlier. From the bay window in the guest room, she'd watched him walk out the front door and around the house toward the garage. He hadn't looked up at her or back at the house. Either he hadn't sensed her watching him or he hadn't cared. Probably a little of both.

It was Friday, now. Jane brushed her bangs out of her eyes and stared at the stack of books in front of her. She was alphabetizing them as she placed them on the shelves. She sighed. Okay. She was alone; she could admit the truth to herself, if to no one else. She was lonely.

Returning to Orchard had sounded so noble when she'd lain awake in her bed in San Francisco. She would unite father and daughter, be a wonderful teacher, provide her child with a warm, loving and stable environment. When she'd imagined the scene, there had been a Joan of Arc sort of glow around her head in reward for all her good deeds.

Reality turned out to be very different. She hadn't seen Adam since Sunday, so she wasn't making any progress on that front. School wouldn't start until early September. She'd planned her lessons before she'd left San Francisco. And as for Billie— She smiled. She'd love to take the credit for her daughter fitting in so well, but it was all Billie's doing. Adam had sent, via Charlene, information on the local softball league. By Tuesday Billie had been enrolled in the park's summer-camp program and assigned to a team. She came home every day with new battle scars from her activities and tales of friends made and adventures experienced.

Jane rose to her feet and walked from the den to the kitchen. White tiles gleamed from her thorough scrubbing. Food filled the pantry. Everything had been unpacked and put away.

Maybe she shouldn't have worked so quickly, she thought as she leaned against the counter and stared out the kitchen window into the backyard. But it had been hard not to. She wasn't sleeping well. Only by staying busy could she keep Adam and the kiss they had shared from her mind.

Back in San Francisco, she'd had friends and activities to fill her time. Here she knew people but—she shook her head—they would ask questions she couldn't answer. Not until Adam knew the truth. She could go see Charlene, but the older woman had her own life. She was currently planning a trip to Greece. A movie about an older woman finding if not love then certainly passion in the beautiful islands had inspired her to travel to the Mediterranean. In addition, Billie had mentioned something about Charlene arranging for a few of her trucker friends to stop by before she left. Jane grinned. She wouldn't want to touch that one.

She remembered the time she had casually asked the

other woman about her visiting male friends. Charlene's frank lecture of the joys of sex had left her blushing for days. When she'd told Adam about the conversation, he'd laughed for several minutes, then had teased that it was her own fault for inquiring. When she'd protested, he'd pulled her close and offered to illustrate some of Charlene's more interesting points. She'd turned away, embarrassed and scared and he'd—

She groaned. It always came back to Adam. Stop thinking about him, she ordered herself. She forced herself to mentally create a list of other chores she could do to fill her time. There was always the mending. Billie destroyed her clothes on a regular basis. And she could tackle the attic. Her mother had left several boxes up there.

She glanced at the clock. Almost twelve. She should do something about lunch. That would fill a few minutes.

The back door banged open and Billie stormed into the kitchen.

"Mom! I'm home!" she announced as she flew across the room and into her mother's arms.

"So I see." Jane hugged her close. "It's early."

"Friday's only a half day at camp and I don't have a game until tomorrow." Billie looked up at her, her baseball hat pulled down so low, she had to crane her neck to see below it. "Can you make cupcakes for after the game?"

"Sure."

Billie grinned. "Great. I told the guys you would." She stepped back and dug out the ever-present softball from her dirty red shorts pocket. "Sometimes boys are dumb," she said.

Jane chuckled. "Interesting observation. Why do you say that?"

"They tell me I can't do stuff 'cuz I'm a girl."

"So?"

"So I threatened to beat them up." She tossed the softball into the air.

If Jane hadn't been present at Billie's birth, she might have questioned whether or not this child was really hers. "Don't throw that in the house," she warned. "Why not just do what they say you can't and show them up that way?"

"Maybe." She walked to the refrigerator and pulled open the door. "I'm hungry."

"I was just about to make lunch."

Billie peered inside the fridge. "Something good, okay?"

"Are you insulting my cooking?"

"Mo-om. I just thought we could forget about vegetables until dinner. It's Friday."

"So?"

"So, I just thought. You know. For a treat. How come we don't have that center thing in our kitchen like Adam does?"

Jane blinked at the quick change in subject. "Do you mean the island?"

"Yeah." Billie shut the fridge and stared around the room. "It has stools to sit at, like a restaurant counter. I eat there at breakfast."

"What?" Her heart lurched. "I thought you were visiting Charlene in the mornings before camp."

"Nope." Billie smiled, unconcerned. "I went over there Monday, but she said she wasn't a morning person and that I should have breakfast with Adam."

Jane felt faint. "You've been there every day this week?"

"Yup."

She didn't sound too panicky. Billie and Adam eating breakfast together? Every day? It was inconceivable. On Monday Billie had bounced out of bed, her normal cheerful self, and had asked if she could visit Charlene before camp. Jane had known the other woman would have shooed the girl away if she was being a pest—but never would she have imagined Charlene sending her to Adam. Here she'd been worried about him having a chance to get to know Billie and it was already happening right under her nose.

"So, Mom, can we have a center island in our kitchen?"

"We don't have room here, honey."

Jane forced her thoughts away from father and daughter sharing a meal and studied the small room. Counters lined two walls, with a built-in stove in the middle of one and the sink in the middle of the other. Opposite the stove stood the refrigerator; opposite the sink, the old-fashioned Formica table with four matching vinyl chairs. She remembered that set from her childhood. The yellow, green-and-orange abstract shapes had reminded her of Crispy Critters breakfast cereal. Her mother had hated the set, but her father had picked it out, so she'd lived with it. Jane recalled that as she ate her solitary breakfast each morning, she used to make up stories about the imaginary animals running across the Formica tabletop.

"But I like the island." Billie tossed her ball in the air and caught it. "Maybe we could make the kitchen bigger."

Jane pulled off the cap and ruffled her daughter's bangs. "One, don't throw your ball inside. And two, we don't have the money. Besides, it's just the two of us. We don't need more room. We already have three bedrooms."

"I like Adam's house better."

So do I, Jane thought, thinking of the large graceful mansion built before the turn of the century. The inside had been modernized, but each room maintained an elegance that couldn't be manufactured today. By comparison, her house was small and dark. Still, it was home to her. The price was right and when she got a couple of paychecks in the bank, she'd be able to make some changes. Her mother had often talked about remodeling. She'd even made some sketches of the new room layouts and had pinned swatches of carpet and wallpaper to the sheets. Jane's father had vetoed the idea, telling his wife that her foolish plans were just a waste of time and money. Her mother had turned away without a word and the sketches had disappeared, never to be mentioned again.

"It's a nice house," Jane said, pushing away her memories. "And ours will be, too. In time. Now you go play while I make lunch."

"What are we going to do this afternoon?"

"What would you like?"

"The pool." Brown eyes glowed with excitement. "And ice cream."

"I think we can manage that."

"All right!" Billie raised her arm and held her hand open. Jane hit it with her own, then paused for the high-five to be returned. "You're the best."

"Thank you. You're somewhat of an exceptional child yourself."

"I know." Billie grinned, then ran from the room.

Jane pulled out sandwich fixings and the salad she'd been planning on having for herself. After spooning the lettuce and vegetable mixture into two bowls, she used raisins to make eyes, Chinese noodles for hair and a ribbon of honey-mustard dressing for a mouth. If the plate looked interesting enough, Billie often forgot that salad meant vegetables. It wasn't that she didn't like green food, it was more that she felt it was her job to protest eating them. Kids, Jane thought with affection and a flash of longing that she could have had four more just like Billie. It would have been a handful, but more than worth the effort. Her daughter brought her joy and fulfillment. She gave her all the love and—

Crash!

"Billie?" Jane called as she wiped her hands on a dish towel and walked out of the kitchen. "I told you not to throw your ball inside. What have you broken?"

"Nothing." But the small girl stood beside the living room coffee table and stared at the broken remains of what used to be a glass. "It slipped."

"You didn't throw your ball?"

Billie shuffled her feet. "Not really."

Jane waited.

The girl sighed. "Yeah, Mom, I threw it." Her shoulders slumped in a defeated gesture. "I'm sorry."

"Thank you for apologizing. However, sorry doesn't replace the glass. We've been over this before. No ball throwing in the house."

"I know." The words came out as a whisper. "Here." She held out her ball.

Jane took it.

"Where do you want me?" Billie asked.

"The hallway. Facing the back wall."

Billie shuffled forward slowly, out of the living room, then down the hall until she reached the far wall. She sank to the floor and stared at the blank space. "How long?"

Jane glanced at her watch. "Ten minutes."

Billie leaned her forehead against the wall. "I really didn't mean to do it, Mom."

"A time-out means no talking."

"Sorry."

Parenting was tough, Jane thought as she moved back into the kitchen and set the timer for ten minutes. The punishment hurt her as much as her daughter, but Billie wouldn't believe that for about fifteen or twenty more years. After sweeping up the broken glass, she continued with the lunch. She finished the last sandwich when the timer went off. There was a shuffling noise in the hall.

Billie appeared at the doorway. Tears created two clean streaks down her freckled cheeks. Her lower lip thrust out as she swallowed.

Automatically Jane held out her arms. Billie flung herself against her mother and held on tightly. "I still love you," Jane murmured against her hair. "You'll always be my favorite girl."

"I'm sorry, Mom," Billie said, then hiccuped. "I didn't mean to break anything."

It was the stress of moving, Jane thought as she blinked away her own tears. Usually punishment didn't faze Billie, except that she found the time-outs boring. But sometimes, like today, they affected her deeply. With her bubbly personality and outgoing nature, it was easy to forget that she was still just an eight-year-old little girl.

"Let's forget about it and eat lunch. Okay?"

"Okay." Billie raised herself up on tiptoe and gave her a salty kiss. "I love you, Mommy."

"And I love you."

Jane gave her a last squeeze and pushed her toward the table. Billie looked at the salad and then at her. A tentative smile tugged one corner of her mouth. "I'm not fooled by the clown face."

"But you'll eat it."

Billie stuck a raisin in her mouth. "Maybe."

Jane poured lemonade for both of them and chuckled. Despite the mishaps, parenting was worth it. She felt sorry for people who couldn't have children in their lives. The ones who were infertile or never married or—

The pitcher slipped from her grasp and she barely caught it. What about the people who didn't know they had children? Guilt swept over her; the strong wave threatened to pull her under.

Adam. He had a child he didn't know about. Apparently Billie had already taken it upon herself to get better acquainted with her own father. Oh, please God, what was she supposed to do about the mess she'd made of everything? She had to tell him. And soon. But how? What would he say? What would Billie say? She preached that honesty was the best policy, but she'd told the biggest lie of all. What was she going to do now?

Billie glanced at her. "Aren't you eating?"

"What?" Jane stared down at her full plate. "Of course." She took a bite of her sandwich.

"What are we going to do until we can go swimming?" Billie asked.

"What do you mean?"

"You know, we can't go in the water until our food has digested. We'll get cramps and drown." She made gagging noises and clutched her throat. "I'm drowning. Save me, save me. Ahhhgg!"

"We could walk around town."

"Can we visit Charlene?"

"Not today." Jane thought about those truckers due to arrive at any time. "Maybe we could—"

The idea popped into her mind fully formed. She couldn't. She shouldn't. She bit into her sandwich and chewed. It was wrong. No, not wrong. In fact she had every right to be there. It was, after all, a business.

"We need to go to the bank," she said.

"Bor-ring."

"I have to open a new checking account and we need to move your college fund out here."

Billie sat up straight. "I have money?"

"For college."

"Oh. But maybe I could—"

"No."

"But you didn't let me—"

"No."

"What if I don't want to go to college?"

Jane smiled sweetly. "Baseball scouts go to college games."

Billie nibbled on a Chinese noodle. "I'm going."

"I knew you'd say that."

"Do I have to come with you to the bank?"

"Yes."

"Where's the bank?"

"In town."

"Which one is it?"

"There's only one. Barrington First National."

Billie frowned. "That's Adam's name."

"It's his bank."

"Here are the changes you requested, Mr. Barrington."

Adam stared blankly at the folder.

"From the loan committee meeting on Monday," his secretary reminded him patiently.

"Of course, Edna." He took the offered pages and smiled. "I'll look at them this afternoon."

She raised her penciled eyebrows until they disappeared under the sprayed fringe of hair that curled to precisely the midpoint of her forehead. "When else?" she asked.

"What? Oh, the reports. Yes, I always read them on Friday afternoon. You're right." He glanced at his watch. "On time, as usual. Thank you."

Edna's narrow lips pursed together. Her heavy makeup and the fitted long narrow dresses and jackets she wore made her look like a time traveler from 1940. She'd been with him since he'd taken over the bank and with his father for who knows how many years before that.

"Are you feeling all right, Mr. Barrington?" she asked.

Despite the fact she'd known him since his diaper days, she always addressed him formally. After fifteen years, he'd given up trying to break through to her softer side. He'd begun to suspect she didn't have one.

"I am a little scattered," he admitted.

She nodded as if to agree. "You don't want to talk about it, do you?" She asked the question because it was polite, but her folded arms and the fact that she was inching toward his office door told him that she really didn't want his confidences.

"No, Edna, I don't."

"Well, I'm here." She smiled quickly and let it fade.

"I'll be at my desk, Mr. Barrington. If you're sure you're all right?"

"I'm fine."

"Good."

She ducked out before he could begin his confession. Adam grinned and turned in his chair to stare out the big window behind his desk. Green grass stretched out on this side of the building. The bank sat on a corner and backed up on the town square. Pecan trees, the oblong fruit just beginning to turn brown, provided shade. Several employees sat in the early afternoon sun, taking their lunch break outdoors.

Orchard was a long way from New York or Los Angeles or Chicago, the places where his university friends had gone after Harvard. At one time he'd thought about leaving for the big city. But his parents had died at the end of his freshman year while he was at Harvard. He'd been the oldest son, and the Barrington heir. With two young siblings to care for, a bank to keep in business and an eccentric aunt who needed as much supervision as she provided, there had been no room for dreams about moving somewhere else. He didn't mind that his fate had been set when he was born, and sealed by the premature death of his parents. But sometimes he thought about what it would have been like if he'd been able to grow up at his own pace. The parties and social events of his freshman year had given way to extra classes and study. He'd graduated a semester early so that he could return home and take over the bank.

Turning back toward his desk, he picked up the report Edna had left him. He knew he was driving his staff crazy. In the last few days he'd wandered around in a fog, upsetting a routine they'd all grown used to. He knew the cause—as much as he hated to admit the fact that he couldn't drive her from his mind as easily as he'd driven her from his house.

Jane.

He stared at a portrait of his father hanging on the opposite wall. "Did Mom ever give you this much trouble?" he asked quietly. Not that Jane was troubling him, he amended quickly. He barely thought about her at all. And when he did, it was with completely justified anger and indignation. He hadn't forgiven her for her childish behavior and the damage she'd done all those years ago. In fact...

Adam shook his head. He was a lousy liar. Always had been. It was his damn Southern upbringing. Too much talk about being a gentleman and the dance lessons they'd made him attend between football practices. He grinned as he remembered Charlene's discussion with Billie about charm school. The girl had been adamant in her refusal, and her mother had backed her up. He wondered if Billie would stay a tomboy long or if the pressure of society would force her to conform. Just this morning, she'd regaled him with stories about her quest for the perfect curve ball. He'd informed her that he hoped she found one that didn't destroy windows.

She'd wrinkled her nose at him. The quick gesture, a mirror of what Jane had done when he'd teased her, had made his resolve to forget falter. Billie had slipped past his guard too easily as well, he thought. With a little help.

On Monday, the morning after— He refused to think about kissing Jane, he told himself firmly. It hadn't meant anything. It had been a flash of temper or an attempt to prove to her that she couldn't affect him. He hadn't kissed her because he'd wanted to. After what she'd done, she was lucky he hadn't run her out of town. Showing up after all this time, with no warning. He didn't care, of course. She meant nothing to him now. He wanted—

Stop thinking about her, he commanded himself. Billie. That was safe. He recalled last Monday morning. He'd been drinking his morning coffee. Charlene had found Billie lurking outside his back door.

"I wanted to say hi to Adam," she'd said. He'd put down his paper, not sure if he welcomed the interruption or not.

"Adam has a very rigid schedule in the morning," Charlene had answered. "He doesn't like to be disturbed." She laughed then and held open the door. "Go right in."

He'd been cursed, he thought, toying with the engraved letter opener that had been his grandfather's. Cursed to endure the women in his life. Charlene. God, someone could write a book about her. And now Billie. A four-foot-nothing bundle of energy who had already wormed her way into his life. She was funny and intriguing as hell. But not as intriguing as Jane.

He pulled out his right-hand drawer and glanced at the brochure lying on top. The neighboring town sponsored a Triple-A baseball team. They were home for the next couple of weeks. Maybe he could get tickets and take Billie. She'd like that. And if her mother wanted to tag along...

Adam slammed the drawer shut. Was he crazy? He didn't want to see Jane. And even if he did, hadn't he learned his lesson? The woman had publicly humiliated him. The only emotion left was anger, and even that didn't matter. He refused to feel anything else. He couldn't. It cost too much.

But the rage, so easily tapped into over the weekend, had faded with the passing week. It became harder and harder to focus on the past and what she had done and not wonder what had drawn her back to Orchard. Why now? Why here? He sensed some secret behind her carefully worded explanations. Had she returned for absolution? A second chance?

He shook his head. Not that. She hadn't cared enough the first time. Why the hell would he think she'd want to try again? And if she did—he picked up the letter opener and stared at the engraving—he wasn't fool enough to get his heart broken a second time. He wasn't interested in Jane Southwick. Not now. Not ever.

Adam rose from his desk and walked to his door. After pulling it open, he stepped into the hallway. To his left were the rest of the offices, the supply cabinet and the lunch room that was only used in the winter. To the right was the bank. A couple of people stood in line. Old man Grayson and his wife hovered by the safety deposit box cage, waiting to get inside. Every couple of weeks or so, they took their box into one of the private cubbyholes and spent a few minutes with their personal treasures. For as long as he could remember, they'd been coming here. He'd give a sizable chunk of his estate to know exactly what was in the box. As a kid, he and his friends had speculated about everything from stolen gold to body parts.

A flash of movement by the front door caught his attention. He turned. And drew in a sharp breath. It was as if his thoughts had conjured her from thin air.

Jane held the door open for her daughter. Billie skipped in and looked around. Adam slipped behind one of the old-fashioned pillars, then cursed himself for being a coward. This was *his* bank, dammit. He had every right to be here. But he stayed where he was and watched them.

Like Edna, Jane was a throwback to another time. While she didn't wear the heavy makeup his secretary favored, she'd never fully embraced the concept of wearing pants or shorts. A white T-shirt, with a V front that made him wonder what happened when she bent over, covered her upper body. A flowing skirt in a feminine print fluttered around her thighs and fell to mid-calf. The long hair that, years before, had haunted his thoughts until his hands ached to touch it and his body had throbbed for hers, had been tied back. No braid this time, but a ponytail that swung with each step.

She looked young, he thought. Innocent. Incapable of the deception she had committed. For the first time he allowed himself to wonder why. Why had she left him? Why couldn't he forget her? In the nine years she'd been gone, he'd managed to push her to the back of his mind. She'd been home less than a week, and she haunted every moment of his day. He must exorcise this ghost from his life, he told himself grimly. There wasn't room for her anymore.

Chapter Seven

Jane glanced around the bank and sighed with relief. No Adam. Funny how at the house, the decision to go see him had sounded like such a good idea. Yet the reality of coming face-to-face with the person who would least like to see her made her squirm.

She glanced around at the old-fashioned lobby. Not that much had changed. On one side of the building stood the teller windows, on the other, the desks for the various departments. The marble floor had been imported from Italy and would outlast the town. The walls looked like they'd received a recent coat of paint, and the woodwork gleamed from constant care. Everything was exactly as she remembered. Even the old couple waiting by the safety deposit box cage looked as if they'd stepped out of a Norman Rockwell painting. *Going Banking,* she thought, giving the imaginary artwork a title, then giggling nervously. Beside her Billie danced from one foot to the other.

"This place is cool," Billie said, her loud voice drifting up to the arched ceiling and echoing.

"Shh," Jane warned, before her daughter could exercise her vocal cords in a serious way. "People are trying to do business here. No talking."

"You're talking," Billie pointed out.

Jane prayed for patience. Taking a deep breath, she located the desk with the New Accounts plaque and headed that way.

The woman behind the desk looked up and smiled. Then her smile faded, and a faint frown appeared between her eyebrows. Jane struggled to put a name to the semifamiliar face. Oh, no. Old Miss Yarns. She'd taught Jane's fourth-grade Sunday School class and had been stern with her requirements and free with her discipline.

"Jane? Jane Southwick?" Miss Yarns rose to her feet and held out her hand. "It has been several years, has it not?"

"Yes, Miss Yarns." The walls of this old institution would probably crack and fall if Miss Yarns used a contraction, Jane thought. "Nine. Years." She grabbed Billie's hand and drew her closer, as much for protection as to be polite. "My daughter, Belle Charlene."

Billie glared at her mother. "Billie," she said, then smiled. "I bet you can slide real good on this floor, huh?" she said, staring at the marble tiles. "You ever take your shoes off and—"

"No." Miss Yarns blanched and resumed her seat. "I had heard you were back in town, Jane. Do you want to open an account with Barrington First National?"

No, Miss Yarns, I came over to New Accounts because of the stimulating company. "Yes," she said demurely, sitting in one of the cloth-covered chairs in front of the woman's desk and pointing to tell Billie to do the same. "I have an account in San Francisco that I've closed." She slipped her purse off her shoulder and onto her lap, then pulled out a cashier's check.

"Very well." She reached into her desk and withdrew an

application form. Miss Yarns didn't believe in rings or bracelets, and she would rather be flogged than wear earrings. Just a plain gold watch and a suit so conservative she'd look at home sitting in on the Supreme Court. "Will this be a joint account?"

"No, it's—" Oh, God. Jane clamped her mouth shut. It was too late. Miss Yarns's perfectly plucked brows rose, and she glanced from Billie, bouncing in her seat, to Jane's bare left hand. Damn small towns, Jane thought. And herself for being fool enough to come back.

"You will be the only person signing on this account." It wasn't a question.

"Yes."

"I see."

They should have gone to the pool right after lunch and taken their chances with drowning. It would have been more fun.

"And the name on the account?"

"Mine."

"I know that, dear. The *last* name."

Jane took a deep breath. In San Francisco, no one had known her well enough to realize Southwick was her maiden name. Everyone assumed she was divorced. Or didn't care. But this wasn't San Francisco. It was her hometown. Maybe Miss Yarns would think she'd gone back to her maiden name because— Yeah, right. It shouldn't matter what this old relic thought of her. In a way it didn't. But rumors got started so easily. And Billie would be the one hurt by them.

"Southwick," she said at last. "Jane Southwick."

Those perfect brows rose a notch higher, as the older woman glanced speculatively at Billie. "I see."

Did she? Jane wondered. What if the town of Orchard figured out the truth before she got the courage to tell Adam?

"Why does that lady keep looking at me?" Billie asked in a stage whisper.

Miss Yarns had the grace to flush slightly and glance away.

"I don't know," Jane lied, knowing she could never explain this to her daughter. Not yet, anyway.

"Need any help here?"

Jane looked up and saw Adam standing beside his employee's desk.

"Adam!" Billie scrambled out of her chair and raced to him. With the trust of a child who knows she will never be allowed to fall, she launched herself upward. He caught her under her arms and swung her around.

"What are you doing here, peanut?"

"Peanut?" Billie wrinkled her nose. "I'm *not* a peanut."

"That's right." He tugged on the bill of her baseball cap. "You're a soon-to-be famous pitcher of our champion Little League."

Jane swallowed against the lump in her throat. It had happened so quickly, she thought. In just five days, they'd become friends. Was it Billie's outgoing nature, Adam's charm or was it genetic? Did they, on some subconscious level, recognize themselves as family? She *had* to tell him, tell them both. Soon. But not yet. There was more at stake than friendship. More than Adam's right to know he was a father. Billie, and how all this would affect her, was Jane's most important consideration.

"You haven't answered my question," Adam said, shifting Billie until she leaned against his chest. Her arms wrapped around his neck and he supported her weight with his left arm. Jane wasn't sure if it was in deference to summer or the fact that it was Friday, but he'd abandoned his suit jacket. His white shirt fit perfectly, the long sleeves showing the ripple of his muscles as he shifted Billie's weight. "What are you doing here?"

"Banking. We're opening an account."

Miss Yarns had watched the greeting and subsequent conversation. Obviously Billie and Adam knew each other well.

Her mouth had opened slightly, as her jaw had dropped farther and farther down.

"Billie is a very outgoing child," Jane said, hoping the other woman wouldn't notice the similarities between the man and the little girl.

"I see that." Her face sharpened as lines of disapproval pulled her mouth straight. "Perhaps we could get on with this form. Your place of employment?"

"I'll handle this, Miss Yarns."

The older woman glanced up at her employer. "Mr. Barrington, I assure you I am entirely capable—"

"I know," he said, with an easy grin. "As a favor. Please."

"Well. If you put it like that, I am sure I cannot say no." She rose slowly from her chair and brushed her hands against her skirt. "I will take my lunch now. If it is convenient?"

"Of course."

She walked away as if her back were made of steel. Jane bit the inside of her lip to keep from smiling. No doubt the old biddy was convinced something sinful was going to happen in front of God and everybody, not to mention on *her* desk.

Jane raised her eyes to Adam's face. Their gazes locked for a second, and he winked. The playful moment, stolen between the reality of their mutual past and present, caught her unaware. She smiled back. In that blink of time—before he remembered who she was and what she had done—they connected.

The heat that filled her chest and radiated out along her arms and legs wasn't about sex. It was about the comfortable, the comforting and the familiar. This is the Adam she had adored while growing up. The man with the quick wit and the ability to laugh at everyone, including himself. These were the flashes of fun, between his days of responsibility, that had made her fall in love and want to be everything for him. He took care of those around him, so she never worried about him not being a good husband or father. It was that he rarely took time to be anything else. That had frightened her the most. What if he had turned out to be like her father? She too would have lost her dreams. She'd been too young to even have many dreams, let alone believe in them.

But he hadn't turned into her father, she realized as he looked away and whispered something to Billie. The need to control was still there, as strong as ever, but so was the joy and the humor. Had she been wrong to not trust him? Was she wrong now to want to try?

"All right." Adam set Billie on the corner of the desk, and sat in Miss Yarns's chair. "Let's see if I remember how to do this. You're opening a checking account?" He looked up at Jane.

She nodded.

"I can do that. I think. Address. I know that. Occupation. Teacher. Employer." He filled in most of the card, asking for her social security number and the new phone number at her house. His thick dark hair showed signs of a recent cut. One stubborn lock slipped down on his forehead. Billie leaned toward him, her hand casually resting on his shoulder. They looked right together.

As he wrote the information in his neat script, joked with her daughter and tossed her the occasional casual smile, Jane wanted to scream. This was the first time she'd seen him since the kiss. He was acting as if nothing had happened between them. As if that passionate moment had been meaningless. Could he just put it behind him? Did he kiss so many women that he could easily forget one or two? Or was it Jane he was so quick to forget?

"That seems to be everything. Do you want to look at the check design book?" he asked.

"I'll just take the standard ones."

"Do they have baseball checks?" Billie asked.

"Not yet." Adam smiled at her. "Maybe I'll call the printing company and make that suggestion." He gave the form a once-over, then frowned. "You want the account in your maiden name?"

As unexpectedly as the good humor and friendliness had arrived, they faded. His mouth thinned and the lines of his body stiffened.

"Yes." She looked around the bank, at the tellers watching their exchange, at the interested faces of the people standing in line, to Billie staring intently. This wasn't the time to tell him she'd never been married.

"What's a maiden name?" her daughter asked.

"It's the name a woman has before she gets married," Jane answered, hoping she wasn't about to dig herself a hole. "Southwick is your maiden name."

"How come girls have to take boys' names?"

Jane offered her daughter a shaky smile. "It's a tradition."

"So if you get married, you get a different last name?"

"Yes."

She thought for a moment. "What if I don't like his last name? What if it's dumb?"

"Then you can keep your own."

Adam shot her a questioning glance.

"She can if she wants to."

He raised his hands up as if to show he wasn't armed. "Hey, this is your discussion. I'm not going to say a word. Far be it from me, a mere man, to interfere."

Billie shifted on the seat and looked at her mother. "Why don't you use your married name? Was my dad's last name dumb?"

"No. It was—" She cleared her throat. Not here. Not in the bank during business hours, with half the town of Orchard watching. "I didn't want to—" It was hard to lie to her daughter. Harder, perhaps, to lie to Adam. "We'll discuss this at home."

"But I don't understand," she whined.

Rescue came from an unexpected source. "I've been wondering what's different about you today," Adam said to Billie. "You don't have your softball with you. Did you forget it?"

Billie shot Jane a glare. "I was a reptile."

"A what?" Adam asked.

"Reptile. Reptile behavior. I broke a glass."

Jane sighed in relief. The reprieve gave her time to think. She leaned forward. "I think she means disreputable behavior. Billie isn't supposed to throw her ball in the house. She broke a glass. Part of the punishment is that I keep the softball for the rest of the day."

"Bummer, huh," Billie said with a heavy sigh.

"That's what you get," he said, then made a fist and lightly tapped her chin. "You'll get it back tomorrow, in time for the game."

"You coming? I'm going to pitch."

Adam's gaze found Jane's, as if asking what she thought. Yes, please do, she answered silently to him, then turned to Billie. "Adam might be busy, honey."

"You *always* say that about people. But everybody likes me. They *want* to watch me pitch. Don't you?"

Adam grinned. "Of course."

"See." Billie placed her hands on her hips. "I told you."

"Where do you get this nerve from?" Jane asked. Then she could have slapped herself. Talk about putting her foot in it. But neither Billie nor Adam followed up on her comment.

He passed the form to her to sign, then handed her a stack of temporary checks. Their fingers came close to touching but didn't. She wanted to reach out and stroke the white cuff of his shirt. She wanted to keep him smiling at her. Instead she took the checks he offered.

"That should keep you going until the real ones come from the printer," he said. "Are there other accounts? What about your savings?"

"I don't have one."

He tried not to react, but she read the surprise on his face.

"I've been going to school to get my teaching credential," she said, her voice a little sharper than she'd intended. "And I've been working, as well. There wasn't very much left over each month. There are expenses with a child and—"

"I'm not judging you, Jane."

She leaned back in her chair and shook her head. "Sorry. I'm overreacting. I guess it's because I have this argument with my parents every time I see them."

"Grandma always tries to give Mom money and she always says no. Sometimes they cry."

Thanks for sharing, Billie, Jane thought ruefully, realizing she'd have to be more careful about what she said and did while her daughter was in the room.

"We do have Billie's college fund," she said, to change the subject. She pulled out the forms. "I guess we need to transfer this, or something. I didn't want to close the account and risk the tax status."

He took the papers. "You don't have a savings account, but Billie has a college fund?"

"Yes."

Something flickered in his brown eyes, something warm and genuine. She willed time to freeze, so that he would go on like this forever, but Billie leaned over them, her foot kicking the business card holder onto the floor and sending Miss Yarns's cards scattering in all directions.

"Oops, sorry." Billie slid to the edge of the desk and jumped to the floor. "I'll get them."

Jane watched to make sure she'd landed safely, then glanced back at Adam, but the contact had been broken. He studied the account information.

"It's pretty standard," he said. "We'll put it in her name, with you ATF."

"Fine."

"What's ATF?" Billie shoved the loose cards onto the desk and reached for the holder.

"As trustee for. It means your mom can handle the account for you."

"I want to take care of my own money."

"You can't."

"Why?"

"You're a child."

"It's for *my* college."

"When you're ready for college, then you'll have a say-so. Until then, it is being kept for you."

Billie tilted her chin up. Adam straightened in his chair.

"How do I know the money will be there? What if someone wants to spend my money?"

"No one will do that."

"How do you know?"

"I'm the bank president. It's my job to know."

Billie planted her hands on her hips. "What if *you* spend it?"

"That's against the law."

"Oh."

Identical pairs of brown eyes flashed with identical fire. Billie's cap hid most of her hair, but Jane knew the color was close, too close, to her father's. Matching shoulders squared against the opponent, similar mouths straightened.

How couldn't they know? Why didn't everyone see it? They were two peas in a pod, a matched set, father and daughter. It was as if a fist closed over her heart and began to squeeze. She was playing with two lives. What would the price of honesty be? Would she lose them both?

Billie gave in first. She looked away. "Then I guess it's okay."

"Thank you."

Billie looked at her. "I'm thirsty."

"There's a soda machine in the lunch room," Adam said, before she could respond. "It's at the end of that hallway. Go pick out what you'd like." He shrugged. "If it's all right with your mother."

"Fine. Thank you." Jane reached for her purse.

"No charge," he said. "The bank gives them to the employees."

"Cool." Billie turned to race away.

"No running in here," Jane cautioned.

"Mo-om."

"You heard me."

"Okay."

Billie moved off at a pace too slow for a run, but too fast for a walk. By the end of the teller line, she was skipping, and when she reached the hallway, she whooped loudly and raced down the slick floor.

Jane stared after her. "Sometimes I think I've failed completely with her."

"Billie's her own person."

"She is that."

She looked back at Adam, then wished she hadn't. Someone somewhere had turned a switch. The friendly man from her past had disappeared and in his place sat the cool, controlled stranger. She couldn't see the wall between them, but she felt its thickness. When she offered a tentative smile, he simply stared.

"You must be very busy," she said, clutching her purse to her chest. "I don't want to keep you."

He blinked and looked at the application form in his hands. Was he wondering about her maiden name or the existence of an ex-husband somewhere? Did she flatter herself with the question?

"You're doing a good job," he said.

"What?"

"With Billie. I can imagine how hard it is to raise a child alone."

He surprised her. She set her purse on the floor and folded her hands together on her lap. "I wanted to be self-sufficient. My parents..." She sighed. "The first couple of years, I couldn't have made it without them. Then I began to realize that I was becoming dependent. I started returning the money they sent, got a better paying job and went back to school."

"All this with a baby?"

"By then, Billie was around two." She laughed. "You can imagine what the terrible twos were like with her."

One corner of his firm mouth tilted up slightly. "I would have liked to have seen that."

His words hit her like a blow to the midsection. What would he think when he found out the truth? "Let's just say, I went through a lot of baby-sitters," she said, hoping her voice didn't tremble.

"She's a wonderful girl."

"I know."

"She reminds me of Dani at that age."

"I hadn't thought about that, but you're right." Did she look like his sister at that age, as well? Don't panic, she told herself. He wouldn't figure out the truth on his own. She still had time; just not as much as she'd thought. She collected her purse and stood up. "Thanks for everything, Adam. I appreciate the personal attention."

He rose and walked around the desk. Her foolish heart fluttered slightly. He'd always been too damn good-looking, she thought, wishing it didn't matter. Her lips tingled as if the closer proximity brought to life the remembered sensations of their kiss. Did he think about it, too? Did he lie awake at night and remember their lovemaking, all those years ago? Did he think about how different it would be now that she was grown and willing to take him on her own terms?

"Charlene said that she'd like to invite you and Billie to dinner on Sunday," he said without meeting her eyes. "Four o'clock. Can you make it?"

The invitation surprised her, but not the way he distanced himself from it. "I..." She wasn't sure she'd be ready to face Adam so soon after today. But she didn't have a choice. She had Billie to consider. "We'd love to."

Maybe another meeting with him would give her the courage to tell him the truth.

He nicked himself shaving. Adam stared in disbelief at his reflection in the mirror. Sure enough, a drop of blood formed just to the left of his chin. As he watched, it trickled down and dripped onto the bathroom counter. He hadn't done that in years. Muttering a curse, he tore off a piece of tissue and stuck it on his cut, then finished shaving. He should have gotten out while he had the chance. An old friend had called to invite him to a play in Atlanta. The old friend—a woman—had included dinner and breakfast in her invitation. He'd been tempted for less than a second.

Jane wasn't the reason he'd said no, he told himself for the hundredth time as he pulled on twill trousers and a polo shirt. He didn't give a damn if she was coming over for dinner. It was Charlene's invitation, not his. Just because his aunt entertained all her friends—except for the truckers—in his house didn't change anything. Hell, he didn't even have to show up. He could work in his study, or watch the game on TV.

That's what he'd do, he decided, as he brushed his hair, then straightened the collar on his shirt. He would watch the game. After slipping on his shoes, he started down the stairs. There was a knock.

"I'll get it," he called to Charlene who was already hard at work in the kitchen.

Just as he reached the front door, he remembered to brush the piece of tissue from his face.

"We're here," Billie said, walking in slowly, a pie balanced precariously in her hands. "Mom made fresh blueberry pie. Yum. I could smell it all morning, but she wouldn't let me have none."

"Any." Jane came in behind her daughter and offered him a shy smile.

"Any," Billie repeated. "Or none. It's the same." She thrust the pie at Adam. "Where's Charlene? I want to say hello. Then can we watch the game?"

"Billie! I told you this was a visit. No sports."

"But the Braves are playing San Francisco. That's my team. I'll *die* if I don't watch."

He took the pie. "In the kitchen," he said, jerking his head in that direction. "Then go on into the study. The TV is already on the right channel."

"Cool." She dashed away.

He stared after her. "No softball, and she's wearing a dress. I'm impressed."

"Don't be. She's wearing shorts under the dress and is convinced you have a hardball somewhere she can play with." Hazel eyes met and held his. "If you do, please don't let her get her hands on it. I can't make any promises about breakables."

"I'll keep it hidden. Please, come in."

She stepped past him, into the foyer. Her perfume followed like a soft floral breeze, teasing his senses and making him wonder what the anger had been all about. Again she offered a tentative smile. This time he returned it.

"You look beautiful." He spoke without thinking.

She blushed, but didn't look away. "Thank you."

A green-and-white dress hugged her curves from shoulder to hips, then flared out around her thighs. The off-the-shoulder sleeves left her neck bare. But it was her hair that captured his attention. For once, she'd left it long. Soft curls cascaded down her back. A small spray of tiny white flowers had been pinned over her right ear. Light makeup made her hazel eyes darken to green and her lips look full and kissable.

The kiss. He couldn't forget it, wouldn't repeat it. His gaze centered on her mouth. She'd tasted sweet, willing. Not the shy timid girl he'd remembered. He would have thought he'd miss that, when he'd kissed her. He'd been wrong. There was something to be said for experience, and a woman who wasn't afraid of what she wanted.

"Adam!" Billie called from the back of the house. "The game's already started. And *my* team just scored a run."

"I'd better go help Charlene," Jane said, reaching out and taking the pie from his hands. Their fingers brushed.

Funny thing about the past, he thought, resisting the urge to touch her face. What they had shared years before made it so easy to forget the distance they'd traveled. He'd thought he'd have to fight hating her. Perhaps he still did. But he'd never imagined he'd have to fight wanting her.

"And I should check on your daughter before she destroys something valuable."

Her tongue swept across her lower lip. His body vibrated with need.

"Charlene is waiting," she said, swaying toward him.

"Adam!" came the call.

"So is Billie."

"I guess I'll see you later."

"Yeah, later."

He stood in the foyer until she walked away, then moved toward the family room.

"Have you broken anything?" he asked as he turned into the room. Large pieces of furniture filled the L-shaped space. One end contained a pool table and wet bar. The other, a huge sectional sofa, large-screen TV and enough audio-visual equipment to stock a small store.

Billie sipped on a can of soda and shook her head. "Not yet. Pretty good, huh?"

"The best." He sat next to her on the long sofa and pulled on the bill of her cap. "That hat doesn't go with the dress."

"I'm wearing shorts." Billie pulled up her skirt to show him. "Mom can be tough about clothes, especially on Sunday. This is our compress."

Compress? "Do you mean compromise?"

"Whatever." She pointed at the screen. "Bottom of the second. Atlanta's up, but the Giants have already scored."

"There's still several innings, peanut. Don't get your hopes up."

She stuck out her tongue. He grinned. When the next batter popped a fly into left field, providing the third out, Billie crowed her pleasure.

"Told you, told you."

With that, she scooted over until she was next to him, then snuggled close to his chest. Adam sat there stiffly, not sure what to do with his arm. Finally he rested it against her slight back. She smiled up at him and sighed with contentment. Such a powerhouse, he thought with amazement, yet still a little girl. Her body felt warm against him. Small and in need of protection, although he could never tell her or her mother that.

"Am I going to talk funny?" Billie asked.

"Funny?"

"You know. 'I declare, chile, you are simply too charmin','" she said in a fair imitation of a Southern drawl.

He chuckled, then stretched out his legs and rested his feet on the coffee table. "Probably."

"Why?"

"This is Orchard, Billie. You're going to hear people speak with accents all the time. You can't help imitating."

"My mom doesn't talk too funny, and neither do you."

"Your mother has been away for nine years. It'll come back to her. And I've never had much of an accent."

"I'm not going to, either."

"It's too late, peanut." He shook his head when she offered him a drink out of her can of soda. "Accept the fact that you'll soon be a Southern belle."

"Well, I'm *not* going to charm school."

He didn't answer. She snuggled closer and they watched the game. At the next commercial break, she pulled away and tucked her feet under her. "Adam?"

She looked serious. "What's wrong?" he asked.

"Do you remember at the bank, we talked about maiden names and dads?"

He nodded, sure he wasn't going to like what was coming.

She stared down at her drink, then up at him. Tears pooled in her dark brown eyes. She was close enough that he could hear her shallow breathing and count the freckles across her nose. The pattern reminded him of something but before he could figure out what, she sniffed.

"Billie?" He rested one hand on her shoulder. "It's all right, peanut."

"I made my mom cry."

"How?"

"I asked about my dad. I knew I shouldn't. It always makes her cry. But sometimes, I just want to know. Where is he? Doesn't he love us anymore?"

As he pulled Billie into his arms, a soft sound came from the hallway. He looked up and saw Jane standing in the doorway. The expression on her face—pure pain—stabbed at him. Before he could say anything, she turned and fled.

He continued to hold her daughter, murmuring words of comfort, but his mind raced. Obviously Jane had heard what Billie said. Obviously her ex-husband had hurt her very deeply. Obviously she still cared for the man.

Chapter Eight

"Are you all right, child?" Charlene asked as Jane hurried into the kitchen.

"What?" She stared at her friend, then tried to smile. "Oh, I'm fine."

"You look like you've seen a ghost. Now don't go getting any ideas. The Carolina Barringtons have always been too well-bred to allow ghosts in the house."

Jane moved through the kitchen and picked up the plates for dinner. "I'm a little tired. That's all."

"Mmm." Those shrewd blue eyes saw more than they were supposed to. Still Jane knew that she was safe. Despite the truckers that visited from time to time and her rather flamboyant wardrobe and ways, Charlene was too much of a lady to pry. "I thought you were going to ask Billie to set the table."

"She's…ah…Adam, that is, they're watching the ball game. I didn't want to disturb them."

"Well then, you'll need to get out the good silver. It's in the middle drawer of the hutch."

Jane nodded, then escaped from the kitchen to the quiet of the formal dining room. Lace-covered windows let in the soft, afternoon light. Underfoot, an antique Oriental carpet provided the color in the elegant room. The beautiful carved table could seat twenty, with all the leaves. Even at its smallest, it was too big for four, but Charlene liked to use the good pieces on Sunday and that meant eating in the dining room. Jane didn't mind; the formal setting, remembering which forks went where, would occupy her mind. If she tried hard, maybe she could forget Billie's conversation with Adam.

It was futile, she admitted, as she smoothed the pressed linen cloth over the table. Her daughter's pain had ignited her own. "Where is my daddy? Doesn't he love us anymore?" Her words echoed over and over again.

"I never meant to hurt you, Billie," she murmured softly, as she folded the napkins. She had hurt her though, and Adam, too. All in all, she'd botched the whole thing. Now what? Should she tell him today? Could she?

"You have to tell him soon. That's what this is all about, isn't it?"

She hadn't heard Charlene enter the room. "Yes," she said, as she continued to fold the napkins.

"You have to tell him," Charlene repeated.

"I know."

"He's going to guess, and if he doesn't, people in town will. She has too much of the Barringtons in her."

"But she doesn't really *look* like him," Jane said, hopefully, as if convincing Charlene would mean putting off the deed for another day.

"You're right. She looks like Dani."

"You think so?"

"Of course. All she needs is to be blond. She's even got the freckles."

"I never thought of that."

"Start thinking." Charlene placed a silver trivet on the table. "Sophia Yarns called me yesterday."

Jane opened the center door of the hutch and picked up a handful of flatware. "She was at the New Accounts desk at the bank."

"She wanted to know if *I* knew you were unmarried and had a child."

"She's just an old busybody."

"She's an influential member of this town. And no dummy. You think you can keep your secret after she spends an hour or two with Billie and Adam?"

"I'll make sure that doesn't happen." She placed the forks at all four places, then went back to collect the knives.

Charlene stepped next to her and laid a restraining hand on her arm. "You can't run forever."

"I know." Jane wanted to crawl away and hide, but she forced herself to look up at Charlene.

The older woman patted her gently. "He'll hate you for keeping Billie from him."

Her throat grew tight. "Yes," she whispered.

"But he *will* eventually understand."

"I hope you're right."

Charlene hugged her close. Jane leaned into the embrace. The scent of gardenias, the womanly figure, the clinking of the bracelets brought her comfort with their familiarity.

"I am right," the older woman said. "He'll forgive you. What I'm worried about is whether or not you can forgive yourself."

They had dessert on the front porch. The sounds of summer, birds, children playing, a soft breeze rustling through the leaves, lent themselves to another time when everything had been easier. If this had been the 1800s, her life would have been different, Jane thought taking a bite of blueberry pie. Back then, despite her concerns about Adam and their pending marriage, she wouldn't have run. Society and circumstances would have forced her to stay and fight for her man. Now, with the vision of hindsight, the lack of opportunity sounded heavenly. If she couldn't risk, she didn't fail. But even as the simpler time tempted her, she acknowledged that the past nine years had made her a stronger person. However much she regretted the pain she'd caused and was still going to cause, she'd arrived in the present as a mature human being. A difficult price to pay, she thought as she glanced up and met Adam's gaze.

He offered her a quick, sympathetic smile. He'd been nice ever since he'd seen her in the doorway, listening to Billie talk about her "missing" father. No doubt he had a few theories of his own as to why she'd bolted. At this moment he probably felt badly, maybe even let himself like her. All that would change as soon as she worked up the courage to tell him the truth.

"This is delightful," Charlene said, picking up her last blueberry in her fingers and popping it into her mouth. "You always did magical things with a crust."

"It's my mother's recipe. I'll pass along the compliment."

"Do that. And give her my best. I should probably call her before I leave for Greece. I've just been so busy what with my various—"

"Charlene—"

"Don't say anything—"

Adam and Jane spoke together. His aunt drew herself up straighter in her wicker chair and frowned. "Why do you always assume I'm going to say something inappropriate?"

"Because you usually do," Adam said wryly.

Billie looked up from her dessert. She'd perched herself on the steps leading up to the porch, while the adults sat around a glass and wicker table. "What's inappropriate?" she asked.

"It means—" Jane paused. "Something that's not appropriate."

"Now that's a clear definition," Adam teased.

"You think you're so clever, you try," she shot back.

"Yes, Adam," Charlene said, putting her plate on the table in front of her. "Go ahead."

"Inappropriate means something that isn't polite."

Charlene shook her head. "I was going to be very polite." She glared pointedly at Jane. "And appropriate."

"All right." Adam took another bite of pie and chewed thoughtfully. "Inappropriate."

"Yes." Billie waited patiently. "Should I go get the dictionary?"

Jane chuckled.

"Absolutely not," Adam said. "I won't be defeated by a word. It means—"

"It means that your mother and Adam think I was about to say something you're too young to hear." Charlene rose to her feet. "And they were wrong. But my feelings are already hurt, so I'm leaving." She held out her hand. "You can come with me, Billie, and help with the dishes."

"Aw, do I have to?"

"Yes. Because I found out that someone here broke one of my prize roses. And I have a feeling it was you. Not—" She glared at Jane, then at Adam. "I repeat, *not* that anyone had the good manners to tell me. I had to find out on my own. The poor thing is crushed beyond repair."

Jane stared intently at her plate and struggled not to laugh. "Charlene, I know how much you care about your roses. I meant to say something earlier. It slipped my mind."

Billie hung her head. "I'm sorry. I'm always breaking stuff."

Charlene squeezed her hand. "I forgive you. Children are supposed to break things."

"I'll be happy to reimburse you," Jane offered.

"No, thank you. But this is a good time to remind you that charm school would take care of many of her problems."

Billie rolled her eyes. "I don't want to go to charm school. It's dumb, girl stuff."

Adam leaned back in his chair and folded his arms across his chest. "Explain that to me, Charlene. You are the least conventional woman I know, yet since you've met Billie, you've been trying to turn her into the Southern ideal of a lady."

Charlene shook her head. Tendrils from the upswept style bounced off her cheeks and her long silver earrings jingled. "Power, Adam. It's all about power." She gave Billie the plates and urged her toward the door. "First you have to learn the rules, then you can break them. That's always been our strength. What was that movie? *Steel Magnolias*. Look at Jane here. Nine years ago she was a child with no direction, confused. Afraid. Now she's grown into a beautiful woman capable of taking care of herself. We're strong. We just don't want everyone to know right off."

Billie balanced the plates in her arms. "I don't understand."

"You will," Charlene said, patting her head. "Learn to be a lady and control the world."

"I'd rather learn a curve ball." Billie thrust out her lower lip. "Do I have to help with the dishes?"

Charlene nodded. "Think of it as repaying me for that rose you killed." She followed Billie inside, then turned back. "You two just sit here and talk. We'll take care of everything else."

"What do you think of Charlene's theory?" Adam asked.

"I think she's right about the rules. I tell my students that in my English classes. You have to know how to construct a sentence before you can start switching things around. As for the power—" She shrugged, then laughed.

"I've never felt especially powerful. Maybe that's saved for the true Southern belles."

He leaned forward and rested his forearms on the round glass-covered table. They sat across from each other. If she leaned forward and rested *her* forearms on the table, their hands would touch. The thought tempted her. Tonight, while Adam was warm and friendly, she found herself needing to play a dangerous game. She wanted to push a little, perhaps find out if he wanted to kiss her as much as she wanted to be kissed. His compassion made him approachable. The night made her bold. That and the knowledge that his friendliness would be gone as soon as he found out the truth.

"Why don't you see yourself as a Southern belle?" he asked. "You grew up here. And if I remember correctly, you went to charm school."

"And dance classes. Yes, everything appropriate."

He grinned at her word choice. Those dark eyes flashed amusement and something else that might have been caring. Lies, she thought. This fragile peace was built on lies. Just tonight, she swore, sending a promise out into the cosmos. Just this one evening when the cold stranger had disappeared and in his place sat the handsome lover she had always adored.

"And?" he prompted.

She placed her hands on the table and held on to the curved edge. Rubbing her thumb against the wicker, she stared at the glass surface. And what? "You have to be pretty to be a Southern belle," she blurted out, then died a little inside.

She didn't dare look up.

"You were always pretty," he said quietly, from the other side of the table. "Sweet and soft-spoken."

"Adam, don't. There's no need to make up things just to make me feel better. I lived my life. I know how much I did, or rather didn't, date in high school. Until you asked me out—'' She shrugged again. "Let's just say I wasn't Miss Popularity."

"Boys can be stupid, going after the obvious and common, instead of what's rare and precious."

She raised her head and looked at him. Rare and precious? Her? She half expected to see a teasing light in his brown eyes. Instead he radiated sincerity. The handsome lines of his face, familiar and strong, made her heart beat faster. One corner of his mouth tilted up.

"Why are you looking at me like that?" he asked.

"Like what?"

"As if you've never seen me before. Did you think I would have asked you out if I thought you were unattractive?"

"No. It's just..." She folded her arms on the table. "That's the nicest thing you've ever said to me."

"I'm not a complete jerk."

"That's not what I meant." The night closed around them, making her feel that it was safe to expose bits of her soul. "I never understood why you did ask me out. I always felt so inadequate."

"Inadequate? In God's name why?"

His genuine surprise made her laugh. "Thank you for that."

"For what?"

"Acting shocked."

"I am shocked." He leaned back in his chair. "I knew you felt young and inexperienced, but I had no idea you felt..." He paused, searching for the right word.

"How about completely out of my element?"

One dark brow raised slightly. "I can't believe that."

"Think about it, Adam. You were the heir to all the Barrington wealth. Too damn good-looking, charming, funny. You always knew what to say and do. Everyone liked and admired you. I was nobody."

He gave her a slow smile that sent heat coursing all the way to her feet. Her toes curled inside her white pumps.

"I had no idea I was looked upon so favorably."

"Oh, stop. You knew it then and you still know it. You were the catch of the decade. How could I not feel inadequate? I kept waiting for you to figure out I was just some gawky teenager who'd had a crush on you since she was twelve."

As soon as the words came out, she wanted to call them back. In all the time they'd dated, even after they'd become lovers, even after he'd proposed, she'd never confessed that to him. A heated blush climbed up her chest and throat, then flared across her cheeks. She started to stand up, but he shot his hands out and grabbed hers, holding her in place.

"Oh, no you don't," he said. "Not after that bombshell. You had a crush? On me?"

"Don't sound so surprised," she said, daring only to stare at their joined hands. His, broad and tanned, next to her paler skin. He turned his wrists so that her fingers rested on his palms. He brushed against the sensitive skin on the inside of her wrists. Electric sparks flew between them. She half expected to see little flashes of light bouncing over the table.

"I *am* surprised. I never knew. You didn't say a word."

She risked glancing up at him. "Why would I have gone out with you if I hadn't liked you?"

"I knew you liked me, but a crush is different. From the time you were twelve." He drew his eyebrows together in concentration. "Did something special happen, or did you just wake up one morning and realize you lived next door to someone wonderful?"

"Stop!" She pulled one of her hands free and hit him on the forearm. Before she could retreat, he grabbed her hand back. His thumbs began to trace slow circles on her palms. "You taught me to swim that summer."

"I remember. You were always so serious. All legs and eyes."

She grimaced. "Skinny and flat-chested."

"You were only twelve."

"Some things never change."

The slow movement of his thumb continued. Jane found herself thinking more and more about his touch and less about what was being said. It felt good to have a man hold her hands. This man, especially. It felt good to be in his company, talking about each other and the past.

"You're not skinny anymore," he said.

"Thanks."

"And I've never understood the importance you placed on breast size. Yours are perfect."

"Mmm." She continued to stare at his hands cradling hers. The circling of his thumb hypnotized her until all she could think about was—

She snapped her head up and stared at him. "What did you say?"

Humor flashed in his eyes. "I said that there is nothing wrong with your breasts. In fact I've always—"

"Never mind." She jerked her hands free and crossed her arms over her chest. "I get the gist of it. Thanks for the share."

"You want to change the subject," he said kindly, his gaze never once flickering below her face. Still she kept her arms in place.

"How'd you guess?"

"Body language."

"Oh." She glanced at her arms. "Pretty obvious."

"Would you feel better if we talked about your crush?"

"No."

"So it was my teaching you how to swim. My sculptured body. The devil-may-care gleam in my eyes."

He was laughing at her, but she didn't care. "Actually, you took the time to be nice."

Now it was his turn to look uncomfortable. He leaned back in his chair and shrugged. "I was just being neighborly."

"I know, but it meant a lot to me. You always had time to smile and say hello. That goes a long way with a twelve-year-old girl." She bit her lower lip. Could she ask him the same sort of questions? Did it matter anymore? A slight breeze whispered against her bare arms, bringing with it the scent of night-blooming jasmine and rich earth. "When did you first notice me?"

"When you were about six months old and screaming loud enough to wake me up at four in the morning."

"Adam! You know what I meant."

"Yeah, I know." He raised his arms and laced his fingers behind his head. The lights from the house highlighted the right side of his face and outlined his profile. "Charlene gave me a party for my twenty-first birthday. She went all out, hiring a band and a caterer. There must have been a couple hundred people here."

"I remember." It had been her first grown-up event. The first time her mother had taken her into Atlanta to buy a formal dress. The white confection of ribbons and lace had made her feel special.

"You danced with Ty," he said. "I watched my brother lead you around the floor, but you couldn't dance in your shoes."

"Oh, God." She buried her face in her hands. "It's not fair that all my embarrassing memories are public knowledge. I'll never live them down. I must have looked like a geek."

"It was very charming."

She shook her head. "Geek."

"I found you out by the garden, walking barefoot, like a nymph from a storybook."

She straightened, smiling at the memory. "You told me I looked pretty."

"You did."

"And that was it?" she asked, surprised that one of her favorite memories might have influenced him.

"You were a little young, but yes, that was it. I kept my eye on you until you were old enough for me to date."

"I fell in love with you that night," she said, daring to look at him. "Out there, under the stars. It was terribly romantic and I was quite young, but I fell all the same."

"So we were heading in the same direction." His features hardened slightly, as if he remembered something more. Like the fact that she left him at the altar.

"I did love you," she insisted, as if her words could keep reality at bay.

"It wasn't enough."

"Adam—"

"No." He rose and walked over to the porch railing. The shadows swallowed him until only a vague outline remained visible. "It's true. You were too young. I see that now. The blame—" He drew in a breath and released it. "You weren't ready."

"No, I wasn't."

"And I pushed you."

"I wanted to be pushed. Sort of." It was so complicated, she thought, standing up as well and walking toward him. "So many things confused me. I wanted to believe that you cared about me, but I was never sure I measured up. You were so perfect, and I was just this dumb kid."

"Hardly that." He shifted until he sat on the railing and looked out into the yard.

When she reached him, she leaned against one of the pillars supporting the covering. They were nearly at eye-level. The darkness made it easier to confess almost everything.

"I wanted to please you," she said. "More than anything, I wanted to be everything *you* wanted. But there was so much that scared me."

"Like me?" He asked the question bitterly.

"Yes," she whispered.

"You could have told me."

"I was afraid of what you'd think and say. I was afraid you'd finally figure out that I wasn't enough."

He looked at her then, regret tightening his mouth. "I wanted to marry you, Jane. No one else. You were exactly right for me."

"We were compatible?" she asked.

"I thought so."

"The perfect banker's wife?"

"You could have been."

Convenience, she thought. While she spoke of love and need, he remembered that she was malleable. Had he loved her? She wanted to ask the question. Had he cared?

"I always thought—" He offered her a quick smile. "I had plans for us. Changes in the house. Trips. A future. I supposed I could have talked more about that. Times were hard for me then. What with the bank, and Dani and Ty needing things." He turned back to face the yard. "I know that I could have been there more for you. We were so suitable, I assumed that you'd know all that. I should have realized your youth would be a problem as well as an asset."

It was as close to a confession of responsibility as she was going to get. Suitable. He thought they were suitable. What about passion? she wanted to cry out. Tell me that you used to lie awake nights and dream about making love with me. Tell me that you ached for my touch. Explain to me how we would grow old together, loving each other more and more each day.

He did none of those. And she didn't ask him to. It didn't matter anymore.

"I'm sorry, too, Adam," she said at last, because there was nothing else to say. It was as she'd suspected. She'd loved with her whole being, while he'd followed a logical course of action. Running had been wrong; not marrying Adam had, however, been the correct decision.

He looked at her. "I feel as if this is a significant moment. A truce of sorts. Maybe we should commemorate it."

"In case it doesn't last?"

She meant the question as a joke but he didn't smile. Instead, he stood up and took the single step that separated them. Before she could move away, he trapped her between the pillar, the railing and himself.

"Adam?"

He reached up and cupped her cheek, then drew his hand to the side, slipping his fingers through her curls. "I never expected to get over the anger. I never expected not to hate you." He gave her a slight smile. "I never expected to see you again."

He took her breath away. His gentleness, the scent of his body, his warmth surrounding her. Except where he wove his fingers through her hair, they didn't touch. She wanted him with a fierceness that threatened to overwhelm her. This was more than a woman's need for man. This was a lethal combination of past and present. She hated that it didn't matter that he'd never loved her. She hated herself for being so weak where he was concerned. But she understood the phenomenon. He was her first love, her only love. He could, with just a look, tap into a lifetime of memories. How could she resist him?

He placed his other hand on her shoulder. His skin felt warm against hers. His pinky slipped under the strap of her dress, his thumb traced a line from her jaw to the hollow of her throat. Slowly, he twisted his fingers in her hair, until she was forced to lean her head back, exposing more of herself to him.

Anger, disappointment, regret, guilt all faded under his sensual assault. She swayed toward him. Tomorrow, she thought vaguely. She'd tell him tomorrow. Please, God, let her have tonight with the man she had once loved with her entire being. Just one perfect night to remember.

The screen door slammed. "We've finished the dishes. Hey, where are you guys?"

Billie!

Adam instantly stepped back. Jane cleared her throat and turned to look out at the yard.

Billie walked over to them. "What are you guys doing over here?"

"Looking at stars," Jane said, hoping her voice sounded normal.

"Why?"

"It's fun. Can you find the Big Dipper?"

Billie came up to the rail and leaned out to look at the sky. "It's there." She pointed.

"Very good."

Billie turned to Adam. "I'm very smart for my age."

"So it would appear." As always, she had the power to make him laugh and forget what was ailing him, Adam thought. This particular time, it was a case of misplaced passion. Jane wasn't a woman for him to fool around with. She'd already wounded him big-time. Giving her a second chance to screw up his life would be idiotic. Telling himself it was strictly physical might sound good, but he knew better. The heart was a very physical organ and had a nasty habit of getting in the way. He didn't want to risk that kind of involvement again. Caring meant losing. Jane was proof of that. So why had he almost kissed her again, and why was he frantically thinking up an excuse to see her? Wasn't he the one who had convinced them both that if they really made an effort, their paths didn't have to cross?

"It's late," Jane said. "We should get this one home. She's got a big day tomorrow."

"Mo-om, it's barely dark. My bedtime's not for a couple of hours."

"Your mother's right," he said, suddenly needing to be

away from Jane before he said or did something he would regret. The control he'd prided himself on for so long seemed to be failing on a regular basis.

"Thank you, Adam." She shifted her weight from one foot to the other, as if not sure what to do with herself. "We had a lovely time. Tell Charlene thank you as well."

"I will."

Billie held out her arms, and he obligingly picked her up and gave her a kiss on the cheek. "You're the best," she said as she leaned forward and rubbed her nose against his. "Too bad Atlanta lost."

"Yeah, we'll get you next time." He squeezed her tight, then set her on the porch. "Oh, I almost forgot." He hesitated, telling himself not to ask. Damn. "The triple-A team is going to be opening a home stand. Would you like to go next Saturday?"

"Sure!" Billie spun in a circle. "Can I, Mom? Can I?"

"Calm down." Jane brushed her daughter's hair out of her eyes. "Certainly, if Adam doesn't mind."

Billie rolled her eyes. "He *asked*, didn't he? Why would he mind?"

"You're welcome to join us," he said, then wondered why the hell he was playing this game. Did he want to see what else Jane could do to him? What exactly was his problem?

"I'm sure you'd rather spend the time alone with Billie."

Billie jabbed him in the stomach. "She's just saying that. She wants you to *really* ask her."

"Billie!"

Her daughter hunched her shoulders. "Sorry. I'm going to go to the house and wait for you, Mom. Maybe I'll start my bath water."

"You do that," Jane said.

Billie scurried between the hedge dividing the two properties, then stomped into the smaller house.

"She can be a trial," Jane said, not meeting his eyes.

"But you love her."

"Of course. She's my daughter." She bit her lip, then stared at the ground. "I should go, too. Thanks for dinner."

She reached up and gave him a quick kiss on his cheek. Her perfume whispered around him, like a sensual ghost.

"You're welcome."

She walked down the steps and toward the hedge. "Oh, Adam, I'd love to go with you to the game. If you're sure?"

He wasn't. About anything. "Of course."

"See you Saturday, then."

"Saturday." He watched her disappear into the night.

Rain fell from the sky. Sheets pounded into the earth as if a permanent rift had been created somewhere in the atmosphere.

"I can't believe you went to all this trouble," Jane said as she studied the contents of the refrigerator. Hot dogs and salads sat on the top two shelves. An assortment of sodas filled the door. A bottle of white wine rested on its side on the bottom.

"I'd promised the two of you a baseball game," Adam said, pulling out the wine and closing the refrigerator door. "What else was I supposed to do?"

"But a barbecue in the rain? We could have rescheduled."

"The porch is wide enough to handle the grill. Besides, did you *want* to have Billie to yourself all day? She strikes me as the type of kid to go stir-crazy in this kind of weather."

"She is a little trying. I was thinking about driving into town to catch a movie with her. It was that or lock her in a closet."

He smiled. "We still can. The movie part. After we eat."

"Sure. Unless you've made other plans for tonight?" She sounded to herself as sophisticated as the twelve-year-old who'd first fallen for him. Get a grip, she told herself.

"Not at all."

When she'd woken up to a gray wet day, Jane had been convinced that Adam would excuse himself from seeing her and Billie today. Disappointment had flared, her distress much stronger than it had a right to be. It had been almost a week since she'd seen him. Every day she'd strolled in her yard after he got home from work and had hoped he might come outside, too. He hadn't, and she'd gone inside each night feeling foolish and lonely. It was worse than being a teenager again. Back then she hadn't known what she was missing.

Billie had been almost as crushed as she was. Adam's phone call had rescued them both from a case of the blues.

In concession to the muggy heat, he wore shorts and a T-shirt. She tried not to stare, but his long lean legs, tanned from his morning jogs, stretched endlessly down to deck shoes. The T-shirt wasn't any safer to study, she thought, taking in the broad expanse of chest and rippling muscles. The man was a walking cliché. Tall, dark, handsome. How had she ever found the strength to walk away?

Upstairs, in the far reaches of the house, something thudded to the floor. Adam looked up. "Should we go investigate?"

"No. Knowing Billie, she's found something to throw, or hit."

"I must admit, I didn't think she'd want to play dress up."

Charlene had sent the girl up into the attic with the promise of chests of old clothes and secret treasure.

"She will. Only don't expect her to come down dressed as a princess or movie star. She'd rather be a pirate. Maybe she'll find the secret Barrington treasure lost during the Civil War."

Adam opened a drawer in the center island of the kitchen and removed a corkscrew. "You've been gone too long."

"Why?"

"It's the War of Northern Aggression."

"Sorry."

"Besides, there isn't any secret Barrington treasure." He opened the wine and poured them each a glass.

"How do you know if it hasn't been found?"

"You have a point." He raised his drink toward her. "To friends?"

It was a peace offering, she realized with a sinking feeling in her stomach. A token that, after their intimate conversation last weekend, left certain doors opened. She was a coward and a liar.

"To friends," she answered, tightening her grip on the stem so that he couldn't see her tremble.

He rested his hand on the small of her back and pressed lightly, urging her toward the front parlor. The thick clouds made the late afternoon seem more like evening. Shadows filled the corners of the rooms. The steady drip-drip onto the porch railing should have soothed her, but the sound of rain only seemed to repeat the same refrain. "Tell him, tell him, tell him." She would. Now.

He seated her on one end of the floral print sofa, then sat next to her. He'd left enough space between them so that they weren't touching, but he hadn't sat on the far end, either. Brown eyes regarded her thoughtfully. What would have happened if Billie hadn't interrupted them? she wondered. How far would his caresses have gone? Would he have hated her more or less when he found out the truth? There was only one way to find out.

"Adam, I—"

"I've been—"

They spoke at the same time.

"You first," he offered.

"No. Go ahead."

He took a sip, then set his glass on the table in front of them. Half-opened shutters allowed in the dusky light. A single lamp in the corner illuminated the area by the hallway door. He turned toward her and rested his arm along the back of the couch, his fingers inches from her shoulder.

"I've been thinking about our last conversation," he said.

That look. She knew it. Sultry brown eyes caressed her face, then dipped lower. The filmy gauze of her tank top provided little protection against what he sought. Her small breasts swelled as her nipples hardened inside her bra.

"Me, too," she confessed.

"Everything between us is different," he went on. "I didn't expect—" He shrugged, as if not sure how to put his feelings into words.

"I know." His long fingers brushed her bare shoulder. She leaned forward. "But first, Adam, I have to tell you some—"

Something heavy thumped down the stairs, followed by clattering footsteps.

"Look what I found!" Billie called. "Hey, where are you guys?"

"In here," Jane said. Timing, she thought grimly. Just when she'd been about to spill the beans. Maybe locking Billie in a closet wasn't such a bad idea. She shook her head. She'd just have to wait until her daughter went to bed. Then she and Adam could be alone and she'd tell him the truth.

"There's a bunch of sports equipment and uniforms. I found this softball and bat. Can I have this jersey, Adam? And where'd you get the wig?"

At last Billie stepped into the doorway. The light from the lamp highlighted her appearance, including the blue and white numbered jersey that hung down to her knees and the long blond wig perched on her head. In one hand she held a softball, in the other a mitt.

Jane felt her breath catch in her throat. That wasn't her daughter standing there smiling proudly. It was another girl. Funny how with dark hair, Billie didn't look much like

Adam's sister at all. But with the long wig, and her old high school team uniform, she was the spitting image of Dani Barrington.

"Well?" Billie asked. "What do you guys think?"

It was like in the movies, when everything suddenly happened in slow motion. Billie's question sounded as if she were a hundred miles away. Jane felt her muscles clench as panic chilled her blood.

He knew.

She didn't have to look at him to confirm her suspicions. She could feel it in the way he sat so quietly and stared at her daughter. *His* daughter.

Without saying a word, he rose to his feet and walked over to Billie. He crouched in front of her and touched her face.

"What?" she asked, puzzled. "Why are you looking at me like that?"

"Billie." His voice sounded hoarse. He kissed her cheek, then took her hand.

"Where are we going?"

"To see Aunt Charlene. You're going to visit with her for a few minutes while your mother and I have a talk."

Chapter Nine

"When were you going to tell me?" Adam asked.

The shock had sustained him for the time it had taken him to walk Billie over to Charlene's. The older woman had taken one look at the girl's outfit and blond wig and had gasped. The look in her eyes had been compassion for him, but not surprise. She'd known, as well. Looks as though he was the only one kept in the dark around here. He'd left Billie with his aunt. He would deal with Charlene and her betrayal another time. Right now all he cared about was Jane.

He leaned against the doorframe and stared into the dimly lit parlor. As the shock faded, cold deadly rage took its place. She'd made him angry when she'd first arrived and pushed him to get in touch with his feelings. Then he'd lost his cool, but nothing like what was about to happen. Images formed in his mind—disconnected pictures of Billie laughing at him, smiling, burrowing in his arms. No wonder they'd gotten along so well.

A sharp pain jabbed his heart. A daughter. He had a daughter. His gaze narrowed as Jane rose from the sofa and walked toward the shuttered window.

"I asked you a question," he said, struggling to keep his voice low and even. "When were you going to tell me?"

She laughed sharply and without humor. "You wouldn't believe me if I told you."

"That's not an answer."

"It's the best I have."

"Come on, Jane. You can do better than that." He folded his arms over his chest. "What the hell kind of game have you been playing? I don't even know where to begin."

"It's not what you think."

"Oh? Billie *isn't* my daughter? You haven't kept her from me for over eight years?"

"I..." She touched the shutter and swung it open. Dim light crept into the room and illuminated her profile. "Yes. Billie is yours."

Her simple answer opened the floodgates. "That's it?" he asked, stepping into the room. "That's the whole confession? After all this time, you calmly announce she's mine? Where do you get off, lady? You stole my kid. You ran away and had *my* child and didn't tell me. How dare you play with my life, with Billie's life?"

"I'm her mother." She glanced up at him, her eyes flashing with temper.

"So?" he asked, taking another step closer to her. "Does that give you the right to lie to her? To me?"

"Dammit, Adam, I made the best decision I could at the time."

"You think I care about you? After what you've done?" He clenched his hands into fists. "You had no right to steal my child from me. You had no right to keep her a secret. How long, Jane? How many years would have gone by until you told me?" He shook his head. "If we hadn't been interrupted, you would have come to my bed last weekend. You would have made love with that lie between us.''

Her gaze faltered until she dropped her head toward her chest. ''There's nothing you can say that I haven't already told myself.''

''So what's your excuse? What reason do you have for cheating me out of Billie? Who gave you the right to make that decision?''

She snapped her head up and glared at him. ''You did, Mr. High and Mighty.'' She pointed her finger toward his chest. ''The day you coerced me into your bed.''

''Don't give me that. I never did anything you didn't want.''

''Now who's lying? I wasn't ready. You scared me. I would never have told you no, and you took advantage of that.''

A small measure of guilt joined his rage. ''What are you saying? Are you accusing me of something?''

She held his gaze. ''No. I'm telling you we both made choices we've come to regret.''

''You regret Billie?''

''Never.''

''Then what?''

The sound of rain filled the room, the steady drumming from the roof, the drip-drip off the porch covering. In the distance, he heard the rumble of thunder.

''I should have said no. Even though we were engaged, I wasn't ready to be your lover. I should have told you.'' She turned away and gripped the windowsill. ''Aren't you curious, Adam, about how I came to be pregnant? After all, you're the one who decided it was time for us to go all the way, so you took me to the doctor and waited while I was fitted for a diaphragm. You're the one who drove me to the next town, because I was too shy to get the prescription filled here in Orchard.''

He didn't like the way the conversation had shifted. This

was supposed to be about what *she'd* done. She's the one who'd lied. Who'd had Billie. He had to focus on that. Instead the past intruded.

"I don't care about any of this," he said.

"I didn't use it." She spoke quietly.

"What?"

"The diaphragm. I couldn't."

"That's the most ridiculous—"

"I was embarrassed."

He turned away and swore.

"That doesn't change anything, Adam."

"Why didn't you tell me?"

She shook her head. "I couldn't talk to you about anything."

"Then what the hell were you doing marrying me?"

"I didn't, did I?"

That one hit below the belt. He struggled to regroup his thoughts. "I'm not the villain in this piece. You're the one who kept the secrets."

"Only one."

"Oh, yeah, just the fact that you were having my child. Is that why you ran? Because you found out you were pregnant?"

"No."

He raked one hand through his hair. He couldn't deal with this. Too much information in too short a time. He felt like exploding or lashing out or— "When?" he asked. "When did you figure it out?"

"When I got to San Francisco." She continued to stare at the windowsill. Lightning ripped across the sky. The brief flash lit up the room. Three seconds later, a boom shook the house.

"Why didn't you come home then? I would have—"

"Would have what? Married me? After I ran out on you? What was there to come home to? This town, where everyone would know I was a pregnant teenager? You didn't want a baby, Adam. Why else would you have gone to all that trouble with the birth control? We'd never talked about kids.''

''Of course I wanted children. Maybe not right away, but that doesn't give you the right to choose for me. Do you think I would have abandoned you?''

She leaned her forehead against the windowsill. ''No.''

He hadn't expected that to be her answer. He glanced at her, then began to pace the length of the parlor. The marble floors gleamed as he strode across them. He reached the fireplace and turned to face her.

''I don't understand. If you didn't think I'd abandon you, then what was the problem?''

''I couldn't come back with Billie. My pride wouldn't let me. I'd run out on the wedding. What sort of person would I be if I'd then come back because I was pregnant? Yes, you would have taken me in, but what was between us had already been determined. We would have had nothing but obligation.''

''That's a tidy rationalization of your actions.''

She sighed. ''I deserve everything you're saying and I'm willing to listen if it makes you feel better. But don't let your anger hide the truth. Telling you about the baby would have meant you'd be there, but only because you had to be.'' She looked out the window and into the storm. ''You didn't care about the relationship anymore. If you'd really wanted me, you would have come after me. You never did.''

If you'd really wanted me, you wouldn't have left, he thought, surprised that her leaving still had the power to hurt him. He should be grateful that he'd learned the lesson so early. Given a chance, people you love will leave you.

''I would have been the perfect banker's wife,'' she said. With one finger, she traced the trail of a raindrop against the glass. Another clap of thunder shook the house. ''Young, easily trained. I wasn't important enough to you.

I realized that before the wedding. That's why I ran. And when I found out I was pregnant, I couldn't bear the thought of being an obligation for the rest of my life."

"You selfish bitch."

She jerked her head around to stare at him. Surprise widened her hazel eyes. Her long braid trailed over one shoulder, but for once the thick silken length didn't catch his attention.

"I realized—I couldn't bear—" He mocked her in a falsetto voice. "It's all about you, isn't it? Did you ever once think about what *I* might want? That I might care about my daughter, want to see her born, watch her take her first step, hear her first word? You've taken a piece of my life away. You've stolen time that I can't recover. Worse than what I might regret, you have stolen your daughter's birthright. Made her suffer when her life might have been easier. There were advantages I could have—"

"Money isn't everything."

He dismissed her with a wave of his hand. "I'm not talking about money. I'm talking about people, a culture. A place to grow up knowing that generations before have walked the same path, lived in the same house. Your decision, blamed on me and circumstance, has destroyed two lives."

"I'm sorry," she whispered. A flash of lightning showed the trail of tears on her cheeks. "You're right."

He turned and hit the fireplace mantel. "That doesn't make me feel better."

"I know."

"Why? Why did you come back? Why are you doing this?"

"I wanted Billie—" Her voice cracked. "I wanted the two of you to meet."

"Was it all a sick game? We met. Big deal. Did you think I wouldn't guess eventually? Who else aside from Charlene knows?"

"No one."

"Your parents?"

"Yes."

He cursed.

"I couldn't tell you." She took a step toward him as if to beseech him to listen. When he glared, she moved back. "When I first arrived, I wasn't sure you'd want Billie in your life. She seems tough, but she's still a little girl. If I'd told you about her right away, you would have been angry and might have said or done something that would have scarred her."

He spun and walked over to stand next to her. "And you haven't? You dare to judge me, when you're the one telling all the lies?"

"I'm sorry."

"So you've said. I don't care about you, or your apologies." He raised one hand to rub his temple and she flinched. He didn't care that she thought him capable of hitting her. "That's right, Jane. Be afraid. You can't manipulate me anymore. You've taken something precious from me and by God, you'll pay."

By ten-thirty that night the storm had passed, leaving behind wet earth and clean damp air. A few stars braved the clouds, peeking out and winking. Now what? Jane asked herself for the thousandth time. Did she leave, or did she stay? A soft breeze cooled her heated skin. She shivered at the slight contact and pulled her knees up closer to her chest. Unlike Adam's yard, hers didn't contain as many trees. From her seat on the front porch steps, she could see out to the street. There wasn't any traffic this late on a tiny street in Orchard. A few houses glowed with lights from within, but most of her neighbors had already retired for the evening. Her porch light didn't chase away enough shadows to allow her to forget.

She felt as broken and battered as a board washed ashore

from a shipwreck. She supposed it was possible to have handled the situation worse than she had, but she couldn't figure out how. After Adam had threatened her, she'd fled the room. Charlene had agreed to keep a bewildered Billie for the night. That left Jane free to deal with her emotions and the tears that refused to be halted. Every time she thought she couldn't possibly cry anymore, she would start again.

Her life lay crumpled around her. She had no one to blame but herself. Adam was right—so many of her choices had been wrong ones. She had deprived him and Billie of each other. Had she been a bad mother as well? She closed her eyes and rested her forehead on her bent knees. She recalled the months she'd struggled to make ends meet, to pay the rent and provide food and utilities for their tiny apartment. Billie's face flashed before her, the four-year-old's tantrums when her mother had left for work. Had she damaged Billie? Had she chosen incorrectly? She was willing to admit to some of the blame, but all of it? She groaned softly. She just didn't know.

Was Adam right? Should she have come home? Was living in a big house better, even if that house didn't have any love to fill it? Could he have learned to care about her and his child? Could she have lived with the knowledge that she was little more than an obligation?

She'd only ever wanted Adam to love her. That's all. Not want her because she was appropriate, or easily trained, or because he'd felt obligated. She'd wanted to be loved. For herself. Was that wrong? Selfish? Wrapping her arms around her legs, she wished she could disappear.

From her left came the soft crunch of footsteps on the path between the two houses. Jane sat perfectly still, as if her lack of motion would make her invisible.

Adam. She sensed it was him even before he sat next to her and she could smell his after-shave and the unique male essence of his body.

"Go away," she murmured, refusing to look up.

"I had dinner with Billie," he said without warning.

Oh, God. Her heart froze in her chest. Had he—

"I didn't tell her."

Thank you, she prayed.

"I wanted to," he said, anger still apparent in his voice. "I was going to blurt it out over the salad. I even thought about kidnapping her and running until you couldn't find us."

She turned her head so she could see him. He sat next to her on the steps of her front porch. Two feet separated them. He mimicked her pose—he'd drawn his legs up close to his chest and rested his arms on his knees.

"I couldn't." He looked at her then. She saw that she'd been wrong about hearing anger in his voice. It wasn't rage—it was pain. The loss he'd suffered deepened the lines around his eyes and the hollows in his cheeks. "I don't give a damn about you, but I couldn't hurt her."

"Thank you."

He looked straight ahead. "Where do we go from here?"

"I don't know."

"You don't have any ideas?"

"No."

"You never planned to tell me."

"Oh, Adam, I can't convince you of it, but for what it's worth, yes, I did want to tell you about Billie. Today, believe it or not. Telling you is one of the reasons I came home. I wanted her to grow up here with a family, like she'd always wanted. But I didn't know how to say it without risking it all. I was afraid you'd use Billie to get back at me. That you'd hate me so much that you'd punish her. The longer I was gone, the more time passed, the harder it got."

"I do hate you."

She forced herself not to cry out. Of course he did. But telling herself that he would and hearing the words were two very different things. He still got to her. She'd been foolish to think she'd escaped that.

"How dare you," he said. "How dare you assume I would punish an innocent child."

She stared at her lap. He sounded cold and angry. Worse, he sounded like a stranger. "You have every right to be furious with me," she said. "I *should* have known you'd never do anything like that."

"Why do you keep agreeing with me?"

"You're telling the truth."

"But it makes it damn hard to hold on to the rage."

"Good."

He turned toward her. The anger and the bravado were gone. "Damn it, Jane, you hurt me."

She bowed her head. The tears flowed fast and hot, trickling down her arms and dampening a spot on her skirt.

"Say something," he demanded.

"I...I can't."

He swore. She heard him slide on the step, then felt his hands on her arms, pulling her close. He angled their bodies so that her head rested on his shoulder. Their legs touched, from hip to knee. She clutched at his T-shirt, bunching the soft fabric in her hands. The tears continued, replenished by the aching in her heart.

"I'm s-sorry," she said, her voice cracking with a sob. "So sorry, Adam. I l—loved you so much. I never wanted to hurt you. Or B-Billie. I was afraid for her, I swear."

"I know. Hush." He enfolded her in his strength, rocking back and forth while she cried. The minutes passed. She struggled for control. Finally the tears subsided.

She sniffed and forced herself to straighten. Unshed tears darkened his brown eyes. His words earlier in the day—his speech about stolen time and memories missed—had made her feel bad, but she hadn't had the chance to really think about what he was saying. Now, seeing him emotionally exposed for the first time in her life, she felt what he felt and knew that her crime was far greater than she'd imagined. It hadn't been a speech. He *had* lost all those times she'd taken for granted. And even meeting Billie now couldn't make up for that. She'd cheated them both. It didn't matter if he couldn't forgive her; she'd never forgive herself.

He cupped her face and brushed away her tears with his thumbs. "Where do we go from here?" he asked, repeating his earlier question.

"I wish I knew."

His touch comforted her. She didn't deserve it, but couldn't bring herself to pull away. Still, when Adam straightened, she forced herself to smile slightly and wipe her face.

"I guess we should tell Billie," she said, shifting on the step.

"What is she going to say?"

"I don't know." Jane thought for a moment. "She'll be happy about getting a dad. She's wanted one since she figured out most kids have two parents. But she'll be angry that I lied to her."

"She'll get over it."

She smoothed her skirt over her knees. "That depends on you. Are you going to say things?"

"What are you talking about?"

"Are you going to tell her that I'm the worst mother since the invention of the institution, that I've deprived her of her birthright and family?" She closed her eyes and waited.

"You must think I'm a real bastard."

Now it was her turn to be surprised. "No. Why would you think that?"

He shook his head. "You don't have a very high opinion of me."

"You're still angry and I thought you might—"

"I don't plan to bad-mouth you to Billie. She's the innocent one in all this. She might be pleased to take my side at first, but in the end it would only confuse her."

"Thank you."

"I'm not doing it for you."

Right. She couldn't allow herself to forget that.

"What about her name?" he asked.

"You don't like Billie?"

"Her *last* name. You didn't give her mine."

"I didn't want you to know. It would have been pretty obvious if I'd named her Belle Charlene Barrington."

He sprang to his feet. "You named her Belle Charlene? After Aunt Charlene?"

"Yes. Is that okay?"

He jammed his hands into his pockets. "I don't even know my kid's name."

Jane wanted to bite off her tongue. She'd already hurt him enough—couldn't she stop saying things without thinking? "Adam, I—"

"Don't," he said. "Don't say anything. We'll deal with the name thing later. What about custody? We live next door, so it shouldn't be a problem. Am I listed as a father on the birth certificate?"

He was moving too fast. All this talk about living arrangements and legalities. "Yes, but we need to deal with this later."

"Why? Are you going to disappear again?"

"I didn't come all the way back just to leave. I had planned to have a life here with my daughter."

"My daughter."

"Our daughter." What was going on with him? Why did he have to—

Control. He was trying to control an uncontrollable situation. Of course. What else would Adam do?

She rose to her feet and moved next to him. When he didn't step back, she risked putting a hand on his arm. His skin felt warm to the touch. Alive. The black hairs tickled her palm. Stubble outlined the strong line of his square jaw. The young woman who'd left him would have been allowed to touch that skin and stubble, but she wouldn't have appreciated the contrast of smooth and rough, warm and cool. She wouldn't have noticed the shape of his mouth, or that his muscles coiled when he was tense. She hadn't learned that losing, even if by choice, was hard to get over.

It had been nine years and Jane still hadn't gotten over Adam.

"Billie is our first priority," she said. "We have to tell her that you're her father."

He stiffened. "Father. How am I going to be her father? I don't know how."

"You'll be fine." She was about to go on with the logistics of where and when to tell Billie, when he cut her off.

"What if I say something wrong? What if she decides she doesn't want me for her dad?"

She stared at him. Adam Barrington, *the* Adam Barrington, expressing doubt?

He shrugged out of her touch. "Why are you looking at me like that?"

"I'm surprised you're worried."

"Why wouldn't I be? I don't know Billie that well and she doesn't know me. What if she doesn't like me?"

"She adores you."

"Maybe."

She shook her head.

"What?" he asked.

"I was just thinking I wish you'd been like this nine years ago."

"Like what?"

"Insecure. Scared."

His eyes met hers and for the second time that night she saw into his soul. "You scared the hell out of me, Jane."

The confession came nine years too late.

"Hell of a day," she said, blinking frantically and ordering herself not to cry.

"You're telling me." He sighed. "Tomorrow, over breakfast?"

"Okay."

"What do you want to say?"

"I haven't a clue." She forced herself to smile. "Maybe we should wing it."

He nodded. "Nine. My kitchen."

"I'll be there."

She stood in front of her house until he walked through the hedges that separated their properties. Her mind raced. Thoughts of Billie and what her daughter would say competed with those eight simple words. "You scared the hell out of me, Jane."

Had he been frightened of losing her? Had he cared? Had she destroyed three lives to get away from a demon that didn't even exist?

Adam stepped quickly through the dark night. He'd grown up on this land, he knew every inch of the path from his house to Charlene's. Even without the moon to guide him, he made his way through the trees and up the bricklined walkway to her back door. He knocked softly and waited. She'd still be up. They had a lot to talk about.

"Come in," she called.

He opened the door and stepped into her kitchen. Charlene stood at the stove stirring a pot. Long red hair tumbled around her shoulders. Her full-length burgundy robe clashed with her hair color. Usually he teased her about the combination. Not tonight.

"Is Billie asleep?" he asked.

"Yes."

She didn't turn around to look at him. The silence between them lengthened. "You knew," he said at last.

"Yes."

"She told you?"

"I guessed."

"When?"

With a sigh she tapped the spoon on the edge of the pot, then placed it on the counter. Turning slowly, she raised her chin and looked up at him. "The day she arrived."

He cursed. All the emotion of the past few hours had left him feeling drained, as if someone had pulled the plug on his energy. He didn't have enough in him to sustain anger. He could only feel disappointment and hurt.

Charlene continued to watch him. Her blue eyes, less vivid without any makeup to accentuate the color, didn't show remorse. "I didn't tell you," she said as she leaned against the counter. "Because that wasn't my decision to make. I warned Jane she didn't have much time. If she didn't say something you'd figure it out."

God, he was tired. "You betrayed me."

"How?"

"You're my aunt. You should have been looking out for me. How dare you keep Billie a secret?"

"Adam, I understand your pain. Believe me, this was not an easy thing to keep quiet about. Yes, you're family. But by virtue of having Billie, so is Jane. It wasn't my secret to share or not. It was hers." She picked up the spoon and began stirring the pot again. "Do you want some cocoa?"

"You can't fix this problem that easily," he said, moving into the kitchen and pulling out one of the chairs in front of the window. "I'm not a kid anymore."

"You haven't been for much too long. But cocoa can still make you feel better. Trust me."

He looked at her.

"Adam, I love you. I also love Jane and Billie. Please don't trap me in the middle."

He wanted to hate her, but he couldn't. There was too much at stake. "I don't know what to do."

"About Billie?"

"About all of it. What am I supposed to say when she finds out I'm her father?"

"When are you going to tell her?"

"Tomorrow. At breakfast."

Charlene took down two cups, then measured out cocoa and sugar. "You'll think of something. Billie is a bright girl. She'll handle this better than you imagine."

"I hope so."

She poured the steaming milk into the mugs and stirred. After handing him one, she took the other and sat opposite him at the round oak table. "You'll be a fine father."

"How do you know?"

"Because I know the kind of man you are, Adam Barrington. Have a little faith in yourself." She picked up her cup. "To fatherhood and one more generation of Barringtons."

They tapped mugs. In the corner of her kitchen, the CB unit squawked. "Breaker, breaker, I'm lookin' for my red-headed Southern belle. Charlene, you listenin' to me, darlin'?"

Adam raised one eyebrow.

Charlene tossed her head as she rose to her feet. "I'm just keeping busy."

Chapter Ten

Adam laid out the dozen cinnamon rolls Charlene had brought over, then set the plate in the center of the kitchen island. He moved them slightly to the left. Next he put out place mats, some fruit and napkins. He was about to check the front window to see if Billie and Jane were coming over yet when he remembered that he had to start the coffee.

He hadn't been this nervous since he— He shook his head. He'd never been this nervous. It wasn't every day a man was introduced to his child. Usually it happened in the hospital while the kid was an infant and too little to make judgments about liking and not liking. Billie was eight and very opinionated. What if she decided she didn't want him for her father? He couldn't force himself onto her. It hadn't taken a hell of a lot of soul-searching to realize how very much he wanted to be part of her life.

He gave the kitchen a quick once-over, realized he'd forgotten plates, then set them on the place mats. As he straightened the napkins, he heard a knock on the back door.

Billie didn't bother to wait for him to answer. She barreled into the room and grinned. "I *told* her we didn't have to knock. We have breakfast together almost every day. I said you were 'specting me."

"*Ex*pecting," he answered, before bending over and giving her a hug.

"Whatever," Billie said as she hugged him back, then wiggled out of his embrace and climbed up onto a stool at the center island. "All right! Cinnamon rolls. My favorite." She picked one up and began licking the icing.

"Good morning, Adam," Jane said as she hovered in the doorway. The shadows under her eyes told him she, too, had had a sleepless night.

The nervousness, anticipation and concern swirling in his stomach didn't leave any room for other emotions like anger or resentment. He and Jane were in this together. The first order of business was to tell Billie the truth. Once that was taken care of, he and Jane would have plenty of time to work through everything else. He knew he'd have to come to terms with what Jane had done. He couldn't continue to hate the mother of his child; not without hurting Billie. And she was his main priority.

"Morning." He waved toward the chairs. "Have a seat."

"Thank you."

She sounded as awkward as he felt. As she walked by him, the hem of her floral-print skirt brushed his bare leg. The cotton tickled. He'd thought about dressing up for their talk with Billie, but had decided shorts and a polo shirt would look less as though he was interviewing for the job of father.

"I made coffee. It's almost ready," he said. "Would you like some juice?"

"That would be nice." She seated herself next to Billie, leaving the chair at right angles to the girl for him.

He poured one glass. "Billie?" he asked, holding up the pitcher.

"Sure." She grinned. "And milk, please."

Icing coated her face from her nose to her chin. Crumbs collected at the corner of her mouth. The ever-present baseball cap had been abandoned on the counter and her bangs stuck up along her forehead. She looked adorable.

Her hair— He stared at it for a second, then glanced at Jane. They didn't have the same color. Jane's was darker, a true brown with no hint of blond or red. Billie's hair was lighter. He finished pouring the juice and gave them each a glass. She had *his* hair color. He peered closer. And his eyes. His heart clenched in his chest, as if a giant fist squeezed it tight. It was real. He couldn't believe he'd never noticed.

"Why are you looking at me like that?" Billie asked.

Adam shrugged an apology, but couldn't take his eyes from the girl. The freckles on her nose looked just like Dani's. Her mouth—he glanced at Jane, then back at Billie—belonged to her mother.

Billie leaned across the counter until their faces were inches apart. "You're still staring at me."

He kissed her forehead. "I'm done."

"Good." She grabbed a piece of watermelon and bit into it. Juice ran down her chin. She caught it with the back of her hand.

"Billie, we have to talk," Jane said.

Instantly Billie set the fruit down. Her smile faded and she looked at Adam.

"Am I in trouble?"

"No." He took the seat on the other side of her. He sat on the end of the island, at a right angle to her. He could see Jane over her head. Their eyes met for a brief moment. He saw Jane's uncertainty. He wanted to promise her that it was going to be okay, but he didn't know *how* the situation would end up.

Jane angled herself toward her daughter and rested one arm on the counter. "Adam and I—"

"I slid down the banister," Billie said, staring at her plate.

"What?" he asked.

"Last week, when you got that phone call from the bank, I sneaked out of the kitchen and slid down the banister."

Adam frowned. "I told you not to do that. It's very high and you could get hurt."

She thrust out her lower lip. "I didn't fall."

"That's not the point. The point is—"

"Adam." Jane shook her head. "Billie, you know better, but that's not what we want to talk about."

She nodded and pushed her half-eaten piece of watermelon across her plate. "I know. I didn't *mean* to. It just happened. I was going to say something." She looked up at Jane. "Honest." She turned back to Adam. "You weren't home, so I couldn't tell you. Then when I came to breakfast, I didn't want you to get mad at me. I'm sorry."

He stared horrified as a fat tear trickled down her cheek. "What the hell are you talking about?" he said loudly.

Billie jumped.

"Adam, don't swear," Jane said.

"Mom, he said a bad word." Billie sniffed. "Adam, you shouldn't say *hell*."

He'd lost control, he thought as he struggled to stay sane. He wasn't sure he'd ever had it, but it was gone now. He slid off the stool and grabbed the coffeepot. After filling two mugs, he handed one to Jane, then resumed his seat. "Okay, let's try this again. Billie, you're right. I shouldn't say—"

Jane raised her eyebrows.

"I shouldn't swear. I apologize. What were you talking about before? The thing you didn't want to tell me."

Another tear rolled down her cheek. "I broke a window in the shed."

"You what?"

"There's no need to raise your voice," Jane said, putting an arm around her daughter. His daughter.

"I'm not raising my voice." He spoke through clenched teeth. "I'm calmly asking Billie to tell me what happened with the shed."

She sighed and sat up straight. Jane kept her arm around the girl's shoulders. "I was playing ball in the back. It was kinda windy, you know?"

"Go on." He sipped his coffee.

"Well, I was working on my curve ball and—"

"This isn't important," Jane said, staring intently at him. "This isn't what we wanted to talk about."

"But I want to know about the window."

"Fine. If you think that's more important, be my guest."

Billie looked from one to the other, her eyes getting wider and wider. "Are you guys fighting?"

"No," he said grimly.

"Yes," Jane answered, picking up her napkin and snapping it open. "Adam is easily distracted. Do you want to talk about the window or should we discuss something more relevant?"

"You're right," he said, wondering how he'd been moved off the subject at hand. "Billie, we'll deal with the shed another time." He took her hand. The short blunt nails needed cleaning. She had a cut at the base of her thumb. A child's hand, small and full of promise. His child's hand. "Billie—"

"Yes?" She looked up. "Do you have tickets to the Triple A game?"

He smiled. "No, honey, I don't."

"Can I have another roll?"

He pushed the plate toward her. She pulled her hand free and grabbed for the sweet.

"I can't," he said, leaning back in his seat. "I don't

know what to say, or how to handle this situation." He looked at Jane. "Any suggestions?"

"I'll try," she said. "I've had longer to think about this than you."

"Think about what?" Billie asked, her mouth full.

"Honey, I've got a secret."

Billie looked up at her mother. "A good one?"

"Yes." Jane smiled weakly and brushed her daughter's bangs out of her eyes. "You've always asked me about a father. Where yours was. Why he couldn't be with us."

Adam swallowed. Here it comes. What would Billie say?

Billie set her roll on the plate and licked her fingers. "You know where my dad is?"

"Adam is your father, Billie. Your real father. I—" Jane cleared her throat. "He didn't know until yesterday. We wanted to tell you together."

Billie glanced at him, her eyes as big as the softball she carried in her shorts pocket. When he offered her what he hoped was a reassuring smile, she dropped her chin to her chest and stared at her lap. "Did you know?"

Jane nodded. "Yes," she said, her voice thick with unshed tears. "I knew Adam was your father."

Billie looked up at him. He tried to read her expression, but couldn't. "Do you want to be my father?"

"More than anything."

She pushed her plate away. "It's okay, I guess."

"Good." He started to lean forward to hug her, but she slipped off the seat and picked up her baseball cap.

"I'm going to go play ball." She stopped by the back door. "Okay, Mom?"

"Fine."

"What about church?"

"We'll try to go tonight."

She ran out without looking back.

He breathed a sigh of relief. The conversation had been anticlimactic at best, but had gone better that he'd hoped.

"She handled that very well," he said.

"I don't think so." Jane stared after her daughter. Her makeup couldn't hide her sudden lack of color or the stricken expression in her eyes.

What had he missed? Panic threatened. "Why do you say that?"

"Billie is bright and inquisitive. At the very least I thought she'd ask how I knew you were her father. Which would lead to...well, you know. But she hardly said a word."

"Would you have preferred her to get upset?"

Jane moved her cup along the edge of the tiles. "I think so. She doesn't understand what we told her. Not really. That will come later. I hope—" she sighed "—I hope she can forgive me."

"For what?"

"You were right last night. I lied to her, for her whole life. I wouldn't talk about her father. It would have been one thing if I hadn't known where he was, but I knew you were here. She's going to figure that out."

He felt vaguely uncomfortable. He didn't want to hear Jane's side of the story; he only wanted to be angry at her. Besides, if the truth were told, he didn't mind if Billie was irritated with her mother for a couple of days. "Maybe you should have thought about that when you chose to stay away all those years. You only have yourself to blame."

The long morning got longer. Jane glanced out the kitchen window and saw Billie sitting under their chestnut tree. The girl had been there for almost an hour. The only time Billie stayed still voluntarily was when she was sick. Even asleep she tossed and turned like a puppy having a dream.

Jane pushed opened the back door and walked down the steps. When she reached the shade, she knelt on the grass and laced her fingers together on her lap.

"How you doing?" she asked.

"Okay." Billie turned her softball over and over in her hand. The bill of her cap hid most of her face.

"You want to play catch?"

"I don't think so. I'll just sit here."

"Do you have any questions?"

"Uh-uh."

Now what? Jane wondered. "We gave you a lot to think about."

Billie nodded. "Is Adam really my dad?"

"Yes."

"Are you divorced from him?"

Jane grimaced. She hadn't seen that one coming. "No, honey. Adam and I didn't get married."

Billie looked up. Her mouth twisted as she wrinkled her nose. It was her I-can't-solve-this-problem expression. "Don't you have to be married to have a baby?"

"Not always. Adam and I were going to get married. But then we decided we shouldn't." It wasn't exactly a lie, she told herself. Besides, the truth was difficult for *her* to understand, let alone an eight-year-old.

Billie rolled her ball along the ground. It stopped in front of Jane and she rolled it back. "You didn't marry Adam, but you had me, anyway?"

"Yes."

"Why?"

"I wanted you."

Billie picked up the ball. "And Adam didn't?"

"Adam didn't know about you, honey."

"Why?"

"I didn't know when I left."

"But you knew later?"

"Yes."

Billie stood up and stuffed her ball into her pocket. "Every Sunday when we went to church, I always asked God for a dad. He gave me one. I guess I'm happy."

"I know it's a lot to get used to."

Billie nodded. "I'm going for a walk, Mom."

"Lunch is in an hour."

Billie shuffled off deeper into the backyard. Jane watched her go. This quiet sedate child wasn't hers. Had telling Billie been a mistake? Was the damage permanent? She wanted to run after her and hug her and love her until all the questions and fears disappeared. It didn't work that way. Billie had to figure this thing out on her own. Nothing would be the same again.

Jane made her way back to the house. Should she invite Adam over for lunch? How were they going to handle that now? Coming home and reuniting father and daughter had seemed like such a good idea in San Francisco. But she'd never thought through all the logistical problems. Where did they go from here?

It was almost two o'clock when Jane burst into Adam's study. "She's not here, is she?"

He looked up from his work and frowned. "Billie? I haven't seen her since this morning. I was going to call you later and see if you thought we could all have dinner."

She turned toward Charlene who was standing behind her. "She's not here. That's it, then. She's run away."

"Who's run away?"

"Your daughter." Jane rubbed her temples. "I last saw her about three hours ago in the backyard. We had a talk about, well, you know. I told her lunch was in an hour. When I went out to get her, I couldn't find her."

Billie? Gone? He glanced at his watch. "And you're just now coming to find me?"

"I wanted to check the yard and then the house. Charlene looked around here while I went to the park."

"And?" he asked, already knowing the answer.

"No one's seen her."

He'd been a parent less than twenty-four hours and it had

been one crisis after another. His first inclination was to tear out of the room and begin a search of his own. "Let's keep calm," he said, as much to himself as to them.

"Calm?" Jane shrieked. "Calm? My daughter is out there. Alone. And you want to stay calm?"

"Jane, please, dear. This isn't helping." Charlene took her arm and ushered her into the room. "Have a seat and we'll all think this through. She can't have gone that far."

"You don't know Billie. She's very resourceful."

"She's also a little girl. And that is what she's going to act like. Now, think. Where would Billie go?"

Jane crumpled into the chair in front of his desk. She shook her head. "I don't know. I *can't* think. Oh, God, she's lost and it's all my fault."

Charlene looked at him. "Adam?"

He came around the desk and crouched in front of Jane. Taking her hands in his, he squeezed them reassuringly. Her skin felt icy to the touch. "This isn't helping Billie. Please, Jane. You must get a grip on yourself. Where would Billie go?"

"I don't know." Her hazel eyes, wide and unfocused, swept the room frantically, as if her child might be concealed in some corner. A shiver racked her body. "She's never done this before."

"She probably wants time to think. Where does she go when that happens?"

Jane jerked her hands free and tried to stand up. "Get out of my way. We need to call the police."

"Not yet." A memory walked along the edge of his consciousness. It stayed tantalizingly out of reach, but there was something familiar. A sense of having been through this before. Dani had disappeared after his parents' funeral. He'd searched for hours until—

"Did you try the old tree house?" he asked.

"What?" Jane stared at him. "Is it still there?"

"Pieces. I think Billie mentioned something about it the

day you arrived. You'd told her stories. Maybe she's there."

Hope brightened her pale face. "You think so?"

"There's one way to find out. Come on."

He grabbed her hand and led her out of the study. Charlene followed on their heels. Most of the two-acre backyard had been landscaped, but a patch of woods still existed in the southwest corner. Adam went first along the overgrown trail. Billie had spent part of her days exploring his yard; it wasn't unreasonable to assume she'd found the tree house.

He kept repeating the thought over and over as if thinking it enough would make it true. The real truth was that he was as anxious as Jane. But after years of dealing with crises at home and at the bank, he was better at hiding his feelings. Be all right, Billie, he repeated like a prayer.

As they neared the tree house, he motioned for them to move more quietly. He wanted to get close enough to see her before she spotted them. He didn't want to give her the chance to run. Jane held on to his hand as if it were her lifeline. He returned her pressure and glanced over his shoulder to give her a reassuring smile.

They rounded a curve in the path. The old cottonwood stood like a battle-scarred warrior among the newer saplings and willows. A ladder hugged the trunk of the eighty-foot tree. Stout branches fanned out. The thickest, about fifteen feet off the ground, supported the remains of a tree house.

At first he didn't see anything. Then the sun caught a flash of red among the leaves. He closed his eyes and pictured her at breakfast that morning. Red T-shirt, denim shorts.

"She's there."

Jane sagged against him.

"Do you want to go talk to her?" he asked.

"We should go together." Jane glanced back at Charlene, as if to confirm her opinion.

"I agree. I'll wait here."

Adam stepped along the path. When they were almost at the tall tree, he stepped on a fallen branch. It snapped. Billie stuck her head over the side of the tree house.

She wasn't crying, but she didn't smile at them, either. "I'm in trouble, huh?"

"You bet," he said, finally realizing the extent of his worry as relief flooded his body. "You're not allowed to go off without telling someone."

She frowned. "How'd you know that?"

"It makes sense."

She nodded and looked past him to her mother. "Am I going to get a whippin'?"

Jane tried to laugh. It came out sounding a little shaky. "I've never hit you."

"I was just checking." Billie adjusted her baseball cap. "You probably want me to come down."

Adam released Jane's hand. "I'll come up."

"Be careful," Jane said, touching his arm.

"I will. I've been climbing this tree since I was younger than Billie."

"When was the last time?"

He hoisted himself onto the first step and looked back. "About nine years ago. Are you saying I'm too old?"

"I'm saying be careful."

He climbed the rungs leading up to the tree house. As he pivoted and lowered himself onto the floor of the open platform, he gave Billie a smile. "Nice view."

"Yeah." She took her ball out of her pocket and studied it.

"With the walls gone, it's not safe up here for you. If you'd like, I'll put the walls back."

She shook her head. "I won't be allowed up here. My mom won't like it."

"How do you know?"

She shrugged. "She just won't."

"Maybe I can talk to her about it."

"Really?" She eyed him suspiciously. "Is that a dad thing?"

Was it? Now he shrugged. "I used to play up here when I was your age. I had a lot of fun. I'd like the same for you."

She offered her first smile since she'd heard the news. "Sometimes famous pitchers need a place to play."

"I bet. I'll talk with your mother in a couple of days. Right now, though, I'd like you to come down with me. Can I give you a piggyback ride to the bottom?"

"Okay."

She walked over to him and leaned against his back. After stuffing her ball back into her pocket, she wrapped her arms around his neck and her legs around his waist.

So small, he thought, fighting the sudden tightness in his throat. So young and fragile. His daughter. His child.

"All set?"

"Uh-huh."

He stepped back onto the ladder and quickly brought them to the ground. Jane met them at the bottom. She pulled Billie off Adam and hugged her close.

"I was so frightened," she said, burying her cheek against her daughter's hair. "Don't scare me like that again."

"I'm sorry, Mom. I'm in trouble, huh?"

Jane continued to hold her tight. "No. You're not in trouble."

Adam expected several reactions, but not for Billie to start crying. The tears fell fast and furious down her face, but she made almost no noise.

"Mommy," she said. She squirmed to get closer. Her hat fell to the ground.

"Hush, Billie. You're safe now. You'll always be safe. I won't let anything happen to you."

"I love you, Mommy."

"I love you, too, baby."

The sobs continued, as if the child's most precious possession had been torn from her. Adam stood helplessly beside the two of them and watched as Billie suffered a pain he couldn't begin to understand. He thought about offering comfort, but to whom? And for what?

Charlene walked over and touched his arm. "We'd better head back."

He shook off her hand. "I don't want to."

"Adam!"

He glanced at her.

"Let Jane handle this."

"She's my daughter, too."

"In name only. Right now Billie needs her mother."

Jane looked up and nodded. "Please, just a couple of hours. Come by around five and we'll talk over dinner."

It was Billie who made the decision for him. He reached over to pat her back, but she shrank out of reach and clung tighter to her mother. It hurt, he acknowledged, allowing Charlene to lead him back to the house. Telling himself Billie was a child and simply reacting to the situation didn't help.

When he reached the curve in the path, he turned and stared at Jane and Billie. The woman who should have been his wife, holding the child that belonged to him. In a moment of passion, he and Jane had made that precious girl. He didn't understand all the ramifications of being a parent, but he would die for that child. As Jane's gaze met his, then slid away, he realized something else. The risk he took. He couldn't stop Billie from finding a place in his heart. It was too late for that; the process had already begun. He had to find a way to keep her from disappearing from his life. He knew the rule; if you love something, it leaves you. He couldn't let that happen now.

Chapter Eleven

She was as nervous as the day she'd arrived. Jane wiped her palms against her skirt and paced the small living room. It was silly, she told herself. Adam was the same man he'd been yesterday, before he'd known. He would be the same tomorrow. He might be angry and hurt and confused, but he was still Adam.

That's what scared her. In the brief time they'd spent together, she'd come to see that the young man she'd run from was not the person he'd become. She'd run from phantoms. Vague fears of a young woman too inexperienced to understand what frightened her and too cowardly to speak about those fears. She freely admitted running had been wrong. But what about not marrying Adam? Had she made the right choice there?

"Mom, I'm hungry." Billie stood in the doorway of the living room. The ever-present softball bulged at the pocket of her denim shorts.

"We'll be having dinner in less than an hour. Adam is due here any minute."

"Is he going to eat with us all the time now?"

"I don't know."

"Maybe we can use his kitchen instead. You know, eat at the island?" Billie smiled hopefully. "I'll be real careful not to spill anything."

"I'll be sure to let him know."

"I'm still hungry."

Jane sighed. "There are a couple of apple slices on the plate in the fridge. But that's all."

"Thanks." Billie stifled a yawn.

"Early to bed for you, young lady."

"Mo-om!"

She followed her daughter into the kitchen. "Don't 'Mo-om' me. I have a feeling Charlene kept you up well past your regular bedtime."

Billie grabbed a slice of apple and slammed the fridge door shut. "Maybe, you know, a couple of minutes."

Jane bit back a smile and leaned against the counter. "And what did the two of you do?"

"Well, we, huh, you know, talked."

"About?"

Billie hunched her shoulders. "Baseball."

"Did you play cards?"

"Cards?" Billie took a bite of her apple. "Can't talk with my mouth full," she mumbled.

"How convenient."

There was a knock at the screen door. "What's convenient?" Adam asked as he let himself in and paused just inside the kitchen.

Jane straightened and told herself not to stare. It didn't help. He'd showered recently. Dampness darkened his short brown hair, and he looked as if he'd just shaved. The smoothness of his jaw made her wonder what it would feel like against her hand. The crisp cotton short-sleeved shirt stretched across his broad shoulders and chest. The open V allowed a few hairs to peek out. She recalled touching that chest, so many years ago. A light dusting of hair, broad at the shoulders then narrowing toward his waist, had teased her fingers. Even now, her fingers curled into her palms at the memory of how he'd sucked in his breath when she'd accidentally brushed her fingers across his flat nipples. It had been a moment of triumph for her, she remembered. A brief time when she'd been able to ignore her fears and reduce this strong man to hungry passion.

His chinos hugged slim hips and outlined the lean muscles in his thighs. Her gaze dropped farther down to the casual loafers, then began to move back up. His carefully constructed wall of control didn't seem to be working tonight, she thought in surprise. She could see his discomfort in the way he shoved his hands into his pockets, then removed them. She studied his face. The square jaw, the firm mouth that had claimed hers so recently, the eyes that he'd passed on to Billie.

Pain flickered in the brown depths. And confusion. And something that might have been longing. For the time lost? For the fact that he'd missed those years with Billie? Or for her? No, she thought. She couldn't allow herself to think like that. It cost too much.

"I'm glad you could make it," she said softly.

"Thanks for inviting me." He gave her a quick smile, then looked at Billie. "How are you feeling?"

"Okay." Billie finished the last of her apple and began to lick her fingers. She yawned suddenly.

"She's a little tired," Jane said. "I think Charlene kept her up last night. Can I get you something to drink?"

"Thanks. Whatever's easiest."

"Beer?"

He raised his eyebrows.

She shrugged. "We went to the market."

"Yeah," Billie said. "She bought this bread. The long

kind." She held out her hands to show him the length. "We're going to make garlic toast. I know how."

"Maybe I could help you."

Billie tugged on the bill of her cap. Jane held her breath. It had been a gesture of friendship by Adam. She hadn't forgotten the look on his face when he'd watched her with Billie that afternoon. The need in his eyes, the obvious disappointment at being shut out. Go on, she urged her daughter silently. He's not so bad.

"Okay," Billie said. "I have trouble stirring the butter sometimes. You can do that."

"Great." Adam tugged off her hat.

"Gimme!"

He held it out of reach. She jumped up and tried to grab the cap. When that didn't work, she grinned. "Please."

"Why should I?"

"'Cause it's mine."

He chuckled and pulled the hat over her head.

"Here." Jane handed him a glass of beer.

Adam leaned against the counter and took a sip. His gaze flickered over her, and she was glad she'd taken the time to shower and change her clothes. The sleeveless sundress with its rows of tiny buttons up the bodice made her feel pretty. And right now she could use all the confidence she could get.

Billie yawned again. Adam frowned. "What time did you go to bed?"

"I don't know."

"Was it past your bedtime?"

Billie's smiled faded. "I don't have a watch."

He glanced at Jane. "I don't like the sound of that."

"Charlene wouldn't have done anything really horrible."

He raised his eyebrows.

"Oh, dear. I guess she would. Billie, did you and Charlene play cards?" Billie pulled out her softball and studied the seams. Jane knew that look. "Just tell me."

"A couple of games."

"Poker?"

"No." Billie shook her head. "We did a counting game. She gave me cards and I had to count them. Whoever got closest to twenty-one won. We played for cookies."

She moaned. "I told her not to teach you card games."

"It's hopeless," Adam said. "She's always been that way. I guess I shouldn't be surprised. She taught me to play poker when I was around Billie's age. It never bothered me much before."

"It makes a difference when it's your kid."

Their eyes met. For a second she regretted her statement. But Adam didn't lash out at her. There was a flash of understanding between them. Something warm and shared that made her long for all the moments they'd missed as a family. Had he been right? Had she deprived Billie of two parents? And what about the things she'd deprived herself of? Sharing the responsibilities made the load seem lighter.

"I see that," he said. He took another drink. "Early to bed for you tonight, Billie. And no more card games."

Her good humor vanished. "You can't tell me what to do."

"I certainly can."

Jane moved next to him. "Adam, I don't think—"

"We've established that point."

Her temper flared. "This is neither the time nor the place to bring that up."

"Don't yell at Adam," Billie interrupted, using her own brand of logic. Jane stared at her. Just seconds before *she'd* been the one saying he couldn't tell her what to do.

"Don't talk to your mother that way," Adam said, setting his glass on the counter. "You may not like what she's saying, but you will listen and respect her. Do you understand?"

Both women stared at him. Jane recovered first. "I think we've had our first fight as a family."

Adam folded his arms over his chest. For a second she thought he was going to stay mad. Then he grinned. "Was it good for you?"

"Yeah, it was."

Billie stared at both of them. "You guys are weird. I'm going outside to play ball."

"Dinner's in an hour. Don't run away this time."

Billie rolled her eyes. "I won't. Geez, Mom. Give me a break." With that, she ran out the back door.

Without her the kitchen seemed smaller. That didn't make sense, Jane told herself, but the feeling persisted. Perhaps it was the way Adam studied her. She walked over to the refrigerator and began pulling vegetables out of the bin at the bottom. "I thought we'd have pasta. I hope that's all right."

"It's fine."

She picked up the broccoli and stared at it. "Thanks for telling her to listen to me. You didn't have to take my side."

"I did it instinctively. The parents against the kids, I guess."

"A united front is best, especially now."

"There's so much I don't know."

She set the broccoli on the counter and looked at him. He shrugged. She saw the worry in the frown lines on his forehead.

"You just have to feel your way," she said. "At first I didn't know what to do, either. A lot of the time, I still don't. I just try and be fair and consistent. I also try not to sweat the small stuff. There are enough big things to worry about."

"Such as?"

When she least expected it, the pain caught her off guard. He stood there, so tall and handsome. In control. A perfect catch. If only he'd loved her. She shook her head. If she had a dollar for every *if only* in her life, she'd own the Barrington mansion and he'd be living next door.

"Oh, nothing I can think of offhand."

Before she could turn away, he reached out his hand and cupped her face. The touch, gentle, concerned, broke through her resolve and her pride. She started to look down, but he moved his index finger along her cheek and jaw until it rested under her chin and she was forced to stare up at him.

"Don't shut me out," he said. "What do you worry about?"

If he'd stopped touching her, she might have been able to lie. But he continued to hold her face, occasionally stroking her cheek with his thumb. The warm caress, more comforting than anything else, wore her down.

"Not Billie," she admitted. "Somehow she got the best of both of our families. I know in my heart she'll be fine."

"Then what?"

They stood alone in her kitchen. It wasn't the least bit romantic, what with raw vegetables scattered around on the counter and the sound of their daughter playing in the backyard. Yet she felt in tune with Adam. Perhaps he *would* understand.

"It's not my finest hour," she said tentatively, waiting to gauge his reaction.

"Are you waiting for a promise that I won't judge you?"

She nodded.

His brown eyes searched her face. He struggled with her request. She saw the battle rage in his eyes. Then she saw victory. Her victory, and it tasted sweeter than she would have imagined.

"I give you my word."

How ironic. She'd given hers once, and it'd had no value. Yet she would risk her life on the strength of Adam's word.

"I'm afraid of losing Billie."

"But you said you thought she'd be fine."

"Not to anything bad. To you."

He frowned. "I don't understand."

She started to step away, but he tightened his hold on her face just enough to let her know he wanted her to stay. She relaxed. He eased her forward, slipping his hand around her neck and under her braid, until she rested against his side. His arm came around to hold her close.

"I've always been first in her life. The only constant in a changing world. That's all about to change. She likes you already, Adam. She can't help but grow to love you."

"You're assuming I'll do well."

"You will."

"I wish I could be as sure." He took a deep breath, then released it. "If you knew this was going to happen, why did you bother…" Now he was the one who stiffened slightly.

She wrapped her arm around his waist and held on. "Don't, Adam. Why did I bother coming back, if I knew the risk I was taking? Is that the question?"

"Yes."

It was easier this way, she thought, closing her eyes and resting her head against his chest. His cotton shirt felt warm and smooth against her cheek. She inhaled the scent of him. Better not to see the emotions in his eyes. Or worse, to see the shutters closing her out.

"I came back because it was time I stopped thinking only of myself. I took the risk because Billie deserves a father in her life and you deserve your daughter. I love her. She loves me. I have to trust that love to last through this. And if it doesn't…" She didn't allow herself to visualize that scenario. "I can't make her care if she doesn't want to."

"Sounds dangerous to me."

She could see why he would think that. After all, his parents had died when he'd been quite young. The next big relationship in his life had ended when she'd run off. No wonder Adam had his doubts about the strength of love.

"You're going to have to trust me on this one," she said.

"That's a big order," he said quietly.

She squeezed her eyes shut against the pain. She deserved the comment, but it still hurt.

"I didn't mean that the way it came out," he said.

"Yes, you did."

He stepped away from her and walked to the other side of the kitchen. The physical rejection hurt almost as much as his words had, but she forced herself to stand upright and not let it show. The hard part was that she felt as raw and exposed as an open wound. The broken promises, fears and lies from their past might never be overcome. And then what?

From the window, he could see out into her backyard. "Look at her," he said.

Jane walked over to stand next to him. She glanced out. Billie had a bucketful of softballs on the ground next to her and was pitching them through an old tire he'd hung in the yard. Her running commentary was barely audible through the glass.

"What are we going to do about all of this?" he asked, as if he could read her mind. "Where do we go from here?"

"I haven't a clue."

"Mom said she'd rather bake something, but there wasn't time, so we're having store-bought dessert." Billie leaned closer to Adam and lowered her voice. "I love my mom's cookies and stuff, but sometimes it's fun to have it from the store. They have that thick icing she doesn't like me to have."

No doubt about it, Adam thought as he returned her grin, Belle Charlene Barrington was a charmer.

"Did she let you pick it out?"

"Uh-huh. German chocolate cake." She licked her lips. "I took a taste of the icing before. It's great."

"I'm sure." He rose to his feet and collected their plates.

Dinner had gone better than he'd hoped. Despite the awkwardness between him and Jane, conversation had been lively at the table. With Billie around, there wasn't much fear of silence. So far she seemed to have accepted him with few reservations, although she did stick close to her mother. Charlene had told him it was perfectly natural in a child her age. He had to bow to her superior wisdom in this area. Funny, Jane was worried about losing Billie, while he was concerned about not being accepted. They were both afraid.

Billie picked up the empty bowl that had contained the pasta.

"Have you got that?" he asked. "Is it too heavy?"

She rolled her eyes. "I'm not a kid."

"Oh? What are you?"

She wrinkled her nose. "Okay, *maybe* I'm a kid, but I'm not a little one."

"Point taken." He held open the swinging door to the kitchen, and she ducked under his arm.

"Are you going to live with us?" Billie asked.

Even though he'd been worried about her handling the heavy glass bowl, he was the one who almost dropped the dishes he carried. He stepped into the kitchen and sought Jane's gaze. She looked about as startled as he felt.

"Live with you?" he repeated.

"You know, in the same house? Families do that. Are we a family?"

Jane took the bowl from her daughter's hands. "Yes, Billie, we're a family. As for living together, there are a lot of details to be worked out."

"What about the houses? We shouldn't have two. Can we live with Adam? I promise I won't slide down the banister."

Jane smiled at the girl. Adam wondered if Billie saw how her mouth quivered at the corner and the panic in her eyes. "I've told you about not making promises you can't keep."

Billie sighed heavily. "I'll *try* not to slide down the banister too often."

"That's better."

"So can we?"

Jane looked at him and silently pleaded for help. He set the plates on the counter and crouched in front of Billie. Without her baseball cap, she looked smaller and more feminine. He tapped her nose. "Your mother and I have to work out the details of this arrangement. As soon as we've come to some sort of agreement, we'll let you know. Agreed?"

"Agreed." Billie peered at him. "Are you my dad forever?"

The lump appeared in his throat without warning. "Yes. Forever."

"You won't go away?"

"What do you mean?"

"Sometimes dads leave. There were two girls in my class last year whose dads left. One of them had to move."

He didn't dare look at Jane. "Sometimes parents do things their children don't understand. But no, I won't ever leave you. Not after I've just found you." He rose to his feet. She held out her arms and he swung her up into his embrace.

"What does a dad do?" she asked.

"I'm not sure. We'll find out together."

"Do you buy me presents on my birthday?"

"Yes."

"And Christmas?"

"And Christmas."

"Like a bike?"

"Billie!" Jane shook her head.

Billie leaned closer to him and whispered, "In case you wanted to, you know, ask what I'd like for Christmas, I'd like a bike."

"I'd never have guessed," he said, holding back a smile.

"Enough," Jane said, planting her hands on her hips. "Billie, finish clearing the table. Adam, do you want cake?"

He lowered Billie to the floor and watched her scurry out of the room. Then he turned back to Jane. Several strands of hair had escaped from her braid and now drifted around her face. She wasn't wearing much makeup, just something to make her lashes longer and her eyes look mysterious. Any lipstick had long since worn away. But that didn't stop him from staring at her mouth.

If he concentrated, he could almost taste her sweet passion. It hadn't been that many days ago that he'd kissed her in anger. Despite the rage he'd felt and his need to punish her, she'd more than met him halfway. It had been a joining of equals, not of teacher and student. A blush stained her cheeks, but he didn't stop staring. His gaze drifted down to her chest and the row of impossibly small buttons marching from the top of the scooped neck down to the dropped waist of the dress. Her loose clothing hid her shape. Nine years ago she'd felt self-conscious about her small breasts. Had another man taught her that it was the soul of the woman that drove a man wild; that her body was simply packaging? Had other hands taught her that size didn't matter, that smaller might be more sensitive, that skin as smooth as hers could only ever be perfect? How many lovers had completed what he had begun? How many had made up for his boorishness?

"Adam?" She spoke his name softly, responding more to his look than asking a question.

He took a step toward her. Billie burst into the room carrying three glasses and a serving plate balanced precariously on top. He leapt toward her to rescue the china. The plate teetered. He caught it as it fell.

"Oops," she said.

"*Oops* is right, kid."

Billie set the glasses on the counter and turned to her mother. "When are we having dessert?"

"Right now."

Jane opened a bakery box and pulled out the cake inside. Billie grabbed forks and grinned. "My favorite part of the meal."

"Mine, too," he said, trying to ignore the panic building up inside. It was all happening too quickly and too easily. Billie liked him; Jane— He drew in a breath. Something was happening there all right. Hormones or memories or both. And it scared the hell out of him. He was risking too much. This whole thing could explode in his face, leaving him worse off than before.

"But I want *both* of you to put me to bed," Billie whined when Jane told her it was time to take her bath.

Jane shook her head and glanced at Adam. "There's still time to back out."

He sat on the sofa with Billie curled up next to him. With a lazy flick of his hand, he sent her baseball cap sailing. She chuckled and ducked after it, then climbed onto his lap.

"I'll take my chances," he said, holding Billie in his arms as he rose to his feet. "How about if I give you a piggyback ride to the bathroom, then *after* your bath, I'll help tuck you in?"

"Okay. But I want a *long* ride. The tub's real big and takes a long time to fill."

Jane watched Adam gallop down the hall, with Billie clinging to his back and urging him to go faster. He ducked to avoid bumping her against the hall light fixture. As they passed under the glow, the hair on their heads gleamed. Identical shades of brown reflected in the light. She forced herself to stand and walk up the stairs to the bathroom.

The raw feeling hadn't gone away, she thought, as she adjusted the water temperature. She needed some serious comforting. As she added bubble bath to the tub, she realized that an hour-long soak and a good book wasn't exactly what she was thinking of. She wanted to be held. By Adam. The trouble with that scenario was that he was part of the problem. A big part. No doubt he was feeling a little on edge himself. Who would he go to for comfort? Was there someone special in Orchard, or maybe the next town, that he could call?

The thought of Adam with another woman fired up her temper, but she told herself she had no right to care. She'd given away that right the day she'd run out on him. She was lucky he wasn't married with a dozen kids of his own. At least Billie would have him all to herself while they got acquainted. Charlene had warned her that Adam hadn't spent the last nine years waiting for her. She would do well to remember that advice.

While the tub filled, Jane went into Billie's room and pulled a clean pair of pajamas out of a dresser drawer. After clicking on the lamp, she drew back the bright red spread and smoothed the sheets. The worn old teddy bear, with one ear missing and most of the fur rubbed off, was the only vaguely feminine thing in a room full of baseball posters and sports equipment. She picked up a couple of dirty T-shirts and dropped them into the basket, then walked to the doorway and surveyed the room. Where would they live when the dust settled on this new situation? The three of them? Here? She shook her head. Adam would never give up his family home; nor did she want him to. He belonged to the Barrington estate; it was as much a part of him as his eyes. Would they continue to live next door to each other? There didn't seem to be much option. She wouldn't move into that big house. She had no right.

Thundering footsteps on the stairs drew her attention away from her thoughts. She stepped into the bathroom and turned off the water, then returned to the hall and watched Adam carrying Billie up the stairs. They were both laughing at something. Billie tugged on his shirt collar as if it were the reins. Her pulling had unfastened two buttons exposing more of his broad chest. Jane felt herself flush and looked away.

"One child delivered for bathing," he said, turning his back on her and grabbing Billie's arm to help her slide down.

"Just in time," Jane answered. "The bath is ready."

"Aw, Mom."

Jane laughed. "We have this conversation every night and I've never changed my mind about your bath. Why do you keep trying?"

Billie grinned. "You might say I don't have to."

"Hope springs eternal." She pulled off her daughter's baseball cap. "In." She pointed to the bathtub. "Now."

Billie glanced up at Adam. "Will you help tuck me in?"

Jane told herself not to look, but she couldn't help it. She glanced at his face. The shutters opened to reveal a longing so intense, it took her breath away. He reached out and tapped Billie's nose. "Yeah. I'll be there."

"Cool." She ducked into the bathroom. "I'm not really dirty, Mom, so this shouldn't take long."

Jane rolled her eyes. "We go through this every night."

Adam smiled. "I can imagine. Call me when she's done."

She watched him retreat down the stairs. He moved with a powerful grace that made her long for a second chance.

"I'm in the tub," Billie called. "I'm splashing."

"I'm coming."

"Now Adam kisses me good-night," Billie demanded royally.

He leaned forward and obliged.

"Enough," Jane said. "No more kissing or conversation. Go to sleep. You're exhausted."

Billie yawned suddenly, then rolled onto her side. "Okay. G'night."

Adam hovered by the bed, as if he didn't want to leave her just yet. Jane waited by the door. Billie sighed, then her eyes fluttered closed. He leaned over and kissed her again, then joined Jane. They shut the door behind them and walked toward the stairs.

"All that energy," he said. "It's hard to believe she's actually going to sleep."

"I know. But as tired as she is, she'll be out in about twenty seconds."

They reached the hallway and stopped. Jane bit her lower lip. She should send Adam on his way. That was the sensible thing to do. They were both emotionally at the end of their ropes and needed the time to regroup. But to be honest—and selfish—she didn't want to be alone. Not yet.

"Would you like some coffee?" she asked, not daring to look at him.

He didn't answer at first. Slowly she raised her gaze to his. Confusion, acceptance and pain swirled in the brown depths. "You have anything stronger?" he asked.

"Brandy?"

"Perfect."

"I'll meet you in the parlor."

Chapter Twelve

Jane found the box of brandy her parents had given her last Christmas and opened the package. After collecting glasses, she turned off the kitchen lights and made her way to the front of the house.

The storm from the previous evening had passed, leaving clear skies and slightly lower temperatures. Even so, the South Carolina summer night swirled around her, bringing with it the scents and sounds that were uniquely home. Night jasmine, her mother's favorite, filled the air with its sweetly sensual fragrance. As she entered the parlor, she saw Adam standing by the front window. As at his house, shutters protected them from prying eyes. He'd pulled them back and opened the windows, but hadn't turned on any lights. A streetlamp provided slight illumination, as did the light in the downstairs hall. Enough to see the size and shape of him, but not his expression when he turned to look at her.

"Can you open this for me?" she asked, her voice a little softer than normal.

He took the bottle. "Are you sure you want to? Are you saving it for a special occasion?"

"I can't imagine anything more special than you finding out about Billie."

Even though he would be as unable to see her face as she was to see his, she turned away, embarrassed at exposing herself to him. She couldn't let herself forget that he was still angry and had the potential to wound.

But all he said was "Thank you." He tore off the protective covering and opened the bottle. She held out the glasses and he poured them each a half inch of the dark liquid.

"To Billie," she said, raising her glass.

"To Billie," he answered. But instead of drinking, he stared at her. She would have sold her soul for the courage to turn on a light and see the look in his eyes.

Uneasily she took a sip of the brandy, wincing as it burned a path down to her stomach. But in a few seconds the fiery heat became pleasant and she felt her tension begin to ease.

"Would you like to sit down?" she asked.

Without answering, he walked to the long sofa opposite the window and sat. Not on the edge, but not in the middle, either. She chose the opposite spot on the same couch. They didn't touch, but they could. If they wanted to.

Don't! she ordered herself. It was the night that made her foolish. Or the man. But it wasn't anything real.

The furniture loomed large in the semidarkness. She picked out the shape of the armoire she had carted with her across the country because of all the memories it contained. Two wingback chairs sat under the big window. In front of the sofa stood a coffee table. She leaned forward and set down her drink.

"Not a brandy drinker?" Adam asked.

"No."

"Me, neither. But it sounded good." He placed his glass next to hers. "Some of this old furniture sure brings back memories. I recognize that." He pointed to the armoire.

"I helped my mother refinish it. I guess I was a little older than Billie." She sighed. "I'm sorry, Adam."

"Don't be. It's been a lot for both of us to deal with. Let's worry about the apologies another time."

It would be easy to accept his kind offer, she thought. Easy to push her shame away and go on with her life. But that was the coward's way, and she'd been doing that for too long.

"No, I *am* sorry. About everything." She shifted on the sofa, turning until she faced him. She tucked one leg under her and spread out the full skirt of her sundress. "I'm sorry for the way I left you."

"But not for leaving?" He sounded bitter.

"I don't know."

"At least you're being honest."

For a change. He didn't say the words, but she heard them, anyway. "I'm trying," she said.

In the darkness she saw his right shoulder rise, then lower. But she couldn't see his face or the secrets in his eyes. She pulled her braid over her shoulder and began to toy with the end.

"My mother went to art school," she said, not looking at him. "She was very talented. There are some pictures of hers in the attic. I keep meaning to go get them down, but I can't. Not yet."

"Why?"

"I'm afraid of what I'll see in her paintings. She loved my father, but he didn't understand her desire to be more than his wife and my mother. He didn't like her painting or changing the house." She pointed at the armoire. "He was furious about that. He liked everything to stay the same. Including her. She wasn't allowed to grow or be her own person."

"I'm not your father."

"I know. But..."

He leaned forward and rested one arm on the back of the couch. "Don't blame me for his behavior. I had nothing to do with that. I would never have prevented you from changing. If you remember, I'm the one who encouraged you to plan on continuing with college after we were married."

"It's not that easy, Adam." She plucked at the ribbon at the end of her braid. When the cloth loosened, she pulled it free, then removed the rubber band. "You wouldn't have *said* anything, but I would have known just the same."

"What the hell are you talking about?" he snapped.

"Expectation. You were looking for the perfect banker's wife. I couldn't be that."

"You said that before. I didn't understand it then and I still don't. There is no 'perfect banker's wife.' I wasn't looking for a job applicant, I wanted a partner."

He sounded hurt. She wanted to go to him and offer comfort, but she didn't have the words and he wouldn't accept the gesture. Not from her. It was the darkness that made her brave, she realized. That and the fact that she was already so exposed to him. There wasn't much more he could do or say to hurt her. What was there to lose by speaking the truth?

"I wanted to be that partner," she said, loosening the braid. "I wanted to be everything. But I was so afraid."

"Of what?" He jerked up one hand in an impatient gesture. "What was so damn frightening about me?"

"Everything."

"That's a big help." He turned his head and she caught the flash of white as he smiled.

"You, Adam. You're what's frightening. You're so damn perfect."

"Perfect? Come on, Jane. That doesn't wash."

"You knew what you wanted and you went after it. I didn't know anything, except how I felt about you. Your direction and intensity scared me. I thought I'd get lost inside of you and never find my way out." She sighed. "That sounds silly."

"No, it doesn't."

She nodded. "Thank you for that. There was so little of me that I'd discovered. I felt that if I became a part of you, there would be nothing left. You wanted so much. What if I couldn't do it?"

She raised her hands and continued loosening the braid. With a shake of her head, she tossed the freed strands over her shoulders. Part of her hair swept across the back of the sofa. He twisted one curl around his finger.

"I wish you'd told me." His voice sounded husky.

"I was wrong not to."

"I'll admit that I could have spent more time with you," he said slowly. "There were difficulties at the bank and with Dani and Ty, but I should have made the time. You were important to me. I never meant to scare you away."

Perhaps it was her admission that freed him to confess his own secrets. She still couldn't see his face or read his eyes, but suddenly that didn't seem to matter.

"I know," she said softly. "I was too young for you. I didn't know at the time. It's only now, looking back, that I see I was—"

"What?" he asked urgently. "Tell me."

"A girl. A fool. You needed a woman, but I couldn't be that." It hurt to confess her shortcomings, she thought, surprised that after all this time it still mattered.

He swore. "You were all I ever wanted. Why can't you believe that?"

"I was too afraid."

"Of me?"

"Of the sex."

He bowed his head. "Now I'm the one who's sorry. Jane, I had no right to—"

Without thinking, she scooted forward and pressed her hand against his mouth. "Don't," she whispered. "I wanted to please you. What I said the other day, about pushing me further than I'd wanted to go...." She shrugged. "I wanted you, too. Maybe not in the same way, but I needed the closeness and to feel you holding me. The rest of it, I'll admit, didn't thrill me...but never believe that you coerced me or hurt me. I came to your bed willingly, Adam Barrington. I loved you. There wasn't any other choice." When she finished her speech, she realized she still held her hand against his mouth. His firm lips moved slightly against her palm. She dropped her hand. "Sorry. I got carried away."

But before she could pull back, he twisted his hand in her hair. "I like it when you get carried away."

"Adam?"

"It's the night," he said softly, staring at her intently. "A time for secrets. Here's mine. You drove me wild. So sweet and funny, so eager to please."

She ducked her head. "You make me sound like a puppy."

"No, just innocent. And beautiful. You stared at me as if I were the most—"

"Perfect man," she whispered. "My fantasy come to life."

Whatever had smoldered between them since her arrival burst into life. Her body leaned toward the flames, absorbing the heat that started another fire deep inside her. This wasn't the time. They were dealing with problems that would only be complicated by a physical relationship between them. But she had to know. She had to find out if the time they had been apart had changed anything. She had to know if being a woman in heart and mind made it different.

"Never perfect," he murmured, lowering his head closer to hers. "I had my share of flaws."

"No. I won't—"

He silenced her with his kiss. She'd wanted this, she thought, as his firm mouth pressed against hers. She'd wanted to be with him, just the two of them, in the dark, with no secrets between them. He continued to hold her hair, as if he were afraid she would try to leave. It was the farthest thing from her mind. Her hands crept up his arms and around his neck. She rubbed the hard strength of him, felt the ripple of his muscles as she kneaded his shoulders. Yes, she thought, letting her eyes drift shut. This is what she'd waited for.

He angled his head so their mouths met more fully. Lips pressed. She leaned forward, encouraging him to take more. His free hand rested on her bare shoulder. His thumb stroked in slow circles, singeing her skin with his heated touch. But still their kiss remained chaste.

She pulled back so that she could look at him. The darkness that had been so kind and allowed them to share their secrets now kept her from reading his expression. Did he want her? Was she looking for something that didn't exist?

"Adam?"

"After you left, I tried to figure out what it had been that had drawn me to you. Was it your hair?" He cupped her face with both hands, then drew his fingers through the strands at her temples and fanned them over her shoulders. She felt the curls as they were drawn across her skin.

"Like silk," he said quietly. "Or was it your smile?" His thumb swept across her lips. "Was it the shape of your mouth or the size or the way the edges curve up even when you're not smiling?" He touched each corner with his index finger. "Was it your body? The gawky picture you made in high heels?"

She didn't move as he ran his hands up her thighs to her

hips. Heat flared wherever he touched, and turned her blood to fire.

"Did I want you because you had no idea about what you were doing to me?" he asked. "Was it the innocence?"

His hands moved up to her waist. She caught her breath but he didn't reach farther to soothe the ache. Her already hard nipples strained against her lacy bra. Her breasts throbbed in time with her rapid heartbeat.

"Or was it here?" He returned his hands to her face. "Inside. Was it your mind? Why were you the one?"

The control slipped away. She felt it flow out of him and disappear into the night. They were lost, she realized. Lost in a cauldron of emotion. Past and present blurred. The grayness of time overlapped until what had been and what was now had no distinction. The flames continued to race through her, but with them came the pain. As the fire burned away layers of facades, she was left with the sharp edges of her soul.

"Hold me," she whispered, feeling her eyes fill with tears. "Hold me tight."

He wrapped his arms around her and pulled her next to him. His heartbeat thundered in her ear. His breath fanned the hair that rested on her cheek. Without breaking their contact, he shifted on the sofa, sliding lower against the back corner, then easing her down until she nestled on top of him.

This felt right, she thought, loving the feel of his body against hers. His hard lines a contrast to her curves. Not even the sensation of his arousal pressing against her hip disturbed her. This was as it was supposed to have been.

"I don't want to deal with the past anymore," she said. "But I can't seem to let it go."

"Neither can I."

She raised her head to look at him. "Help me. Let's try to forget together."

He stiffened. "Like this?"

"Yes."

"I don't think that—"

"Don't." She shook her head. "Don't think about it anymore. Please. You want me." She rocked her hips and felt him strain against her.

"Tough to deny the obvious."

"Then what is it?"

He stared at her. "How much of that girl remains? Are you doing this for me or for yourself?"

He wanted to know if she was still afraid, she realized. The stigma of what had happened nine years before stood between them, an almost uncrossable barrier of guilt and conscience.

She sat up and tossed her hair over her shoulder. When he moved his head to follow the movement, she did it again. Without saying a word, she rose and crossed to the parlor door, then closed it. The clicking of the lock sounded loud in the still room. Only their breathing filled the continuing silence.

She reached for the small floor lamp in the corner and flipped on the switch. The sudden light made her blink. The look on Adam's face made her heart stop. Etched in the lines of his handsome face, desire and guilt battled for control. Everything else faded as the primal emotions raged inside him. She walked back to stand in front of the coffee table. He sat up straight on the sofa. She could tell him not to feel guilty about the past. He wouldn't listen. Better to show him the truth. There had been a time when he *had* frightened her. With her naïveté, she hadn't thought she could ask him to go slower. She wasn't that child anymore. She was a woman, with a woman's need. She slipped her hands up through her hair and fanned it over her shoulders. Slowly, so that he couldn't mistake her meaning, she reached for the first button of her dress. She never made it to the second.

He crossed the few feet between them and gathered her

into his arms. His mouth slanted across hers, pressing, seeking, probing as if she were his only lifeline. She parted her lips to admit him and he pushed his tongue inside.

Her hands clutched at his shoulders and back. His hands pulled her closer. Their tongues mated, slipping together, circling, brushing back and forth, drawing sustenance from the contact. She slipped her fingers through his hair. The short strands teased the pads of her fingers. His hands slid down to her derriere and gently squeezed her curves. Fire licked through her. She strained to get closer, but he held their hips apart. She punished him by forming an O around his tongue and sucking gently. She felt more than heard the moan in his throat and instantly he ground his pelvis into hers.

The hard ridge of his desire pressed against her stomach. She raised on tiptoes to move it toward her needy center. He tore his lips away and took her ear lobe in his mouth. Even as he bent his knees to oblige her wish, he nibbled the sensitive skin.

The combination of sensations—his mouth trailing down her neck, his hands rubbing her derriere, his need rotating against the apex of her thighs—made her feel like screaming.

She spoke his name over and over again, as if the sound would save her from the coming storm. He raised his head and looked at her. She saw the question hovering in his eyes.

"Yes," she said.

He straightened and reached for the front of her dress. His knuckles bumped her breasts as he worked the small buttons.

"Stupid design," he muttered.

She reached under his hands and easily opened the front of his shirt. "You're right."

He stopped long enough to step out of his shoes and

socks and pull the shirt free of his pants. She kicked off her sandals.

When he freed the last button, he drew the sundress off her shoulders. Jane felt a flash of concern. She'd grown up in the last nine years, but not out. Still, he'd known that before they got started here. She squared her shoulders and shrugged out of the dress. It paused at her hips. She gave a slight wiggle and it fell to the floor. Adam's shirt joined her dress. But instead of looking at her body, he stared into her eyes.

"You still doubt yourself," he said, tracing the line of her jaw from her ear to her chin. "Hasn't anyone taught you that you are exactly right?"

She shook her head.

"Then they were fools."

This was probably the time to tell him that there hadn't been a lot of men to do the teaching. She'd dated some, in the nine years they'd been apart. Some of those dates had included heavy petting. But none of them had progressed to lovemaking. At the time she'd blamed it on lack of chemistry or dealing with a toddler or being busy with school. Now she wondered if it was because none of them was Adam.

He moved behind her. When she started to turn to face him again, he held her in place.

"Trust me," he said.

He moved her hair off one shoulder. From the sweet spot behind her ear, down to her bra strap, he kissed her heated flesh. Shivers racked her body, and her skin puckered. He licked her shoulder, then moved back to gently bite her neck. Her breasts swelled. Her nipples, already hard and eager for his touch, jutted out even more. Her hands fluttered in front of her. She didn't know where to put them. She started to reach behind her, but he pushed her away.

"Not yet," he murmured. "Trust me."

Did she have a choice?

He drew his hands around her waist, then up. She held her breath in anticipation. With one finger and his thumb, he released the front hook of her bra. The white lace drew back, only to catch on her nipples. The friction made her inhale sharply. He pulled at the straps until the garment slid down her arms and fell. Then he wrapped his arms around her waist and drew her back.

"Lean on me."

"Why?"

"Because I'm going to make your legs tremble and your body weak."

That statement practically did the job for him, she thought as she sagged against him. His bare chest felt warm against her back. She rested her hands on his forearms and closed her eyes.

"Watch me," he said, his mouth breathing the words into her ear. "Watch me touch you."

She lowered her head to look.

His hands moved up and engulfed her breasts. His palms moved in slow circles, completely covering her. At last, she thought as pleasure shot through her body. It was as if each individual cell had screamed out at his touch. Her head lolled back on his shoulder.

He raised his hands until just his fingers touched her. They circled around and around moving closer to her nipples. Her eyes fluttered.

"Watch!" he commanded.

She did. Her nipples strained forward, eager for their own pleasure. Moisture surged between her legs. Her muscles trembled, as he had promised.

At last he brushed his fingertips across the tips of her breasts. She felt the lightning all the way down to her toes. Her grip on his forearms tightened, and she moaned. Again and again he caressed the puckered skin, making it harder and tighter. Her hips began to rotate in a dance of their own. Her knees threatened to buckle. Her hands longed to touch more of him. But she didn't want him to stop.

"Adam," she said breathily.

Moving quickly, so she didn't have time to register exactly what he was doing, he turned her, then lowered her to the carpet. His shirt and her dress provided a barrier to the rug. Barely pausing to settle her, he continued to touch her breasts. The magic his fingers created made her strain toward him. Pressure built inside. No one had ever taken the time, she realized, to show her how sensitive her body could be.

He lowered his mouth to hers. Wanting to pleasure him, as she was being pleasured, she wrapped her arms around him and went on the attack. When his tongue would have found hers, she sought his out and battled him within his mouth. She traced the edges of his teeth, nipped the inner smoothness of his lips, then sucked on his tongue until he drew back to gasp for air.

And still his hands played with her breasts. At last, when she wondered how long she could endure the glory, he trailed his mouth down her chin and neck and across her chest. She drew in a breath and rose toward him. He pulled away his hands and looked at her.

"Perfect," he said.

She blushed.

"Still the innocent?" he teased.

She didn't answer. If only he knew.

He continued to moisten her skin as he moved closer to her breasts. At last, his mouth closed over one throbbing nipple. The damp heat caused her to jerk and her pelvis to rise toward his. Her hands clutched at him. He suckled her, then circled the beaded tip. Her other breast swelled in anticipation. He didn't disappoint. As his hand continued the game his mouth had begun, he laved the other side with equal attention.

When she had no breath left, he lifted his head and

smiled. She touched his face, the smooth-shaved cheeks, the straight nose, the firm mouth, still wet from his loving her. The rightness of their mating made her fearful of the future, but she pushed away the concerns. They were for later. This was her only point of sanity in a world gone mad.

"You make me tremble," she said.

"As you do me."

He drew her panties from her hips and peeled them off her legs. He had done this before, she remembered. Touched her there, before claiming her. It had been mildly pleasant. She was about to tell him he didn't have to bother, when his finger slipped between her damp curls. He touched some secret spot and she jumped.

He grinned. "I guess that means you're ready."

"For what?"

He started to laugh, then saw she wasn't kidding. His smile faded. "You've never had an orgasm."

It wasn't a question. They were adults. She was already naked. It shouldn't have embarrassed her. It did. The heated flush began somewhere around her toes and climbed all the way to the top of her head.

"I can't," she whispered, turning her head away.

He lay down beside her on the rug and touched her hair. "Who told you that?"

"No one, but I know."

"Have you tried?"

She closed her eyes. "I never did with you."

"Thanks."

His wry tone made her turn back to him. "It's not your fault. I was—"

"Yeah, well, could we *not* talk about my lack of performance and get on with the rest of it?"

"I don't want you to think it was your fault."

His self-deprecating smile eased her embarrassment. "It

was only the two of us, Jane. And you were the virgin. Whose fault was it?''

"Oh."

"Yeah. Oh. What about the other men?"

She pulled her hair over her shoulder and studied the ends. "I've done a few things but I never—"

"Had an orgasm?"

"Went all the way."

"What?"

She swallowed. "I didn't feel the need."

"It's been nine years."

"I can count, too."

"Jane?" He sounded confused.

"Don't read more into it than it is. It just never felt right."

"Does it feel right now?" He touched her breast. She gasped and arched her head back.

"Oh, yes."

"Good."

She wanted to wipe that self-satisfied male smirk off his face, but he continued to tease her breasts and it became more and more difficult to remember why.

He moved his head to her chest and trailed his fingers down her stomach. This time she was prepared for the jolt when he brushed that secret spot. She wasn't prepared, however, for him to keep touching it. The contact created an aching pressure inside. She shifted her legs as if that would help her ease her need.

"Adam?" she asked, confused by what was happening inside. She needed him to stop. No, that wasn't right. She needed him to never stop.

"Hush. Trust me. Just feel it. I won't hurt you. And I won't let you fall."

Fall? She was lying on the floor. Where was there to fall to? Then he began to move faster and she didn't have the presence of mind to ask questions. Her world shrank down to his mouth and his hand. She vaguely felt his erection pressing into her leg. She should let him satisfy himself, she thought as her hips began to rotate in time with his fingers. Not just yet, she told herself as the pressure built.

Her breathing came in short gasps. His fingers danced around and around working their magic until she couldn't move, couldn't breathe, couldn't do anything but feel.

Falling. He was right. She could fall because he took her so high. Her muscles tightened until she thought she'd snap. He moved faster. She was going to fall. It was the only thing that would save her. But she was afraid. She didn't understand this or know what to do. Her hands clenched into fists at her sides. Adam.

She drew in her last breath and exhaled his name. He sucked deeper on her breast and the ground shifted. Her muscles rippled as she sailed out into nothing and began her free-fall back to the world. Pleasure surrounded, supported, carried her forward. Adam caught her as she neared the bottom of her descent. He held her close and promised she'd be safe forever. She'd known that, she saw in a moment of clearness. That's why she'd come home.

"Be in me," she whispered, parting her legs in invitation. "Feel this with me."

He quickly shed his trousers and briefs, then positioned himself between her thighs. Their gazes locked. Need and desire and pleasure at her release lit his dark irises. She wondered if she looked as satisfied as she felt. His hardness probed. She lifted herself toward him. He withdrew and frowned.

"What's wrong?" she asked.

"I don't have any protection with me. This wasn't planned."

"Don't worry." She smiled shyly. "I'm okay."

"Good. Because I didn't know how I was going to stop."

He plunged inside her, filling her with his arousal. This wasn't the uncomfortable pressure she remembered. Her body shivered as a last wave of her pleasure rippled through her. Adam groaned.

"You could feel that?" she asked.

He lowered himself until they could kiss. "Every quivering muscle. It's heaven. You're heaven." His mouth claimed hers.

He continued to thrust into her, the long slow strokes causing her to tighten around him. Every time he moaned his satisfaction, she felt her insides tremble. She drew back her knees and closed her eyes. The ascent began.

This time she knew what to expect from the journey. She reached forward, grasping his buttocks and pulling him closer. His thrusts grew faster, deeper.

"More," she gasped out, her lungs barely able to draw in enough air. She met him stroke for stroke. In her mind's eye, she saw the frightened girl she'd been, lying limply beneath Adam's hungry body. She remembered the ineptness and feeling of failure that had swept over her as he'd groaned his release. She'd been afraid and confused and too much in love to risk voicing her concerns and displeasing him. She'd grown up, she thought as she surged forward to meet him. His body grew harder, thicker inside her. His hips bucked under her hands.

She opened her eyes. His face, a tight mask of tension and raw desire, made her own need increase tenfold. She was his equal now.

He looked at her. The shutters fell away as if they'd never been in place. He smiled slightly, then held her hips and pressed in farther. She was so close. Too close. He reached one hand between their bodies and touched her. His thrusts stopped suddenly as his fingers circled her secret core. Then he moved faster, deeper and she sailed out into the ecstasy. The ripples within her milked his hardness. He cried out her name.

They held each other as they fell.

* * *

Even the crickets were silent. Adam pulled the sheet up over Jane's shoulder and watched her sleep. It was hours past midnight. Sometime after they'd first made love, they'd climbed to her bedroom. There, against the soft cushion of the mattress, she'd shown him that she was a quick study. Even now, his body hummed with the pleasure of her touch.

He was weary. Pleasantly so from their lovemaking. And emotionally from all that had happened. In less than thirty-six hours, he'd found out he was a father, been accepted by Billie and made love with Jane. The latter, he acknowledged, was a reaction to the former. They were both too near the edge to not succumb to the temptation. It didn't mean anything.

He rose to his feet and pulled on his clothes. Better for him not to be discovered in her bed. They discussed it, but she had protested she wasn't ready to let him go. So he'd waited until she'd fallen asleep.

He leaned over and kissed her cheek. Then, taking his shoes in his hand, he crept down the hall and opened Billie's bedroom door.

The girl—his daughter—slept on her back. An old teddy bear rested against her chest. Moonlight drifted across her cheek and made her look as sweet and innocent as an angel. He chuckled softly. Billie was a lot of things, but angelic wasn't one of them. Still—

He closed the door and stepped back. He could feel himself sinking in deeper. What was he going to do? Not caring didn't seem to be an option anymore. If he couldn't turn away from them, he'd have to find a way of keeping them with him. If he wasn't careful, they'd leave. Love meant losing. Jane had already proved she could leave him. This time he might not survive.

No matter what the cost, he had to find some way to get control and keep them here. If he didn't, he would lose them forever.

Chapter Thirteen

Jane looked over the stack of boxes in the attic.

"There's a ton of stuff here," Billie said, "but Charlene has lots more. Are there any clothes for me to play dress up?"

Jane shook her head. Not that again. Look at the trouble it had created the last time. Then she smiled. No more secrets, she thought. There was nothing to hide, nothing to fear. "I don't think my mother kept anything like that, honey. Grandpa didn't want her to save old clothes."

It was late afternoon. The sun had slipped behind a large tree in the yard, putting the attic in shade. A couple of bare light bulbs hung from the rafters and provided light, as did a window at the front of the room. Dust motes floated in the air. They'd left a trail of footprints from the door to the boxes where they stood now.

Billie knelt next to the small window at the front of the attic. "You can see Adam's house from here. The whole thing. It's big, huh?"

"Yes. It's big." Without meaning to, she joined her daughter and stared out at the Barrington mansion. The wings stretched well past where her own house ended. Windows gleamed from constant care. It was a lovely home, she acknowledged. At one time it was to have been hers. With a sigh she shifted until she was sitting on the dusty floor and staring up at the underside of the roof. She hadn't seen Adam since Sunday. She smiled. Okay, technically Monday morning. When sleep had finally claimed her, he'd crept out of the house.

Yesterday a crisis had kept him tied up at the bank. He'd called to explain and sent a huge bouquet of roses. But she hadn't really talked to him since they'd made love.

Had it been a mistake? Was it about the past or the present? Were they going to repeat the experience?

Just the thought of his hands and mouth touching her was enough to make her heart pound and her body flush. She'd spent most of yesterday wondering how she could have missed out on the wonder of it all for so long; and she'd spent most of today fearing that her feelings weren't so much about sex as they were about Adam.

"Whatcha thinking about?" Billie asked, rolling over to sit next to her.

"Your father."

"I like Adam."

"I'm glad. I like Adam, too."

Billie pulled the softball out of her shorts pocket. "Are we going to be a real family?"

"We're going to try. And don't throw that in the house."

Billie's sigh was long-suffering. She stuffed the ball away in her pocket. "If Adam's my father, how come I don't have his last name? Didn't you say that kids get the boy's name?"

The questions were inevitable, Jane told herself. So far she'd gotten off pretty light. But Billie was a verbal child and very bright. She couldn't walk around the truth forever.

"Usually. But Adam and I didn't get married, so I didn't take his name. I gave you mine so that we would have the same name and people would know we belonged together."

"How are people gonna know I belong to Adam?"

Interesting question. "We'll work something out. Come on." She rose to her feet. "Let's get to work on these boxes."

"What are we looking for?" Billie scrambled up next to her.

"Paintings. Your grandmother took several art classes. She's very talented. I know she did a couple of seascapes and a few watercolors of the area. I'd like to find them and hang them in the house."

Billie frowned. "I've never seen Grandma paint. She won't even do finger paints with me."

"I know." Jane opened the first box and peered inside. Old tax records. She closed the box and reached for another. "She had a dream, but she had to give it up."

"Why?"

Oh, that was hard. "Sometimes we want to do something, but we know it will hurt someone else, so we don't do it."

"Like throwing my ball in the house."

Jane smiled. "Something like that. Grandma wanted to paint, but it made your grandfather unhappy."

"Why? If the pictures are pretty wouldn't he want her to make them?"

"You'd think so. Grandpa is a different kind of person than Grandma." She pulled off a cover and peered inside. "Oh, look. Here's a couple." She carefully drew out several flat canvases. The first watercolor painting showed a garden in full bloom. Luscious colors blended harmoniously. Small, sure brushstrokes added depth to the plants and a gazebo in the corner.

"I like this one," Billie said, leaning against her arm. "What are the others like?"

Jane showed her, one by one.

"That one is like the roses Adam sent you."

She was right. Pale peach-and-cream flowers floated in a glass bowl. She had a dozen of the same roses downstairs in the parlor. She'd placed them deliberately so that when she looked at them, she saw the patch of carpet where they'd first made love.

"Are we going to hang these up?"

"Yes."

Billie touched the corner of the painting. "I don't understand why Grandpa wouldn't want her to do this. It's nice. Can I have one in my room?"

"Sure." Jane placed the watercolors on the floor by the door of the attic. "I think there might be some more pictures. Let's look for them for a little longer, then I'll go start dinner."

"Is Adam coming over tonight?"

"I hope so."

She needed to see him and reassure herself that what had happened between them had been as perfect and right for him as it had been for her. She wanted to see him and touch him and—

"Should I call Adam 'Dad'?" Billie asked. She wiped her hand down her face and left a trail of dust.

The question shouldn't have been unexpected, but it was. So many changes. Still, she'd done this for Billie. And Adam. "If you want to."

Billie shrugged. "I guess. I'm glad I have a father now. I wanted one for a long time. But when I think about him in my mind, he's Adam. I'm afraid I'll say it wrong."

"It's up to you." Jane smiled at her daughter and ignored the small tug at her heart. It was going to be hard to learn how to share the affection of this eight-year-old. She'd been the only one for so long. "You could practice for a while. Soon you'll start thinking of him as Dad instead of Adam and that will make it easier to say."

"Okay. Dad." She tried out the word. "Dad, Dad, Dad." She twirled in the room, bumping into boxes and chanting the word like a song. She stopped and stared at her. "Did you love Ad—Dad?"

Where had that come from? It would be easy to make up a story, but she was so tired of the lies. "Yes, Billie, I loved your father with all my heart."

"Then why did you leave?"

That was tougher. She wasn't so sure anymore. At one time the answer to the question would have made a lot more sense. "I didn't think I was ready to be married. Adam was all grown up, but I wasn't. Relationships between men and women require that both people are ready."

"Did he want you to go?"

She thought of all that he had told her. The bald way he talked about having to pick up the pieces of his life, the details of the failed wedding, the anger when he spoke of her betrayal. "No, Billie, he didn't. I hurt him very badly."

"Are you sorry?"

"Yes."

"Did you 'pologize?"

She smiled. "Yes, I did."

"Then it's okay. You always told me 'pologizing helps make it right."

Jane held open her arms. Billie rushed into her embrace. She hugged her daughter close. "You're a smart girl."

"I know. This is going to be great. You and me are going to have Adam now. He loves us and we love him."

Jane released Billie and walked to the window. Did she? She thought about her decision to come home from San Francisco. She recalled the way she'd pushed to have a confrontation with Adam, how she'd resisted telling him the truth because she didn't want to face what she'd done. So many of her concerns had been about keeping Billie safe. Had those genuine fears allowed her to hide another truth? She thought about how easy it had been to make love with him. And it had been making love, she thought with a sureness that surprised her. It had been more than sex, because Adam was more than just a man from her past. She hadn't developed a relationship with anyone else, because she'd been waiting and growing up. When she was finally ready, she'd returned, willing to pay any price to set the past right.

She loved him.

It didn't matter that he might not want her now. It didn't matter that he wouldn't easily let go of his need to control. It didn't matter that she had nine years to make up for. She loved him. That's why she'd come back to Orchard. She'd come home to Adam.

"Something smells good."

Jane turned at the sound of Adam's voice. He stood in the doorway of her kitchen. She hadn't heard him knock, but Billie had been playing out front and had probably told him to go in.

It was a little after four. He'd obviously come straight from the office. He'd removed his jacket and rolled up his shirtsleeves, but had left on his tie. Stubble darkened his jaw and highlighted the firm lines of his mouth. She wanted to run to him and kiss him and tell him how much she'd been thinking of him. She wanted to have him whisper those words back to her.

Instead, paralyzed by a sudden burst of shyness, she hung back. "I'm trying a new recipe. It uses chicken and—"

He crossed the room in three long strides. "I wasn't talking about the food." With that he gathered her close.

Her arms went around his neck. She raised her head and he brushed her lips with his.

"I missed you," he said, then kissed her again.

"Me, too."

"You're all I've thought of."

"Me, too."

"I thought this day would never end."

"Me, too."

He grinned. "Is that all you can say?"

Now that he was here, holding her, the shyness fled, chased away by desire. "No. I can ask why you feel the need to talk so much."

With that she held his face still and raised herself up on tiptoe. She brushed her tongue across his lips. He tasted wet and warm and wonderful...like Adam, she thought, closing her eyes and leaning closer. His hands moved from around her waist up, until he cupped her breasts. Instantly, her nipples hardened and he teased them.

She broke away. "Billie's outside."

"I know." He planted one last quick kiss on her mouth, then stepped back. "How about something to cool me down?"

"There's still beer in the fridge."

"Thanks." He walked across the room. "I'm sorry I couldn't get over here yesterday. It was one crisis after another. I didn't want you to think it was because Sunday night didn't mean anything to me."

"You explained this on the phone as well as with the roses. They're beautiful."

He twisted the top off the bottle and shut the refrigerator. After taking a swallow, he looked at her. "I wanted to make sure you understood."

He was so damned decent, she thought, feeling her love for him swell inside of her. For a moment she toyed with the idea of telling him what she'd realized that afternoon in the attic. But it was too soon. There was still so much to work out. Besides, she wasn't sure that Adam was interested in her love. He hadn't had time to come to grips with all the sudden changes. Neither of them had. And he had a lot more forgiving to do than she did.

"I understand. Do you want to stay for dinner?"

"I'd love to."

"Should I invite Charlene?"

"She's busy with her packing tonight. I don't know that she'll have time."

"I'll call and ask. When does she leave?"

"In the morning."

Jane smiled. "I admire her. Going to Greece. Alone. At her age."

"I'm not so sure she's going alone."

She turned back to the counter and continued dicing the vegetables she'd been working on when he arrived. "Then with whom?"

"I haven't a clue. Maybe one of her trucker friends. I was thinking about Billie," he said, approaching her from behind and resting his hands on her shoulder.

"She's been thinking about you, too," she said. She tilted her head and rested her cheek on his hand.

"And?"

"She wanted to know about calling you Dad." She smiled up at him. "I hope you don't mind that I encouraged her."

He swallowed. "I'd like that."

"She said that it would take a little getting used to, but I don't think it will be all that long."

He picked up the beer bottle and took a drink. "Speaking of Billie, I thought I'd better bone up on this whole parenting thing."

"What does that mean?"

"I'll show you." He walked into the hallway and returned with a bag from a local bookstore. "I picked up a few books on raising children. Just to give me a frame of reference."

He spread them out on the counter. She scanned the titles, then wiped her hands on a nearby dish towel and picked up the top one. "*Assertive Discipline For Children.* Don't let Billie see this one."

"She's going to need a firm hand."

Jane shook her head. She didn't like the sound of that. "Billie is her own person."

"She'll be a teenager in a few years."

"She's only eight."

"I've done a little reading. It's important to control—"

"Stop." She held up her hand. "I know *control* is *your* favorite word, but it's not mine. I want you to be a part of Billie's life, but that means we'll be working together, Adam."

"I've been thinking about that, too."

"And?"

"What about her last name? Shouldn't it be mine?"

First Billie and now him. Did they have some sort of psychic communication she didn't know about? "I don't think that's important."

"It will be." He stared down at her. The warm lover who had greeted her with a kiss was disappearing and in his place stood the cold stranger she'd come to fear. "School starts in a few weeks."

"I'm aware of that. I have a planning meeting next week."

"My point is Billie isn't going to keep quiet about me."

"So?"

"Orchard is a very small town. As soon as word gets out, people are going to talk."

She covered her face with her hands. "I know. I didn't want to think about that, but you're right."

He touched her arms and lowered them to her sides. "I'm not trying to be difficult, Jane, but these are things we have to talk about."

"But do we have to deal with them now?"

"Why not?"

Because I've just realized that I never stopped loving you, she thought. Because I want you to hold me and love me and promise me this time we can make it. Because I need to hear that I'm not too late. "I just thought—" She shrugged.

"What about her birth certificate?"

"What about it?"

"Am I listed as her father?"

"We went over this already. Of course."

"Good. Then we won't have to deal with the formalities of an adoption."

"Adoption! What on earth are you talking about?"

He folded his arms over his chest and leaned against the counter. "I want to legally recognize Billie as my daughter. I'm meeting with my lawyer and changing my will. Everything will be left to her—in a trust of course. There are certain family heirlooms that will go to Dani and Ty, but the bulk of the estate—"

"Stop!"

She walked out of the kitchen and down the hall. He followed. When she reached the front parlor, she instantly regretted leaving the safety of the other room. The scent of roses filled the parlor. The soft light from the lamp caught their peachy color and made the individual petals look as if they glowed.

"You're going too fast," she said, without turning around. "We have to handle this situation one crisis at a time. The first item is dealing with the three of us as a family."

"But I want Billie to be taken care of."

"I've done that." She spun to face him. "She's been taken care of just fine. By me. I've been responsible all these years and we've managed to survive without you."

"That isn't necessary anymore."

She saw by the stubborn set of his jaw that she wasn't getting through to him. "We don't need your money."

"Don't let your pride interfere with what's best for the child. There's medical insurance, contributions to her college funds. I want to take care of the details. You shouldn't have to do it on your own. Billie is my daughter, too."

Where had he gone? she wondered as she looked searchingly at his eyes. The deep brown gave nothing away. But sometime between the last time she'd seen him and this, she'd lost her ability to find his vulnerable side. The need to control had returned in full force.

"You want too much, too soon," she said, rubbing her hands up and down her arms. Despite the muggy heat, she felt cold.

He leaned against the doorframe. "I'd also like to go with you when you meet with her teachers."

"Dammit, Adam, are you listening to me?"

"Of course."

"Adam, I'm not a child anymore. You can't push me around."

He frowned. "I don't understand why you can't be reasonable."

"Reasonable?" It hurt so much, she thought as the tears formed. She blinked them back. "You can't win this by controlling us. You can't make me stay or Billie care about you by giving her your last name or putting her in your will. That's not what matters. It's the people. Us. You. Me. Billie. Love us. Let us love you. That's how we'll make it work."

He turned away, but not before she saw the fear in his eyes. He couldn't, she realized with a sense of panic. He couldn't do it without the control. To him that's all he had. She'd grown up while she was gone, but he hadn't learned that love without trust, without freedom, could never survive.

"Oh, Adam." The tears fell. She didn't bother to brush them away.

He looked at her then. "No," he said coldly. "You're not going to run this time. You're not taking Billie away from me."

She shook her head. "You don't get it. That's not what this is about. It's about letting yourself love somebody, and trusting them to love you back."

The front door banged open. Billie ran in.

"I'm hungry, Mom," she called. "When do we eat?" She came to a sudden stop and glanced up. "M-mom?"

Jane reached up to wipe her face, but it was too late. "I'm fine," she said through the tears, then turned and fled up the stairs.

Billie stared after her, then swung her gaze to Adam.

"You made my mother cry!"

Adam felt as if he'd taken a sucker punch to the gut. "Billie, I didn't mean—"

"Why'd you do that? I hate you."

She ran at him and began punching his thighs. The blows were too light to cause damage, but they hurt him as much as if she'd stabbed him with a knife. Every touch of her fist was a dagger to his heart.

"Billie! No! Stop, please! This isn't what you think." He dropped to his knees and grabbed the girl's hands in his. She squirmed to get away.

"I won't let you hurt her. I won't!" she cried.

"Hush, Billie. Listen." She tried to twist out of his grasp. "Please. Just listen."

His quiet voice finally got through to her. She stopped moving and stared at him. Tears rolled down her cheeks. Her nose was red and her hat askew.

"I didn't hurt her on purpose," he said, taking the chance and releasing her. "I'm going to go up and talk with her, but first I need to make sure you understand."

"You made her cry," she repeated stubbornly, wiping the back of her hand across her face.

"I know and I'm sorry. Sometimes it's easy to hurt people we care about even though we don't mean to. Have you ever made your mother cry?"

She stared down at her feet. "Yes." Her voice came out as a whisper.

"Do you remember how it made you feel?"

"Bad."

"That's how I feel inside. I'd never hurt you or your mother on purpose. I'm going to apologize to her. Do you understand?"

She nodded without looking up.

"Billie?" He touched his index finger to her chin. She raised her head. "Are we okay?"

"Yeah."

"Promise?"

She gave him a watery smile. "Yeah. We're okay."

"Can I have a hug?"

She hesitated for a second, then flung herself at him. She spoke so softly that he couldn't hear the word at first. Then it sunk in.

"Dad."

She'd called him Dad. The coat of armor he'd been building ever since Jane had barreled back into his life cracked a little bit more. He was losing ground fast here. First with Jane and now with Billie. He couldn't stop thinking about keeping the two women in his life. But at what price? Billie had just shown him that her temper could easily explode. What happened if she decided that she didn't want him as her father anymore? What if Jane refused to listen to his plans for the future? How was he going to keep them from leaving?

He held Billie tighter, as if by hugging her close, he could hold the world at bay. He was losing a war and he didn't even know who the enemy was.

He felt her ease back, then kiss his cheek. "I'm gonna go outside till dinner, okay?"

"Okay. I'll go talk to your mom."

She ran out the front door.

He rose to his feet and turned to go upstairs. When he

reached the landing, he paused. He couldn't lose them. Not now. What was he going to do?

A thought burst into his mind. He ignored it at first, then began to wonder if it wasn't true. Perhaps the reason he was going to lose this war was that the enemy was himself.

Jane knocked on Charlene's door. When the older woman called for her to come in, she stepped into the living room and laughed.

"I can't believe you're going to need this much luggage," she said, looking at the suitcases open around the room. Clothes stood in piles on every available surface.

Charlene sighed. "I'm not a light traveler, dear. I always think of something else I just might need. So I pack it all."

"I've come to say goodbye."

Charlene raised one auburn eyebrow. "I assume you mean because I'm leaving in the morning."

"Why else?"

Charlene didn't answer. She folded the silk nightgown she was holding and laid it in the nearest suitcase.

"Oh." Jane grimaced. "As opposed to my leaving because everything here has gotten so awful."

"I *was* going to ask about that, but now I won't."

Jane cleared off a space on the floral-print sofa and dropped down. Charlene handed her several camisoles. She began to fold them. The older woman's small house provided a haven for all of them, Jane thought. Billie had stayed here. Who knows how many times Adam had run here, and now she was doing the same. It was better than being home.

She sighed as she recalled Adam's stiff apology for making her cry. He hadn't said he was sorry for what he'd wanted to talk about, though. She'd noticed that distinction. And then dinner had been strained and awkward with Billie talking to the two adults, but them not talking to each other.

When he'd offered to read to Billie and put the girl to bed, Jane had gratefully accepted and had fled to Charlene's.

"There are problems with the adjustment," Jane said. "It would have been foolish to assume otherwise. Still—"

"You were foolish?" Charlene smiled.

Jane shrugged. "Let's just say things are about what I should have expected if I'd thought this thing through."

"What exactly does that mean?"

"He's still the same. He's still trying to control people by controlling the circumstances."

"In what way?"

"He wants to talk about changing Billie's last name, putting her on his health coverage, adding to her college fund. That sort of thing."

The older woman nodded. "I understand perfectly. I can't *believe* he'd be so self-centered. I hope you put him in his place." She took back the camisoles Jane had folded and packed them next to the nightgown.

"I told him—" Jane looked at her. "Wait a minute. That didn't sound completely sympathetic."

Charlene winked. "You always were a bright girl."

"What are you trying to say?"

Charlene shrugged and headed for the bedroom. "Nothing, really."

"Sure," Jane muttered under her breath.

"I heard that."

Jane chuckled. "Okay, go ahead. Say what you're thinking."

Charlene returned with an assortment of lingerie. She shook out a long, pink, gauzy gown and smiled. "Are you sure you want to give me that much license?"

"Speak."

"You say that Adam hasn't changed, but maybe you're the one living in the past. You've had over eight years to get used to being Billie's mother. Adam has had three days.

Under the circumstances, I'd say he's acting pretty decently." She sighed. "The Barrington men have always been strong. I remember when his mother was first dating—"

"Charlene! Could we please stay on the subject?"

"If you insist." She picked up another negligee, this one black, with more lace than fabric. "Have you considered the possibility that you're overreacting to his very normal concerns about his child? Wanting to make sure she has medical insurance and a decent college fund hardly seem like offenses that deserve your outrage."

"Maybe." Jane leaned forward and rested her elbows on her knees. "I hadn't thought about that. He came in with his list of things to change and I—"

"Reacted. Sit up straight, dear. That position does nothing for your posture."

"I'm twenty-eight, Charlene. I can sit how I like." But she leaned back, anyway.

The older woman smiled. "Very pretty. Now, about Adam." She shoved aside a pile of caftans and settled on the arm of the couch. "If you could have seen him that day at the church, when we found out you'd left. He was very hurt. I remember thinking it would have been kinder if you'd shot him."

Charlene spoke in a matter-of-fact tone. It took several seconds until her words sunk in. Jane blanched. Shot him? Was she kidding? But the older woman shrugged.

"He loved you, Jane. You abandoned him. Why are you surprised that he might feel that pain?"

"Did he love me?" She folded her arms across her chest. "Did he tell you that? Did he say those exact words? I've thought about it, you know. Tried to remember everything from the past. He never told me."

"What?"

She looked up. "That he loved me. Not once. Not even when he proposed. 'We're well suited,' he said to me that afternoon. Then he kissed me and promised he'd make me happy. He didn't have to try hard. I worshiped him already. But he never said 'I love you.' Did he to you?''

"Don't be silly, Jane. Of course he cared." Charlene began to bustle around the room, picking up toiletries and tossing them into a smaller carryon bag.

"But did he say the words?"

"Not those exactly, no. But you mustn't read too much into that."

"That's what you told me when I first came home. Maybe you're wrong, Charlene. Maybe I was just a convenience. Maybe Adam can't love, maybe he can only control people."

"He didn't have to say the words," Charlene said sharply. "I watched him suffer. He lost weight. He couldn't sleep." She blinked several times. "He begged me to tell him why. When I couldn't answer, he told me I was never to speak of you again. And we never did. But I saw it in his eyes. Perhaps he controls his world because without that barrier, it hurts him too much." She turned away. "That sounds like a man who loved very much. To me, at least. But then I'm an old woman. Feel free to ignore me."

"Charlene, don't." Jane rose and walked over to her. She reached out to touch her arm, but Charlene shrugged her off.

"Besides, what about what he's done for Dani and Ty? He raised those two on his own. He worked for them, gave up his dreams about learning banking somewhere else."

Jane stared at her in surprise.

"Oh, you didn't know about that, did you?" Charlene asked. "Adam hadn't always planned to come straight back to Orchard. Before his parents died he'd been considering doing an internship in one of the big cities. Maybe working there for a few years and returning to Orchard when he was older." She leaned close to Jane and pointed her finger. "What about the dreams Adam has had to give up? Who cares about that? Who's taken the time to find out what he's suffered? You? Did you bother?''

''I—'' Shame flooded her. ''No. I didn't find out. I never thought to ask.''

''I love you, Jane. You're family now. But don't ask me to choose sides. I can't take a stand against you, but I won't take one against Adam, either. If you don't like how he's handling the situation, tell him. But before you go complaining about the man he used to be, maybe you should take the time to learn about the man he's become.''

Chapter Fourteen

"I really appreciate this," Jane said as she stuffed a few more papers into her briefcase. "I would have made other arrangements, but with Charlene gone this last week—"

"Hey." Adam reached out and touched her arm. "It's okay. You didn't know the meeting was going to continue this evening. Billie's my child, too. I'm happy to look after her for a few hours. We'll be fine."

She nodded. "I shouldn't be too late. Nine o'clock. There's just a couple more things that need to be discussed."

He leaned back against the kitchen counter and grinned. "Stop explaining. I've said yes, I've said I understand. What else are you looking for?"

He'd meant the question teasingly, but Jane looked at him so seriously, he began to get uncomfortable. He held her gaze for a couple of seconds, then let it wander over her face and body.

She always wore dresses or skirts and blouses, so her

outfit didn't surprise him. She'd pulled a blue jacket over a white dress cinched at the waist with a belt the same shade of blue. Sensible low-heeled shoes gave her an extra inch or so, but she still stood well below his eye-level. Her hair—long and silky, smooth and perfect—had been pulled back in one of her fancy braids. If he concentrated, he could recall the feel of those strands in his hands, against his chest, stroking him as she had— He shook his head to dispel the thoughts. They weren't productive. He shifted slightly to conceal the rapidly growing hardness between his thighs. All right, they *were* slightly productive.

Her hazel eyes met and held his. What was she searching for as she looked so intently, he wondered. Her mouth, wide and soft, shaped to looked innocent, but designed for pleasure, trembled at one corner.

"What are you thinking about?" he asked softly, not wanting Billie to hear. The rain trapped the tomboy inside and she had reluctantly settled down in front of the TV.

Jane glanced down at the papers she was holding. "Nothing important." She stuffed them into her briefcase. "Just remembering something Charlene told me about you."

He grimaced. "I'm not sure I want to know."

"It was all good."

"I doubt that."

She straightened and shoved her hands into her jacket pockets. "Adam, if your parents hadn't died, would you have come back to Orchard after you graduated from college?"

"No."

She smiled, but didn't look especially happy. "Just like that? You don't have to think about your answer?"

"Why would I? I'd already started making plans." He shrugged. "I wanted to try a big city. New York, Chicago. Dallas."

"Dallas?" She raised her perfect eyebrows. "Really?"

"Don't you think I'd make a good cowboy?"

Her gaze swept his body. Her attention was as tangible as a touch, and heat flared inside. "You'd look great in jeans."

"Thanks," he said wryly. "That's always been a priority in my life."

"I'm serious," she said, looking up and smiling. He saw the laughter lurking in her eyes.

"So am I." He moved closer to her, stopping when he was only inches away. Her chest rose and fell in time with her breathing. "Why all the questions?" he asked.

"I only asked one."

"Today." A strand of hair had escaped the confines of her braid. He tucked it behind her ear. "Over the last few days, you've done nothing *but* ask questions."

She stared at his shirt collar as if it were the most fascinating thing she'd ever seen. "I don't know what you're talking about."

"Liar." He grinned.

She made a fist and tapped his arm. "Don't call me names."

"So why all the questions?"

"I'm taking Charlene's advice."

"Now we're in trouble."

She shook her head. "She told me to get to know you. That's what I'm trying to do."

Get to know me in bed, he thought, but didn't speak the words. Since the evening he'd made her cry, they'd slept apart. In separate rooms in separate houses. He longed for her as a thirsty man longs for water. He thought of nothing but her. But he wouldn't ask and she didn't offer. He wanted her to get used to him, to them. He'd apologized and she'd accepted that apology. Now they were feeling their way through a mine field of emotions. It would have been easy, he thought, seeing the need on her face. But he wanted her to be as hungry as he was. In the past, he'd pushed her farther and faster than she was willing to go. He wasn't going to do it again.

"Why?" he asked, stepping back.

"Why what?"

"Why are you getting to know me?"

She lowered her eyes. "Because I'm not sure I ever did." She picked up her briefcase. "I've got to run. Billie should be in bed by eight-thirty. She'll probably hassle you."

"I can handle it. Drive safely."

"I will."

Jane offered him a tentative smile, then escaped out the back door. The rain pounded on the roof of the house. He waited until he saw the headlights of her car sweep down the driveway and disappear.

"Adam, this TV show is dumb," Billie called from the family room. "Can we play a game?"

"Sure," he answered. Something physical, to tire her out. "What did you have in mind?"

"Hide-and-seek?"

She appeared at the doorway to the kitchen. The once-white T-shirt had been stained with an assortment of colors. Despite being trapped indoors all day, her shorts were equally dirty. He'd seen her first thing in the morning and knew that she'd started out with clean clothes.

"How do you do that?" he asked.

Billie frowned. For once, her hat had been left in her bedroom. Her brown hair, exactly the color of his, hung around her face. "Do what?"

"Get so dirty."

She glanced down at herself and shrugged. "I'm a kid."

He picked her up and swung her in the air. She laughed and clung to him. "More!"

He continued until they were both dizzy. "All right, kid. I'm going to count to twenty."

She rolled her eyes. "Twenty! How about a hundred? Give me some time to hide."

"Thirty-five," he countered.

"Fifty."

"Forty."

She wrinkled her nose. "Forty-five."

"Done." He closed his eyes. "One, two—"

"Don't peek."

"You're wasting time. Three, four—"

With a screech, she ran out of the room. Adam continued to count. She was an indescribable joy. He'd been blessed many times in his life, but never with anything like her. He regretted the time lost, he acknowledged. When he was alone, usually late at night, he hated what Jane had deprived him of. But the emotion decreased slightly each day and had recently become tinged with sadness.

Some part of the blame was his. He had underestimated the needs of the frightened young woman he had asked to marry him. Instead of a relationship, he'd offered maintenance. She'd left him, yes. She'd been wrong not to tell him about Billie, but he shared some of the responsibility.

"Forty-five!" he called out loud, then gave her a couple of seconds for good measure.

He'd heard her go upstairs, but had then heard a soft whooshing noise. Had she slid down the banister to trick him? He crept along the hallway, stepping on the edge of the carpet to avoid the creaking boards. In the parlor, he checked behind the sofa and inside the armoire. A slight breeze blew in from the rainy night. He stepped closer to the window to close the shutters. A flash of white caught his attention. She'd tucked herself in the corner, behind the wing chair. He took another step toward the window. Billie huddled deeper into the shadows and kept her eyes closed, as if her not seeing him would mean he couldn't see her.

He was about to speak her name, when he realized it would spoil the game if he found her so easily. He closed the shutter, turned his back on her and walked out of the room.

Several minutes later, after combing the house, he called out to concede his defeat. Billie emerged from the parlor.

"You walked right by me," she said triumphantly. Her brown eyes glowed. "I was in the corner."

He pretended dismay. "I thought I heard you go upstairs."

"I did, but then I changed my mind." She covered her eyes. "Okay, your turn."

They continued to play for almost an hour. Adam called it quits and started to fix cocoa. Billie turned on the TV in the other room. He'd just taken the milk off the stove when there was a crash. He set down the pot and sprinted toward the noise.

Billie stood in the hallway. Beside her, a small table lay on its side, along with the smashed remains of a vase. He crouched down beside the mess. On top of the broken china rested her softball. He picked it up and carefully wiped away the glass. Now what? He wanted to go get one of his child rearing books and read the chapter that covered this, but there wasn't time.

"It wasn't my fault," Billie said, thrusting out her lower lip.

He raised one eyebrow. "I don't see anyone else here."

"I wasn't *throwing* it. It slipped." She planted her hands on her hips. "I'm *not* in trouble."

"Are you allowed to play with your softball indoors?" he asked, knowing the answer.

"Yes."

"Billie?"

"No." She hung her head.

"You knew the rules and you broke them."

"You gonna tell my mom?"

"Yes." Why couldn't Jane be here now? What was he supposed to do? He couldn't bring himself to spank Billie. So how did he punish her? A vague thought passed through his mind. Something about time-outs and— "I want you to sit in the corner for twenty minutes," he said, hoping he was doing the right thing.

She stared up at him, her expression outraged. "No way."

"Yes, way. Now." He took her by the shoulder and guided her to a corner in the dining room. He pulled out a chair and slid it behind her.

"Sit."

"I'm not gonna stay here. You can't do this. You're not my mom."

Her words hurt, he acknowledged, but that didn't change a thing. "You're right. I'm your father. You've disobeyed and now you must face the consequences."

"You can't make me."

He looked at her. Slowly Billie lowered herself into the chair. He pushed it until the edges touched the wall. She bounced her feet on the rung. "I'm not going to stay here."

"Then you'll have to be punished for that, as well. It's your choice."

She turned her head away from him.

He left the room. His heart pounded in his chest and his palms were damp. Was he doing the right thing? Was he scarring her for life?

He cleaned up the glass then put the milk back on the stove. The time passed slowly. He heard Billie hitting the toe of her athletic shoes against the wall. He wanted to tell her to stop, but wasn't sure of all the rules for a time-out.

When the twenty minutes were up, he walked into the dining room. Billie sat hunched in the chair. "You may get up now."

She slid the chair back and climbed down. Her dark eyes accused him. "I thought you were my friend."

He wanted to be. But more than that, he needed to be a parent. This was the fine line those books he'd read had talked about. The reality of caring about someone enough to do what was best, even if it made her unhappy. "I'm your father."

"I don't want you for my dad."

He'd seen it coming, but that didn't stop the pain. "I'm sorry you feel that way, Billie," he said quietly. "Come into the kitchen."

"Why?"

"You're going to write a letter to your mother explaining what you did and that you're sorry. I'll give it to her when she gets home."

Billie followed him silently. When he placed a sheet of paper and a pencil on the small table, she sat in the chair without saying a word. He poured cocoa and set a mug next to her. She ignored it.

He wanted to say something. But what? She deserved the punishment. Didn't she? His chest ached from the hurt inside. It seeped all through his body, making him feel beaten. It was happening, just as he'd feared. He cleaned up the pot he'd used and put away the ingredients. Behind him, Billie wrote on the paper. Her pencil scratched slightly with each letter. He heard a sniff. He turned around, and she was brushing away her tears.

"Billie?"

She didn't look up. God, he wasn't ready for this. Before he could decide what to do, she pushed back the chair. "I'm done."

"Fine. Would you like—"

"I'm going to bed." She wouldn't look at him.

"I'll come up and tuck you in."

"No!" She raised her head and glared. "I hate you. You're not my dad. My dad would never do what you did. Go home."

With that, she marched out of the room.

He'd lost her, he thought grimly. He'd had her for less than two weeks and now she was gone. "I hate you." The words repeated themselves over and over in his mind. He could see the tracks of her tears, hear her voice, see the rage in her small body. He'd lost his child. If he'd ever had her.

Was it all an illusion? Jane, Billie, the chance to be part of a family—his family? Everyone left eventually. Why hadn't he learned that lesson? Billie was gone; Jane wouldn't be that far behind. He took Billie's untouched mug and poured the cocoa into the sink. He couldn't let it happen, he realized. He couldn't let Jane go. He had to hold her with him. Being left a second time—he shuddered—he would never survive.

He turned off the lights in the kitchen and walked toward the parlor. There was only one way to convince her to stay.

Jane arrived home a little after nine-thirty. Adam heard her car in the driveway.

"Hi," she said, as she swept into the kitchen. Drops of rain glistened on her smooth hair. "It's still raining."

"So I noticed." He smiled slightly and wiped the moisture from her cheek. "You should have taken a jacket."

"You sound like my mother." She wrinkled her nose. "Besides, it's too hot out there. I won't melt." She set her briefcase on the counter. "Is Billie asleep?"

"Yes. I just checked on her." He didn't mention that he'd spent the better part of an hour sitting in the dark and watching his daughter sleep. She clutched her teddy bear so tightly to her chest. Was that her normal position, or was she still traumatized from what had happened before? He knew *he* was. His stomach clenched tight as her words again echoed. "I hate you."

"How was the meeting?" he asked.

"Great. I really like several of the programs they have here for the students." She slipped out of her jacket and hung it over one of the chairs, then sniffed the air. "Coffee?"

"Decaf." He motioned to the pot. "Want some?"

"Thanks. Anyway, they have a real commitment to education. And a few surprises. I heard about the Barrington scholarships."

He walked over to the cupboard and pulled down two mugs. "So?"

"So? It's wonderful. You're offering ten scholarships to kids who otherwise wouldn't have a chance."

"It's no big deal."

"Of course it is." She moved to stand next to him. Even more hairs had escaped from her braid. They drifted around her face and tempted him to touch her. Her hazel eyes glowed with admiration. "Ten regular students. Not the most athletic, not the brightest, just ten kids that have the grades but not the money to go to college. I think it's terrific."

He shrugged off her praise. "Super smart students get academic scholarships and jocks go on athletic ones. I wanted to help the students that fell in between. Like I said, no big deal."

She leaned closer and kissed him on the cheek. "I don't care what you say, I'm impressed."

Her scent enveloped him. It was late in the day and the fragrance should have faded by now, but it hadn't. Her hand, resting on his shoulder, provided a warm connection between them. He turned slowly until he faced her. Behind him, the coffeepot hissed. He ignored it. Hazel eyes, wide with no hint of blue, met his. Her mouth curved up at the corners. Lipstick stained the sweet flesh, darkening the color to a deep rose.

He had forgotten. All the time she'd been gone, all those years, he'd let himself forget. The work, his responsibilities, the women who came and went without touching past the first layer of skin, had allowed him to pretend that it didn't matter anymore. To have come so close a second time and then to have lost it all. How was he going to survive?

"What is it?" she asked, smiling up at him.

"Nothing."

She swayed slightly, toward him. He read the invitation. He wasn't sure she knew what she was asking. He'd promised himself not to push her, that he'd let *her* say when. But could he wait? Could he risk it all?

No! Not if there was a chance of tipping the scales in his favor. He reached up and placed his hands on her shoulders. Slowly, so that she would know what he intended, he lowered his mouth to hers. She didn't back up or pull away. Instead she rose onto her tiptoes and met him more than halfway.

He'd planned a gentle kiss. His partially formed idea had included seducing her with soft touches and gentle words. Instead, the moment their lips touched, he lost control. He had to have her. All of her.

His mouth angled against hers. Without asking, he swept forward with his tongue. Instantly she parted her lips to admit him. Instead of shying from his assault, she counterattacked with her own plunges. They began a different sort of hide-and-seek with pleasure being the prize for both players.

Jane strained against him. She wrapped her arms around his waist and pulled him toward her. Their bodies touched from chest to knee, but it wasn't enough.

He reached for her braid and yanked off the ribbon. The elastic band quickly followed. Raking his fingers through the long silky lengths, he combed her hair free. When it was loose around her shoulders, he buried his hands in the warm satin. It tickled his skin and aroused him. His groin already throbbed with painful readiness, and the feel of her hair slipping through his fingers, trailing along his arms, made him grind his hips against hers.

She pulled back slightly and looked up at him. He read the questions in her eyes.

He could lie. He could confess his fears. He could even tell her what had happened with Billie. Each would require more explanation than he could provide right now. He released her hair and stepped back. A voice inside said that she must come to him of her own free will. If he didn't allow her that, all would be lost.

"I need you," he said simply.

She bit her lower lip, then smiled. "That's all you ever had to say." Lacing her fingers with his, she led him out of the kitchen and up the stairs to her bedroom.

In the darkness, with only the sound of the rain to distract them, he undressed her. When her clothes fell to the floor, he lowered her onto the bed. He touched each inch of her. His fingers traced the delicate skin on the inside of her elbows and behind her knees. He tickled her insteps until she begged her surrender. When her hands reached to caress him, he captured them and held them above her head. This was for *her*.

Still holding her arms up against the pillow, he plundered her mouth. When her tongue chased his back into his mouth, he gently bit on the pointed tip. At her gasp, he sucked on her lower lip. She grew limp. He pressed his leg against her secrets and felt her ready moistness.

Before he reached for his own clothing and removed it, he took her twice up to the edge of passion and caught her as she fell. Only when she had cried out his name over and over again did he allow himself to be buried in her waiting warmth. And not until her third release rippled around him did he give in to the need that pulsed within him. With heavy-lidded eyes and a satisfied smile, she moved her hips in a way designed to reduce his control to ashes. As the fire consumed him, as he reached the pinnacle and prepared himself for his own flight, he wondered if he'd indeed won.

"I'll have to leave more often," Jane said as she settled back against the pillows. "I like how you welcome me home."

Adam didn't respond, he just continued to hold her close and pray for a miracle.

"Why now?" she asked.

"Why not?" It was avoiding the question and the truth, but what else could he do?

"I wasn't sure." She snuggled closer to him. Her hair fanned out over his chest. One of her legs rode up against his and her arms held him tight. "After the last time. You never said anything about doing it again."

"I wanted to give you time."

"Oh."

He looked down at her. "*Oh?* What does that mean?"

She shrugged. "I knew that it was better that we try to get used to the arrangement without complicating it with, you know, sex, but—" She shrugged again.

"Jane." He touched her chin and forced her to look at him. "What are you saying?"

Her eyes, dark now in the stormy night, refused to meet his. "I wasn't sure you wanted me again."

"You're kidding?"

She shook her head.

"Why would you think that?"

"I wasn't very experienced." She rested her head on his shoulder. "I wasn't sure I pleased you."

"Do you still have doubts?"

He felt her mouth curve against his skin. "No. You took care of them nicely, thank you."

If only you could take care of mine, he thought. They continued to hold each other. His hands stroked her bare body, loving the feel of her skin. Warm living satin, he thought. He couldn't leave her. He didn't deserve to stay.

"I had a problem with Billie tonight," he blurted out.

"What happened?"

"She played with her softball inside and broke a vase."

Jane groaned. "Which one?"

"The one in the hall. On that little table. It was completely shattered. There wasn't anything to save."

"That little— I've told her and told her. What did you do?"

He closed his eyes against the memory. "Gave her a twenty-minute time-out and had her write you a letter of apology."

Jane squeezed him. "Welcome to the world of parenting."

"Did I do the right thing?"

"Yes. I especially like the letter. It's a nice touch. I usually take her ball away for the rest of the day, but seeing as it was so close to bedtime, it's no big deal."

He nodded. At least he hadn't scarred Billie for life, he thought grimly. "She said she hates me."

Jane raised herself up on one elbow. "What?"

"After I punished her. She told me I wasn't her father, that she wanted me to leave. And that she hates me."

"Adam, I'm sorry."

"It's not your fault."

"Don't take it too seriously. She's a kid. She's just reacting to the situation. You've gone from being a friend to being an authority figure in a very short time. It'll take some getting used to."

He turned away. "What if she doesn't get used to it? What if she decides to hate me forever?"

"Billie's attention span isn't that long."

"This isn't humorous to me."

"Adam." She touched his cheek. "Are you upset?"

"Of course. What did you think? That I'd take this lightly? My God, Jane, I've known her two weeks and she already hates me."

"She doesn't. I promise. Billie thinks the world of you."

"It's not enough."

He stared into the darkness. There had to be a solution.

"Adam, please. She's just a little girl. She often says things that she doesn't—"

"Marry me."

"What?"

He hadn't meant to say that, but now that he had, it felt right. He leaned over her and brushed her lips with his fingers. "Marry me, Jane Southwick. Live with me in the big house. Be my wife."

He hadn't planned the proposal enough to have formed thoughts on her reaction, but he never expected her to jump out of bed and glare at him as if he'd suggested something disgusting.

"How dare you?" she asked in a low cold voice. "That is the cruelest thing you've ever said to me."

"I asked you to marry me."

She walked over to the closet and pulled out a robe. After slipping it on and tying the belt tight, she clicked on the lamp on the nightstand. Her hazel eyes flashed with fire and something that might have been pain.

"Why?" she asked. "Why do you want to marry me?"

"Because—" He paused. "It's the right thing to do."

"No!" Her hands closed into fists. "Damn it, no! Not that, Adam, please. Tell me you love me. Tell me you can't live without me. Tell me—" She sighed and collapsed onto the edge of the bed. "Tell me anything but that," she whispered.

"I do need you." He moved behind her and took her in his arms. "Please, Jane. You've got to understand. All of this. It's too—"

"Too what?" She spun out of his embrace. "Too scary? For me, too. I'm terrified. It's almost like those nine years never happened. We're still connected with each other. But those nine years are real. I'm not that frightened girl who ran away. I'm all grown up. I know what I want."

And it's not you. She didn't have to say the words; they echoed loudly enough already. He'd lost. It didn't matter how or why, but it was over. He rose and walked to the window. Keeping his back to her, so she couldn't see how much it hurt, he asked, "What *do* you want?"

"You."

He couldn't have heard her correctly.

"Then why—"

"I love you, Adam. I've never stopped loving you. I had to leave to find out everything I needed was right here at home."

Hope flared inside of him. He turned to face her. "Then—"

"No." She shook her head. "It's not that easy. You don't trust me."

"That's crazy."

"Is it? You want to marry me to keep me from running away again. And I'll bet it has something to do with forcing Billie to be with you as well. That doesn't sound like you trust us very much." She stood up. Her gaze traveled from the top of his head to his feet. He stood naked before her and prayed that she would find him enough. She didn't. "I could probably forgive you for not trusting me, if you loved me."

"I—" He couldn't say the words.

"See." Her smile was sad. "You never told me then, and you can't say it now. You won't risk loving me, because it's the final risk. Everyone you've loved has left you."

She walked over to him and touched his chest. "Here, in your heart. This is where I want to be. But you won't let me in. You won't trust me enough to stay. You won't love me enough to give me the chance to prove I'm not going anywhere."

"You're wrong."

"Am I?" She smiled sadly. "Tell me you trust me."

"I trust you."

"Tell me we can stay together without getting married."

"Why won't you marry me?" he asked in frustration. "What's so wrong with that?"

She shook her head. Her long hair swayed back and forth on her shoulders. "You don't get it. Look me in the eye and tell me you trust me enough to stay without the commitment of marriage."

He couldn't. He didn't.

"Adam Barrington, I love you. It's taken me nine years to figure that out. I'm going to prove it to you, too." She folded her arms in front of her chest. "I'm going to live next door to you. I'm going to love you. I'm going to tempt you into my bed. When you can risk my leaving enough to confess your feelings—when you can tell me you love me, I'll marry you."

Chapter Fifteen

Adam sat on the old wicker chair in the corner of Jane's front porch. He should go home, he told himself. But he couldn't. Not yet.

It wasn't the rain that kept him in place. The storm had passed, leaving only a few sprinkles. It was his personal band of demons that kept him close. He couldn't bear the thought that, in a matter of hours, he'd lost them both. The pain, a hollow emptiness inside that seemed to be sucking in his soul, grew with each breath. He felt as if he would disappear in the void. He leaned his head back against the chair and sighed. The truth wasn't that eloquent. He wouldn't disappear. He'd keep on going, day after day, knowing he'd lost the two people he cared about most.

He shouldn't have proposed. He realized that now. But he'd panicked about Jane hating him as Billie did. Marriage had seemed an easy solution. Jane had seen right through him.

He shook his head. Damn, she'd grown into a beautiful

woman. Not just on the outside—as much as he adored her body close to his—but in her heart. She'd become independent and capable. Those fears about losing herself in another person wouldn't matter to her anymore. She'd conquered them. And him.

Give me strength, he prayed silently. And then asked— for what? How did he want to be strong? Did he want to walk away and not regret what he'd lost? Or was he looking for the power to follow in Jane's footsteps and conquer his fears?

The front door creaked open. Adam half rose from his chair. But instead of Jane's willowy form, he saw Billie stepping cautiously on the damp porch.

"Billie?"

She turned to look at him. The lamp above the door cast a harsh pool of light. The child looked pale and drawn.

"Adam? Is that you?" she whispered.

"Yes. What are you doing up?"

"Oh, Adam!"

She ran across the wooden floor and flung herself at him. He grabbed her as she leapt and pulled her next to him.

"I'm sorry," she said, then sniffed. "I'm sorry I was mean."

"Hush." He held her tightly, her small head nestling against his chest. Inside, the pain around his heart eased some, allowing him to draw a full breath. She felt warm and soft in his arms, and smelled of sleep and little girl. He shut his eyes as a burning began behind the lids.

"I kept waking up," she whispered, then tilted her head to look at him. "I had a dream that you really went away. I woke up scared. That's why I came to find you." She wrapped her arms around his neck. "I'm glad you didn't go home."

"My home is with you," he said thickly, touching his cheek to hers.

"I don't hate you."

"Thank you for that."

"Are you mad at me?" Her lower lip trembled.

"No, Billie."

"You won't go away like in my dream?"

"No," he said, recognizing that they shared the same fears. "I promise I'll stay with you."

"Forever?"

It was like looking into a mirror, he thought, staring into eyes that were so much like his own. "Forever," he answered.

Her arms tightened around his neck as she clung to him. "I love you, Dad."

His heart filled with gratitude. "I love you, too."

As he spoke the words, he knew they were true. She was his daughter; how could he not love her? He kissed her forehead and waited for the wave of fear. He'd said the words; now it was just a matter of time until she left him.

He held her until she fell asleep, then he picked her up and carried her back to her bed. After tucking the worn teddy bear under her arm, he pulled up the covers and whispered, "Good night." She didn't even stir. On his way out, he passed by Jane's door. He thought about knocking, but she might be asleep as well. Certainly she wouldn't want to see him. He crept down the stairs and out the front.

It wasn't until he reached his own house that he realized there was no fear. He felt wonder that this child was his, and gratitude that he had the chance to be with her now. But no fear.

He stared up at the sky. Clouds drifted by, exposing the beauty of a starry night. He held on to Billie's words, repeating them over and over like a prayer. "I love you, Dad," she'd said with the sincerity of one who still believes. It gave him hope, he realized. Hope that there might be a way out of this after all.

Jane stared blurrily at the coffeepot and begged it to hurry. Her night had been long and sleepless. She'd dozed off for a short time, then had spent the rest of the predawn hours staring at the ceiling.

Had she pushed him too far? Was she asking more of Adam than he could give? Could she settle for less? She shook her head. No. Not for herself or for Billie. She could handle his fears if he would meet her halfway. All she wanted was to know that he loved her. Easy enough. Why didn't she just go ahead and change the tide while she was at it?

Billie came bouncing into the kitchen. She'd already dressed herself. Her softball bulged from its usual pocket.

"How are you?" she asked, remembering what Adam had told her about the previous night.

"Fine."

She bent down to receive Billie's kiss. "Fine? That's it. What about the vase?"

"Oh, that."

"Yes, that."

Billie shrugged. "I've already been punished." She grinned. "And I wrote a letter." She thrust it at her mother.

"What about Adam? I understand that the two of you had some words."

Billie laughed. "He's fine. I talked to him last night."

"When?"

"After I'd been asleep. I had a bad dream that he went away because I told him to." Her smile faded as she remembered. "I was sad when I woke up, so I went to find him."

Jane frowned. "You left the house in the middle of the night?"

"No. He was outside. On the porch." She put her baseball cap on her head. "You know, on the chair out front. We talked."

"And?"

"I 'pologized." She wrinkled her nose. "He said he'd always be my dad. I told him I love him. Is that okay?"

"Yes, honey, that's fine." Billie was growing up so fast, Jane thought sadly.

"Good, 'cause he loves me, too."

"I know he does, Billie, but sometimes people aren't comfortable saying the words."

"What words?"

"I love you."

She shook her head and skipped toward the door. "He said 'em. I'm going over to see Adam for breakfast. Bye." With that, she slipped through the back door and headed toward the hedge that separated their property.

He said them? "Wait," Jane called after her, but it was too late.

He said the words? Adam Barrington said "I love you" to his daughter? Was it possible? Jane poured herself a cup of coffee and sat at the kitchen table. She smiled to herself. Maybe, just maybe they were going to get through this.

Adam stared out his office window. Give it up, he told himself as he tossed his pen onto his desk. He wasn't fooling anyone. For the last week he'd existed in a fog; going through the motions of his life, but not really participating. He wasn't kidding anyone. He shook his head. That wasn't true. He *was* kidding everyone else; he wasn't kidding Jane.

He thought about the routine they'd slipped into. Billie appeared at his house for breakfast. He went over there for dinner. They spent the evening as a family, but as soon as Billie went to bed, he returned to his own place. As Jane watched him leave, she asked him silent questions. He still didn't have any answers.

She'd threatened to tempt him into her bed. So far she hadn't tried anything, but that didn't mean he wasn't tempted. It only took a look, a brush of her hand against his arm, or the scent of her perfume and he was hard and ready to take her. So far he'd managed to resist. Not out of any moral strength. Rather it was a feeling of self-preservation and the sensation that he was on the edge of a great discovery. He just had to hang in a little longer. He hoped.

The late afternoon had turned hot and muggy. Despite the air-conditioning in the bank, he felt uncomfortable. He swore out loud. He couldn't stand it anymore. Rising from his seat, he grabbed his jacket, then headed for the door. He met his secretary in the hallway.

"Mr. Barrington?" Edna asked as she stared at him.

"I'm leaving."

"Now?" She sounded scandalized. "It's only three o'clock."

He grinned at her. "I know, Edna. Why don't you take off early, too?"

"I couldn't." Her heavily painted mouth formed a moue of disapproval.

"Your choice."

He walked through the bank and out the back door.

The trip home took about ten minutes. After opening a cold beer, he loped up the stairs toward his room. Once he'd shed his suit, he felt better. The house was oddly quiet. It was because Charlene was gone, he told himself. Even though she didn't actually live with him, she was in and out enough for him to miss her. He wondered what Greece thought of Charlene Standing of *The* Carolina Standings.

He pulled on shorts and a polo shirt and picked up his beer. But instead of going downstairs to his office, he turned left and continued down the hall. One of the small rooms at the very end, in what used to be the maids' quarters, housed a few of his boxes. There were his sports trophies from high school. Some old clothes, his letterman's jacket. His lucky jersey and a football helmet.

He pushed open the door and stepped inside. He wasn't interested in anything from high school, or even college.

Adam crouched by a small box tucked in the corner. He set his beer on the floor and touched the white cover. Taking a deep breath, he lifted it up and stared inside.

White roses. They still carried their scent, he thought as he inhaled the sweet smell. Two dozen, in the shape of an oval. Yellowed ribbons circled the arrangement, and it all sat on a cloud of tulle. Jane's bouquet.

He sat down and picked up the flowers. They'd dried perfectly. A couple had crumbled at the edges, but other than that, they were exactly as he remembered.

It had been after the guests had been told there would be no wedding. He'd stood in the back and watched them file out. A couple had walked over to him to offer condolences. He'd been too numb to respond. Jane's mother had approached him last. Her hazel eyes, so much like her daughter's, had avoided his. Without saying anything, she'd pressed something small and hard into his hand. The ring.

He looked into the box and saw the velvet jeweler's case in the corner. He'd taken the ring and held it tight. When the last person had left, he'd walked through the church. There had been so many questions. Why had she left? Why hadn't she said anything? What could he have done to keep her?

Then he'd seen them. The flowers. She'd left them on a chair by the church's side door. He'd picked up the bouquet with the intent of throwing it into the garbage. In the end, he couldn't. He'd stared at the flowers every day for two months, until they'd dried up and he'd finally packed them away. With the ring.

He set the flowers on the floor and picked up the velvet box. Inside a two-carat solitaire diamond winked at him. A ring fit for a princess, he'd thought when he'd seen it in the store window. He'd bought the ring months before he'd proposed because he'd known it was perfect for Jane. He'd practiced what he'd planned to say. The romantic phrases had sounded silly, so in the end he'd told her they were suited.

Suited. He shook his head. *Not* that she drove him wild with her smiles. *Not* that he wanted to watch her grow large with their children and raise them together. *Not* that he dreamed about building a life with her for years to come. *Not* that he loved her. Because he couldn't say the words. If he loved her, she would leave him.

She'd left him, anyway.

He snapped the box closed and took another drink from the bottle. So the system had its flaws. Nothing was perfect. Nothing was forever. Nothing was guaranteed. He could make it easy or he could make it hard. In the past, he'd chosen the difficult path. By listening to the voice inside, by giving in to the fear, he'd lost the only woman he'd ever loved.

And here he was again. Damn close to losing her. He was supposed to be the smart one. When was he going to learn?

He rose and walked over to the small window. He could see Jane's house from here, and her yard. Her car stood in the driveway. She was right there, he thought. All he had to do was reach out and take what she offered. A single step of faith. Three small words. How much easier could it be?

Jane stared in the refrigerator. There wasn't anything decent for dinner. Maybe she should suggest that the three of them go out to eat. Not a good idea, she thought, swinging the door closed. It had been awkward between her and Adam lately. There would be enough gossip without speculation that their undefined relationship was already falling apart. She glanced at the clock on the wall. There was still time to go to the store before Billie came home from her day camp. Maybe a nice roast.

Someone knocked on the front door. She walked through the house and pulled it open.

"Adam?"

She stared, not at him, but at what he was holding. She recognized the dried flowers and crumpled tulle. Her bouquet! She'd wondered about it. Her mother had saved her dress and veil, but had told her the flowers had disappeared. Had Adam kept them all this time?

She looked up at him. His brown eyes gazed warmly at her, but she couldn't tell what that meant.

"Can I come in?" he asked.

She stepped back. "I don't understand."

"About the flowers?"

She nodded.

"I kept them." He set the flowers on the table in the small foyer, then shoved his hands into his shorts pockets. They were standing so close that she had to tilt her head to look at his face.

"Why?"

"At first they reminded me of what you'd done. They fed my rage. Then I kept them because I couldn't bear not to. They were all I had. The flowers and this."

He pulled his hand out of his pocket and held it out. Automatically she raised her palm up to take what he offered. She gasped. Her ring.

She stared at the circle of gold, the sparkling diamond. Tears burned, but she blinked them away. What did it mean? Her heart thundered in her chest.

"Adam?"

He touched his forefinger to her chin and nudged her until she raised her head. He stood so tall and handsome. A special man she had loved her whole life. Just him, she thought, knowing she would accept whatever he offered. She had no choice. There would only ever be Adam.

His gaze caressed her face. He brushed his thumb across her lips. "I love you," he said.

She stared, mute, not able to believe.

"I love you, Jane. I've always loved you. Even when you were gone and I told myself I hated you, I couldn't let go of what we'd had together." One corner of his mouth lifted. "You don't have to marry me, but will you come live with me in my house? The two of you. Can we be a family?"

"Oh, Adam." She flung her arms around him. "Yes, love, yes. I'll live with you. I'll even marry you."

He clutched her upper arms and held her away from him. "Really?"

She nodded.

He leaned forward and kissed away the tears she hadn't felt fall. Then his mouth captured hers. Warm and probing, his tongue swept her lips before plunging inside. She gave herself up to him, clinging to his strength, knowing that her world was at last complete.

A gagging sound broke through her passionate haze. Adam lifted his head.

"You're kissing," Billie said, sounding more disgusted than unhappy. "Gross."

Jane held out her hand. Billie shuffled forward, but refused to be drawn close.

"I don't like this kissing stuff," she said.

"You will." Jane smiled at her. "We're—" She glanced at Adam. "You tell her."

He took her hand, the one that held the ring. He slid it on her finger and kissed her palm, then crouched in front of Billie. "Your mother and I are getting married."

"Really?" Billie grinned. "So we'll be a real family?"

"Yes," Jane said. "And we even get to live in Adam's house."

"With the island in the kitchen and the banister? Cool." She looked up. "I won't slide down the banister, of course."

"Yeah, right." Adam rose and tapped her nose.

Billie tugged off her cap and frowned. "Does this mean there's going to be a wedding, like when Auntie Jolie married Uncle Brad?"

Adam looked at her. Jane smiled. "A friend of mine back in San Francisco. Yes, Billie." She glanced at her daughter. "But a lot smaller."

"I'm not wearing a dress," Billie announced.

"Where?"

"At the wedding." She frowned. "No way."

Jane kissed Adam's cheek. "There's still time to back out. She's a handful."

Billie held out her arms. Adam bent over and picked her up. Jane wrapped her arms around his waist. "I wouldn't change her for the world," he said.

"Good." She leaned her head against his shoulder. "Because I want four more just like her."

He coughed. "Four?"

"Yes. Do you have a problem with that?"

"No. Four is a nice round number."

"All right!" Billie pumped her arm. "Four. Enough for an infield."

Adam groaned.

"I warned you," Jane said.

He shifted Billie so that he could support her with one arm and hug Jane with the other. Pulling her close, he murmured, "I can handle it."

"Brothers," Billie interrupted, just before his mouth touched Jane's.

"What?" Adam asked.

"I want all brothers. No girls."

Adam smiled at Jane. She felt her insides start to melt. They were going to make it, she thought, feeling the happiness flood her heart. They were going to make it just fine.

Adam looked at his daughter and winked. "Brothers? I'll see what I can do."

* * * * *

Finally a Father
MARILYN PAPPANO

MARILYN PAPPANO

brings impeccable credentials to her writing career—a lifelong habit of gazing out of windows, not paying attention in class, daydreaming and spinning tales for her own entertainment. The sale of her first book brought great relief to her family, proving that she wasn't crazy but was, instead, creative. Since then she's sold more than forty books to various publishers and even a film production company.

She writes in an office nestled among the oaks that surround her country home. In winter she stays inside with her husband and their four dogs, and in summer she spends her free time mowing the garden that never stops growing and daydreams about grass that never gets taller than two inches.

For Judith Banks.
Thanks for making our move
to Jacksonville so much easier.
Here's to many more Thursday nights
and lots of laughs—
but, no more crisps.

And, as always, for Bob…
one of the finest of the
Marine Corps' few good men.

Chapter 1

Quin Ellis was a lazy person by nature. Even though she was pushing thirty and found her weight tougher to maintain by diet alone, her favorite form of exercise was settling into the old porch swing out front with a cinnamon roll and a glass of sweet tea, and giving the swing a shove now and then to keep it in motion. But, my, oh my, she did enjoy watching the marines in her Jacksonville neighborhood engage in *their* favorite exercise. At all hours of the day, winter or summer or in between, come rain or shine, joggers passed her house as regularly as clockwork, and the hotter it got, the less they wore.

And this July was pretty darned hot.

My, oh my, oh my.

She was in her favorite spot this warm Saturday morning, the roll already eaten, the tea on a table beside her. Through the picture window behind her, she could hear the shrill voices and exaggerated sound effects of cartoons, punctuated occasionally by Cady's giggles. Every Saturday she teased her daughter about watching cartoons at her age, and every Saturday Cady gave her an older-than-the-hills look along with some remark about half-naked marines and hard bodies. Then she promptly plopped herself in front of the TV in her nightshirt and ate a breakfast of ice cream and fudge sauce to the accompaniment of animated friends.

Ah, Saturday mornings in the Ellis household.

As Quin reached for her glass, the phone rang inside. She listened for a moment, but there was no bellow of *"Moth-er"* from her sweet, small child. Apparently, the call was for Cady. At nine years old, the girl got more phone calls than Quin. Heck, at nine years old, she had more of a social life than Quin.

Sometimes Quin felt positively ancient. She had married David Ellis at nineteen and had been widowed only a few months later. She had given birth to Cady at twenty and had raised her alone. She occasionally dated, but most of the men in town—eighteen and nineteen and twenty-something marines—were young enough to make her feel like a lecherous old woman. The few she met who were single and old enough to comfortably lust after all too often weren't interested in commitment or permanence or raising another man's daughter.

But that was all right. None of them interested her enough to get serious.

None of them could make her forget her husband—Cady's father.

But they certainly were fun to watch, she thought, as two lieutenants from down the street ran past with a wave.

Burdened with a sudden restlessness, she left the swing and walked to the top of the steps. It was warm this morning, already in the mid-eighties, and promised to get even warmer. Her grass needed mowing, but she would save that chore for the cooler evening hours. She would save the watering for then, too, even though everything was already looking a little parched. It was a mystery to her how the humidity could stay so high that the outdoors was like a giant steam bath and yet so little of that moisture made its way from the air to the soil.

Finally a Father 9

She moved down the steps, then stepped off the sidewalk and into the grass. They had moved into this house when Cady was five, young enough to be easily entertained and fond enough of her mother to want to spend time with her. With her help, considerable for a five-year-old, Quin had dug up all the shrubs that had fronted the house and replaced them with flower beds from one end of the house to the other, along the sidewalk to the driveway and in great circles around the two gum trees and the single pine.

Unfortunately, Cady's interest in gardening—and in hanging out with her mother—had faded by the time she was seven, which left Quin with a great deal of work to do through the summer. In another year or so, she figured, Cady would be mercenary enough that her assistance could be bought for a reasonable sum. Until then, the grass, the flower beds and the weeds—well on their way to outnumbering the flowers—were all hers.

She wandered out along the driveway, bending to pluck a handful of weeds from the periwinkles, then headed for the curb to collect the paper from its faded red box. Unfolding it, she had just scanned the front page headlines—politics and the Marine Corps—when the thud of footsteps on the pavement caught her attention. Knowing that Cady would laugh, she surreptitiously peeked over the top of the paper as the jogger, wearing worn shoes, faded red shorts and nothing else, came into view. Hard bodies, Cady usually said with the superior sniff of a female who hadn't yet fallen prey to the charms of the opposite sex. Beautiful bodies, Quin thought with a healthy smile. Especially this one. Long legs, slender hips, narrow waist, broad chest. Muscled and lean.

And familiar.

Her smile faded as her assessing gaze reached the runner's face. Oh, God, no. *Too* familiar. She almost called his name to confirm her suspicion, but she didn't need any more confirmation than the sudden shock racing through her and the clenching of muscles deep in her stomach.

Mac McEwen.

Dear God, it was Mac.

She had thought she would never see him again. For a time she had prayed she wouldn't, had prayed for him to disappear from her life. Then, when that had happened, she had prayed he would come back.

It seemed her prayers had been answered.

Too bad she had quit offering them nine years ago.

Mac.

She hadn't seen him since the day his and David's battalion had shipped out to the Middle East ten years ago, part of a Multinational Force and Observers peacekeeping group. She had kissed David goodbye while Mac watched, had told her husband of five days that she loved him and would miss him while Mac listened with a skeptical look in his ancient eyes.

The battalion had left that day, and she had never seen either of them again. David had died in that distant, strife-torn country, along with more than half the men in their company, killed early one winter morning by a terrorist's bomb. She didn't know by what miracle Mac had escaped unharmed. He hadn't contacted her after David's death. He hadn't come to tell her he was sorry when he got back to Jacksonville. He hadn't dropped her a note, hadn't called her, hadn't cared at all about how she was coping. He had been David's best friend and more—oh, God, so much more—and yet, after David died, he had acted as if Quin didn't even exist.

He ran with long smooth strides, passing her neighbor's driveway, now only yards from her own. Only yards from *her*. Shock gave way to something uncomfortably close to panic. She didn't want him to see her, didn't want to meet him this way—unprepared, stunned, off balance. Oh, God, she didn't want to meet him with Cady in the house and liable to pop out at any moment.

Awkwardly, her feet feeling leaden, she began edging her way toward the house. Out of the street, into the driveway, past the lavender periwinkles, even now with the white ones.

Finally a Father   11

She was going to make it. If she could keep forcing each muscle to work, each foot to take its proper step, she would reach the safety of her house, and he would never know....

"Hey, Quin," her neighbor across the street called. "Thanks for loaning me your car yesterday."

The steps stopped abruptly—both hers and the heavier, more rapid ones in the street. For a moment she stared straight ahead; then, with a sickly smile, she slowly turned around and responded to Casey's call with a listless wave. The woman got into her car, backed out of the driveway and drove off with a wave of her own. When she was gone, Quin stared at the pavement as long and as hard as she could, biting the inside of her lip, pretending Mac hadn't stopped, wishing he would go on as if he hadn't seen her, as if he hadn't recognized her. She wished she had run to safety the instant she'd seen him. She wished she had found some safe refuge where she could remember and feel and suffer in private. Alone, the way she'd been the past ten years.

The way he'd left her.

For a time he just stood there, a blur in her peripheral vision. She could hear his labored breathing—because the morning had become so quiet? Or because she was still so tuned in to him? Ten years ago there had been a curious connection between them—a link that had alerted them to each other's presence, an awareness that no one else, not even David, bless his trusting heart, had ever noticed. Could that have survived everything that had happened—her marriage, David's death, Cady's birth—all these years?

Wrapping her fingers tightly around the rolled-up newspaper, she considered turning and walking away. It wasn't so far from here to the house—from here to safety. She could go inside, and he wouldn't stop her. After all, it had been his choice to stay away.

But before she could gather her courage and go, before she could move, he did. His shoes came into her field of vision first—leather, expensive, well broken in. David had remarked once that Mac ran so damned much, he wore out a pair of shoes in no time. He had teased him about what he was running from, never noticing that Mac wasn't amused, that he never answered. Never figuring out that maybe he really had been trying to outrun something.

But Quin had noticed. Worse, she had known part of what Mac was trying to avoid. She had *been* part of what he wanted to avoid.

Breathing heavily from exertion and the heat—and surprise?—he came to a stop a dozen feet away. "Hello, Quin."

He was ten years older and over a hundred deaths harder, but his voice hadn't changed. It was still strong, deep, guarded. She had never heard much of it before, not considering the amount of time they'd spent together, but she remembered it. She still heard it in her dreams. In her guilt.

I won't hurt you, Quin.
Trust me, Quin.
You don't love him, Quin.

"Hey, Mac," she said, her own voice failing her, coming out soft and scratchy and hoarse.

Before shifting her gaze to some safe point beyond him, she stole a glance at him—at his strong jaw, his dark eyes, his straight nose, his unsmiling mouth. His hair was dark brown and short—not practically shaved like so many young marines, but high and tight. Often, long ago, she had wondered what it was like when allowed to grow to a normal length, if it was silky and soft, or coarse. She had wondered how it would feel beneath her fingers if it weren't so regulation-Marine-Corps short, and she had been ashamed of herself for wondering. She had been David's girl, and David's girl wasn't supposed to wonder such things about David's best friend.

But David's girl had done much worse things with David's best friend than wonder.

She had hated Mac for it, had hated herself and even David.

Finally a Father

For a time she had hated everyone...except Cady. Innocent Cady.

"I didn't know you were still in Jacksonville," he said flatly.

Clutching the paper in one hand, she folded her arms across her chest. "How could you? After the battalion shipped out, I never heard from you again."

That earned her a sharp look. She could feel it, even if she couldn't meet it. "When would have been a good time, Quin? When David's body came home in a coffin? When you buried him?"

Ten years ago, if he had looked at her like that, she would have run to safety. She had been afraid of him back then.

No, that wasn't exactly true. He would never have deliberately hurt her. In spite of his toughness, in spite of the harshness of the life he'd lived, he'd shown her a curious tenderness that even David had never matched.

No, she hadn't been afraid of him, but of the things he'd made her feel and think and want. Afraid of what those feelings could make her do. But even now, all grown-up and mature and well acquainted with more of life than she'd ever wanted to know, running away was still exactly what she wanted to do.

But she didn't run. She didn't back down. "You could at least have said you were sorry."

"Sorry?" he repeated. "What was it you wanted me to apologize for? Being alive when David was dead? Or..."

With a scowl, he looked away without finishing. He didn't need to say it. She knew all too well what *or* led to. So it still bothered him, too. Those few hours they had spent together—two, maybe three—still nagged at his conscience. Two, maybe three, hours. That was all they'd needed to prove how unworthy a best friend and a girlfriend could be.

"You could have said you were sorry David was dead."

"You knew I was."

When she dared to look, she saw that weariness of the spiritual kind shadowed his eyes, and it made her feel petty. She did know. He had loved David. They had been best buddies. They had worked together, trained together. They had known that one day they might go to war together, might have to fight together, might even have to die together. But David had died without Mac. Not alone. No, there had been a hundred and seventeen men killed with him—but without Mac. And, dear God, no, she didn't want an apology that he had survived when David hadn't. Knowing that Mac was alive and unhurt had been her only comfort when she'd gotten the news.

She wasn't sure she could have endured it if he had died, too.

"So…" She exhaled heavily. Why didn't you call me? she wanted to ask. Why didn't you come to see me? Why didn't you love David enough to visit his widow? Why did you cut me out of your life?

Compressing her lips, she kept all those questions in and searched for something else, something harmless, to say. It wasn't easy. Small talk was one thing she and Mac had never indulged in. It had been too safe, too meaningless. No, when it came to indulgences, they had gone right to the big one. The hurtful one. The sinful one.

Thank God David had never known.

"Do you live around here?" she finally asked. It was a simple question, not likely to hurt either of them, and one whose answer mattered. Surely he didn't live in her neighborhood. Fate couldn't be so unkind after all these years as to let him move into a house near her own. He had always liked long runs—five, six, even eight miles. Maybe he still did. Maybe he lived safely far away from here.

"I have an apartment down the street."

Fate *could* be unkind. She passed those apartments every day—on her way to work, to the grocery store, to the credit union, to the gas station. Everywhere she went took her right by where he lived.

"Are you…?" She hesitated again. She didn't want to ask

Finally a Father

the question, but she needed to hear the answer. For herself. For Cady. "Are you married?"

He answered her with a quick, hard look. She would take that, and the absence of a wedding ring, as a negative reply. She waited for him to ask if she had remarried, or if the ring she wore was David's. She'd worn the diamond band for ten years. In the beginning she couldn't take it off—it had been her only link to David—but now it was habit. She got up, showered and dressed, and she put on her watch, earrings and wedding ring. Every morning. Just habit.

But he didn't ask. Maybe that was his way of telling her he didn't care.

Why hadn't he stopped caring *before* they had betrayed David? she wondered wistfully.

She shifted on the warm pavement. A part of her wanted to bring this meeting to an end, wanted to go inside and convince herself that she would never have to see him again.

The stronger part couldn't let him go that easily.

Because of Cady.

"How long have you been here?"

"Two weeks."

For two weeks he had been living down the street from her, and she had never suspected it. She would have found out eventually. For all its people, Jacksonville was still a small town. There was only one mall, only so many grocery stores and so many restaurants. If she didn't run into him around town, she would have seen him at the exchange or the commissary on base. She would have bumped into him at the credit union or the post office, or they both would have had business at the Naval Hospital at the same time. Sooner or later she would have found out he was stationed here again. Living here again.

Sooner or later she would have seen him again.

"You must have about fifteen years in now."

"Sixteen."

"You decided to make a career of it, huh?"

"It's all I know." His accompanying shrug drew her gaze to the muscles rippling across his chest. Cady teased her about her fascination with nice male bodies, but Quin always insisted it was just a healthy appreciation. She never wanted more than to look. She never wanted to touch, to find out if those muscles were as hard as they seemed, if the skin was as soft and warm as it looked.

Until now, she thought as she guiltily looked away.

Mac drew a line back and forth across the pavement with the toe of his shoe. The muscles in his legs were tight and warm. It wasn't smart stopping so abruptly after nearly six miles. He had run enough thousands of miles and suffered enough improperly worked muscle strains to be a big believer in warming up and cooling down. But he had heard the woman across the street call Quin's name, had seen her standing there, and it had knocked the wind from him. He couldn't have run another ten yards if his life had depended on it.

Ten years ago he had thought his life depended on getting close to her, as close as two people could be. It hadn't mattered that she'd been scared half to death of him. It hadn't mattered that she belonged to someone else. It hadn't even mattered that that someone else was his best friend in the whole damn world. He had wanted her—had needed her—for himself, and he had taken her, only to discover too late that all those things did matter. What he had thought would be his salvation had instead been his damnation. He had paid for it every day of the past ten years. He was still paying.

Aware that she wasn't looking, he risked a quick glance her way. Ten years hadn't changed her much. She had traveled the distance from nineteen and innocent to twenty-nine with remarkably little to show for it. There were a few fine lines at the corners of her eyes, and, although she was still slender, there was an overall softness, a roundedness, to her body, that had been missing before. Other than that, she looked the same. Short brown hair. Deep dark eyes. Soft, full mouth.

She was still beautiful.

Finally a Father   17

Damn her for that.

Feeling the discomfort of the silence mount, he finally asked, "What do you do?"

She seemed grateful for the question. "I'm a schoolteacher," she said with an uneasy smile. "Fourth grade. And in the summer I work for a friend who owns a real-estate agency, overseeing rental property."

Schoolteacher. He had no problem seeing her in the role. It was such a respectable position. If things had turned out differently, if David had survived the bombing, he would have finished his time in the marines, and then he and Quin would have returned to their little hometown. She would have taught school, and he would have gone to work in his father's insurance agency, and they would have been highly regarded members of the community. They would have had the perfect little family, and when David's father retired, David would have taken over the business. They would have been solidly middle-class all the way, well liked and respected and absolutely perfect.

The image made him feel sick.

He never could have given her any of that.

But, oh, he had wanted to. He had wanted to give her everything. In the end, he had taken everything from her, instead.

Even David.

Did she know? Did she suspect the role he'd played in David's death? Was that the reason for the bitterness that had tinged her voice when she'd first spoken? *After the battalion shipped out, I never heard from you again.... You could at least have said you were sorry.... You could have said you were sorry David was dead.*

Forcing the guilt and the pain back into their place deep inside, he focused his narrowed gaze on the house behind her. It wasn't anything fancy—brick, two stories, a nice porch and a yard with lots of flowers. It was a little big for one person, but it wasn't anything David's life insurance wouldn't have covered. "Do you live here alone?"

Not that it mattered. He didn't care who shared her life now. He didn't care if she had married again—although he recognized the only ring she wore as David's—or if she had a roommate or, damn her, a lover. *He didn't care.*

"No."

She replied hastily, guiltily, almost defensively, and her cheeks were shaded a soft pink. So she was living with some guy, he thought darkly, the tightening muscles in his stomach disproving his earlier assertion that he didn't care. He wondered why they weren't married—if the bastard didn't want to marry her, or if she was reluctant to give up her status as David's widow. Although his life insurance would have been paid out in a lump sum, there were certain other financial benefits still coming in—privileges at the commissary and PX, free medical care on a space-available basis and medical insurance when space wasn't available.

There were other benefits to remaining David's widow. No doubt she got a great deal of sympathy whenever anyone learned she had been widowed at nineteen and a great deal more when they learned her husband had died in a terrorist bombing. Ten years ago the entire nation had watched the events of the terrorist attack unfolding on television. The entire nation had mourned those deaths and offered their sympathy to the families. There was even a memorial in town honoring the men who had died in the Middle East, a memorial that, simply by being David Ellis's widow, Quin was a part of.

There wasn't a memorial to those who had survived, to those who had seen their friends die, to those who, through fate or luck or an act of God, had escaped injury in the blast. Every buddy he'd had in the battalion had died in the rubble of the barracks. He had helped in the rescue effort, had helped recover body after mangled body. He had helped recover David's body, and he had wondered why in the hell *he*—with nothing to live for, with no one waiting for him, no one loving him—had survived when David, with so much to go home to, hadn't.

Finally a Father 19

God's idea of a sick joke.

Before he could think of anything else to say—always one of his problems with Quin—she began backing away. "I— I've got to go," she murmured with an awkward little smile. She had never smiled at him the way she had at David or any of the other guys who'd come. Her real smiles were charming and warm and sometimes teasing. Her smiles for him were painful, wary gestures.

He watched her, her pace increasing with each step until she fairly ran up the steps and onto the porch. At the door, she hesitated, looked back and offered another of those uneasy little smiles. Then she disappeared inside.

Uneasy. Some things never changed. In all the time they'd spent together, there had been only one time when she hadn't been uneasy. For a few short hours, she hadn't wished he was someplace else, hadn't wished he was some*one* else. For those few sweet hours, she had welcomed him—had welcomed *him*—into her life.

He wished it had never happened.

He wished he hadn't wasted ten long years wanting it to happen again.

Dear God, he wished he had never known her.

Well, he couldn't change the past, but he could damn well control the future. Now that he knew she was here, he would know to avoid her. He wouldn't run past here again, wouldn't drive down this street. Hell, after going through the hassle of getting permission to live off base, when the lease on his apartment was up, he just might move *into* the barracks. The base was self-contained. He could spend the rest of his assignment there without ever having to leave it.

He had stayed away from her for ten years, just as he'd promised David he would. He would do whatever it took to keep that promise for the next three.

Turning away from the neat house and the sweet-scented flowers, he walked back out to the street and headed for home. His steady walk turned into a jog, then a flat-out run, as if that would get him anywhere. It seemed he had spent the better part of his life running, and it never helped anything. It never changed anything. When he stopped, he was still who—and what—he'd been trying to get away from.

He was sweaty when he reached his apartment. He kicked off his shoes and stripped out of his clothes, then stepped into the shower, leaving the water cool until he began to shiver. Turning the faucet toward hot, he leaned his head against the tiles and let the water beat down.

Damn Quin.

He'd had a tough enough time accepting his orders back to North Carolina. How could he come back here when all his memories of this place were bad? He would as soon have gone back to Philadelphia, back to where he'd grown up, back to the family who hadn't wanted him then and wouldn't want him now.

But he had checked with Information for a listing for Quin, and the operator had had nothing. He'd told himself that meant she wasn't there. After all, Jacksonville had no more been her home than it had been his or David's. She had moved there to be close to David. Once he was dead, there was no reason for her to stay. She should have gone back to Morehead City, back to her family and David's. Back to her home.

How many times in his life had he been wrong?

Every time, it seemed.

Picking up the soap, he scrubbed, then rinsed and dried off. He wasn't going anywhere today, so he didn't bother shaving, didn't do more than run a comb through his hair before dressing in a clean pair of running shorts and a T-shirt. Then, a bottle of juice in hand, he stretched out on the couch, the television tuned to Saturday morning cartoons, and very softly, very viciously, muttered a curse.

It wasn't that seeing Quin this morning had made a failure of his efforts to forget her. He'd given up on that long ago. He had accepted that, thanks to David's death and other circumstances, he was never going to get her completely out of

Finally a Father 21

his thoughts. But thinking of her, nineteen and beautiful and far, far out of reach, was one thing; knowing she was living half a mile down the street, twenty-nine and still beautiful, was another entirely.

Reaching for the remote control, he flipped through the channels, searching for something interesting enough to redirect his thoughts. But there was no other direction to take. Quin filled all of them.

Just like the first time they'd ever met. David had asked him if he would help her move into her apartment, and Mac had agreed. He'd had nothing better to do with his Saturday afternoon, and besides, he was curious. In the two years he'd known David, he had heard a lot about Quin Austin. He had heard tales about their growing up together, in houses that sat side by side on Bogue Sound. He knew that their parents were best friends, that their younger brothers and sisters were also extraordinarily close. He knew that Quin and David had been best friends since they were kids, that starting to date when they were old enough had been as natural as breathing, that they had never dated anyone else. He knew that they were planning to get married as soon as David's four years in the Marine Corps were up. He had wanted to meet the girl David spoke so fondly of.

They had spent the afternoon helping her move a worn assortment of furniture and personal belongings into the small one-bedroom apartment, and, as thanks, she had offered to fix dinner for them. It had been nearly midnight when they'd returned to the barracks, and Mac had gone back knowing two things for certain: there wasn't anything more than friendship—unusually strong and deep, but merely friendship, all the same—between David and Quin.

And there could be a hell of a lot more between *him* and Quin.

From the beginning, she had knocked him off his feet. He had never wanted any woman as quickly, as intensely, as surely, as he'd wanted her. And from the beginning, he had never done anything to fulfill that need. He had accepted David's regular invitations, he had been polite and as friendly as he knew how to be and he had never done anything out of line. After all, Quin had been David's girl, the woman he was planning to one day marry.

Even if there was something wrong between them.

Mac had had more than a few girlfriends of his own, so he knew what the word meant, and Quin's relationship with David never qualified for that status, no matter what they thought. They had never gone out, just the two of them. Every single time David went to her apartment, he had always invited someone else along—usually Mac, often a couple of other guys from the battalion, as well—and Quin had never seemed to mind. She had never hinted that she would like to cut their group outings from three, four or five down to only two.

Although David had had a definite affection for women, he'd shown about as much interest in Quin romantically as if she were his sister. He had never given her much more than a brotherly kiss good-night. There had never been any passion, any desire, any jealousy, between them.

There had never been any lovemaking, either, not until they were married. Mac knew that for a fact, in the most intimately positive way possible.

He had thought they were together because it was familiar, comfortable, safe. They had been together all their lives and, according to David, nothing would have made their families happier than to see them become husband and wife. They had known for as long as either of them could remember that they would one day marry.

They were settling, Mac had known, for companionship instead of love. For security instead of risk. For comfort instead of passion.

But none of that changed the fact that, in love with him or not, Quin had been David's girl.

It didn't change the fact that Mac had seduced his best friend's girl.

Finally a Father

It didn't make him any less guilty, any less a bastard.
It just made him sad.

Quin leaned against the door, the knob pressing against her back. Her eyes were closed, and her heart was beating loudly enough to dim the noise of the television fifteen feet away in the living room.

Mac.

It seemed she had always felt this way when she'd seen him, had always gotten quivery and unsteady, had always been grateful when he was gone. From the first time David had brought him over, when he had introduced them and Mac had turned that haunting dark gaze on her and said in that quiet, strong voice of his, "Hello, Quin." From that very first meeting, she had always felt anxious, apprehensive. Excited. Guilty. Ashamed.

So ashamed.

And she'd had good cause to be ashamed then: David. She had been unfaithful to him in her heart long before that night with Mac.

She had even better cause to be ashamed now. She needed to take only a few steps and look through the double door that led into the living room to face it.

Pushing herself away from the door, she took those steps, then stopped. Cady was lying on the floor, a pillow from the sofa beneath her stomach, her feet in the air, her chin propped on her hands. She was tall for a nine-year-old, and thin in the way that only young girls could be. Still a tomboy, she opted for simplicity in her life: her hair fell straight down her back, and her bangs lay straight across her forehead. Her wardrobe consisted of shorts, jeans and leggings, T-shirts and sweaters, with only one dress shoved into the back of the closet for the occasional church service or formal affair. Little-girl jewelry? She didn't wear it. Makeup? She wasn't interested. Boys? They were great playmates—as long as they didn't mind being outrun, outpitched, outscored and outbiked by a girl.

She was part of Quin's biggest shame.

Her biggest secret.

Her biggest love.

She was a lovely child, everyone said. *She looks just like her mother.*

But everyone who said that—her family, David's family, their friends—saw what they wanted to see. What they needed to see. They saw no trace of David with his blond hair and sweet blue eyes in Cady, and so they all agreed, *she looks just like her mother.*

And they were wrong. Like most children, Cady bore a resemblance to both parents. Her hair was Quin's—brown, silky and straight—and her eyes—dark and expressive. Her bone structure was also Quin's, as was her Cupid's bow mouth. But her coloring came from both parents—dark—and she got that jaw, that quirky smile and that straight, strong nose from her father. She got more from him: her quiet nature, her seriousness, her cool practical manner.

No one but Quin had ever noticed her strong resemblance to her father, but they could be excused for it.

After all, none of them had ever seen her father.

None of them had ever met Mac.

Smiling bittersweetly, Quin turned away and went down the hall to the kitchen. She tossed the paper on the table, then went to the sink to wash her hands.

Ten years ago she had tried to tell the truth—sort of—about the baby she was carrying. She had sent a letter to David, confessing everything except the name of the man she'd been unfaithful with. She had written how sorry she was, how deeply she regretted it and had pleaded with him to forgive her. If he wanted a divorce, she'd written, she understood, but if he would give her another chance, she would make it up to him. She would spend the rest of her life being the best wife a man could ever ask for.

Tears in her eyes, she had taken the letter to the post office, where she couldn't change her mind and reclaim it from the

Finally a Father

box. Six weeks later, it had been returned to her unopened, and by then she hadn't cared, because she'd been mourning her husband's death. He had died, never knowing that she was pregnant with his best friend's child.

Ten years ago. She'd been nineteen and on her own for the first time ever. Nineteen was a time to be foolish and young and carefree. She had managed the first two, all right, but, oh, such cares she'd brought upon herself—she and Mac. Her partner in crime. Her partner in parenthood.

Only he didn't know it.

He was living just down the street from the daughter who'd inherited his jaw and his nose and his rare sweet smile, and he didn't know it.

Oh, God, what was she going to do?

Cady wandered into the kitchen, ice cream bowl in hand, her bare feet making little noise on the linoleum. "Who was that guy you were talking to?" she asked, laying the dish on the counter and picking up a cinnamon roll from the plate nearby.

Quin stiffened, then forced a smile into place as she shut off the water and faced her daughter. "Someone I used to know years ago," she replied, drying her hands on a towel.

"'Years ago,'" Cady scoffed. How could a nine-year-old girl scoff as easily as she did? "You make it sound like ancient history. You're not that old, Mom."

"It was before you were born, kiddo. That was a long time ago."

"So who is he?"

"I told you—"

"What's his name?"

Her smile slipping, Quin turned back to the sink to rinse Cady's dishes. "His name is Mac McEwen. He's a marine."

"No kidding. I can recognize a jarhead when I see one."

"Don't use that word," she said automatically, shutting the water off and adding the dishes to the dishwasher.

"Did you used to date him or something?"

"No," she replied too quickly, too sharply. There had been no dates for her and Mac. Just a little *or something*.

"Did you used to date anybody besides Daddy?"

Quin flinched. It came out so easily, so naturally, this intimate reference to a man Cady had never known. She hadn't taught her that. David's parents had, and Quin's mother and father, and all their brothers and sisters. From the time Cady had started talking, they had shown her pictures of David and coaxed her into saying the word. *Daddy, Cady. This is your daddy.*

And Quin had encouraged it because she hadn't known what else to do. She'd been twenty years old—such a child, she realized now—with a tiny baby girl. Her husband had died, and Mac had cut her out of his life. She had needed the families' support, and they had needed Cady. David's parents, especially, had needed the granddaughter who linked them to their dead son. At the time, she had lacked the courage and the emotional strength to tell them they were wrong, and later, when she was stronger...

She had remained cowardly. By then the Ellises had loved Cady too much. It would have hurt them too much. And so Quin had taken the easy way—easy for Cady, for her grandparents, easy for herself. She had kept her secret. She had lived her lie.

And now Mac was back.

Now it felt wrong to hear Cady call another man Daddy.

It *was* wrong.

"No, honey, I didn't date anyone else."

"So how'd you know this Mac guy?"

Wishing her daughter had the short attention span of so many of her students at school, Quin tried to deflect her interest. "My, we're nosy today, aren't we?"

Cady wasn't offended. She rarely took offense at anything anyone said. "We're nosy every day. If we don't ask questions, we never learn anything. So how'd you meet him?"

Quin faced her. If she avoided answering much longer, Cady

Finally a Father 27

would figure she had something to hide. The fact that she *did* have something to hide aside, she didn't want to give Cady the idea right now that—*please, God, forgive me*—there was anything special about Mac. "He was a friend of David's."

Then, desperate to change the subject, she brushed her daughter's hair back, fixing it behind her ear, then pinched her cheek. "Why aren't you dressed yet? And why are you still eating?"

Her head tilted to one side, Cady eyed her for a moment, then apparently decided to let her mother brush her off for now. "I'm a growing girl."

"You keep eating like that, sweetie, and you'll grow, all right. You'll be as big around as you are tall."

Swallowing the last of the roll, Cady licked her fingers clean. "What do you want to do this afternoon?"

"Go to the library?"

"Nah. Let's go to the beach."

"How about a movie? We can sit in air-conditioned comfort."

"Nah. I'd rather go to the beach."

"We haven't been to the mall in a while."

"The beach, Mom."

Quin considered it. The beach on base was a pretty place, but it was a long drive, and it was sure to be busy on a hot Saturday afternoon. Worse, lying on a towel would leave her with nothing to occupy her mind but old memories—like the first time she, David and Mac had gone to the same beach and she'd worn her new bikini to show off for David. Only it was Mac who had noticed. Mac who'd given her a long, appreciative look. Mac who'd made her feel for the first time in her young life like an attractive woman.

Old memories and new worries. A lethal combination if ever there was one.

"You get much more sun, kiddo, you're going to disappear in the dark."

"Moth-er." Cady gave her a chiding look.

Forcing a smile, Quin capitulated. "All right. We'll go to the beach—but only for an hour. Then we'll come home and weed the flower beds."

Any other child in the world would have immediately agreed, but not hers. Cady wasn't selfish; she simply wanted what she wanted on her own terms. She considered her mother's offer, then made one of her own. "Two hours at the beach, and I'll do the weeding by myself. A couple hours, Mom. What could it hurt?"

Quin's smile slowly faded. In a couple of hours, she and Mac had changed their lives. They had betrayed David. They had sentenced Quin to ten years of secrets and lies. They had managed to cause plenty of hurt.

But they'd done something else in those few hours, something she would never regret, regardless of who else was hurt by it.

They had given Cady life.

Chapter 2

Traffic coming off Camp Lejeune and onto Highway 24 was heavy at the end of every workday, and Tuesday was no exception. Although Mac's apartment was only two miles from the main gate and seven miles from the battalion area, getting home was an annoyance from the time he entered the traffic circle near battalion headquarters until he turned onto Pine Valley Road six and a half miles later.

What the Marine Corps needed, he decided, was some sort of flexible schedule. Other services had tried it with success, and he would willingly come in to work earlier or stay later if it meant missing rush hour. It wasn't that he was so impatient to get home—there was nothing for him to go home to. He just didn't like waiting. He didn't like being trapped inside his car with nothing to do but think.

He didn't like thinking about Quin, and lately it seemed he couldn't think of much else. Whatever he did somehow reminded him of her—watching television, cooking, cleaning, reading. Even his daily run reminded him of the one time David had coaxed her along, when she had collapsed in the grass after less than a quarter of a mile and breathlessly announced that she wasn't going one step farther.

And she hadn't. They had gone on for three miles—an easy run for Mac but just about David's limit—and had returned to the apartment to find her stretched out on the couch with a bag of chocolate kisses, smugly lazy and watching an old movie on TV.

Last night he had even pulled out the only thing she'd ever given him—a paperback book, the then-new release by an author he had once mentioned as his favorite. It hadn't meant anything to her—she had seen it in the grocery store and tossed it into the cart, much the way she would have tossed in a bag of David's favorite chips—but it had meant something to him.

It had meant the world to him.

A paperback book. That was all he had to show for that fateful summer...that, and a load of guilt he would never get out from under.

Seeing her on Saturday had given him a jolt. Maybe the gods had decided that he'd gotten too comfortable with the guilt and the anger and the emptiness, that he needed shaking up, needed old wounds made fresh again. Or maybe this was some new phase of his punishment for what he'd done to David—yes, and to Quin, too: having to live with the knowledge that she was there, right down the street, practically a neighbor.

Having to live with the knowledge that after ten hard years, even now, he still couldn't have her.

I'll stay away from her, David, I swear I will.

Even now? *Especially* now.

Traffic came to a complete stop, and he impatiently drummed his fingers on the steering wheel. Times like this made living in the barracks again an appealing notion. That was where he'd spent the better part of his adult life. It was convenient, close to the office and the price was right—free, in exchange for the quarters allowance he'd given up.

Funny how things had worked out. When he'd decided sixteen years ago to enlist in the Corps, he'd had no intention of making a career of it. He certainly hadn't intended to live, eat,

Finally a Father

sleep and breathe the Marine Corps by taking up permanent residence in the barracks. No, he had merely been looking for an escape from a home life that was rapidly going from bad to worse. He'd hated leaving Chelsea behind, but there had been no help for it. His sister had just turned seventeen, a year away from finishing school.

He would spend that year living in the barracks, he had decided, and save every penny he could. As soon as she had her diploma in hand, she would come, and they would get a place together. He had promised her that the day he left Philadelphia.

One year. It really wasn't so long. Anyone could endure anything for a year.

But not Chelsea.

Finally he made it through the last stop light, shut off so MPs could direct traffic merging from the cross street. In a matter of minutes he was off base and headed toward home. Traffic was worse, it seemed, on Lejeune Boulevard, but light on Pine Valley, where he drove slowly past his apartment and on down the street. Toward Quin's house.

He wasn't going to stop, wasn't going to hope for some glimpse of her. He was just going to look. Just going to rub salt in the wounds that seeing her had opened.

The house was quiet when he passed, the driveway empty, but the neighborhood wasn't. A half dozen kids, five boys and one dark-haired girl, were gathered in one yard, all sitting astride bicycles, chattering loudly among themselves. When Mac returned after a turnaround at the end of the street, the girl was pedaling hard across the lawn. When the yard abruptly ended at a retaining wall, she jerked hard on the handlebars and sent her bike soaring through the air. Upon landing, she skidded the rear wheel in a spray of dust, faced the boys and grinned triumphantly.

She was quite a tomboy, he thought with a faint smile. He hadn't known any tomboys when he was growing up. Of course, in his neighborhood, mothers had kept their daughters close to home. It was the only way to keep them safe...but even that wasn't always enough.

It hadn't been for Chelsea.

Passing the kids, he shifted his attention back to Quin's house. His fingers tensed around the steering wheel seconds before the realization that she was home now registered in his mind. In the few minutes it had taken him to drive to the end of the street and back again, she had come home, gotten the mail and was now on her way to the porch.

Knowing it was stupid—that it was wrong—and not caring, he pulled across the street and to a stop at the curb in front of her house. He didn't shut off the engine, didn't call her name or do anything to draw her attention. All he did was watch as she climbed the steps, pulled open the screen door and turned the key in the lock. All he did was look.

And that was enough.

She glanced over her shoulder and went still. After a moment she pushed the door open, laid the mail and her purse inside, then slowly returned to the top step.

Down the street, the kids yelled, and in his rearview mirror, he saw the dark-haired girl go flying through the air again. When he looked back toward the house, Quin was approaching.

She wore a summery print dress, cool and flattering, and her hair was pulled back and held with a wide white clamp. She'd worn a summery dress that night so long ago, too, a red one in exactly the same shade as the shirt he'd worn. She'd had combs in her hair that night, tortoiseshell combs that had easily slid out when he pulled, spilling her hair over his hands.

Damn her. She had no right looking so pretty and fresh after a full day's work. She had no right making him remember that summer night, making him wish he could have just one more night.

But *he* was the one with no rights here. No damn rights at all.

He rolled the window down, then cut the engine off as she reached the mailbox. She rested one arm on the wooden post

Finally a Father 33

that supported it, brushed a strand of hair back and quietly said, "Hey, Mac."

"Quin."

She looked down the street, watched the kids for a moment, then glanced at his uniform. "On your way home from work?"

"I was. I missed my turn."

One corner of her mouth lifted at that; then she looked away again. She was restless, always restless, around him. He wondered, as he had so many times in the past, what it would take to put her at ease. Could he be nicer, softer, more harmless? Could he talk more, be less serious, care less? Could he be more like David?

But all he could be was who he was—and who he was hadn't won him many admirers in the past. His friendships growing up had only been surface deep, except for Chelsea. He hadn't seen his family in more than fifteen years; as far as they knew—or cared—he could be dead. As for his relationships with women... The only woman he'd ever wanted anything permanent with had been Quin. Quin, who clearly didn't want to be standing here talking to him. Sweet Quin, who could hardly bear to even look at him.

But then she did just that. She looked at him, *really* looked at him. She met his gaze, almost smiled and asked, "How does it feel to be back in Jacksonville?"

"I would prefer to be almost any other place in the world."

His honesty made Quin smile. When she'd first seen him sitting there, she'd gotten that quivery feeling again, but it was manageable now, especially since Cady and her friends had abandoned their bikes and gone inside Matthew's house to play. Especially now that there wasn't much chance of her coming home before Mac left. "Jacksonville's not a bad place," she remarked evenly, knowing as she did that it wasn't the town he'd wanted to avoid but the memories of his time here. "It used to be your home."

"No, it wasn't. It's just one more place where I've lived."

She moved to sit on the curb, gathering her full skirt close around her legs. From here, looking up rather than down at him, she had a better view. From here she could better appreciate the dark good looks that had left her darn near breathless the first time—*every* time—she'd seen him. She had always thought he was gorgeous and attractive and appealing. She just hadn't known what to do about it. He'd been older. So serious. So intense. So mesmerizing. And she'd been young. Oh, my, yes, so young.

"What other places have you seen since you left here?" she asked, determined to keep her thoughts in line.

"South Carolina. California." The look in his eyes turned distant and old. "Saudi Arabia. Kuwait. Africa."

"You're well traveled for a boy from Philadelphia." Her teasing fell flat, and so did her smile.

"Where have you been?"

"Right here." She sighed softly, sadly, wistfully. "I've always been right here, Mac."

The questions she'd wanted to ask Saturday, all the *whys,* came back. *Why didn't you call? Why didn't you come? Why didn't you want me?* If he had come back when she was pregnant, maybe he would have guessed the truth. If he had been with her when Cady was born, surely he would have known. He would have counted the months and realized that she had been pregnant when she'd married David, that her baby had been conceived a month before, and he would have known, damn him, would have known beyond a shadow of a doubt that her baby was his.

Surely he would have wanted his daughter, and he probably would have taken Quin, too, to get her. And with him at her side, with his strength to lean on, she could have told everyone the truth. She could have endured their condemnation and their anger. She could have shouldered their blame and their disappointment if only Mac had been there to help her.

She could have avoided ten years of lying.

God, how was she going to set things straight now?

She could start by telling Mac that she had a daughter. Not that *they* had one, but that *she* did. And then she could introduce them, and he could take one look at Cady and see himself in her sweet features and...

She shuddered. Heavens, she was in trouble.

"When will your roommate be home?"

There, Quin, she told herself. There's your opening. All she had to say was, "I don't have a roommate, Mac, I have a daughter." But when she opened her mouth, the words wouldn't come. Only one made it past the tightness in her throat. "Soon."

"Is he a marine, too?"

For a long time she stared at his car, gray and dusty, relatively new and lacking the usual dings in the door. Why did he automatically assume that she was living with a man? Why did he think so little of her?

Maybe because she'd slept with him when she was planning to marry David. Because she'd told him afterward that it had merely been curiosity on her part. That any man would have done. That he had simply been convenient.

To this day she remembered the awful look in his eyes before he'd gotten dressed and walked away.

He was waiting for her to reply, watching her intently. Did it matter to him? she wondered bleakly. Logic told her no. He didn't still want her. He didn't still care about her. He didn't even want to know her now.

But those ancient dark eyes of his offered another answer. It mattered. He didn't want it to. He didn't want to give a damn about her living arrangements, but somewhere, on some level, he did.

"No," she replied softly. "She's not." The words that should obviously come next—*she's a nine-year-old girl, too young for the Corps*—stayed in her heart, unspoken.

He looked away, watching as a car passed, then just barely glanced at her again. "Why did you stay in Jacksonville? Why didn't you go home to your family?"

She'd been asked that question before, and she'd found multiple answers. She liked Jacksonville. She liked being close to the base and the benefits it afforded her. This was where she and David had begun their marriage.

This was where Mac had left her.

She chose an answer she rarely gave, though it was just as true as the others. "If I'd gone home, our families would have smothered me. As it was, they hovered around me. They treated me as if I might break. They wanted to do everything for me. If I had moved back home the way they wanted, it would have been so easy to let them. I needed someone to lean on, but I don't think I would ever have *stopped* leaning on them." She paused briefly, only long enough for a quick breath of courage, then asked, "Why didn't you call me when you got back?"

He didn't say anything. He simply stared straight ahead, his jaw set tight.

"I remember when the battalion came back. They made such a fuss over the homecoming—the returning heroes, the survivors. It was in the news for days. I watched it on TV, and I read about it in the papers, and I kept thinking that surely you would call me. I kept waiting."

Finally he did look at her. At that moment, he couldn't have looked more the stereotypical tough-as-nails marine if he'd tried. The expression in his eyes was cold, the set of his jaw hard, the lines of his face carved in granite. "We had already said everything there was to say. There was nothing left." Reaching down, he turned the key, and the engine roared to life.

Quin stood up and brushed her skirt off, then bent so she could see him through the open window. "Maybe you had nothing left to say, Mac. But I did. There were things I needed to know. Things I needed to tell you. Things…" Things she couldn't tell him right now, not like this. Shaking her head, she broke off and took a few steps back. "Forget it. Take it easy, Mac."

Without another word, he drove away. He was only going a few blocks down the street, but she couldn't shake the feeling that, once again, he was running away.

Finally a Father

Sighing, she watched until he was out of sight, but out of sight definitely didn't mean out of mind. He hadn't been out of her mind one minute since Saturday morning. With Cady spending Sunday with her grandparents and two slow days at work, Quin had had plenty of free time since Saturday morning—time to think, to remember, to consider—and she had reached a few inescapable conclusions.

Mac had a right to know he had a daughter.

If he was interested in being a father, Cady had a right to know him.

And because she couldn't put her daughter in the position of keeping such a secret, that meant everyone had to know the truth: her parents, her sisters, David's brothers and, God help her, his parents. She had to tell them how she had lied, and she had to pray that all of them—Cady and Mac included—could forgive her.

But she didn't think Mac had much forgiveness in him, and what she'd done, after all, was pretty unforgivable.

She was walking up the driveway when Cady came tearing past on her bike. At the garage she jumped off, let the bike fall to the ground and came racing toward her mother. "I'm glad you're home," she greeted her, throwing her thin arms around Quin's shoulders.

What she'd done, Quin thought, a lump in her throat. She had deprived Mac of this kind of welcome home every day for the past nine years. Knowing how utterly alone he was, she had hidden all knowledge of his daughter from him. She had passed his daughter off as belonging to another man, a dead man, had given Cady nothing for a father but an eight-by-ten picture on the nightstand. She had denied Mac the love and pleasure and delight that were every father's right. She had stolen nine precious years from him and Cady that they could never get back. *Never.*

What she'd done was indefensible. Under the circumstances, it was silly of her to worry about whether he could forgive her for it. There was no question of that.

He was going to hate her for all time.

* * *

He had promised himself he wouldn't come this way anymore, but Saturday morning found Mac jogging down the street toward Quin's house once again. He didn't question why. He didn't remind himself of the promise he'd made to David so long ago. He didn't warn himself that it would be smarter by far to pretend she didn't exist. He didn't acknowledge that coming around like this was going to end only one way: in heartache.

He didn't consider any of those things. He simply ran his usual six miles, arrived back at his apartment and continued on down the street.

It was already uncomfortably hot, and his clothing was soaked with sweat. It coated his skin, ran in rivulets down his back and chest, and dripped from his hands. Heat like this was dangerous for physical activity unless you were acclimated to it. He was.

The muscles in his stomach clenching, he caught sight of Quin's house ahead. It was a comfortable place—not as nice as David would have given her, although probably about the best *he* could have afforded. He wondered how long she'd lived there, whether she rented or was buying, whether she intended to stay there forever. If he came back to Jacksonville when his time in the marines was up, would he find her still there?

He was almost even with the house now. The flowers were drooping a little, as much in need of a drink of water as he was. The yard was pretty the way she'd landscaped it—emerald-green grass, lavender and white flowers edging the driveway, red, orange and gold ones around the trees, shades of pink and blue in front of the house. He had always wanted a place like this—a big yard that needed regular cutting, a comfortable house that required occasional repairs, a garage for puttering around in and a wide porch for relaxing on. It was so typically middle-class American, so normal, so real. It was a world away from the place where he'd grown up.

Quin was sitting on the porch swing, the newspaper open but ignored. When she saw him, she stood up, sections of

Finally a Father

paper falling in all directions, and walked to the top of the steps. She didn't speak, didn't wave, and neither did he. He didn't slow his steps, but he watched her intently until he had passed.

Life wasn't fair and never had been. He'd learned that lesson when he was nine years old and his father had died. He'd understood it when his mother had remarried only weeks later and brought home her new husband, who'd hated every reminder of her first marriage, including Chelsea and Mac. *Especially* Chelsea and Mac. He'd gotten a refresher course, fifteen years ago, when he heard the news about Chelsea.

But falling in love with his best friend's fiancée had been the most unfair. Being granted only those few hours with her, then living with the guilt for ten years. Wanting her and knowing he could never have her. Accepting that, then finding that she was back in his life again. Those were the biggest injustices of all.

He reached the end of the street, where a housing subdivision had recently gone in, and turned around. There were ways back to his apartment without passing her house, ways that, if he had even the slightest instinct for self-preservation, he would take. But, with a sense of fatalism, because he knew exactly what he was going to do, he headed back the way he'd come.

She was still sitting on the swing, holding the paper once more. She laid it aside as his steps slowed and he turned into the driveway, then moved up the walk. Once again she left the swing for the top of the steps, leaning against the post there as she watched him.

The five steps between them left her maybe three feet above him. His hands on his hips, his breathing heavy and ragged, he looked at her, and she looked back for a long time before hesitantly smiling. "You look like you could use a pitcher of water."

He shrugged just a little.

"Sit down. I'll get some."

When she opened the door to go inside, he heard the sounds

of Saturday-morning TV. They faded to an indistinct murmur when she closed the door behind her.

Sit down, she'd invited. There was the swing, still swaying from her leaving, a wicker chair with a faded, dusty cushion, and an old rocker, weather-beaten and smooth. They all looked inviting.

Passing a few moments on a hot July morning with Quin on her porch was entirely too inviting.

He sat down on the top step, the rough surface of the brick biting into his skin. Resting his arms on his knees, he let his head fall forward and listened to the uneven tenor of his breathing, concentrating on slowing it, evening it out. By the time he heard the door open behind him, his heart rate was about as normal as it was going to get with her around.

She brought a pitcher and a glass, and over her shoulder was draped a hand towel. Without speaking, she offered the towel first, and he dried his face, then his throat, catching a scent of lemony fabric softener. When he was done, she handed him a glass of water.

"I admire a man who's dedicated enough to exert himself in heat like this," she remarked as she moved past him to sit a few steps lower. "When the heat and humidity are both over ninety-five, it's all I can do to sit in the shade and read."

He drained the glass, and she refilled it before setting the pitcher on a step between them. "Do you always sit out here on Saturday mornings?"

"Usually. I'm a creature of habit."

"So I recall." Even at nineteen, she'd been more comfortable with routines than with spontaneous activities. She had liked knowing when David was coming over and who he was bringing with him, had liked knowing that the only times he invited anyone but Mac had been on weekends. She had liked not being bothered before eleven o'clock on Saturday and Sunday mornings, her only days to sleep late, had liked knowing that Sunday afternoons were for baseball games on TV, Tuesday nights for going out to the movies, Friday nights for poker games.

Finally a Father

"As I recall, so were you. I always thought you were well suited to the Marine Corps, because you appreciated organization, order and routine. You didn't mind showing up for work at precisely the right time with your uniform starched and pressed and your boots polished, or following orders or doing things exactly the way they were supposed to be done."

"Whereas David's attitude was a little less rigid."

She smiled faintly. "David didn't take the Marine Corps seriously. He signed up on a whim. If he got along okay, great. If he didn't, hey, it wasn't any big deal. It was only for four years." Then her smile faded. "He should have taken it more seriously. Maybe he wouldn't have gotten killed."

For a moment she had sounded relaxed, comfortable, and he had started to relax himself. But her last words made his muscles go taut again. She was wrong. The Marine Corps hadn't gotten David killed. Even that terrorist's bomb couldn't have done the job, not without help from Mac. *He* was the one responsible.

"Where is...?" He trailed off, looked away, then back again. "Where is his grave?"

"In Morehead City. His parents wanted it there, beside generations of Ellises. His mother puts fresh flowers on the grave every week, and his father replaces the little American flag whenever the sun bleaches out the colors." She spoke softly, comfortable again, as if she'd made peace with David's death. As if it no longer hurt to think or talk about him.

It still hurt Mac. He had never learned to accept death. He'd had so few people to lose, and he still mourned every one of them.

"I couldn't..." He used the towel to mop his forehead again, then focused his attention on the glass he held. "There was no way I could have come for the funeral. We had to finish our deployment. We couldn't come home early."

"I know," she said gently.

"The battalion held a memorial service, and then...we had to go back to work." Then it had been business as usual...

except that more than half of his two-hundred-man company was gone.

"There was also a memorial service here. I met Jimmy's wife and Tex's sister."

His fingers tightened around the glass. He hadn't heard those names, hadn't even let himself think them, in so long. Jimmy, a scrawny, red-haired kid from Georgia, was a farm boy who hadn't been away from home long enough to forget his mama's manners. It had been his last-minute marriage to his high school sweetheart, Mac had believed, that had inspired David to do the same.

And Tex... His name was Enrique, and he was from Miami, but he'd always intended to move to Texas one day. He'd never been west of the Mississippi, but he'd already adopted a Spanish-flavored drawl and had rarely worn anything but jeans, cowboy boots and a beaten Stetson. He had bragged about his sister, the prettiest woman in all of South Florida, and had insisted that one day he would bring her to Jacksonville to meet Mac.

So she had finally made it to town, only Mac hadn't been there to meet her.

And Tex had never known it.

"I remember seeing a photograph," he began slowly, "of all the transfer cases lined up, row after row of them, each one draped with a flag. There were so many of them, and I knew every one." It had been a powerful picture, one that had haunted him for months afterward.

"I still have the flag presented at David's funeral, folded exactly the way they handed it to me, tucked away in a dresser drawer. I wanted to give it to David's parents, but they told me to keep it for—" Abruptly she broke off and pressed her lips together. After a moment's silence, she looked up at him and smiled crookedly. "This isn't pleasant talk for such a pretty morning, is it?"

"No," he agreed.

They were both silent for a few minutes; then he asked,

Finally a Father

"Does your roommate stay inside all day, or is she already out and about?"

Given the choice between talking about David's death and talking about Cady, Quin thought uneasily, she would prefer the former right now. She wasn't yet comfortable with the idea of telling him that she had a daughter. She wasn't sure she could hide her guilt, wasn't sure she could act normally enough that he wouldn't immediately suspect her secret.

Eventually there would come a time, of course, even with just brief, casual visits like this, when she would no longer be able to hide Cady's existence. After all, hadn't she already decided that she had to tell Mac he had a daughter? But she wanted that time to be later, when things were maybe a little easier between them. When there wasn't such tension. When she was sure he would be around for Cady.

"Why do I get the feeling you don't want to talk about your roommate?"

His voice was pitched low and shadowed with the same suspicion that darkened his eyes when she met his gaze. She didn't want him to look at her that way, as if he didn't quite trust her. But why should he trust her? He already knew she was capable of deceit. After that hot August night with him, she had continued her relationship with David as if nothing had happened, as if nothing had changed.

He didn't know, though, just how deceitful she could be. He didn't know that she had married David knowing that it was a mistake, that it was sinful considering the way she felt about Mac. He didn't know that, upon discovering she was pregnant with his baby, she had promised David in her letter that she would devote her life to being a good wife if only he would accept Mac's child as his own.

He didn't know that the past ten years of her life had been based on lies and deception. But soon he would find out.

Soon he would hate her.

And it was time to take the first step now.

Standing up, she bent to pick a bloom from a mound of delicately hued impatiens before facing him. She wished she was brave enough not to dread this. She wished she was cowardly enough to avoid it.

"I don't have a roommate, Mac," she announced, meeting his gaze and holding it only through sheer will.

"But you said—"

"I have a daughter."

It took a moment for the news to sink in, and she gave it to him, rolling the fragile blossom back and forth between her fingers and waiting, her chest so tight that it hurt, for his response.

"A daughter?" he repeated at last, sounding a little dazed. "You have a daughter?"

"Yes."

"Who's her father?"

Oh, God. No one had ever asked that question. When she'd told the Austins and Ellises that she was pregnant, they had rejoiced. Oh, they had counted back and realized that she'd already been pregnant for a month when she and David got married, but they hadn't cared. They had naturally assumed, every one of them, that David was the father. Some of their relatives had even believed that had been the real reason behind Quin's moving to Jacksonville—not to attend school, but so she and David could have the opportunity and the privacy to indulge the more intimate side of their relationship.

Mac, only Mac, had thought to ask what everyone else assumed.

She chose her words carefully as she tore apart the blossom she held. "I was pregnant when David died."

He simply looked at her, understanding absent from his expression.

"He never knew. That's why you never knew. I told him about it in a letter that I mailed the sixth of December."

He recognized the significance of the date, she saw, remembered that the barracks had been destroyed only three days later. Of course he remembered. Everyone he'd cared about had died that day.

How had he felt? How had he coped with the deaths of so

Finally a Father 45

many friends? Had he blamed himself for surviving when they died? Had there been anyone to comfort him?

She would have offered him comfort if he had let her. If he had come to her. If he hadn't turned his back on her.

"That was what you meant about your family smothering you," he said stiffly.

"I was nineteen and pregnant, and my husband had just died. They were concerned."

"When was she born?"

"Early summer." Deliberately she didn't specify the month. If she told him that Cady had been born on May second, exactly nine months from the very night that they'd made love, he would guess what no one else had. Of course, he knew what no one else had even suspected. "The morning after she was born was the first time I knew beyond a doubt that I was going to survive all this. Sometimes I think she saved my life."

"The dark-haired girl on the bike the other day," he murmured. "That was her, wasn't it?"

She nodded.

"Why didn't you tell me then? Why didn't you just point her out and say, 'By the way, Mac, that's my little girl'?"

Because she had been afraid of what he would see, afraid of what he might recognize.

"Why didn't you tell me ten years ago?" Finally there was emotion in his voice. Passion. Anger. "You had the battalion address. You'd been writing all those damned letters to David. Why didn't you let me know that he—that you were going to have his baby?"

"Would it have made a difference?" she countered. "If you had known that I was pregnant when he died, would you have called me? Would you have come to see me?"

"*Yes.*" He rose from the step, towering over her, as if sitting still was no longer possible. "It would have made a hell of a difference. He was my *best friend.* I owed him—" He broke off, muttered a curse, then continued, "I owed him everything."

"So you would have come back for David's baby, but not

for me." Quin had never known it was possible to be jealous of her own daughter, but the tight, hurtful feeling deep in her stomach proved that she was. Climbing the steps, she didn't stop until she was at the top, now two steps above Mac, eye-to-eye with him. "*I* was the one you said you needed. *I* was the one you said you would sacrifice David's friendship for. Did you know I believed you? That I actually considered telling David I couldn't marry him because, God forgive me, I wanted *you* instead?"

Feeling her throat tighten, she looked away and drew a deep breath before facing him again. This time her voice was quieter. "Thank God I didn't, because it was just talk, wasn't it? Three months later you forgot all about me. When *I* needed *you,* you were nowhere to be found."

She gave him a chance to speak, to say something, *anything,* but he didn't. His expression had become closed off, and his eyes were distant. Cold. Sometimes he could be so cold.

With a shiver, she turned away, going to stand at the end of the porch. A hummingbird feeder hung overhead there, and a tiny angry bird fluttered about before retreating to the safety of a nearby dogwood's branches. When she heard the creak of a floorboard behind her, signaling his approach, she sighed wearily. "It wouldn't have made a difference, Mac," she said. "Cady needed her father, not one of David's friends, and what I needed…"

She sighed again. "You couldn't have given."

Chapter 3

Mac dipped the sponge into the bucket, then brought it out, water streaming, to the roof of his car. It wasn't even noon yet, but he'd been up more than six hours and had already done a day's work. After an eight-mile run, he had cleaned his apartment, done his laundry and washed last night's dinner dishes. He had run a couple of errands and cleaned out his car inside. Now he was washing it.

And when that was done, he decided, he would get some lunch, then find something to do with his afternoon. Maybe, if he was lucky, he would sleep it away. He could certainly use some sleep after the restless night he'd had. But he knew that if he tried to fall asleep, it wouldn't happen. He would lie there, thinking. Remembering. If he did finally doze off, he would dream.

He hadn't had that dream in a long time. He suspected it was Quin's announcement yesterday that had brought it back. *I have a daughter.* David's daughter. And she hadn't seen any reason in all these years to let him know. He was hurt that she hadn't shared one of the most important occasions in her life with him. She must have known that he would care, that he would want to know. She must have known that, his promise to David notwithstanding, he would have done anything in the world for David's baby girl.

Quin had a pretty little tomboy of a daughter.

Not only had he made her a widow, he had also taken Cady's father from her. *Cady needed her father, not one of David's friends....* Like all kids, she'd needed a father, and thanks to Mac, she'd never had one.

And he thought he'd known what guilt was before.

That—the guilt, the surprise, the hurt—had led to the dream. It wasn't a dream so much as a detail-perfect replay of the explosion that had killed David. It was like watching a videotape, only more real. He could feel the concussion as the bomb exploded, could smell the smoke and the dust, could hear the screams and the cries.

He could feel the blood.

David's blood.

He had been a half mile from the barracks when it happened, running, working toward sheer exhaustion so he wouldn't have the strength to be angry or frustrated. The curses had become a litany that matched his steps. *Damn Quin. Damn David. Damn, damn, damn.* He had run, hating Quin for marrying David when he knew she didn't love him and hating David for having her. Most of all, he had hated himself because David was the best friend he'd ever had, and he had let his need for Quin poison that friendship.

They had been three months into the deployment—three months, for Mac, of bitterness and resentment, of anger and guilt and loneliness—oh, God, the most incredible loneliness he'd ever known. He had thought that losing Chelsea had left him the emptiest he could ever get, but he'd been wrong. Losing Quin had been worse.

Even though she had never been his to lose.

She had always belonged to David, ever since she was a little girl. It was David she had married. David she had kissed goodbye. David she had written almost daily. Sometimes there

Finally a Father

had been no mail for days at a time—never any for Mac—and then a bundle of letters would arrive. All her news, all her concern, all her love. All for David.

There had been mail the day before the explosion. Five letters and a package.

For David.

Mac had run that winter morning, mile after mile, wishing he had never met David, wishing he had never touched Quin. At the same time, he had bleakly wondered if there was any way he could ever get her back. He had wondered if their marriage would last—how could it, when they weren't in love?—and he had wished there was some way to get David out of the way. If he were gone, there would surely be a way to reach Quin. If David were out of the middle, she would have to see that there was something special between her and Mac. She would have to realize that he could give her things David never could.

If only David would disappear.

Then the bomb had gone off.

And David had died.

Mac's wish had come true, and he had realized in his grief that he'd been horribly wrong. David would always stand between him and Quin.

Always.

He was trading the bucket and sponge for the hose when a red Pontiac pulled into the parking lot. Even though he'd seen it only three times, always as part of the background, hardly worth noticing, he recognized it immediately. He was more than a little surprised. He had figured that, after the way they'd left things yesterday, he wouldn't be seeing her again for a while. He certainly hadn't expected her to come looking for him.

She parked across from his car and got out. For a moment she simply stood there beside the car, sunglasses hiding her eyes, her hair pulled back from her face into a ponytail. In her tailored knee-length shorts and yellow shirt, she looked cool and aloof and incredibly young. Though there was only six years difference in their ages, she had always been far too young for him.

Was she thinking better of whatever impulse had brought her here? Or was she waiting for him to come to her? He could do that. He could put the hose down and walk across the parking lot to her.

But before he could move, she approached. Mindful of the spray, she stopped a few yards away, out of range, and shoved her hands into her pockets. "Hey, Mac," she said, her voice subdued.

That was the way she'd always greeted him, right from the very beginning. But he had never been comfortable with the casual, very Southern *hey,* not with her. "Hello, Quin."

She stood there for a moment, obviously uncomfortable, then remarked, "I like your car."

"Thanks."

She watched as streams of soapy water rushed from the car to the ground. It pooled there, then ran toward the center of the parking lot. "I wasn't sure I would be able to find you. I don't know which apartment you live in."

"This one." He gestured with a nod to the one directly behind them. It was on the end of the building, one bedroom and one story, looking like a tacked-on afterthought to the two-storied building. "What brings you looking?"

She shifted restlessly, regretting the impulse, he was sure. Impulse had led her into bed with him—that and curiosity, he remembered with a twinge of long-ago pain. She had been a virgin, and she'd wanted to know what sex was like, even though David was insisting that they wait until they were married. When David canceled out on their plans for that night, she had decided it was a good time to satisfy her curiosity, and Mac had been adequate for the job. He supposed anyone else David might have sent over that evening would have been deemed just as suitable, probably even more so, but she'd had to make do with what she'd gotten.

"I'm meeting Cady in half an hour for lunch," she said at last. "She spent last night with a friend, and Kelli's mother is

Finally a Father

going to drop her off at the restaurant. Would you like to join us?"

He crouched in front of the car and blasted the suds from the headlights. Sunday dinner with Quin and David's daughter. He would like that. He would like to meet Cady, would like to see what kind of child the two people he loved—and hated—most had produced.

He would like to see if she was all right, growing up without a father.

He would like to know that the harm he'd caused her hadn't been irreparable.

"All right." He stood up, gave the car one final rinse, then eased his finger off the trigger pull on the sprayer. "I'll have to clean up first." He was wearing faded gold gym shorts and nothing else, and the shorts were stained with grease and soap.

She nodded once.

"Where should I meet you?"

"I'll wait, if you don't mind."

Mentally, he placed her inside his apartment, sitting on his furniture, touching his things. It was an image he found entirely too appealing—so appealing that he knew he shouldn't allow it. He didn't need her presence there. He didn't need any memories that would linger. Still, after he shut off the hose and coiled it underneath the faucet, he opened the door and gestured for her to enter.

The apartment was cool and dim, the miniblinds on the broad living room window turned at an angle to restrict any line of sight from outdoors. Clenching her keys tightly in one hand, Quin walked to the center of the room and hesitantly turned. The living/dining room and the kitchen were cleaner than she ever seemed to manage in her own house. The only thing out of place was the Sunday paper, scattered in sections across the coffee table and the couch. Of course, it wasn't fair to compare this immaculately neat place with the mess and clutter of her own home. After all, Mac wasn't living with a nine-year-old child.

Although he very well might be, once she told him everything. He could insist on sharing custody of their daughter, could bring her here to live half the time. Even worse, he could demand full custody to make up for the nine years Quin had denied them. She couldn't blame him if he did, but, heaven help her, how could she make it without her daughter?

"I'm going to take a shower," he said from his position near the door. "Make yourself comfortable."

She nodded as he went into the bedroom, which opened off the living room, but she didn't move from where she stood. How could she get comfortable when she was taking him to meet his daughter for the very first time and lying all the way?

Deliberately she forced her attention to the room again. It wasn't quite what she'd expected. Having no ties the way he did, she'd thought his apartment would be rather sterile and functional. Not pleasing. Not welcoming. But the colors were soft—cream and pale greens and blues—and there were plants on the corner tables. On the walls were plaques, citations and paintings—originals, she thought, mostly in the lovely spare Japanese style. To the right of the TV and VCR was a stack of tapes, all neatly labeled, mostly old movies, and a bookcase, filled to overflowing, except for the top shelf.

That shelf was reserved for photographs. She tried to ignore them, but they drew her across the room for closer study. For the most part they were old. There were several black-and-white shots of a man with a strong resemblance to Mac. His father? she wondered. Cady's grandfather? And there were three pictures of Mac and David. Two had been taken before they had come to Camp Lejeune, and the third had been snapped in front of an all-too-familiar building: the last barracks where their company had been quartered. She had seen few shots of it like this, standing unharmed. Most of the photos she'd come across consisted mainly of rubble: a few walls standing here and there, twisted steel support beams, a giant crater filled with bricks, concrete and pieces of everyday life—bunks, desks, bits of clothing. Quin picked up that photograph and cradled it in both hands. The two most important men in her life, she thought with a sigh. One she had loved dearly, as

Finally a Father 53

dearly as any best friend was ever loved, but not as a husband, and the other…

Her feelings for Mac had been so confused. He had shaken up her perfect little world. Her life had been planned for years—by her parents, by David and his parents, by the naive child she had been. There had been no room in it for one tough, intense, dark-eyed man.

She had loved David, but she had come dangerously close to falling *in* love with Mac. He had excited her in ways that David couldn't. He had mesmerized her, had enticed and frightened her. She had wanted—oh, heavens, how she had wanted—him, but she had been afraid. He had been too different, too serious, too much the loner. David was such a sure thing, and Mac was totally a mystery. David was comfortable and familiar.

Mac was definitely *un*comfortable.

In the end, she'd gone for the sure thing, only it hadn't been. Too bad she hadn't reached that conclusion before she'd found herself standing in a church in Morehead City, wearing a hurriedly shopped-for wedding gown, after the deed had been done. The families had believed she was teary-eyed because she was so happy, because she had achieved her life's dream, because she was now Mrs. David Ellis. And Quin had let them. She'd never told anyone that the tears were for Mac.

Her hand unsteady, she returned the frame to the shelf, then picked up the next one. It held an eight-by-ten portrait of a girl, a school picture in the same unnatural pose that Quin remembered from her own senior picture. But where Quin had smiled in her picture, this girl was solemn. Sad. Her hair was long and straight, dark brown, parted in the middle. Her makeup was too heavy, her eyes too hopeless, but she was a lovely girl.

Who was she? A relative, maybe a sister? Mac had never mentioned a sister, but then, he'd never mentioned any family at all. As far as she knew, he had no family to offer Cady— no grandparents, no aunts or uncles or cousins. He had no one but himself...but that was more than enough. That was all she needed.

Or, came the sly thought, maybe this girl was an old girlfriend. One who he still cared enough about to display her photograph after all these years.

Jealousy really was an ugly feeling.

"Are you ready?"

Still holding the photograph, she turned to see him standing in the bedroom door. He had on jeans now, softly worn and snug, and a red T-shirt. He wore red a lot—he'd worn it that fateful night. She had always wondered whether he simply liked the color, if he knew how well it set off his dark good looks, or if he chose it because red and gold were Marine Corps colors. Marines did tend to have a little excess esprit de corps.

His gaze dropped to the photo, and she looked down at it once more, at those sad, sad eyes, before returning it to its place on the shelf. He had to know that she was curious, but he didn't volunteer any information about the girl, about who she was or why she was sad or what she meant to him, and Quin didn't ask. She didn't have the right.

He opened the door as she crossed the room, then locked it behind them. "Want to take my car?"

She gave the sports car a wistful look, then shook her head. "I have to bring Cady back. We'd better take mine."

It wasn't far to the restaurant—a few miles down Western Avenue, another mile on Marine. Cady was already there. While Mac waited beside the car, Quin claimed her daughter and her gym bag, thanked Kelli's mother and evaded a few none-too-subtle questions about Mac. As she and Cady walked back across the parking lot to leave the bag in the car, her daughter asked, "Is the jarhead the reason we're eating out today instead of at home?"

"Don't use that word."

"Were he and Daddy good friends?"

"Best friends."

"Then why haven't you ever talked about him?"

Finally a Father 55

"I haven't seen him in a long time," she hedged. "I didn't know where he was or what he was doing."

"Do I have to call him Mr. McEwen?"

Quin's steps slowed, the question bringing a stab of pain so real that she winced at it. The good manners of the South had been instilled in Cady from the time she was little. She said please and thank you, she was respectful to her elders—in spite of her affection for the mild epithet of *jarhead*—and she never called an adult by his or her first name only. *Never.*

But Quin would be damned in hell forever if she made her daughter call her father "Mr."

She removed Cady's baseball cap, letting her hair fall free, then slipped her arm around her shoulders. "If it's okay with him, I think it'll be all right if you call him Mac."

It was still wrong, still sinful, but better.

Sometimes people had to be satisfied with merely better.

Mac moved away from the door on which he was leaning and watched them as they approached. David's daughter. *Quin's* daughter. Oh, hell, yes, she was Quin's daughter. He had expected some mixture of her parents—lighter hair, lighter skin, maybe blue eyes—but her mother's coloring was dominant. She was slender and long-legged, not much shorter than Quin—a lovely girl with the promise of true beauty in her face.

After tossing the nylon bag and the Braves cap into the trunk, Quin brought the girl closer. She seemed both expectant and uneasy, nervous. Did she think he would get angry again because she'd hidden this part of her and David's lives from him for so long? Did she think he would lose his temper in front of Cady? Or did she dislike feeling compelled to do this, to share the most important part of her life with someone who had never been important?

Probably.

The admission hurt somewhere deep down inside, in that place only Quin had ever touched. It was a familiar ache, one he had once endured for weeks on end, one that had become such a part of him that he had missed it when it was finally gone.

"Mac, this is my daughter." She drew the girl a few steps closer. "Cady, this is Mac McEwen."

Cady's composure matched her mother's uneasiness measure for measure. She extended her hand and politely said hello. Shaking her hand—so small, her fingers thin, her palm callused—he returned her greeting.

"Mom says if you don't care, I can call you Mac instead of Mr. or... What's your rank?"

"Gunnery sergeant."

"Do they call you Gunny?"

"Sometimes."

"I'd rather call you Mac."

He liked the way she said it, liked the way she was so serious about it. "All right."

"And my name is Cady. That's *C-a-d-y,* not like Katie-short-for-Katherine. People get confused all the time." Releasing his hand, she slid her arm around Quin's waist. "I'm hungry, Mom. Can we go in now?"

Inside, the waitress showed them to a booth. Cady sat beside Quin, ignoring the menu, and fixed her attention on him. "Mom says you knew my dad."

"Yes, I did."

"He's dead, you know."

Mac swallowed hard. She spoke so matter-of-factly, without grief or sorrow. Maybe it was difficult feeling grief for someone you'd never known. To her, David couldn't be more than just a name, a picture. She had never heard him laugh, never felt his arms around her, never known what it was like to have her father's love.

And she had Mac to thank for that.

"Were you over there with him when he died?"

"Cady." Quin laid her hand gently on the girl's arm and gave a warning shake of her head.

The girl turned to look at her, her head tilted slightly to one side. "You said he was Daddy's best friend. If I can't talk to him, then who *can* I talk to?"

"If you have any questions, you can ask me."

Finally a Father

The angle of Cady's head increased until she was looking up from beneath her eyebrows. "You weren't there," she pointed out with exaggerated patience. "He was."

Yes. He sure as hell had been.

He waited until they'd given their orders to the waitress, then asked, "What is it you want to know?"

She thoughtfully considered, her chin resting in her hand, then asked, "Why did he have to die? And why didn't you?"

"Cady!" Quin admonished. Looking from her daughter to him, she said, "Mac, I'm sorry—"

"Haven't you wondered the same thing?" His smile was faint and bitter. "I know *I* have."

He expected her to look away again, but she held his gaze, and he saw in her sweet dark eyes that, yes, she had wondered why he had lived when David had died. She wondered what twist of fate had saved him—the least worthy of them all—when better men had lost their lives. Would she have traded his life for David's? Absolutely.

But then, he would have, too.

Cady was waiting, her attention locked on them, her expression curious and just a little confused. Could she feel the tension? he wondered. Did she wonder at its cause?

He broke the contact with Quin and gave her daughter a reassuring look. "Your dad liked to sleep in late. He would shower and shave and get his uniform ready at night so he could sleep as late as possible the next morning. That's where he was when...when the explosion happened—in bed asleep."

"So he probably never knew anything was wrong," she said solemnly.

"Probably not." He hoped she found some measure of comfort in that. He didn't.

"Where were you?"

"I get up early every morning to run. I was on my way back when..."

"When the bomb blew up. I know all about that, and about the people who did it because they don't like the United States and how no one was ever caught." Again she spoke so matter-of-factly about things that little girls should never have to know about. "Why do you run every day? Do the marines make you?"

"Sometimes, but not every day. I just like doing it."

She grinned abruptly. "You ought to. It saved your life."

With that, she went on to other questions, easier questions. Where are you from? Have you ever been in a war? Where have you been stationed? What was Okinawa like? Did you learn to speak Japanese? Have you ever been married? Do you have any kids?

Finally Quin teasingly covered Cady's mouth with her hand. "You are the nosiest child I've ever known."

Cady forced her hand away. "You always say that the only way to learn something is to ask." In an aside to Mac, she said with a hint of dismay, "She's a schoolteacher, you know. Fourth grade. *My* grade. At *my* school, starting this year."

"It won't be so bad," Quin assured her.

"Yeah, right. You could have waited two more years before transferring there. After all, *I* was there first."

"Ellis is a common enough name. I'll pretend I don't know you."

This time Cady rolled her eyes—eyes so like her mother's that no one could be fooled. "Yeah, right. Can I go watch the baseball game?"

"Only until lunch is served."

Cady slid out of the booth, started away, then stopped abruptly. "Want to come, Mac?"

"No thanks. I'll keep your mother company." He watched until she disappeared through the door into the second, smaller dining room, where a giant screen TV was tuned to the game. She left a curious quiet in her wake.

"She's a nice kid," he said at last.

Regret flashed in Quin's eyes, quickly replaced by the familiar nervousness. Why regret? he wondered. Maybe because she didn't want him to like her daughter? Because she didn't want him to be even a small part of Cady's life?

"Sometimes I think she forgets she's a kid. It's been just

Finally a Father

the two of us ever since she was born, and I'm afraid I've always treated her more like an adult than I should have, but I think she turned out okay. She's very bright, a little too serious, but she gets along well with both grown-ups and kids." Realizing that she was rambling, she stopped abruptly and drew a deep breath. "I'm sorry for all those questions about David. She forgets that, for people who knew him, it's sometimes painful to talk about him."

"All she has of him is other people's memories," he said flatly. "She's entitled."

His response seemed to make Quin even warier. He wanted to shake her, wanted to make her see that he wasn't a threat to her, that he wouldn't hurt her for the world. He wanted to force her to relax and to treat him—please, just once—the way she would treat any other man.

But he didn't reach out. He didn't touch her.

He wasn't sure he could handle touching her.

"For the record, Mac..." Her voice was steady, low, but her hands were clasped tightly enough to hurt. "I always wondered how you managed to survive the explosion uninjured. When the casualty assistance officer came to notify me of David's death, I asked about you, but he wouldn't or couldn't tell me anything. It wasn't until the complete list of casualties was printed in the newspaper that I knew for certain you were alive." She broke off and gazed out the window for a time before continuing. "I wondered what miracle had saved you. But I never wondered why you lived and David died. I never wished you had died instead of him. I never would have sacrificed your life for his."

He stared, his face hot, at the tabletop. She never would have sacrificed anyone, but *he* would have. He would have destroyed everything—his friendship with David, Quin's relationship with him, their future, their plans, their hopes—if she had given him the slightest encouragement. He would have spelled out for David exactly how they had betrayed him. He would have destroyed the best friend he'd ever had if, in return, he could have had Quin.

Would have?

He *had* destroyed him.

He *had* sacrificed him.

And for the rest of his life, he had to live with that knowledge.

With that guilt.

The ceiling fan made a soft humming sound, pushing cool air down onto the bed and ruffling the pages of the magazine that lay open on Quin's lap. She had showered and put on her nightgown an hour ago, then climbed into bed, intending to read only until she got sleepy.

Instead she'd been thinking of Mac.

So what else was new? she thought with a wry smile.

Pushing the magazine aside, she rubbed her fingers across the coverlet that she used for a bedspread. It was a grandmother's fan quilt, made ten years ago by her mother as a housewarming gift for Quin's new apartment in Jacksonville. The ribs of each fan were cut in shades of rose, pale blue and soft green, in solid fabrics and in prints, pieced together and sewn with lace edging to a background of pale salmon. Every seam was perfectly matched, the stitching precise, the mitered corners of the ivory borders forming perfect angles.

Quin had loved the quilt from the first time she'd seen it. On her first day in her apartment, she had made up her bed with her grandmother's eyelet-embellished sheets, this quilt and an even dozen pillows lavished with lace and ribbons and bows. With that single act, the strange new apartment had become her home.

The quilt had done the two things quilts were supposed to do—had kept her warm and had provided her with sweet memories: of her mother, working for hours on end, meticulously measuring, cutting, sewing and stitching. Of her father, never much of a handyman, making the large wooden frame so her mother could properly quilt the layers together.

Of Mac, teaching her things that, in her innocence, she had only imagined.

Finally a Father

Cady tapped on the partially opened door, then stepped inside. She was carrying a book, her finger stuck inside to mark her place. Without waiting for an invitation, she climbed up onto the bed beside Quin. She had outgrown bedtime stories, she had announced a year ago, and so they had replaced the routine with time here on the bed. Cady brought a book, and Quin usually had a book, a magazine or papers from school to grade. It was a nice way to end the day, a time for being quiet, for sharing, for talking if there was something to discuss.

Tonight there was.

"I like Mac."

The sudden tightness in Quin's chest hurt. "I'm glad, honey."

"He liked me, too."

"Of course he did. Everyone likes you."

"I know. Everyone spoils me—Grandma and Grandpa Ellis, and Grandma and Grandpa Austin, and everyone. I think it's because Daddy's dead. They're trying to make it up to me 'cause I never knew him." She brushed a strand of her hair back. "Mac feels bad that Daddy died."

Quin had to swallow over the lump in her throat to reply, "Yes, he does. He and—" *Your father.* She couldn't say that. God help her, she couldn't. "He and David were very close."

Cady turned a page in her book, then, with a sigh, closed it and turned onto her side to face Quin. "How would things be different if Daddy was still alive?"

"I don't know. It's hard to say."

If David had survived, there would have been so many possibilities. He might have forgiven her, might have accepted Cady as his daughter. He might even one day have come to believe that she was. He had been a generous man, full of love and willing to give it away.

Or he might have stayed married to Quin, might have accepted Cady but never forgiven her mother. He might have held her affair against her for the rest of their lives. He might have punished her forever for it. After all, just how generous could a man be?

Or he could have divorced her and told everyone that her daughter wasn't his. They would all have been disappointed in her, would all have been angry with her. They wouldn't have made Cady suffer for her mother's sins, but *she* would have suffered.

As it was, she *would* suffer. When the truth came out, she would have to endure her parents' disappointment, her in-laws' disillusionment. She would lose the Ellises' respect and their love. She would prove herself unworthy, so unworthy.

Mac would hate her.

And Cady…

Closing her eyes on the tears that had suddenly formed, she whispered a silent prayer for her daughter. She could endure whatever bad things her family and the Ellises felt for her. She could handle the guilt and the blame, the sorrow and the shame. She could even survive Mac's hatred. But she couldn't bear it if Cady hated her, too.

God help her, that would be too much.

"Would he still be a marine?"

After a few calming breaths, Quin opened her eyes again. "I don't think so. He was planning to get out when his enlistment was up and go to work for his father."

"Would we live in Morehead City?"

"There, or maybe Beaufort or Atlantic Beach."

Cady considered that for a moment, then wrinkled her nose. "We'd be close to the beach and the aquarium, but I like Jacksonville better." Moving closer to Quin, she snuggled in against her. "He would teach me to throw a baseball better, wouldn't he?"

Quin pressed a kiss to the top of her head. "Probably."

"I bet Mac could do that."

"I think you already throw a baseball pretty darn good—better than any of the boys in the neighborhood."

Cady tilted her head back to give her a chiding look. "There's always room for improvement, Mom."

With some effort Quin managed to laugh and sound rela-

Finally a Father 63

tively normal. "You sound more like a schoolteacher than the teacher does, kiddo. Maybe you'll be one when you grow up."

"Not me. Too boring."

"What sounds more exciting?"

"Anything," Cady replied drily. "Maybe I'll be a pilot. Or an astronaut. Or a marine biologist. Maybe I'll be a marine." In a quiet, thoughtful voice, she added, "Like my dad."

Unable to sit still a moment longer, Quin nudged her daughter away, pushed the covers back and got to her feet. "It's bedtime, baby. You go brush your teeth, and I'll meet you in your room to tuck you in."

"It's barely ten o'clock, Mom."

"Go on." She shooed her away, then, after a moment's silence, followed her down the hall to her room.

Another of Janice Austin's quilts graced the bed, a geometric pattern in primary colors. Quin removed it, folded it and laid it across the wicker chair in the corner. Cady was a warm-blooded child; all her covers always ended up on the floor. So did the stuffed animals she insisted on sleeping with—a ragged-eared puppy, a dirty white rabbit and a black-and-white cow David's brother had picked up on a trip to Maine.

Across the hall in the bathroom, the water taps were turned on. With a sigh, Quin sat down on the bed to wait. When she did, the first thing she saw was David.

When Cady had been old enough to choose, Quin had offered her her choice of dozens of pictures of David for her room. She'd chosen this one, taken while he was in boot camp in South Carolina. He wore his dress blue uniform and looked as stern and tough as a sweet, good-natured boy of twenty could.

Maybe his joining the Marine Corps without ever discussing it with her should have been a tip-off that things between them weren't what they should be. A man in love simply didn't make that sort of decision—a four-year-long commitment—without including the woman he loved in it. But she had been seventeen, naive and foolish. Whatever he had wanted was fine with her. Joining the Corps. Not seeing each other for months at a time because of it. Abstaining from sex until they were married. Putting off their marriage until he was out of the Corps. The hasty wedding before he shipped out. Those had all been his decisions, and she had meekly complied with each of them.

Giving up her virginity to his best friend...that had been *her* decision. Had David even noticed on their wedding night that she wasn't a virgin? She didn't think so. He hadn't seemed surprised or disappointed. He hadn't hinted about it. He hadn't said a word.

Mac had definitely noticed that she *was*.

It had been madness that had led her into bed with him. Passion. Need. The kind of breathless, heated, achy longing that she had thought existed only in fantasy. She had lain down with him, snuggling underneath her mother's quilt, expecting... She hadn't been sure exactly what, maybe the same kind of passion and fiery need.

And she'd gotten it. But she hadn't expected gentleness. She hadn't expected the most exquisite tenderness. She hadn't expected patience and caring and something so damn like reverence.

She had never suspected that Mac—tough, hard, distant Mac—was a gentle man.

Such a gentle man.

Reaching out a trembling hand, she touched the glass, drew her fingers lightly across the image underneath and whispered, "I'm sorry, David. I'm sorry I was unfaithful to you. I'm sorry I wasn't honest with you. But most of all..."

She broke off as the bathroom door opened and Cady padded barefoot across the hall.

Most of all...I'm sorry I married you.

Chapter 4

Mac gingerly lowered himself to the sofa, leaned his head back and, with an inward sigh of relief, closed his eyes. He was in good shape, better than most men his age, but this Wednesday afternoon every muscle in his body ached. His feet were tender and throbbing, his shoulders sore, his neck stiff, and he smelled worse than just about anything he could imagine.

A forced march in ninety-degree heat with full gear could do that to you.

Fifteen years ago a fifteen-mile hump through the wooded training areas on base had been a walk in the park for him. The distance was the same now, the pace no more grueling, and the terrain hadn't changed. It was the years that made the difference.

Slowly he leaned forward to untie the laces on one boot. He'd just completed that task when a knock sounded at the door. "Go away," he muttered. It had to be a solicitor or someone equally unimportant. He hadn't yet met his neighbors, he never got any mail except bills that would easily fit in the box and no one at work knew where he lived.

But Quin knew.

He forced himself to his feet, wincing as pain radiated through them. It was only a few steps to the door, and he took them carefully. He twisted the lock, opened the door and, in that instant, damn near forgot what sorry shape he was in.

"Hey, Mac." Quin smiled hesitantly. "Is this a bad time?"

"For what?" When her smile disappeared and a guarded look came into her eyes, he raised his hand to stall any reply she might make. "Come on in."

As she'd done the last time, she moved into the center of the room and just stood there. She had apparently come from work. She wore a fitted linen skirt in pale yellow and a soft, rounded-neck blouse the color of sunshine, and her hair was pulled back and secured with a yellow bow. She looked good. She smelled good, too, he thought, catching a whiff of her fragrance as he limped past her to the couch. She had smelled so good that long-ago night, so sweet and sexy and...

Innocent. She had been so damned innocent before he touched her.

"Are you all right?"

"The battalion had a forced march today. Fifteen miles in under four hours." He carefully sat down again, then began loosening the laces. When he judged they were loose enough, he pulled at his boot, wriggling his foot free, swearing out loud in the process.

Before he realized what she intended, she came closer and knelt in front of him. She eased his boot away, freed his sock from beneath the garter that held his trouser leg in place and peeled it off. Lowering his foot to the floor, she repeated the process with the other one. There was something oddly intimate about a woman—this woman—kneeling there and removing his boots and socks. It made him remember all too well the night she had helped remove the rest of his clothing. His shirt. His jeans. His briefs.

All too well.

Finally a Father

Finished, she sat back on her heels. "You've got some blisters," she remarked solemnly.

He knew that—had known they would form the first time he'd crossed water and his boots had gotten wet—but for a moment he couldn't feel them. All he could feel, even though they no longer touched him, were her hands—soft, gentle, cool.

She rose from the floor but didn't go far, choosing to sit on the edge of the coffee table. With a faint smile, she asked, "Do you ever think you might be getting too old to play these games?"

He affected a stern look. "I'm a marine. Marines are tough. They never get too old."

"Uh-huh. So enlighten a civilian. What is the purpose of a fifteen-mile forced march in this kind of heat, beyond ruining your feet?"

"Damned if I know. I follow orders. They tell me to march, and I march."

Her smile grew stronger, and for a moment all he could do was look. There wasn't anything hesitant or uneasy about it. It wasn't forced or shadowed with emotions that robbed it of pleasure. It was sweet and lovely, and it was directed at him.

Damn.

"I don't normally make a habit of dropping in on people unannounced," she said apologetically, "but I don't know any other way to get in touch with you. But I see this *is* a bad time, so..."

He repeated his earlier question. "For what?"

"Cady and I would like you to come over for dinner sometime, and I thought maybe tonight, but you're obviously not up to it."

Although he winced at her *obviously,* he silently acknowledged that she was right. The only things he wanted this evening were a long hot soak in the bathtub, some aspirin and his bed.

No, correct that: he wanted a long hot soak, some aspirin

and his bed with Quin in it. He would feel better if she touched him again. He would sleep better if she lay beside him.

Sleep? he silently scoffed. After ten years of wanting her, if he finally got her into bed again, they for damn sure wouldn't sleep, no matter how stiff and sore he was. He would satisfy ten years of wanting, of hunger, of need.

He would satisfy a lifetime of need.

"How about tomorrow evening? Will you be feeling better then?"

"Yeah, that would be fine."

She shifted restlessly, as if in preparation to stand up, and he felt a brief flutter of disquiet. Now she would set a time for dinner, say goodbye and leave as quickly as possible. He tried to think of something to say, anything to keep her here a little longer.

But she didn't stand up. She didn't refer just yet to dinner. "Cady told me Sunday evening that she liked you, and she was utterly convinced that you liked her, too."

She liked you. It shouldn't mean anything. Cady was nine years old; she probably liked just about everyone she met. But it did mean something. It meant a hell of a lot. It touched him, warm and sweet, way down inside where he hadn't been touched in far too long. "I do like her," he admitted. "You've got a great kid."

On Sunday, in the restaurant, he had complimented her on her daughter, and for a moment she had looked regretful. It was there again—contrition. Then, like before, she quickly hid it. Why? Why didn't she want to hear him say anything nice about the daughter she and David had created?

"Mac—" She broke off and took a deep breath, opened her mouth again, then closed it and looked away.

"Am I that hard to talk to?" he asked softly, searching her face.

Her gaze met his, darted away, then came back again. "Yes," she said with a reluctant smile. "Always. From the very beginning. I never knew what to say to you or how to treat you."

"How about like a friend?"

"But we were never friends. We went from acquaintances straight to—to—"

Lovers. He willed her to say the word, to say it just once. To acknowledge just once the intensity, the rarity, the sheer *specialness* of what they had shared that night.

But, her cheeks pink, her smile quavering, she didn't say it. She left it hanging, trusting him to fill in the blank, and went on. "We never developed a friendship. We hardly ever even talked. I didn't know anything about you."

"You never asked."

Bolting to her feet, she paced the length of the room. At the door, she stopped and faced him again. "I was afraid."

She said it softly, shamefully, as if admitting some great secret. Did she think she'd hidden anything from him all those years ago? She had been naive and innocent and as transparent as air. Everything she'd felt had shown on her face and in her all-too-expressive eyes. Every need. Every desire. Every fear.

"No kidding," he said drily.

She stood motionless, as if caught off guard; then slowly, unwillingly, she smiled. "Of course you knew. You knew too much."

"And you didn't know enough."

"I was very young."

Grimacing at the increasing stiffness in his joints, he got to his feet and carefully walked toward her. A few safe feet away, he stopped. "You're still very young."

She shook her head. "I'm twenty-nine going on fifty."

He imitated her action. "Fifteen, maybe."

"The last ten years have aged me significantly."

She meant because of David's death. The grief that was never far gone tightened in his chest. "I'm sorry, Quin," he said bleakly. "I'm sorry David died. I'm sorry you have to raise his daughter alone."

She reached out as if to touch him, and he sucked in his breath, waiting. But her hand stopped inches away, then slowly dropped back to her side. "I'd better go."

Swiftly she opened the door and stepped outside. Staring hard at the silly yellow bow that somehow looked so right in her sleek dark hair, he thought about the dinner invitation she seemed to have forgotten and about an accusation she had made that first Saturday. *You could at least have said you were sorry... You could have said you were sorry David was dead.*

Was that all she had wanted from him? An apology? And now that she'd gotten it, she had no further use for him?

Then, just as abruptly, she turned back. "You should take some aspirin and get off your feet. Come over anytime after five tomorrow, unless you don't feel up to it. If you don't, we can reschedule."

Feeling a little numb inside, he murmured, "I'll be there."

With one last smile, she went to her car, parked beside his. He leaned against the door frame and watched as she drove away. Even when she was out of sight, he still stood there, silently reviewing the past few minutes.

Quin had touched him, had smiled at him, had talked—really talked—to him. She had invited him to dinner, had shown him compassion, had opened up to him.

She had actually referred to the night they'd made love.

So what if his feet were blistered and his body ached like hell?

This wasn't such a bad day after all.

Quin was dawdling in front of the bathroom mirror Thursday evening when the doorbell rang. "I'll get it!" Cady bellowed from the living room, and a moment later the thud of her tennis shoes could be heard on the parquet hall floor. It was a little after five-thirty, and Quin was wearing the third outfit she'd tried on since arriving home at five.

This was silly, she scolded herself. It wasn't a date, for heaven's sake. It was just Mac coming over to have dinner with her and Cady.

Just Mac. The man she'd spent the most exquisite few hours of her life with.

Finally a Father 71

The man she should have chosen over the one she'd married.

The man she'd had a daughter with.

The man she'd never forgotten.

Oh, no, there was nothing silly about her nervousness. Mac McEwen had had a stronger impact on her life than any other person. His relationship with Cady could have more impact on the future than anyone else. He could destroy her.

She tugged at her T-shirt—black, roomy and long over soft gray leggings—and adjusted the glittery gray band that held her hair in a ponytail, then switched off the light and headed downstairs. Her bare feet made no sound on the carpeted steps, so she was able, for just a moment, to gaze into the living room unnoticed.

The television was tuned into late-afternoon cartoons, the volume too loud, but Cady was ignoring the show in favor of Mac. She was showing him something—a baseball, Quin thought—and gesturing as she talked. Sunday evening, when her daughter had talked about learning to throw a baseball better, she had said, "I bet Mac could do that." Apparently, she'd wasted no time asking.

Entering the living room, Quin hit the mute button on the television as she passed. As Cady bounced the ball in the air, Quin reached out and caught it. Before the inevitable protest could come, she shook her head. "The least you can do is let your guest get comfortable before you start demanding coaching lessons."

"I wasn't demanding, Mother. I was explaining my weaknesses."

"Uh-huh. Take your ball and your glove—and, honey, take your cap off in the house—and put them in your room."

Cady pulled her Braves cap off, shook her hair free, then, in a stage whisper, told Mac, "She'll have to go into the kitchen eventually. We'll pick this up then." Then, ungraciously, she took her ball, ducked down to snatch her leather mitt from the floor and left the room.

Which left them alone.

Experiencing a queasy little attack of nerves, Quin greeted him softly. "Hey, Mac."

"Quin." He was smiling faintly, as if amused by her exchange with Cady. Someday, when the truth was out and he shared parental responsibilities, when he told Cady for the hundredth time to put away her things or take off that ratty baseball cap, he wouldn't find it so amusing.

When he shared parental responsibilities... What would that be like? she wondered. Just how much sharing would they do? Would he be satisfied with weekend visits from their daughter, or would he want more? Would his job allow more? Would they take turns caring for Cady—a week here, a week there—and having little or no contact that didn't involve her?

And when he was transferred... Oh, God, what would happen when his time at Camp Lejeune was up and the Marine Corps sent him someplace else? He could wind up at one of the nearer bases—Quantico, Virginia; Cherry Point, North Carolina; or Beaufort, South Carolina—or he could be on the other side of the country...or the other side of the world.

Cady could end up on the other side of the world.

Pushing away that unwelcome thought, she offered him a weak smile. "Have a seat, Mac. How are you feeling?"

"Okay."

But she caught a barely noticeable limp when he walked to the couch and a wince as he sat down. "Does everyone get stiff like this after a march?" she asked as she chose the easy chair angled near the couch. "Or is it just you older guys?"

"Hey, at least I finished. About twenty of those eighteen-to-twenty-year-old kids in my company dropped out. They couldn't go the distance."

She wasn't surprised to hear that he had succeeded where kids half his age had failed. Sheer stubbornness would carry him through. He worked hard and never gave up.

Except with her. He'd given up too easily on her. After hearing that she and David were getting married before the battalion shipped out, if he had applied a little more pressure—a little sweet talk, a few kisses—he probably could have con-

Finally a Father 73

vinced her to give him a chance. Maybe she wouldn't have broken things off with David completely, but at least she would have put off marrying him until she'd dealt with her feelings for Mac. Until she'd given those feelings a chance to develop into something permanent or to wither and die.

But the battalion still would have left. David still would have died. She still would have been pregnant and alone, only this time without the benefits of marriage, income and medical care. Upon Mac's return, she would have needed him more than ever.

But once he'd gotten her, would he still have wanted her?

In the hallway there was a rush of sound, forcing Quin's attention away from unpleasant thoughts. Cady slid halfway down the banister, jumped three feet to the floor and yelled, "Mom, I left my bike at Matthew's. I'm gonna go get it."

"Okay, but come straight back and don't slam—" The slamming door stopped her. This time Mac made an effort to hide his amusement—but not much of one. "She listens to me almost as well as my students do."

"Probably as well as any nine-year-old listens to her mother," he pointed out.

She murmured in agreement. "Look, don't hesitate to tell Cady that you're not up to playing coach this evening. She's a pushy kid. If you don't tell her no and mean it, she'll have you out there after dinner running all over the yard."

"She takes after her father."

Quin gave him a narrowed look. "Her father?"

"David could talk anyone into doing anything. He was a charmer."

"Yes." Her attempt at smiling failed. "He was. Personally, I think Cady has very little in common with David—maybe because she never knew him."

"Does that bother her?"

She sighed softly. "She misses having a father. Most of her friends come from two-parent homes, but she's just got me. And there are things a father would do with her that I can't or don't like to—play baseball, coach soccer, fish, tinker with things. She says I'm a good mother but pretty lousy as a father. She also says she doesn't care, because she's got her grandfathers and her uncles, but I know that's not the same. As far as never knowing David..."

Again she sighed, and this time she lowered her voice. "I'm not sure David is a real person to her. All she's ever seen are photographs, and all she's ever heard are family stories. I think sometimes that he's become something of a legend in her mind. He was this tall, big and brawny, golden-haired, blue-eyed hero who lived the perfect life, had no flaws, was kind and generous and just, and was universally loved by all who knew him."

"Sounds about like the David I knew."

"No, it doesn't." She gave him an admonishing look. "David was a nice guy. If he'd lived to grow up, he would have been a good man. He was kind and generous, charming and sweet, and he was well liked. But he was immature. He was like a kid in junior high with his jokes and his teasing. He was impulsive to a fault. He joined the Marine Corps on a whim. He married me on a whim. He refused to take life seriously. You knew him better than almost anyone else, Mac. Do you think he would have married me if you guys hadn't been deploying? Do you think, when you came back from the Middle East, that he would have been ready to settle down and be a husband? Do you really think he was ready to be a father?"

Her questions made him uncomfortable. Did he feel guilty for taking part in this conversation? she wondered. Did he think it was wrong to criticize David when he couldn't defend himself? Did he believe it was especially wrong, after what he and Quin had done, to speak badly of David? His reply made her believe the answers were yes. "He would have adored Cady."

"Yes, he would have," she agreed. "He would have thought she was the sweetest thing. He would have loved watching her sleep and making her laugh and playing with her. He would have loved showing her off to his buddies—this precious, darling, living little plaything. But he wouldn't have

Finally a Father 75

been thrilled about being awakened two or three times a night, about the messy diapers and the baby-sitting while I studied, or the feedings when she spit up more than she kept down. He certainly wouldn't have been pleased by the responsibility. There wouldn't have been any more loud parties or late-night poker games. No more long days at the beach. No more spur-of-the-moment nights at the clubs. No more movies, no more dancing, no more spending his money on whatever he wanted."

"So he would have grown up a little quicker than he wanted," Mac said flatly. "He would have learned to accept some responsibilities. *You* did it. You were young, younger than David. You were no more ready to be a mother than he was a father, but you adapted. You accepted it."

She smiled a little sadly. "I didn't have a choice. David would have. He would have had the option of ending the marriage and leaving the baby to me. Men do it all the time—walk out, free and easy, and leave the children to their mothers."

He wanted to ask something—she could see it in his expression—and she was pretty sure she knew what it was. Her earlier words—*I didn't have a choice*—had raised a question in his mind. Go ahead and ask it, she silently encouraged him. Remind me that I did have a choice. Ask me why I didn't have an abortion.

Not that she could be totally truthful with him. Truth was, she had considered it. It had been the first thought in her mind, once she'd gotten past the denial. Past the prayers to God to please don't let her be pregnant, and if she was, please don't let the baby be Mac's.

Of course she *had* been pregnant, and there had been no denying that Mac was the father. Heartsick, she had considered the consequences, and she had determined that if she wanted to preserve her marriage, abortion was the best solution. There were several reasons in favor of it—David, their marriage, their families, her pride and her shame—and only two against it: the baby and Mac. Even if she had bungled the rest of her life, in this child she would always have a part of Mac.

In the end, the decision had been simple. David hadn't been a consideration when she'd gone to bed with Mac, and he couldn't be a consideration in dealing with Mac's baby. She had wanted the baby, even if it ended her marriage. Even if it cost her her best friend and the respect and love of his family. Even if it cost her her own family.

She had *wanted* the baby.

But Mac didn't ask the question, and after a moment he looked away. She was disappointed. Maybe if he had asked and she told him how much Cady meant to her and how deeply she had wanted her, then maybe she could have led into a related subject. Maybe she could have told him not simply how much she had wanted the baby, but how much she had wanted *his* baby.

Rising from the chair, she moved to sit at the opposite end of the couch. "Let's not talk about David any more this evening, all right? Just once, let's spend an entire evening without bringing him into it."

The look he gave her was wary, and his voice when he spoke was underlaid with resentment and just a touch of sarcasm. "We did that once before, and look what it got us."

It hurt—his words, his tone—just a little somewhere down inside. Quin wanted to treat it lightly, to make the sort of silly joke David had been so good at. She wanted to ignore his comment and change the subject to something harmless. She wanted to tell him exactly what their evening together had "gotten" them.

Instead, she got to her feet to go into the kitchen. When she drew level with him, she looked his way and evenly, quietly, said, "I'm sorry you regret that evening, Mac."

When she would have gone on, he stopped her with his hand on her wrist. "Don't you?"

Regret finding out for the one and only time in her life how wonderfully passionate and intense making love could be? Regret the intimacy they had shared that evening?

Finally a Father 77

Regret the few hours that had given Cady life?

"No." She saw that her answer surprised him, and that made her smile faintly. "No, Mac. I wouldn't give up that evening for anything." Tugging gently, she freed her hand. "Here comes Cady. She'll keep you company while I start dinner."

Mac wanted to follow her into the kitchen, but a glance out the picture window behind him showed that she was right. Cady was tearing across the yard on her bike like a bat out of hell, skidding to a stop on the sidewalk, jumping off and rushing up the steps. By the time she slammed the door and came into the living room, Quin was already down the hall. Out of sight.

Out of reach.

No, Mac. I wouldn't give up that evening for anything.

But maybe not too far out of reach.

Maybe not as much as he'd always believed.

Cady settled cross-legged on the couch, facing him with an expectant look on her face. "I have my dad's catcher's mitt. It's kind of old, but I take real good care of it. He played baseball in high school, you know. He was really good. Want to use it?"

"Not tonight, kid. I'm still a little stiff from yesterday's march. How about if we do it this weekend?"

Tilting her head, she studied him as if judging whether he could be trusted to make good on his offer. Whatever she saw must have satisfied her, because abruptly she nodded. "Okay. Why are you sore?"

"Because fifteen miles is a long way to march carrying a full pack."

"Yeah, but you're a marine. Marines are supposed to be real hotshots—you know, a few good men, the few, the proud, men with the mettle to be marines?"

He grinned at her. "Has anyone ever told you you watch too many commercials?"

"My mom says I watch too much TV, period, but Grandma says she watched just as much when she was my age. Grandma says Mom was lazy when she was my age. When it got hot, all she did was lie around in the air-conditioning and watch TV. Even now she doesn't like to go to the beach very much because she says it's hot. Well, *of course* it's hot. It's the *beach*. So…'' Cady glanced across the room at the television, still turned on but the audio muted. "Want to watch TV?"

"Doesn't matter. If you want to, go ahead."

"Nah. Do you like to play cards?"

"Sure."

"Can you shuffle good? I like to play, but Jeffrey down the street says I shuffle like a girl. Can you teach me how?" Before she finished speaking, she was rolling off the edge of the couch. She landed lightly on her feet, stepped over the coffee table and took two decks of cards from the shelves where the television sat, then came back.

Mac held one deck in his right hand, tapping the cards against his knee to line up the edges. After cutting the deck, he shuffled the two halves together, then neatly aligned them again with one tap. Cady mimicked his actions, but when she tried to bend each half just enough so that the cards would slide into place, they flew out of her hands and fell all over the couch.

"No one gets it on the first try," he said, helping her pick them up. "Let's try it again."

She got the same results with the second attempt and the third, but on the fourth about half the cards fell into place before the other half fell apart.

"What grade will you be in this fall?" he asked, idly cutting the deck he held while she tried yet again.

"Fourth."

"Hold the cards with your thumb here and this finger here." He adjusted her hand accordingly. "What's your favorite subject?"

"P.E.," she replied without hesitation.

He chuckled. "Yeah, that was mine, too."

"I like math, and I'm pretty good at science." Looking up,

Finally a Father

she offered him a charming grin. "My spelling is atrocious, but I have a heck of a vocabulary."

"So I've noticed. It won't really be so bad having your mom teach at your school, will it? She's not such a bad teacher that all the kids hate her, is she?"

"Nah, she's pretty good. Most kids like her—except this boy named Roger Black from her old school. Our phone number used to be in the book, but he got mad at her because she got him in trouble once, and he began making a lot of phone calls—ten, fifteen times a day and in the middle of the night, and he gave our number to his friends, and they'd call, too. So that's why it's unlisted now." She stopped to rub her nose, then, a little clumsily, shuffled the cards together. "What was your favorite subject?"

"I liked English because I like to read. I didn't have much interest in anything else. I knew I wasn't going on to college, so I didn't care much about my grades. I just wanted to graduate."

"Why? If you didn't like school, why didn't you just quit?"

"Because I promised my father I would finish. It was important to him."

"Does he still live in Philadelphia?"

"No," he said quietly, thinking briefly about his father. He and Cady had that much—growing up without a father—in common. But at least he'd known his father. He had spent the first nine years of his life with him. She had nothing of hers—nothing but photographs and other people's memories. "My father is dead."

"When did he die?"

"When I was your age."

Something in his voice must have touched her, because abruptly, the cards forgotten, she laid her hand on his forearm. It was such a simple gesture, but it made the muscles in his stomach clench and tighten. "I'm sorry. Usually when I ask too many questions or get too personal, Mom says, 'My, we're nosy, aren't we?'" She did a credible imitation of her mother's softer voice before lapsing back into her own no-nonsense tone. "Want to play a game while we wait?"

"I don't know many kids' cards games," he warned, feeling a little odd and disconnected by her touch.

"That's okay. I don't like kids' games." She grinned wickedly. "I want to play poker."

"I used to play poker with your dad every Friday night."

"Did he win?"

"Not as long as Mac was in the game," came the dry reply from the doorway. Mac's gaze automatically shifted in that direction, to Quin, leaning against the jamb, her arms folded across her chest. In the soft cotton leggings that gloved her long legs like a second skin and the too-big shirt, she looked more like Cady's older sister than her mother. She was even more beautiful than she'd been ten years ago—the lines of her face a little softer, her eyes a little sadder, her expression a little wiser.

"So you were good, huh, Mac?" Cady asked.

"I did okay."

"Okay?" Quin repeated. "Look at that face—carved from stone. The term *poker face* was invented with him in mind. He took your father's money—along with everyone else's— regularly."

"What about you, Mom?" Cady asked with that wicked grin of hers. "What did he win from you?"

Quin's gaze met his. Her smile quavered, and a sorrowful look touched her eyes. What had he won from her? he asked himself. The list was short and almost sweet. A few kisses. A little of her attention. The pleasure of her body for three all-too-brief hours. A lot of her passion. But it was the things he hadn't won that had haunted him. Her affection. Her devotion. Her heart.

The look in her eyes warned him that she didn't have an answer to her daughter's question, but her lips parted, as if she intended to give one anyway. Mac stalled her by offering his own response. "Your mother wasn't much of a gambler back

Finally a Father   81

then," he replied evenly. "We never could get her to play with us."

"Aw, Mom." Cady sounded disappointed.

"You can't take risks if you can't afford to lose," she replied, her attention still on him.

She had believed she had too much to lose if she got involved with him, and, he acknowledged, she had been right. David had been a sure bet. Marrying him had given her everything she had ever wanted. He, on the other hand... He could have given her a home—he'd had all that money he had been saving for Chelsea, plus an additional five years' savings—but it wouldn't have been anything special. He couldn't have offered her a family to replace David's family, who were as much a part of her life as her own. He couldn't have brought her new friends, the way David had. He couldn't have guaranteed the acceptance by her old friends that David had gotten. He couldn't have fit so easily, so naturally, into her life.

But he could have treasured her.

He could have made love, so sweet and hot, to her.

He could have been a good husband to her, could have been a good father. She wouldn't have had any worries about whether he was ready to be a father, wouldn't have been concerned that he might not accept the responsibilities, would never even have considered that he might possibly leave her to raise their children alone.

He could have loved her.

Oh, yes, he could have loved her in ways David had known nothing about.

Finally, she broke free of his gaze and he saw her smile hazily at Cady. "Go wash up, honey. Dinner's just about ready."

Quin had opted for an easy meal: grilled chicken sandwiches, coleslaw and potato salad from the deli, and fresh strawberries with real whipped cream for dessert. It made cleanup easier.

So did listening to Mac's and Cady's voices in the dining

room next door while she rinsed the dishes. With Quin's permission, he was explaining the finer points of poker to her. She liked the idea of them together—liked the totally natural way they responded to each other. It hadn't occurred to Cady to be wary or uneasy or nervous around Mac, the way *she* had been for so long. And Mac... She had never known he could warm up to anyone as quickly as he had to Cady.

It made her heart hurt.

Drying her hands, she filled two glasses with iced tea and carried them into the dining room. As she set one beside Mac, her daughter looked up at her. "Look, Mom, I won. This is going to be neat. Wait until I show Matthew."

"You can show him, but no gambling, remember?" She tugged Cady's hair, then shooed her from the chair. "Enough cards. Why don't you watch a little TV? Bedtime's not far off."

"Thanks, Mac. We'll play some more Saturday, okay?"

Once Cady was gone, Quin eased into the chair she'd vacated at the head of the table. "She'll probably wind up beating all the neighborhood kids out of their weekly allowances," she remarked with a sigh. "I came home one afternoon last spring and caught her taking bets from the kids on whether she would jump her bike off the Simpsons' retaining wall and, if she did, how long she could stay airborne. I put a stop to that right away."

Mac, taking a drink of the tea she'd brought him, swallowed wrong and coughed. Studiously avoiding her gaze, he asked, "To which one? Taking bets? Or riding her bike over the wall?"

"Both," she replied emphatically. "The parents were annoyed about the money, and considering that the navy hospital here doesn't generally provide orthopedic services to dependents, any bones she broke would have to be treated in town by civilians. Who can afford it?"

What little she could see of his expression was so clearly lined with guilt that a tingly little feeling started on the back of her neck and slowly inched down her spine. Lacing her

Finally a Father 83

fingers around the glass, in her best teacher's voice, she ordered, "All right, out with it."

He gave her a sidelong look that was as wary as any she'd ever given him. "I'm no tattletale."

"Is she taking money again, or playing stuntwoman on the bike?"

Another of those looks. "You didn't hear this from me."

Quin couldn't help smiling. "You're an adult. Cady expects adults to tell tales. What was she doing?"

He studied her for a moment before finally replying. "Let's just say the first time I saw her last week, she was in the air—about four feet in the air."

"She *promised* me she wouldn't do it anymore," she said with an aggravated, frustrated sigh. "Sometimes I don't know what to do with her. I don't want to be overprotective, but I can't stand back and let her do something that very well might hurt her."

Mac's voice was quiet, reasonable and faintly chiding. "Didn't you ever do anything your parents considered reckless when you were her age? Or did you always lie around in the air-conditioning and watch TV?"

So her daughter was a tattletale, too. What other embarrassing little family matters had she offered up to Mac? Quin wondered. Drawing her foot onto the seat, she wrapped her arms around her knee. "Once, when I was about ten, my best friend and I tied opposite ends of a rope around our waists. Then she got on her bike and I got my roller skates, and she towed me down the street." She watched him watch her, his expression calm, his manner intense. He was one of the few people she knew who listened—*really* listened—when someone else spoke. He made her feel as if what she was saying was important, instead of a silly story about two silly girls.

"It worked out really well until Mary Kate started down this hill. When the road dead-ended at the bottom of the hill, she stopped okay, but I went flying head over heels. I wound up with a bad case of pavement rash on my arms, legs and face, a broken skate, a twisted ankle and a sentence of confinement to my room for the next week."

"So you weren't always stuffy."

Stuffy. The word conjured up images—bankers in three-piece suits, accountants, conservative people. People who didn't know how to laugh or love or live. She didn't like having it applied to her, even good-naturedly. "Am I stuffy?" she asked curiously.

Gathering the cards Cady had left scattered across the table, he methodically straightened them, turning each playing card faceup, unbending ragged corners, before answering. "Let's just say you lack a sense of adventure."

"I don't know about that." She waited until there was nothing more he could do with the cards, until her silence drew his gaze to her, and then she gently smiled. "I went to bed with you. For a naive, virginal, sheltered and very young girl with my background, that was the biggest adventure of all."

He continued to look at her, his eyes dark and searching, his mouth unsmiling. Slowly, bit by bit, her smile drooped, then faded. She wanted to apologize for bringing it up. She wanted to tell him she was sorry for the way that evening had ended. She wanted to call back the hurtful words she'd said after they'd made love the second time, when the need had been sated and the passion had faded, when reality and understanding and the shock of what she had done with David's best friend had set in.

She wanted to tell him she had lied, that she hadn't used him, that she wouldn't have made love just as easily with any other man—not even David. She wanted to make him remember only the good from that night, to help him forget all the bad.

She wanted to do it again.

"Do you really regret it, Mac?" she asked softly, hesitantly. "Do you regret what we did?"

He looked angry, and frustrated because he had no outlet for that anger. "David was my best friend. You were planning to marry him."

Finally a Father

"I'd been planning to marry him since I was eight years old. It wasn't official. We weren't really engaged."

"Is that how you justify it, Quin? It wasn't *official?* You were his girl. You'd never dated anyone else. You moved to Jacksonville to be close to him. As soon as his enlistment was up, you were going to marry him. You *belonged* to him, and I…" Looking away, he swore viciously.

Her hand trembling, she laid it on his arm. Immediately she felt his muscles stiffen. She waited a moment, expecting him to pull away, to reject her touch. When he didn't, she made the most of that small contact, gently squeezing, massaging away the tautness, releasing the stress. "*We,* Mac. What we did, we did together. You're no more…" What? Guilty? She didn't like the implications of that word. Hadn't they both suffered enough guilt in the past ten years? "You're no more responsible than I am."

Finally he did push her away. "What we did, Quin," he said harshly, "was wrong. Nothing in the world can change that."

Maybe she *was* simply justifying things. Maybe she was amoral. Or maybe she was just tired of the unhappiness of the past ten years—the sorrow, the guilt, the grief. But those few hours she and Mac had spent together had been too good, too special, to be wrong. Not telling David immediately that she was interested in another man—that had been wrong. Agreeing to marry him when it was Mac she'd wanted—that had been wrong, too. Going through with the wedding, writing all the letters, playing the loving wife, planning the future, being the grieving widow, passing Mac's daughter off as David's—all those things had been terribly wrong.

But they were *her* wrongs, not Mac's.

And they didn't include her evening with him.

"Do you regret it?" she asked again. She had wanted to believe that his answer was no, that on some level their lovemaking had meant as much to him as it had to her. And she wanted to hear him say so. She needed to hear him say it.

He wouldn't look at her, wouldn't even glance her way. She

knew that if he did, his eyes would be cold and hard. But he simply stared at the table, recruiting-poster tough. He wasn't going to yield one bit. "It was wrong," he said quietly, each word carefully formed, strained and tight.

"But do you regret it?"

Finally he did look at her, and his eyes, so dark and intense, damned her. "Yes," he said flatly. "Every day of my life."

Chapter 5

There had to be a special hell reserved for people who deliberately hurt other people. Mac's was remembering the wounded look in Quin's eyes when he'd lied to her Thursday night. It was seeing the single tear that had welled, heavy against her lashes, until she blinked and turned away. It had been saying an uncomfortable and abrupt good-night to Cady long after Quin had left him sitting alone at the dining room table.

And he *had* lied. The only thing he regretted about that evening was the way it had ended. He regretted that the man she'd been engaged to—not *officially,* but engaged all the same—had been his best friend. He regretted that he hadn't done more to try to stop her marriage, even if it was to his best friend. He regretted a million things, but making love to Quin wasn't one of them. God, he would give anything to be able to do it again.

He wasn't even sure why he had lied. Why he hadn't simply looked at her and truthfully replied, "No, Quin, I've never regretted it."

Maybe because there were things she didn't know, such as his role in David's death.

Or because there was that promise he'd made to David. *I'll stay away from her, David, I swear I will.*

Or because he found himself getting greedy again. He'd done that before, and he had suffered the consequences—God, how he had suffered! Only this time would be worse. This time he wanted not only David's girl but also his daughter. He wanted to be a part of their lives—lives that he had forever and unforgivably altered ten years ago. Lives that he had no right to touch now.

He wanted to take David's place in their family.

And *he* was the reason that spot was open.

But none of that excused lying to Quin.

Nothing could ever excuse hurting her.

But hurting her seemed to be all he was capable of doing.

Going into the closet, he took down a box from the top shelf. Periodically when he moved he cleared stuff out—old clothes, old books, unimportant keepsakes—but this box made every trip with him. It, and its contents, had survived sixteen years of moving about—had even survived, thanks to the metal locker where he'd stored it, a terrorist's bomb. A hundred and eighteen people had died, and countless others had been injured, but this ratty box with its meager contents had survived unharmed.

Returning to the bright light of the bedroom, he laid the box on the bed and opened it. These items, along with the photographs Quin had been looking at in the living room, were his treasures. These were the good times of his life.

Not much to show for thirty-five years.

There were more pictures: of his mother and father, of him with Chelsea, a few more of David and one of Quin. It was of poor quality, a snapshot someone had taken at her apartment one night. The lighting was bad, the room smoky, but damned if she wasn't beautiful anyway.

There was a model airplane that his father had helped him complete only days before his death, and the paperback book

Quin had given him. The pocket knife that had been a gift from his father. All of Chelsea's cards and letters—nearly a year's worth before they had stopped coming. The athletic letter, in his high school colors of blue on white, that he'd earned on the track team. A few medals for races he'd won.

And in the corner of the box, his goal: a baseball. It was grubby, no longer white, the writing that had once been stamped on the side now rubbed off. With that ball, he had been the captain of every baseball team he'd ever played on as a kid. Equipment for games had been hard to come by in his neighborhood, where most families' paychecks stretched enough for rent and food but not much else. He who owned the equipment ruled the game, and Mac had been the proud owner of this ball.

With a sigh, he left the ball on the bed and returned the box to its place in the dark closet. It was Saturday afternoon, and, unless Quin had told her otherwise, Cady was expecting him. It didn't seem he could keep from letting Quin down, but if Cady was going to be disappointed today, it would be her mother's doing, not his.

When he got to their house a few minutes later, he found Cady in the driveway, bouncing a basketball against the side of the house in the sort of slow, rhythmic thud guaranteed to drive a mother crazy. When she saw him, she tucked the ball under her arm and faced him. "I thought you weren't coming," she announced.

"We didn't set a specific time, did we?"

"I thought maybe you'd want to go to lunch with us—we go to the pizza place down from where you live every Saturday for lunch—but Mom said no. Did you guys have an argument?"

He shoved his hands into his hip pockets. "What makes you think that?"

She gave him a dry look. "Because she went upstairs and left you sitting at the table alone Thursday night? Because she didn't come down to say good-night when you left? Mom believes in manners. She's never rude to anyone—not *anyone,* no matter how badly they behave.''

So Quin was gracious to everyone in the world except him. What else was new?

He moved a few steps closer. "You want to forget about this, Cady, I'll leave. I came because I told you I would and I always—" *I'll stay away from her, David.* "I try to always do what I say I will. But it's okay if you want me to go."

She gave it a moment's consideration, then abruptly bounced the basketball to him. "I have to ask Mom," she said as he caught it. Going to the front door, she knocked politely instead of racing inside. A moment later he saw the door open and Quin move just barely into sight. They talked for a moment, mother and daughter, then Cady returned, ignoring the steps in favor of a leap from the porch railing. "She says it's okay."

He wished she had at least stepped outside and looked his way. He wished she had at least let him see her, even if she wasn't interested in seeing him.

"Do you usually knock at your own door?" he asked as he followed her around to the backyard.

"Mom's cleaning the wood floor, and she doesn't want me walking on it, so she locked the door. I'm supposed to use the back door until it's done."

The backyard wasn't as meticulously cared for as the front. There were more trees, mostly gums and oaks, along with enough tall pines to dump a load of needles on the roof, the gutters and the deck that jutted out from the narrow, screened-in porch. The only flowers back here were in pots on the deck, red geraniums and white petunias, although in the spring there would be plenty of color in the dozens of azaleas. The grass was sparse—too hard to grow in so much shade—and the summers were too hot to give up such cooling shade.

Cady got her gloves from the deck—two of them, he noticed, even though she'd thought he was going to stand her up—but left her baseball behind in favor of the one he'd

Finally a Father

brought. He slid his hand easily into David's glove. It was a little loose—David had been a big man—but he could use it.

Cady's pitching arm was strong—even through the glove, he felt the sting of a couple of catches in his palm—but her accuracy needed work. He offered her a few tips, but mostly just gave her a target to aim at.

"Do you play on a team?" he asked after a while.

"Nope." She paused to retuck her hair under her ball cap before firing off another one. "Mom said I could only play one sport because it took so much time, so I chose soccer. But I'm kind of bored with it. I like football, but it's too easy to get hurt, and if I did, Mom would make me stop playing everything."

"Do you ever play with dolls or anything like that?"

"Why should I?" She threw a particularly hard pitch at him.

"Because that's what girls are *supposed* to do?"

"Hey, I didn't say that. I was just asking."

Pulling her glove off, she wiped her hand on her shirt. "Grandma Austin—that's Mom's mother—says I should act more like a girl. She keeps buying me frilly dresses and bows for my hair and the kind of shoes that pinch your feet, and Grandma Ellis keeps making her take them back for something better. She says it doesn't matter how I act as long as I'm not misbehaving."

Mac would have expected such treatment if he'd given it any thought. Quin's mother had raised only daughters, all three of them pretty, feminine and far from being tomboys. Mrs. Ellis, on the other hand, had raised three boys, all rowdy and athletic. Obviously Cady's looks came from her mother's side of the family, her athletic interests from her father's side.

"Do you see your grandparents a lot?" he asked, tossing the ball to her once her glove was back in place.

"Pretty much. They only live an hour away. A lot of times my aunts pick me up on Saturday afternoons and I spend the night up there. And every summer my grandfathers take me deep-sea fishing. Mom went with us once, just to see what it was like, and, man, did she get sick. She spent practically the whole trip in the head—that's the bathroom on a boat, you know. She said if they didn't take the boat back in soon, we might as well just throw her over and let her drown 'cause she couldn't get any more miserable.''

She threw a pitch that went over his head and to the right, then raced him to the ball, sliding in only inches ahead of him. Hot and sweaty, Mac joined her on the ground.

"Have you ever gone out on the ocean?" she asked, drying her face with her sleeve.

"I went on a Mediterranean cruise once."

Her look was skeptical. "A real cruise? Or on a navy ship?"

"On a navy ship."

"When I was a kid and heard people around here talk about Med cruises, I thought they meant pleasure cruises—you know, like the commercials you see on TV. I thought that must not be too bad, to join the navy and sail across the ocean and have a pool and entertainment and all that food. It would be like being on vacation all the time. Then I found out it wasn't anything like what you see on TV."

She sounded so serious, but Mac couldn't help laughing. "And when did you stop being a kid, Cady? You're only nine years old now."

"Mom says I'm nine going on forty-nine. Granddad says I was born old."

Behind them, across the lawn, the back door creaked as it opened. "Cady," Quin called. "Come here a moment, please."

"Let's pretend we didn't hear her," she suggested. "If I go in, she'll have something for me to do—she always does when she's polite—and I'd really rather just sit out here in the shade."

Mac handed David's baseball glove to her, then stood up. "You pretend you didn't hear her, and I'll see what she wants. I need to talk to her, anyway."

"Are you going to apologize for being awful the other night?"

Finally a Father 93

He tugged the bill of her cap down to cover her face. "Your mother's right. You *are* nosy."

"If I change my mind and come inside, you're not going to be kissing or anything like that, are you?" she asked warningly, pushing the cap back just enough to peer out from under it. "'Cause I don't like watching stuff like that except on TV, where I can turn it off."

He'd gone only a few feet. Now he came back and crouched in front of her. "And do you see stuff like that a lot around here?"

Her sly smile was at odds with the sweet tone of her voice. "I'll never tell."

"Brat." Tugging her hat off, he mussed her hair, then started across the yard. A moment later, her ball cap came flying past in a good-natured toss.

The deck was small and square and held a redwood picnic table, a lawn chair and a gas grill. Three steps led to the porch, occupied by a woven hammock and a battered wicker rocker, and another step led into the house. He found himself in the laundry room, just across the hall from the kitchen, where Quin was working.

Her back was to him, and she was singing along with the radio on the counter. She wore a man's shirt in pale blue, its bigness emphasizing the slender lines of her body, and a pair of snug-fitting white jeans. Her feet were bare, giving her a vulnerable air. For a moment he stood there in the doorway, just looking; then, before it started to hurt too much, he walked into the room.

"Took you long enough," she said without looking. "Get a couple of glasses from the cabinet, sweetie, would you, and fill them with ice—oh, but first, hand me those lemons on the table."

He got the lemons and crossed the room to her, placing one in her outstretched hand. Her fingers closed around it and, because he didn't let go, around his own fingers. Almost immediately she went very still.

For a moment there was silence—even the music from the

radio seemed to fade away to nothing—then, slowly, she exhaled. "Sorry," she said, not sounding as if she meant it. "I thought you were Cady."

"I didn't think you were calling *me* 'sweetie.'"

He was standing close to her, behind and slightly to the side, so close that he could smell her perfume and hear her breathing and feel her uneasiness. Her hand was trembling against his, and her muscles—in her arm, in her neck, in her jaw—were growing taut. He wondered if she would relax if he stroked her arm or the graceful line of her neck.

He doubted it. He didn't think he had the ability anywhere in his soul to make this woman relax.

"Quin—"

She interrupted in a rush. "I was just making some lemonade. I know it's awfully hot outside, and Cady's been playing in the sun for so long. She likes fresh lemonade with a lot of sugar, and she's so skinny that I figure it can't hurt—"

"Quin."

Just as abruptly, she stopped. He drew the lemon from her hand, laid it on the counter with its mate, then slowly turned her to face him. The position was no more intimate than it had been a few seconds ago, but it seemed so. Maybe because now they were face to face. Maybe because, the way she was staring down, his gaze was drawn most naturally to her mouth. Maybe because he kept hearing Cady's teasing warning about kissing and stuff like that.

"Cady tells me my behavior must have been pretty awful the other night to make you behave rudely."

"She knows better than to tell an adult that," she said stiffly, barely moving her lips.

"But she's right. I lied to you, Quin."

She didn't respond to that. She simply continued to stare at some point in the center of his chest.

He touched her hesitantly, laying the tips of his fingers against her cheek. Her skin was soft, warm, flushed. He had always wanted to touch her, from the very first time they'd met when he had extended his hand, forcing her to accept it

Finally a Father

or leave David wondering why not. Making love to her had been special, but his real pleasure that night had been touching her—not just sexual touches, but innocent ones like this, too. He could have lain there the entire night doing nothing more than holding her, stroking her hair or rubbing her back or caressing her face.

If only she had given him the entire night.

"I have a great many regrets, Quin," he said softly, his fingers sliding away from her face. "But that evening with you isn't one of them. No matter how wrong it was, no matter how unfair it was to David, I don't—I've never regretted it. Even knowing how badly it all turned out, if I could go back and do anything differently, I wouldn't."

After a long, still moment, Quin turned back to her task on the counter. She sliced the lemons he'd handed her in halves, then began squeezing one on the juicer. She was aware that he was watching her intently, but she didn't look at him, didn't dare meet his gaze. She worked methodically, squeezing all the lemons, taking out the seeds, emptying juice and pulp into a tall glass pitcher. She poured in sugar, then slowly added cold water, stirring until the sugar dissolved. When that was done, when the knife had been rinsed, the counter wiped, the lemon rinds thrown in the trash, she finally dried her hands, then faced him.

"There are a lot of things I would change if I could."

"What things?" he asked warily.

"Things I said." She watched that long-ago-but-never-forgotten look flash through his eyes and knew he remembered her insults. Her accusations. The blame she had heaped on him. She had felt so guilty, and she had been convinced that if she could somehow place all the blame on him, then she would be absolved. She had tried, hurting him deeply in the process, and she had failed. The attempt had just given her that much more to be ashamed of.

"Things I said," she repeated. "Things I did and didn't do. I used to think if only I'd been five years older, I could have handled you and David. That I wouldn't have made such a mess."

"If you'd been five years older, you and David would already have been married."

She turned away again, taking three glasses from the cabinet to the left of the sink. She filled them with ice, then with lemonade, and handed one to him. "If we'd had time for a real marriage, I don't think it would have lasted," she admitted with painful honesty. "Remember what you said the last time you came to my apartment?"

She saw by his expression that, like everything else, he remembered the details of that meeting all too clearly. That conversation had also taken place in her kitchen, only a few hours after he'd found out that she and David were getting married in four days. He had been angry, and desperate to talk her out of it. She had been afraid and, oh, so desperate to talk herself into it.

You don't love him, Quin, not the way a woman loves a man.

You won't be happy with him.

He won't satisfy you. He can't make you feel the way I do. You'll never want him the way you want me.

Getting nowhere with his words, he had kissed her, and he had proven his point. The heat had been instantaneous. She had wanted him immediately, shamefully, right there in her tiny kitchen, and she had almost gotten her wish. But he had stopped, and she had come to her senses—or so she'd thought. She had sent him away, and when he was gone, she had cried because, deep in her heart, she was desperately afraid that he was right.

Four days later, standing in the church in the town where she'd grown up, wearing white satin and lace, she'd been sure of it.

"David was my best friend," she said quietly, "and always had been. I loved him dearly, but you were right, Mac. I didn't love him the way a woman loves a man. You were right about everything."

Finally a Father

"I didn't want—" At the sound of the back door opening, he broke off.

Quin smiled faintly. "Don't be apologetic. Go ahead and say 'I told you so.' What I got was no more than I deserved. You tried to warn me, but I wouldn't listen."

Cady came into the room, both catcher's mitts and baseballs tucked under her arm, and made a beeline straight for the third glass of lemonade on the counter. After draining half the glass in one gulp, she grinned at Mac. "Well, you aren't kissing or anything, but at least she doesn't look mad anymore."

"*Cady,*" Quin scolded.

"Heck, Mom, was I not supposed to notice that you were pouting because of him all day yesterday and today?"

"What you're supposed to do is mind your own business," Quin retorted, trying to ignore the flush that warmed her face. "And take that—"

Before she could finish, Cady snatched her hat off, saluted her mother with it, then sent it sailing toward the laundry room door. When it landed slightly askew on a hook there, she gave an exultant laugh and spun around in a circle. "Do I have a good arm or what?"

Aggravated, Quin slid her arm around her daughter's shoulders. "A good arm, a big mouth and a swollen head."

"I know," Cady shamelessly agreed. "But I'm your only child. You gotta love me."

"Uh-huh. If you're inside to stay for a while, take your lemonade and go wash up."

"Then we can play poker, okay? You, too, Mom?"

"I don't know much about poker, kiddo."

"Mac will teach you."

Quin stole a look at him, leaning against the counter, arms folded loosely across his chest. He neither accepted nor rejected Cady's offer. That, the hint of a smile in his eyes suggested, was up to her. "Don't you appreciate being volunteered for hopeless causes?"

"What makes you think it's hopeless?"

"You said it yourself—I'm not much of a gambler." But

she disproved that with her next, softly spoken words. "I never know what to keep and what to discard."

She had wagered that he would catch her meaning, and the shadows in his eyes confirmed that, indeed, he had. "Maybe I can teach you."

The lessons she had learned from him in the past had been both bitter—her own fault—and sweet. The ones he could teach her in the future might be more of the same...or harder, heaven help her, than anything she'd ever had to endure before.

"Come on, Mom." Cady tugged her hand, demanding her attention. "It'll be fun."

"All right. But you get cleaned up first." She waited until her daughter's steps could be heard on the stairs, then sighed. "Sometimes I think she's a juvenile delinquent in the making."

"Nah, she's a good kid. You should be proud of her."

His offhand words filled her with pleasure and an equal amount of pain. They should *both* be proud of Cady. They should both love her and like her and feel protective of her. They should both share the incredibly sweet bond of family with her. She had to find a way to tell him that.

She *had* to.

And she would. Soon.

But right now she needed more time. She needed to get to know him again. She needed to spend more afternoons like this with him. She needed to talk to him, to apologize to him, to make up to him for all the wrongs she'd been guilty of. She needed to indulge herself with the sweet pleasure of his friendship. She needed to delay giving him reason to hate her.

Giving him the means to destroy her.

"What's the problem, Quin?" he asked grimly, startling her out of her thoughts. "Every time I say something nice about Cady, you get this look like..." He searched for the proper words, then shrugged impatiently when he didn't find them. "It's almost as if you don't want me to like her, or you don't want her to like me."

Finally a Father

Numbly she shook her head. "That's not true. I want you two to be..." Friends? That was an insult to both of them. The connection between them was so much stronger, so much more important, than mere friendship. Family. Father and daughter. Oh, yes, that was what she wanted.

The only problem was that she wanted that family to include a mother. She didn't want to be left out.

"I do want you to like her," she said awkwardly. "She's my daughter, Mac, and you're..." *My first and best lover. My passion. My obsession. My daughter's father.* In the end, she chose the most cowardly, the least telling, of her possible answers. "You're David's best friend."

"So why those looks?"

"I don't know." She forced a smile, aware that it was feeble but unable to make it better. "Next time I do it, tell me and I'll stop, okay?"

He didn't relent. He could be the hardest and coldest person she'd ever met.

And the gentlest, she reminded herself. The most unselfish. The sweetest.

She tried cajoling. "Come on, Mac. I said I was sorry, didn't I?"

"No. You didn't."

She closed the distance between them and laid her hand over his, her fingers wrapping tightly around his. "I *am* sorry, Mac. I'm sorry for everything I ever said, everything I should have done but didn't, everything I did but shouldn't have. I'm sorry I was young and foolish and selfish. I'm sorry I was afraid to take a chance. I've been sorry for the last ten years, and I'll be sorry for the next fifty. Satisfied?"

His gaze dropped to their hands, and Quin looked to see what he saw. His skin was a shade darker than hers; hers was a whisper softer. His palm was calloused, his fingers long. There was a great deal of strength in his hands, raw power that could soothe pain as easily as inflict it, that could quickly arouse and oh, so, slowly satisfy. His were strong hands. Working hands. Gentle hands.

Tentatively, as if he didn't really want to but just couldn't resist, he shifted his hand, turning it so that now he was the one doing the holding. "It takes a whole lot more than that to satisfy me."

Clasping his hand had been an impulse. Holding it had been a pleasure. Now, with his fingers slowly closing around hers, slowly moving back and forth, sending little shivers across her skin and dancing up her arm, it became a threat. Sweet, tantalizing and full of promise, but a threat just the same.

With a breathless little laugh that revealed more of her anxiety than she would have liked, she tugged free and headed toward the nearest cabinet. "You've gotten greedy, huh?" she asked, her bright smile making her face and her jaw and her teeth hurt. "Don't forget, I fed you for two months. I remember what you like. I'm prepared with a bribe."

From the top shelf she took a box of caramel popcorn, the kind with lots of peanuts, and a package of his favorite cream-filled chocolate cookies. He looked at them for a moment, and she wondered if he was going to be difficult, if he was going to force the issue, to make her explain her guilt. The good Lord knew, he was entitled to an explanation. She was simply afraid that there weren't enough words in the world to make him understand.

She was pretty sure there wasn't enough understanding to make him forgive.

But after a moment the granite lines of his face softened, and he reached out to take the popcorn from her. "I haven't gotten greedy, Quin," he disagreed softly. "I was always greedy when it came to you. I took everything that you could give, and I still wanted more. I wanted it all."

The demand was on the tip of her tongue: Define *all*. Exactly what had he been offering back then? An affair? Great sex, passion, excitement? Or more? She had been too afraid to find out, too convinced that it was David she loved—hadn't she said so all her life?—and David she had to marry—hadn't everyone expected it for years?

More. Romance. Caring. Sharing. Building a future together

Finally a Father 101

with Mac. How different their lives would have been if she'd given him the chance he'd asked for, if she had explored the things she felt for him. She had no doubt he would have come back to her when the battalion returned to Camp Lejeune. He would have married her when he found out she was pregnant. They would have given Cady a real family right from the very beginning, a mother *and* a loving father. Quin would have been spared these ten years of lies and of loneliness, and Mac would have had someone to come home to.

He started across the room, then came back and plucked the bag of cookies from her fingers. "I bet Cady likes these, too. Grab your lemonade and come on into the dining room. Your daughter and I are going to teach you how to play."

He disappeared down the hall. A few seconds later, she heard the scrape of a chair against the wooden floor in the dining room and, a moment after that, Cady rushing in.

More. Yes, she had wanted more. She just hadn't understood that until it was too late.

Now it would forever be too late.

They had long since given up any attempt at a serious poker game when Quin finally tossed in her cards. "You guys go on and play," she said, pushing her chair back and collecting empty glasses. "I'll see about dinner."

Chewing on one of the toothpicks they'd been using in place of money, Mac watched her leave the room. Across the table, Cady gathered the cards and shuffled them, then set the deck down for him to cut. He picked up the top card instead. It was the queen of hearts. Appropriate. "I think we've had enough for today, don't you?"

She grinned knowingly. "Are you going to send me off to watch TV while you go in the kitchen?"

He relied on the carved-from-stone poker face Quin credited him with as protection. "You're welcome to come into the kitchen, too. I'm sure there's something you can do to help with dinner."

"No, thanks. I believe I'll watch a little television, after all." She scooted her winnings together with his larger pile of toothpicks, then left for the living room. A moment later he heard the TV, the volume turned too loud.

Rising from his seat, he gathered what was left of their snacks and took them down the hall to the kitchen. Quin was chopping vegetables while a piece of meat thawed in the microwave. "You were right," he remarked, leaving the nearly empty box on the counter and tossing the cookie wrapper into the trash. "You *are* hopeless."

"Hey, I won two hands," she protested.

"Yes, but you won them because you didn't know what you were doing." He moved to stand beside her, turning on the water to wash his hands. "The idea is to use strategy to win, not to fall into a winning hand by mistake."

"A win is a win, no matter how you come by it." She waited until he dried his hands, then automatically offered him the knife so he could dice the onion on the cutting board. It had been ten years since they'd cooked a meal together, he thought, suppressing a grin, but she acted as if it were just last week.

Opening the microwave, she poked the piece of steak there with her index finger, then transferred it from the plate to a bag filled with smoky-flavored marinade. "Besides," she continued, "I'm only hopeless at cards."

"And sports," he added. "And Cady says you're a terrible sailor. And you're not much at taking risks."

"Oh, sure, gang up on me with my daughter." The smile she gave him was lighthearted and teasing. "And are you so much better? What risks do you take?"

"I came over here today, didn't I?"

"Ooh, as if that took courage."

He finished with the onion, scraped it into a waiting bowl, then reached for the peppers she'd left in the dish drainer—one green, one deep red and the third pure, unblemished gold. "Being around you takes tremendous courage," he replied as the knife slid easily into the skin of the sweet red pepper.

"Why?" The teasing disappeared from her smile, and it

became smooth, sultry and sensuous. "I don't bite, you know."

"I seem to recall that you did—once, at least."

"I seem to recall that you liked it."

Liked it? Damn, yes. He had liked everything she'd done that evening. He had liked her hunger, her passion, her need. Her kisses, sweet and none too skilled. Her caresses, occasionally too eager, occasionally too rough. Her ardor, her curiosity, her delighted satisfaction.

And he had loved her innocence.

Hell, he had loved *her*.

"So…" Eager to change the subject before they got bogged down once again in the past, he grabbed at the first topic of conversation that came to mind. "What are we fixing here?"

"Fajitas. You do still like Mexican food, don't you?"

"You bet. The whole time I was in Okinawa, I had cravings for good Mexican food."

She stole a strip of yellow pepper, and munched on it, leaning against the counter to watch him work. "Did you like it over there?"

"Yeah, I did. It's a good place for families. I'd go back in a heartbeat."

"You ever regret not having one?"

He looked at her, wondering where that pensive look had come from. "I assure you," he began drily, "my heart's beating just fine." Maybe even a little *too* fine when she was around.

"Do you ever regret not having a family?"

After cutting the last pepper into neat strips, he dried his hands and turned to face her. There was no room for teasing now, no place in this conversation for lightheartedness. "I always thought I would get married, have kids and spend the rest of my life deep in debt for a house, cars and vacations, day care and braces, college educations and weddings. I never intended to be thirty-five and single."

"What happened?" she asked quietly, still looking sad and now sounding it, too. "What went wrong?"

He answered honestly—more honestly, probably, than she had wanted. "You. I wanted you. You wanted David. End of story."

Abruptly she moved away, snatching up the plastic bag with the meat inside, grabbing a platter from the cabinet and a pair of tongs from the drawer. Before he could say anything else, she was across the hall and out the door. He stood where he was for a time; then, slowly, he turned to look out the kitchen window.

She was on the deck, standing beside the gas grill, her back mostly to him. Her shoulders were rigid, but her head was bowed. Occasionally the flames, turned to high, flared, casting their reddish gold light on her before dying down again, and the thin breeze that caused the flare-up lifted her hair from her neck and ruffled her clothes.

After a moment, he followed her outside. He knew she was aware of him—the back door creaked, as did the steps leading to the deck, and his footsteps sounded hollow against the wood—but she didn't turn. She didn't do anything at all except grow a little more rigid.

"Would you prefer that I lie?" he asked, stopping behind her. "Would you rather hear that I'd never wanted to get married, that I'd never cared a damn about having a family? Do you want me to say that I'm happy being alone? That I'm too set in my ways to be a good husband, that I'm too selfish to be a good father?"

"No. I don't want you to lie."

He barely heard her whisper over the breeze and the soft hiss of the gas in the grill.

"It shouldn't be a surprise, Quin. You always knew I wanted you. I think I made it pretty damned clear there toward the end." He smiled faintly at the memory. Yes, begging—for that was exactly what he'd done that last afternoon in her apartment—did tend to be pretty unambiguous.

Her feelings had been pretty clear then, too. *How could I possibly want you when I already have David? He's everything*

Finally a Father 105

I could ever want in a man. And you? You were fine for a few hours in bed, but not much else.

"You should have stayed away from me," she said softly, still staring into the glowing coals in the grill. "I'm more trouble than I'm worth."

He moved a step closer. "Maybe." But he doubted it. He'd seen the issue from both sides—having her, however briefly, and not having her—and he much preferred the having.

"I've hurt so many people," she whispered sadly.

One step nearer. "Who?"

"You. David. Cady. Our families."

"David died without ever knowing what we did. He loved you, Quin, and he knew you loved him. That was all he ever wanted. As for Cady, she's the best-adjusted kid I know. You haven't done anything to her."

"She's never known…"

Never known her father, Mac silently filled in. But that was *his* fault. It was *his* guilt. Not Quin's.

He took the last step and, acting purely on need, slid his arms around her from behind. She didn't stiffen or pull away, as he half expected, but instead came to him willingly. Resting her head on his shoulder, she sighed and just sort of leaned back against him. "Don't you ever wish you'd never known me?"

"And what would that have gotten me?"

"A wife. Kids. A lifetime of debt for a house, cars and college educations."

Maybe she was right. Maybe if he hadn't met her first, he would have fallen for someone else. Maybe he would have loved one of the women he'd dated in the past ten years. Maybe he would have gotten married and fulfilled those long-ago expectations.

And maybe he wouldn't have. Maybe he never would have loved anyone. Maybe he would still be alone, but without ever having experienced the brief, intense passion he and Quin had shared.

"No," he replied evenly. "I don't wish that. You were one

of the good times in my life, Quin, and I didn't have enough of those to give up even one.''

They stood like that a long time; then finally, reluctantly, Quin pulled free of his embrace. Opening the plastic bag, she used the tongs to pull the meat out and laid it on the grill. There was a sizzle, a wisp of smoke, and the aroma of steak filled the air almost immediately. She adjusted the heat, sat down on the picnic table, then looked at him. "I don't know much about you."

"You know plenty."

She shook her head. She knew the important things—that he was a good man. That he was honest and decent. She knew that their evening together had cost him dearly in terms of pride, shame and guilt. She knew he was as tough as any marine and as gentle as any man. She knew that his touch was arousing, that his effect on her was potent. Even just now, when he'd held her to comfort her, she had found things far more intimate than comfort dancing through her mind.

She knew that he would be a good father to Cady.

She knew that he would have been good to her, too, had she not lied to him. Had she not chosen to deceive him for ten long years.

She knew that he was going to break—no, *she* would be responsible for the breaking of her heart, not Mac. It was her lies, her deception, her selfishness, her cowardice.

Later, a soft voice whispered. She would think about those things later. For now she chose a safer topic, one she didn't mind asking about, one he couldn't mind answering. "For instance, I know you like to run, but I don't know why."

"For exercise? To stay in shape?"

She shook her head, not accepting those answers.

He pulled the lawn chair closer, slumped down in it and propped his feet on the table beside her. Speaking of running…his shoes were an old pair, broken in and broken down, no longer worthy of the top-quality name emblazoned across the leather but probably entirely too comfortable to throw

Finally a Father

away. How many miles had he put on them? she wondered. Hundreds? Thousands?

"I was on the track team in high school," he remarked.

Initially she was surprised. David had been a talented athlete—had lettered in football, wrestling and baseball, had been the captain of the football team, the pitcher of the baseball team. People had always just looked at him and automatically thought *jock*. But Mac... He'd never shown much interest in sports, and he wasn't much of a team player. He'd always been distant and more than a little aloof, even with the marines he had considered friends.

But after she considered it a moment, her surprise faded. Track wasn't much of a team sport; the events, except for the relay, were mostly individual competitions. No doubt Mac had excelled in things he'd done by himself for himself.

"Why track?" she asked. "I don't imagine many little boys say, 'I want to be a track star when I grow up.'"

He grinned. "I doubt it, but then, not many little boys grow up where I did. In my neighborhood, it paid to be fast on your feet. If you weren't, you stood a good chance of getting arrested or shot—or worse."

What could possibly be worse to a teenage boy, she wondered, than getting arrested or shot? Something totally foreign to the life she'd lived.

Suddenly serious again, he went on. "The part of Philadelphia where I grew up was pretty tough. You see places like it on the news—in New York or Miami, Baltimore or Boston. They're all the same. They look like something in a war zone. Half the buildings are condemned, and the other half ought to be. The stores are boarded up, windows are broken, half the tenements don't have heat or water. *Slums*. That's a good word. You don't know how well it fits until you've lived there."

Quin swallowed hard. She had long suspected that the life he'd lived before joining the marines hadn't been an easy one. That would have explained his maturity, considerable even for a twenty-five-year-old. It would have helped explain that ages-old look in his eyes that had haunted her from the very first time they'd met.

"I started running when I was a kid. It gave me something to do, kept me busy and out of the apartment—and with my stepfather, staying out of the apartment was my number one priority. There wasn't a track anywhere close by, so I ran on the streets. I discovered that, within a few miles in any direction, there was an entire new world out there—places I hadn't even known existed. When I was running, I could be anyone and I could be from anywhere. I didn't have to be this poor kid from the projects. It was freeing—an escape from a life that wasn't the greatest."

"And what are you trying to escape now?"

"I've been trying to run away from you for ten years—from you, from David, from myself—but it doesn't work. That was the first thing I learned back when I was ten years old. It doesn't really change things. When you quit running, you're right back where you started. It doesn't take you anywhere."

"I don't know." Sliding to her feet, she smiled faintly. "It took you places you hadn't even known existed. And more important…" She paused to turn the steak on the grill, then crouched beside his chair and clasped his hand.

"It brought you here."

Chapter 6

Quin was getting dressed on Sunday morning when the phone rang. Since Mac was due to pick them up any minute now for dinner, she stepped out into the hallway, leaning over the railing at the top of the stairs to hear her daughter's voice. She hoped it wasn't him, hoped he wasn't canceling or postponing. She was anxious to see him again.

Yesterday had been an extraordinary day. He had held her, had smiled for her, had admitted that he'd cared for her. Heavens, he had even opened up about himself, sharing a few confidences from the mystery that was his past.

She was curious to see what today might bring.

"Hey, Granny." Cady's greeting drifted up the stairs, and Quin gave a sigh of relief. It was her mother, who, no doubt, was wearing one of those aggravated looks that she managed so well. It was her own fault for letting Cady know how much she hated the title of Granny; now—even though Cady called her Grandma to everyone else—Janice would never hear anything from her but Granny. Kids were funny that way.

Quin was turning back toward the bathroom when her

daughter's next words stopped her. "We're having lunch with Mac—he's Mom's new friend—and he's supposed to be here soon. He's never late—he's a marine, and they're not allowed to be late, you know. He's taking us out somewhere, and then I don't know what we'll do."

Thank you, Cady, Quin mouthed as she went into the bathroom and closed the door. Now her mother would want to know who this new "friend" was. She would want to know everything about him, and she would ask six million questions in that sort of worried manner she always affected when the subject was Quin and a man.

Sometimes she thought her mother didn't want her to ever fall in love again. She wanted her to spend the rest of her life as David's widow, a brave soul who'd lost her one true love and spent the rest of her days pining for him. She was comfortable with things as they stood: it was just the Austins, the Ellises and Quin and Cady. If she ever remarried, her husband and his family—provided he had one—would upset the balance. The Ellises would be pushed out of their proper place, and her mother, Quin was fairly certain, wouldn't like that.

She'd told her mother once that she had no cause for worry. The few men she'd gone out with in recent years hadn't presented a threat of any sort to the Ellises' status in the Austin family circle. None of them had inspired the sort of friendship that she and David had shared; none of them had come close to igniting the passion that Mac had created within her.

But when she'd told Janice that, David had been dead and Mac only a dream from the past.

But now he was back.

Facing her reflection in the mirror, she pulled her hair back, securing it with a heavy wooden clasp. Then she sprayed on perfume and began putting on her jewelry: a pair of dangly wooden earrings, a funky little lapel pin on her left shoulder, a watch around her left wrist and a gold chain around the right. The only thing left in the white ceramic dish where she kept her most frequently worn jewelry was her wedding ring.

David's ring.

Finally a Father

Hesitantly she picked it up, holding it to the light. It needed cleaning; the diamonds had lost a little of their dazzle. It was a lovely ring, more than David could ever have afforded on his Marine Corps salary and with his extravagant spending habits. She had always suspected that his parents had paid the major portion, but she had never asked, and they had never mentioned it.

Slowly she slid it into place on her left hand, then removed it and tried it on the right. It was too loose there; her right fingers were a half size smaller than her left.

Too loose on her right hand, too wrong on her left.

Clenching it inside her fist, she went into her bedroom, opened the small wooden jewelry case on the dresser and laid it inside. And as she closed the lid and turned away, she remembered Mac talking last night about freeing experiences. Now she knew exactly what he'd meant.

For the first time in ten years she truly felt free.

She was halfway down the stairs when Cady called, "Telephone, Mom." At the same time, the doorbell rang. "Tell your grandmother I can't come to the phone right now," she instructed as she headed for the door.

Instead of obeying, Cady dropped the phone to the floor and raced to meet her. "I'll get the door. You talk to your mother."

"Cady, do as I say."

Her daughter gave a drawn-out, put-upon sigh. "I'm not going to lie to her."

"I didn't ask you to lie. Tell her I've got company and I'll talk to her later." Much, much later, if she could manage it.

She waited until Cady returned to the living room before she opened the door. Mac was standing on the porch, talking to one of her neighbors out in the street. When she joined him, he brought the conversation to an end, then gave her a slow look. She had chosen the longer, loose-fitting khaki shorts and the snug white tank top for comfort and coolness, but with that one look, she discovered that she was much warmer than she would have been, covered head to toe.

"Nice," was all he said, but he said it in a way that made

her breath catch right in the middle of her chest, and he looked at her in a way that made her think she might as well be stripped naked.

Oh, didn't she wish!

"Hey," she greeted him huskily.

Slowly he brought his gaze back to her face, and just as slowly he smiled. "Hello, Quin."

"'Hello, Quin'?" she echoed. "You look at me like that and then say, 'Hello, Quin'? Isn't that a little formal?"

"Look at you like what?"

Taking a step back, she subjected him to a similar inspection, and the tightness in her chest spread down into her stomach. My, oh, my, but he was handsome. Lean and hard, dark as sin and twice as lethal. He made her weak inside. He made her hungry.

He made her ache.

"Ah, that look," he said with a grin. "The one that makes me want to—"

Before he could go on, the door flew open and Cady burst out onto the porch. "Hey, Mac. Where're we going for lunch? I'm hungry."

It took him a few seconds to draw his gaze from Quin, seconds that set her nerves tingling and doubled the heat already flowing through her. "That's up to you and your mom," he replied finally, when he was looking at Cady.

"How about someplace up in Beaufort?" she suggested.

"Beaufort," he repeated, mimicking her long *o* pronunciation. "I went to boot camp in a town by the same name in South Carolina, and down there we call it *Bewfort*."

She gave him a decidedly patronizing look. "Well, down there, they are wrong. *Bofort* is the proper French pronunciation."

"It is, huh?" he asked with a grin. "Okay, so fill me in. What's in Beaufort?"

"Nothing," she replied with an innocent smile.

Quin slid her arm around her daughter's waist and pulled her close. "Gee, Cady, I bet the tourism folks up in Beaufort

Finally a Father

will be glad to hear that." To Mac, she explained, "It's a lovely old waterfront town that has a good number of historical sites and some wonderful restaurants and, best of all, it just happens to be only a short distance from my parents' house in Morehead City."

Looking absolutely guileless, Cady said, "Mom's right. Beaufort does have some wonderful restaurants, and if we should happen to go near Grandma's house... Grandma said I can come up and spend the night, and if Mom takes me up there today, she'll bring me home tomorrow."

Mac leaned back against the railing, his arms folded across his chest. "You said you go up there a lot, so why is this something you have to approach obliquely instead of just asking?"

"Obliquely," she repeated, drawing out the syllables. "I like that. Well, I have to approach this obliquely because Mom's in trouble with Grandma for refusing to talk to her on the phone this morning. She told me to tell her that she wasn't here—"

"Cady," Quin interrupted in her best chiding voice, but her daughter didn't notice.

"And that she'd been rushed to the hospital—"

"*Cady.*"

"But instead I told her that she was out on the porch with her boyfriend, and that since I'm just a young, naive child, it was probably best if I didn't see what she was doing out there."

"Cady Elizabeth, that's enough," Quin admonished, her cheeks turning pink. "Do you want to spend the night with your grandmother?"

"Gee, didn't I make that clear already?"

"Then run up and pack your bag. Don't forget your toothbrush—and leave that ratty baseball cap here."

As the door banged shut, she closed her eyes for a moment, then gave a great sigh. "That child is such a treasure," she said dryly.

"You know she is. I used to wonder about you—about what

it was like without David. I wondered how you were getting along. If I'd known you had Cady, I don't think I would have worri—wondered so much.''

Worri...? He had worried about her. His slip touched her. "I wish you had called me sometime in the last ten years, Mac," she said wistfully. "I wish I had called you."

"You didn't know where I was."

But she could have found him. At any time during those years she could have gone out to Camp Lejeune, could have explained the situation to someone out there, and they would have notified him. They would have found him wherever he was stationed and informed him that he was a father, that he had a little girl who needed him very much.

Her guilt that she had never done it saddened her.

But he didn't let her stay sad long. "So what misfortune has brought you into trouble with your mother?"

"Cady exaggerates, but her basic story was true. I used you as an excuse to avoid talking to Mama. Listen, Mac..." She hesitated. She had hoped to spend as much time as possible with him today, but if he accepted the offer she was about to make, that wouldn't be possible. Still, she had to do it. It wouldn't be fair if she didn't. "I can take Cady to Morehead City after lunch. You don't have to go along."

Mac studied her for a moment. His first impulse was to think she didn't *want* him to go along, but there was nothing in her expression to indicate that. She looked uneasy and a little embarrassed, but not reluctant. Not ashamed.

"Is there some reason why I wouldn't want to go?"

"They wouldn't be rude, I'm sure, but... You see, I haven't dated very much since David died. I can't even remember the last time I went out."

That was nice to know. Of course, he wasn't much better off. He remembered his last date, but only vaguely. Only because the woman had given him an ultimatum: get serious or get out. He'd gotten out and had never regretted it.

"Anyway, the point is, my parents—especially my mother—still think of me as belonging to David."

Finally a Father

"And they might resent seeing you with another man."

She shrugged.

If he looked at it from a skewed enough viewpoint, what she was saying was something of a compliment—that her parents might think he was a danger to her status as David's widow. Straight on, though, it looked a little different. It looked as if, instead of competing for Quin against David himself, as he'd done ten years ago, now he was going to have to compete against her parents and, worst of all, against David's memory.

He hadn't been able to defeat the man in the flesh ten years ago. How could he compete now against the legendary hero he had become?

"What do you think, Quin?" he asked. "How do you think of yourself? As David's widow? As Cady's mother? Or as a woman?"

She looked down at her hands, and for the first time he noticed that the diamond ring was gone. It had left a circle of pale skin behind. He reached for her hand and drew his fingertip over that skin, feeling a slight indentation. She had worn that ring for years—over thirty-six hundred days—and now she had removed it. Now she had put it away.

"David is dead," she said softly, wrapping her fingers around his. "But I'm not. We were married less than three and a half months. We actually lived together only four days. And for ten long years, I've been his widow. It's time."

Time to put the ring away? Time to move on? Time to start living again? He didn't ask. He was satisfied with the absence of the ring. That was a good enough start.

"So..." Using her hand for leverage, he pulled her closer. "Do you want to have lunch here, in Beaufort or in Morehead City?"

It was a simple question to bring such a sweet smile. "There *are* some nice places in Beaufort."

"All right," he agreed. "We'll eat in Beaufort."

After lunch Cady directed Mac, driving Quin's car, back across the bridge into Morehead City, through town and to her grandparents' house. He'd been there a few times before, on the day he and David had moved Quin into her apartment. At the time, not having met her yet, he'd been more interested in the Ellis house next door. His introduction to Quin had changed all that. No one had interested him as much since.

The Austin house wasn't showy, but it was impressive all the same. Big, three stories, with great pillars and a wide veranda, it was set in the center of a broad lawn that sloped down to the sound in back. The house was incredibly white, the grass incredibly green, the whole picture so perfectly Southern.

It was the perfect place for Quin.

Cady jumped out of the car as soon as Quin got out and went racing for the house. Quin was shaking her head when she met him at the trunk, where he'd gone to get Cady's bag. "She acts as if she hasn't seen them in ages."

"It probably thrills them to know she misses them that much." A few items had spilled from the bag, and he leaned over to pick them up: a toothbrush, a candy bar, her Braves cap and her stuffed cow. Sliding the forbidden cap underneath the cow, out of sight, he returned everything to the bag. "Funny. I never figured her for stuffed animals."

"She would die if any of the kids at home knew she still slept with them. I guess they're just her version of a security blanket. She has her stuffed animals, I have my quilt."

Mac stood motionless for a second. *My quilt.* Jeez, that brought back memories. Once all of Quin's furniture had been moved into her apartment, David had gone to the store for cold beer and snacks, leaving Mac to reassemble her bed... with her help. They'd gotten it together, and she had immediately set about making it with frilly sheets and pillows and that quilt. When she was finished, they had both stood there for a moment, simply looking at it, imagining... No doubt she'd been thinking about her first night in that bed with David. And *he* had been considering what he wouldn't give to have just a few hours with her there.

In the end, he'd gotten those few hours, and he'd discovered

Finally a Father 117

there wasn't anything he wouldn't sacrifice for them. Not even David.

And in ten years nothing had changed. There still wasn't anything he wouldn't sacrifice for a relationship with Quin. Not even himself.

Aware that she was waiting, he pushed the stuffed cow deeper into Cady's bag, then began zipping it. He was almost finished when Quin spoke softly.

"You sneak. Don't think I didn't see that cap you tried to hide."

He gave her a look that admitted no guilt. "What do you have against baseball caps?"

"Nothing, but I do have something against the filthy, shapeless, torn and disreputable piece of garbage in that bag. She has other caps at home—new ones that aren't sweat-stained—but she prefers this one."

"It must hold some significance for her." Like Quin's quilt did for him. "Don't you hold on to anything special that no one else understands?"

She pretended to consider it, then shook her head. "Nope. The only thing special in my life that no one else understands is Cady."

As he closed the trunk, movement across the manicured lawn caught his eye. Cady and her grandparents had come outside onto the veranda, and in the double doorway were two young women—Quin's sisters? So the whole family had turned out for this meeting. He should be lucky, he supposed, that David's family hadn't been called in for reinforcements. "You know," he began softly, "I can just wait out here while you talk to them."

She followed his gaze to the house. "Coward." Then she grinned. "My family wouldn't be so easily deterred. They can come out here and talk in the driveway just as easily as they can in the house. Come on."

She waited until they had reached the sidewalk before she added, "Oh, by the way, Mac, did I tell you that even when I was dating, I never let any of those men meet Cady?"

Which meant that her parents were going to see his presence here as something special. As something significant. Hell, he hoped it was. He'd been waiting all his life to have something significant—something of more than three hours' duration—with Quin. "No, you didn't."

She gave him her most charming smile. "Then consider yourself warned."

Her father was friendly, Lorna and Rochelle were downright flirtatious, and her mother was polite—and polite from Janice Austin, Quin knew from experience, wasn't a good sign. It took her mother twenty minutes to maneuver her into the kitchen on the pretext of fixing tea for everyone. Quin took advantage of the time to prepare herself for her mother's questions.

She just wasn't prepared for all of them.

"All right, so this man used to be a friend of David's," Janice said for the second time. "But what is he to *you*?"

"He's a friend," she replied stiffly.

"Do you like him?"

"I like him very much. He's a nice man."

"But do you *like* him? I mean, after all, Quin, you're letting him spend time with Cady, letting her call him by his first name. Just how involved are you?"

"Mama, I'm twenty-nine years old," Quin said, impatience slipping into her voice. "I don't need to be cross-examined—I don't *deserve* to be cross-examined—every time I become friends with a man."

Janice paused in filling the glasses with ice. "I don't think I like the way he acts toward Cady. He's gotten much too close to her, considering the short time you've known him."

"I've known him ten years—a third of my life!"

"And I don't like the way he looks at you."

Quin's attention drifted back to her front porch and the conversation Cady had ended with her untimely interruption. *Ah, that look. The one that makes me want to—* She could cheerfully have strangled her daughter for not waiting just one more minute. The look that made him want to do what? She could

Finally a Father

fill in a dozen blanks with things *she* wanted, but she wanted to hear *his* answer.

"Quin." Her mother's voice, somehow making two frustrated syllables out of her name, provided another unwelcome distraction.

"What, Mama?"

"Fill these glasses, will you? I'll get a tray and some nap—" Suddenly her mother froze, her startled gaze locked on Quin's outstretched hand. Quin moistened her lips, then picked up the pitcher of tea and began pouring.

"Having your ring appraised?" Janice asked, struggling to sound calm and patient.

"No, Mother."

"Is it being cleaned or repaired?"

"No. It's in my jewelry box at home, and that's where it's going to stay. That's where it belongs."

"I see. So this man comes back after ten years and you're ready to forget all about David."

It was on the tip of Quin's tongue to tell her that she and Mac had forgotten all about David months before he died and to point out how lucky it was for everyone that they had, because otherwise there wouldn't be any Cady. But she swallowed the angry words and instead very carefully said, "'This man' has a name, Mother. It's Mac. If you can't bring yourself to call him that, you can call him Mr. McEwen or Gunnery Sergeant McEwen, or you can call him nothing at all. Now...forget about tea for us. Mac and I have to get back home."

She made it as far as the door before her mother stopped her with the sharp sound of her name. "Quin, are you sleeping with him?"

Now it was Quin's turn to freeze. She stared hard at the raised panels on the door, concentrating on controlling her breathing, refusing to turn around until she knew she could talk to her mother without screaming.

"That's none of your business."

"Is he staying at your house? Is he spending the night there, with my granddaughter right down the hall?"

Quin laced her fingers tightly together. "When David died—" and Mac didn't come back to me, she silently added "—I relied very heavily on you and Daddy, and on Mr. and Mrs. Ellis. I needed a great deal of help and support. Unfortunately, I forgot that I was an adult, and I let you forget. I let you all treat me as if I were a helpless child, and you're still doing it. You still think you have the right to make decisions for me, to tell me how to live my life."

"You were nineteen when David died, Quin. That's hardly an adult."

"I was married! I was a wife, and I was about to become a mother!" She paced the length of the room, then back again, stopping across the island from Janice. "Do you ask Rochelle about her sex life?"

Her mother brushed her off. "Rochelle is different. She's more…"

"More what? Mature? Responsible? I've been widowed since I was nineteen. I've raised my daughter alone. I've supported her and myself without any help from anyone. Don't tell me that my twenty-four-year-old sister who still lives at home is more responsible than I am."

"Experienced," Janice said firmly. "Rochelle is more experienced in dealing with men."

Quin's laughter was choked. "You bet she is. She's had more relationships in the last two years than I've had in my entire life."

"And that's precisely my point, Quin. You've lived such a sheltered life. You never had any boyfriends but David. You never went out with any other boys. You were never involved with anyone else. Yes, by the time you were twenty, you had been married, widowed and given birth, but you were so innocent. You still are."

Quin's sigh of resignation shuddered through her. Speaking calmly, angrily, quietly, she said, "I will not live the rest of my life alone because you think that's best for me, Mother. I

Finally a Father

will not spend the rest of my life as a living memorial to David Ellis because it suits you. I don't know where this relationship with Mac is going. That's up to him and to me. You don't get a say in the matter. If, as you say, your concern is for Cady, then don't worry. My daughter is healthy, happy, well cared for and very well loved. I've never done anything that might harm her, and I never will.''

Once more she walked to the kitchen door, and once more stopped there. ''If you bring Cady home while I'm still at work, leave her at Jenny Simpson's house. And don't forget to make her brush her teeth.''

With that, she walked out.

She took a long, slow walk through the house to the sun room on the east side, where the rest of the family was waiting. By the time she got there, her smile was almost natural. ''Come and give me a kiss, Cady.''

''Leaving already?'' her father asked.

Quin sat down on the arm of his chair, and Cady wriggled in to hug her. ''Are you kidding? It's been weeks since you invited this little monkey up here. I'm going to enjoy my vacation away from her.''

Cady gave her an all-too-knowing look. ''You're going to miss me every minute.''

''Don't be too sure of it, sweetie.'' To the others, she announced, ''You don't know what silence is until you've lived with Cady—and then sent her away. Pure gold.'' She gave her a hug. ''Obey everyone.''

''Even Aunt Lorna? She's not much more than a kid herself,'' Cady protested with an exaggerated groan, and Quin's twenty-year-old sister threw a pillow at her from across the room.

''Even Aunt Lorna. I love you, sweetie.'' She pressed a kiss to Cady's forehead, then gave her father a kiss, too. ''Mac?''

In spite of protests from her family, she got Mac out the door and to the car without having to see her mother again. She was feeling quite relieved and patting herself on the back for not letting on that something was wrong when Mac dryly remarked, "It must have been pretty bad."

"What?"

He backed out of the driveway and headed for the road that would take them back to Jacksonville. "The scene with your mother."

She gave an aggravated sigh. "She means well. I understand that. But sometimes she drives me crazy."

"Mothers are supposed to drive you crazy." He shrugged. "She loves you. What do you expect?"

"She loves the little girl I used to be more than the woman I've become. My mother understands nothing about birth order. She's never figured out that parents are supposed to let the oldest child get away with murder, ignore the middle one and coddle the younger one. She lets Rochelle do anything, ignores Lorna and tries to live my life for me."

"Under the circumstances, I can see why she feels a need to watch out for you. You experienced some major traumas when you were very young."

Quin fiddled with the stereo, seeking a station that wasn't broadcasting baseball or stock car races. "Thanks, Mac. Take her side," she said sarcastically. Finding a country song that she liked, she leaned back in her seat. "What about your mother? Was she overprotective?"

"Not of us. She didn't care much either way about us."

"If you turn left here, we can avoid the beach traffic," she suggested, but her mind was on his answer. After that last comment, would it be insensitive of her to press for more details? Maybe. Probably. But how could she ever find out anything about him if she didn't ask? "Tell me about your family."

"What do you want to know?"

"Do you have any brothers or sisters?"

"One sister, three half brothers."

"You mentioned a stepfather last night. Were your parents divorced?"

Finally a Father

"No, my dad died when I was nine. My mother remarried about four weeks later."

"You weren't close to your stepfather. What about your father?"

There was a distance in his smile. Of course, his memories were more than twenty-five years old. That was a long time. "My dad was a great guy. We spent a lot of time together, did a lot of things together. He worked hard—he had a factory job—and all his free time was family time. He didn't go out with his friends, didn't do anything that we couldn't do with him. He was thirty-three when he died. There was an accident on the job."

"That must have been hard for you and your sister."

He nodded. "Chelsea was seven. She didn't even really understand what death meant. She was convinced that he was just gone somewhere, that one day the door would open and he would come walking in. Then my mother remarried, and her husband came to live with us."

And that, Mac thought grimly, had been the beginning of the end for Chelsea.

"That photograph in your apartment—the girl with the sad eyes. That's your sister, isn't it?"

Sad eyes. He remembered a song that had once been popular, a lament about sad eyes. Yeah, that had been Chelsea in the last few years of her life. "Yes, it is. She wasn't always like that. When she was a kid…" When she was a child, she had been happy, carefree and full of Cady's brand of gotta-love-me confidence. She had loved everybody, and everybody had loved her in return. Their father's death, coupled with their mother's remarriage and their stepfather's intense dislike of them both, had started a downhill slide in his sister that had never stopped.

"She used to be as funny and as self-assured as Cady. She had the same coloring as Cady, too—dark hair, dark eyes—but she wasn't a tomboy. She wore dresses and lacy socks and ribbons in her hair, and she loved to play house with her dolls."

Across the car, Quin sighed softly. When he glanced over, he saw that she was staring out the side window, her head turned away from him. "She's dead, too, isn't she?" she asked in a whisper.

"Yeah. She died a year after I joined the marines. She was seventeen."

"I'm sorry. Mac, I didn't mean— We don't have to talk about this. I know it must hurt...."

Only like hell. "We were very close," he said. "She was my best friend, but this is the first time I've talked about her in nearly sixteen years."

Quin remained silent, and so did he for a few miles. When he began speaking again, he was almost surprised by what he chose to tell her. "I had to join the marines. I was out of school, working, but not making much money, and my stepfather was going to kick me out of the house. The service seemed my only option. I promised Chelsea that she could come and live with me as soon as she finished school. About ten months later, I got a letter from her. She wanted to quit school and come then. She said she couldn't stand it at home any longer. She hated it there. And I told her no. She had to wait until she graduated."

Not yet, Chelsea. Just two more months. You can stand it for just two more months.

"A couple of weeks later, I was at work when the chaplain came looking for me." He remembered clearly the details of that day—so normal, so routine, until the moment the chaplain spoke his name. He'd known immediately from the older man's manner that it was bad news and that it concerned Chelsea. But even that certainty, even the distress that had been evident in his sister's last letter, hadn't prepared him for the news of her death.

"She'd been found in an abandoned building with a needle still in her arm. The coroner said it was an accidental overdose."

Quin touched him, her hand warm and small against his thigh. "You don't believe that?"

Finally a Father

He gave her a regretful smile. "I'd like to. I'd like to believe she didn't mean to kill herself. But the coroner didn't know her. He didn't know how unhappy she was. He didn't know how desperate she was." But he had known.

Damn it, *he* had known.

"It's not your fault. Maybe it was accidental. But even if it wasn't, even if she chose that path, you're not responsible, Mac."

"If I had let her come..."

"She very well might have done it anyway. If Chelsea was that troubled, you couldn't have helped. You could have loved her, but you couldn't have forced her to want to live. You couldn't have dealt with her problems for her."

"If I—"

"Mac, you can't accept responsibility for someone else's actions. We're all born with brains and common sense, with logic and free will. We make our own decisions for our own reasons, and we have to live with them. You didn't make your sister unhappy. You didn't influence her decision to use drugs. Whether it was for recreation or relief, temporary escape or suicide, it was her choice—hers and no one else's."

He slowed for a red light ahead. They were on the outskirts of Jacksonville, with Camp Lejeune's main gate just a few miles ahead, his apartment and Quin's house only a few miles beyond that. When the car had stopped, he shifted his gaze to her. "I like your philosophy," he admitted grudgingly.

"You just can't embrace it."

"I think I could have helped her. If nothing else, I could have gotten her out of the house and away from our stepfather. If I had done that, just that and nothing else..."

She gestured toward the light, and he realized it was green again. "You were nineteen years old," she said flatly as he pulled away from the intersection. "You weren't old enough to be responsible for your teenage sister."

"You were barely twenty when Cady was born—and, honey, I was a hell of a lot more responsible at nineteen than you were at twenty."

"Quit arguing with me."

"You wouldn't be annoyed if I didn't have a valid point."

She gave his thigh a hard squeeze before withdrawing her hand. "The point, Mac, is that Chelsea made her choice. It was her life, her decision. No matter how badly it hurt you, you can't take responsibility for it."

Slowing, he turned onto Pine Valley Road and drove past his apartment to her house. In the driveway, he shut off the engine, then turned and looked at her. "Are you sure of that? What if something I did—or didn't do—hurt *you?* Would you still be so damned certain that I'm not to blame?"

Quin looked puzzled. "The only thing you've ever done—or not done—that hurt me was stay away when you guys came back from the Middle East. That's hardly the same thing."

"What if…" His fingers were clenched tightly around her car keys, the serrated edges biting. With an effort, he released them and laid them on the console between them. "What if I told you that I could have kept David alive? Would you still say that it was his life, his decision? Would you still say that I'm not responsible?"

She held his gaze for a long time, then looked uncomfortably away. "It's getting stuffy in here," she said unevenly, reaching for her keys. "Let's go inside and set the air-conditioning for frigid."

She had already opened the door and swung her legs out when he laid his hand on her arm. "No answer, Quin?" he asked softly, bitterly. "It's easier to be philosophical when you don't give a damn about the people in question, isn't it?"

Pulling away, she got out and closed the door. By the time he opened his own door and stood up, she was waiting there. "All right, Mac. Tell me how you killed David."

Her words made him flinch. God, why hadn't he kept his mouth shut? So she wouldn't blame him for Chelsea's death. Did he have to keep pushing until he found something she *could* blame him for?

No. But he did have to tell her the truth. Before things went

Finally a Father

any further, before they got any more involved than they already were, he had to tell her about David's death. Then...

Whatever happened then was up to her. She might never want to see him again. She might never forgive him.

And maybe she would.

"Do you want to have this conversation out here or inside?"

"Inside."

She led the way into the house, tossing her purse on the hall table and adjusting the thermostat before finally settling on the sofa in the living room. He didn't sit near her, though. Instead, he walked to the shelves and picked up the only photograph of David in the room.

David. Big, brawny, blond. Funny as hell, the nicest guy you would ever want to know. Everybody's friend, everybody's buddy. Cady's father. Quin's husband. Her lover.

"You know the bomb exploded early in the morning, around 6:20." There was no need for vagueness. He knew exactly when the explosion had occurred: 6:17. The day had turned out bright and sunny, as if nature was unaware that one hundred and eighteen men had died that morning.

"You were running, and David was asleep," Quin remarked. "Like most mornings. He did like to sleep in late."

He was still studying the photograph. It had been taken at David's parents' home—he recognized the house—at some sort of gathering, and David was laughing. He had always been laughing. He was, their friends had all agreed, the cheeriest son of a bitch they'd ever known.

"Not like most mornings," he went on. "Sometimes he went with me. He was supposed to be with me that morning."

"So he changed his mind. Heaven knows, he did that often enough. He took pride in being the laziest man in the Marine Corps."

Finally he put the picture down, settling the frame exactly as it had been before. He turned around to look at her. "He didn't change his mind, Quin. *I* changed it for him. I was supposed to wake him up, to get him out of bed to go running. But I didn't want him to go. I knew all he would talk about was you, because he'd gotten a pile of letters from you the day before, and I didn't want to hear him go on about you and your future and the things you two were going to do when he got home."

He paused for a moment, staring into the distance, remembering the shock of the blast, the horror as the realization sank in. "I left without him that morning, and as I ran, I kept thinking one thing—that if he would only go away, I'd stand a chance with you. If he would get out of our lives. If he would disappear."

At last he moved, sitting in the armchair nearest her, leaning toward her in an unspoken plea. "Do you understand what I did? I left him there in bed asleep. If he'd been with me, the way he was supposed to, he wouldn't have gotten so much as a scratch. He would be here today. But because I was angry, because I was jealous, I left him." He broke off, took a deep breath, then, damning himself with every word, he finished.

"I left him there to die, Quin."

Chapter 7

The air conditioning seemed unusually loud in the room. When it finally cycled off, the ticking of the wall clock became audible. Underlying that, Quin could hear her heartbeat and her slow, unsteady breathing.

So Mac expected her to blame him for David's death. It wasn't necessary. He was already blaming himself. What a tremendous burden he carried—his sister's death, his affair with her and David's death. How incredibly strong he must be to survive all that guilt.

Did she want to blame him? No. What good would it do? It wouldn't bring David back. It would only add to Mac's suffering.

And she couldn't blame him even if she wanted to. She'd known David, had known how incredibly lazy he could be. So what if he'd said, "Hey, Mac, wake me in the morning and I'll go running with you"? That didn't mean he would actually have done it. When morning came and he was faced with the choice of leaving his comfortable bed to exert himself or remaining where he was, more often than not, she knew, he would have chosen to remain right where he was.

Mac was waiting for her to speak—to condemn him. It must have been difficult for him, living all these years with the belief that he had caused his best friend's death. Was that part of the reason he'd avoided her when the battalion returned? Was that why he'd never contacted her—because he felt responsible for her husband's death? Probably. She could even make a plausible guess at his reasoning: she was available because David was dead, but he couldn't have her because he was to blame for David's death.

"How many times a week did David offer to go running with you?"

Her question took him by surprise. He had to consider his answer a moment. "I don't know. Three or four."

"And how often each week did he actually go?"

"Once, twice. Sometimes not at all."

"So chances weren't great he would have gone that morning."

Mac responded with a scowl. "He told me to wake him."

"But you woke him plenty of times when he told you to, and you wound up running alone anyway, didn't you?"

He didn't answer.

"I'm sorry, Mac," she said at last. "I just don't see that that makes you responsible. Maybe if you had awakened David he would have gone with you, and if he had, maybe he would still be alive. Maybe if I had voiced more of an objection when he joined the Marine Corps, he would have changed his mind, and if he had, he would have been safe in Morehead City when that bomb blew up. Maybe if his father hadn't been a marine himself in Korea, David never would have considered the Marine Corps, and if he hadn't, he would still be here. But we can't live our lives on maybes, Mac. What ifs, might have beens, if onlys—they'll drive you crazy, and they won't change a thing. The fact is, David is dead, and the terrorist who planted that bomb is the one who killed him. Not you."

"It's not that easy to wash away the guilt, Quin."

Finally a Father

"I know. But if you're looking for me to add to it, I won't. I can't. You didn't choose to let David die. You would have died yourself if it would have saved his life."

"Sometimes I wished I had," he murmured wearily.

Quin stiffened. *Wished,* she repeated silently. Past tense. Not now. "Don't say that, Mac," she admonished him. "Your life is every bit as valuable as his was."

"Right." His sarcasm stung. "He had a wife, a baby on the way, a family. No one would have given a damn if I had died instead of him."

"*I* would have. Losing David hurt, hurt more than I'd thought anything possibly could. But losing you... Losing you would have broken my heart."

That ancient, haunted look was back in his eyes as his gaze met hers. *Sad eyes.* At that moment the expression applied to him as well as his sister. At that moment she wanted desperately to give him something to make him smile, something to bring him hope.

She wanted to tell him about his daughter.

She drew a deep breath, wondering what to say, how to prepare him, how to explain. But whatever words she chose would be inadequate, so she simply said, "Mac—"

And then words failed her. There were so many ways to start: Mac, I need to talk to you about Cady. Mac, remember the night we made love, when we didn't use any birth control? Mac, Cady isn't David's daughter. Mac, for ten years you've had the best reason of all to live. Mac, you have a daughter.

So many simple, easy words, and she couldn't say any of them.

She couldn't give him up yet.

She couldn't watch their friendship, their attraction—their relationship—wither and die before it had a chance to live.

She couldn't turn whatever he felt for her to hatred.

She couldn't lose him—not yet, not now, when she just might be starting to love him.

Realizing that once again he was waiting for her to say something, she gave him a self-conscious smile. "How about some of that tea my mother offered and I so ungraciously refused?" She didn't wait for him to accept, but left the couch and went straight down the hall to the kitchen.

She would tell him, she promised herself as she took two glasses from the cabinet and filled them with ice. She would tell him everything, and she would do it soon.

Soon.

Tuesday evening found Mac waiting in line at the traffic circle on Camp Lejeune for his turn to join the endless stream of cars heading home. In spite of the afternoon heat, the car windows were rolled down, letting in the pleasant scents of a heavy summer afternoon, tempered by exhaust, the sounds of engines revving and the too-loud stereo from the car behind him.

Ordinarily he would be sitting here, sealed inside the car, the air conditioner running and the stereo turned on, frustrated and impatient to get home to his empty apartment and get started on a long, empty evening. This evening, though, he was taking Quin and Cady, back from her visit to her grandparents' house, out to dinner, and that—having someone waiting for him, someone to spend the next few hours with—oddly enough lessened his frustration. He was going to have too enjoyable an evening to start it off with frustration.

Things were getting entirely too enjoyable with Quin. He had spent the rest of the afternoon and all evening with her Sunday. They had watched TV and talked, although about nothing important. She'd told him stories about Cady, about her experiences as a teacher, about dealing with her family, and he'd talked about the past ten years of his own life—the places he'd been stationed, about living in Okinawa and serving in the Persian Gulf. It had been pleasant, comfortable—the sort of getting-to-know-you that they had never indulged in before.

He wouldn't see her for the rest of the week—the next day the battalion was going out on field exercises that would last through Friday—and he hadn't been able to see her last night.

Finally a Father 133

Her mother had returned Cady and stayed for dinner, no doubt wanting another chance to try to run Quin's life. If she ever succeeded, he would bet her first priority would be running *him* out of it.

So he would have to make sure she didn't succeed.

He inched forward in line, then shifted in the seat to blot the sweat trickling down his spine. Back when he was in boot camp, he had heard this base referred to as Swamp Lejeune—sort of like the pot calling the kettle black, he'd always thought, since Beaufort, where the Marine Corps Recruit Depot was located, was surrounded by marshland itself. They didn't call that part of South Carolina the Low Country for nothing. Climatewise, he didn't much care for either base. The mild falls and winters were nice, but the springs were wet, and the summers could be nearly unbearable. It wasn't the heat, as the old saying went, but the humidity. Damn straight. Ninety-degree heat and ninety-percent humidity could kill you.

From the car behind him the sounds of a familiar song drifted on the air, distracting him from the weather. He recognized the tune immediately, in an instant placing it in the context that gave it significance. It had been ten years ago, give or take a few weeks, and a warm, muggy Saturday night. They had gone to a local club—him, Quin and David. She had wanted to dance, but David had wanted to join a few friends at a table, kick back and drink a few beers. Dance with her, Mac, he had suggested, escorting them to the dance floor and literally pushing her into his arms. She had tried to protest, but David had been insistent, and Mac... Hell, he hadn't been about to give up his best chance yet to get close to her.

This was the song that had been playing that night—slow, sad, haunting. The dance floor had been crowded, and he'd held her closer than she'd wanted to be held. She had trembled all through the dance, like a frightened little bird that suddenly found itself in the claws of a big, mean cat. When the song had ended, before he'd had a chance to speak, before he'd even thought about letting her go, she'd torn loose and rushed to David's side.

Mac had stood on the dance floor, watching her go, and for the first time ever, he had realized with absolute certainty that one way or another, she was going to break his heart.

And he'd been right.

He wondered if, by seeing her again, he was setting himself up for a replay of those events.

He didn't think so. She was older now, more mature, less afraid. Although she was still very young, still very innocent, she had undergone a great deal of emotional growth in the past ten years. She no longer had her misguided loyalty to David to contend with.

But *he* had his promise to David.

He had lived by that promise for nearly ten years, and in the past few weeks he had thought of it often. How binding was a promise given to a man who had never asked for it, to a man who had never even heard it? How binding was a vow made to a dead man?

In seeing Quin, he was breaking his word. He had told himself in the beginning that it was all right, that he wasn't getting involved with her. He was just looking out a little for her and for David's daughter. David would expect as much from his best friend, wouldn't he?

But that was just rationalization. He was getting involved. He wasn't simply looking out for her and for David's daughter. He was trying to take David's place in their lives. He wanted to make David's family his own. So his motives weren't good and decent; they were selfish as hell.

And selfishness wasn't a good enough reason to betray David again.

It wasn't a good enough reason to break his promise, to sacrifice his honor.

So he wasn't an honorable man, he admitted with a scowl. He cared more for himself than for his integrity.

And he cared more for Quin than anything.

At last it came his turn. Three-quarters of the way around the circle, he turned onto Holcomb Boulevard and headed to-

Finally a Father 135

ward the main gate. Once he finally made it home, he showered, then dressed in jeans and a knit shirt. Quin had told him she would be home around five-thirty today. He was ready to go fifteen minutes before that, so, without giving it another thought, he left the apartment for his car. So what if he appeared eager? She must already know just how eager he was to spend time with her and Cady. He was damned near desperate for it.

Desperation and helplessness. Chelsea had inspired both in him, especially there toward the end, with her letters. She had been so sad, and he hadn't been able to help her. He hadn't been able to save her.

Quin had inspired both emotions, too, so long ago. She had been so elusive—right there, an everyday part of his life, but a world away from him. He hadn't been able to reach her, to touch her. That time it was himself he hadn't been able to save.

Now the need was of almost desperate proportions—almost—but the helplessness was lacking. I wanted it all, he'd told her Saturday, and this time he just might be able to have it.

All.

He parked on the street of Quin's house and got out. Across the street and down a few houses—the Simpsons' house, she'd said; Matthew Simpson was Cady's best friend, and his mother her baby-sitter—a group of children were gathered in a huddle near the retaining wall. Scanning each face and finding only boys, he turned away and started along the driveway to the house, intending to wait in the shade on the porch. He'd gone only a few yards, though, when he stopped abruptly and looked again.

There was something odd about that small gathering, something still and strangely edgy. Then he saw the bicycle a half dozen feet beyond the kids, lying upside down, balanced precariously on the seat and one handlebar grip. It was a silvery gray bike, sturdy, but battered by its owner's daredevil tendencies.

It was Cady's bike.

He moved across the yard and into the street, waiting for a car to pass before crossing. As he approached, he could hear soft sniffles, a woman's reassuring voice and one distressed boy's question. "Are you okay, Cady? I didn't mean to make you fall."

When he reached them, the boys silently stepped aside, leaving an opening for him. Cady sat in their midst, her knees scraped, her eyes suspiciously bright and her left arm cradled to her chest. She tried to smile when she saw him, but her lips twitched as if to cry instead. "Hey, Mac." She greeted him feebly.

"Cady." He crouched beside her, looked at her bloody knees and her arm, then at the offending bicycle, and he managed a faint smile. "Got your wings clipped, didn't you?"

"I've done this dozens of times without any problems," she said in her own defense. "I just got distracted." That last came with a scowl for the boy who had earlier apologized.

"You want me to help you home?" He was surprised by how calm his voice was, because he sure as hell didn't feel it inside. He had experienced more than his share of physical pain in his life, but somehow a child's pain—*this* child's pain—seemed far worse.

"I can walk," she insisted. "If you'll just get my bike..."

When he stood up, so did the woman on her other side. "You're Quin's friend," she said. "I called her office, but they said she's already on her way home. Tell her I'm so sorry. I've told the kids not to ride their bikes off this wall, but..."

"Don't worry about it." He helped Cady to her feet, then brushed grass and dirt from her clothes. "Cady knew better. She just thought it was worth the gamble. Didn't you, kid?"

She rewarded him with a grin. "You should have seen me, Mac. It was going to be my best jump ever. I was going to *fly*."

"Well, you're grounded now."

Just as quickly, the grin disappeared. "In more ways than

Finally a Father 137

one, I'm afraid. Miss Jenny, I'm sorry. I won't do it anymore, I promise. Mac, can we go home now?"

He got her bicycle, then crossed the street at her side. She was still holding her arm carefully, and she was limping, favoring first one leg, then the other. When they reached his car, she slowed, then softly asked, "Are they watching?"

A glance over his shoulder confirmed that the boys had gotten their own bikes and were riding away. "No. You're in the clear."

Her shoulders sagging, she gave him a plaintive look. "Can you help me?"

Leaving the bike on the grass, he scooped her into his arms and carried her across the yard and onto the porch. When he set her on the swing, though, she didn't let go. Tightening her good arm around his neck, she pressed her face against his shirt. "My arm hurts, Mac," she whispered, and he felt the first tears soak through the fabric.

"I know, honey."

"I think it's broken."

So did he.

"Mom's gonna be so mad."

He knelt beside the swing, seeking a more comfortable position. "She's going to be grateful you didn't break your leg or land on your head," he said, then conceded, "And maybe a little annoyed that you did something you'd been told not to do. But she won't be angry with you."

"Oh, Mac, it hurts."

For a moment he simply held her. It had been a long time—a lifetime—since he'd offered comfort to anyone, and he'd just about forgotten how to do it. Then he felt the sobs shake her thin body, and instinctively he drew her closer, stroked her hair and simply patted her.

"Mac, you're early." Quin's voice came from the steps, soft and pleased. As soon as she took in the picture, though, pleasure changed to concern. "Cady, what's wrong?"

The girl abandoned him immediately for her mother—a perfectly normal response, he reminded himself. Even if it did leave his arms empty. Even if it did make him feel a little empty inside as he got to his feet.

Even if being in Quin's arms seemed the best and safest place in the world to him, too.

"I'm sorry, Mama," she whimpered. "I didn't mean to get hurt, I really didn't, and I know you told me not to, and Miss Jenny said don't, but it's just for fun, and Jeffrey was saying I couldn't and…oh, Mama, my arm is broken." She finished abruptly, trading words for more tears.

Holding her, Quin met Mac's gaze. "Do you know what happened?"

"Picture Cady on her bike in the Simpsons' yard."

The image formed immediately and brought a grim set to her features. "Oh, honey, I *told* you…" Sighing, she pushed her daughter back a bit. "Are you hurt anywhere besides your arm?"

"Her knees," Mac said when Cady didn't answer. "And her pride. We'd probably better take her to the emergency room."

Concern darkened her eyes. "Do you think her arm…?"

He nodded. "Give me your keys. I'll drive, and you can sit with Cady."

Although traffic was still heavy on base, most drivers were leaving, not coming. By the time they reached the emergency room at the Naval Hospital, Cady's tears had dried, but she was still subdued when Quin helped her out of the car. She was still in enough pain to want Mac to carry her inside.

While Quin went down the hall to register, Mac sat down with Cady in the waiting room. "Hey, Mac?" she asked. She turned sideways in her chair, leaning back against him, her head on his shoulder. "Why don't you have any kids?"

Because of your father, came his initial silent reply. If he could have had Quin, they would have had a half dozen children by now. And because of Quin. Since he couldn't have her, he hadn't wanted anyone else.

But if he'd won Quin ten years ago, if he had talked her

Finally a Father   139

out of marrying David, then *this* child wouldn't be here. Cady was well worth ten years of being alone.

"I just never did."

"Don't you want kids?"

"Sure. But I'd have to find a mother for them first."

"Haven't you had girlfriends?"

He settled her more comfortably against him, then slid his arm around her shoulders, holding her there. "Yes, I've had girlfriends."

"So why didn't you marry one of them and have kids?"

"Because I didn't want to marry any of them."

"Weren't you in love with at least one of them?"

"What is it your mother says when you get too personal?" he asked dryly, then mimicked her rendition of Quin. "'My, we're nosy, aren't we?'"

Cady giggled. "And that's my cue to shut up or change the subject, right?" She raised her arm to look at it, and her momentary cheerfulness slid into a wince. "Do you think they'll put a cast on it?"

"I don't know, honey. If it is broken, you'll get the cast later, but probably just a splint tonight."

"I want a cast. I want plaster. Real hard plaster. And then I'm going to hit that stupid Jeffrey with it. It's his fault I got hurt in the first place."

He suppressed a grin. Her plan sounded all right with him—exactly like something he would have done when he was her age. But he wasn't her age anymore, and he couldn't let her think it was all right—even if stupid Jeffrey did deserve to get hit. "Maybe Jeffrey is partly responsible, but it's your fault, too, kid, for doing something you weren't supposed to do. And even if they put a cast on, you're not going to go around thumping people with it."

"Not even Jeffrey?"

Mac couldn't help but chuckle at the hopeful note in her voice. "No, Cady. Not even Jeffrey."

Unnoticed by Mac and Cady, Quin stood at the door to the triage room, across the hall from the waiting room, waiting for a nurse and watching them. Just the sight of them together made her hurt inside. Cady was leaning heavily against him, and he was holding her and stroking her hair from time to time as they talked. They looked like any other father and daughter in the world.

How could Mac not know? she wondered despairingly. How could he look into Cady's face, as he was doing right now, and not see himself there? How could he respond to her so openly, so naturally—so *differently* from everyone else in his life—and not feel the bond between them?

How could he and Quin talk as much as they had about the night they'd made love without him wondering even once if Cady could possibly have resulted from that interlude rather than the few nights she'd spent with David a month later?

Finishing up with her other patient, the triage nurse took Cady's record, then asked to see her. From that point on it was a matter of waiting—for her name to be called, for a trip to Radiology for X rays, for the films to be developed and read, for the doctor to show them the fracture on the X ray, for a trip to Orthopedics for a splint. Cady held up better through it all than Quin did; by the time Cady was finally released, it was Quin who needed Mac's shoulder to lean on.

Unfortunately—no, fortunately, very fortunately—it was already taken.

Shifting the X rays and the consultation for a civilian orthopedist in town from one hand to the other, Quin watched as he carried Cady to the car once more. "You know, I think she can walk now. It's her arm, not her foot."

Over Mac's shoulder, Cady made a face at her. "My knees hurt when I bend them, Mom, and it's awfully hard to walk without bending them. Besides, I never get carried anywhere. You started saying I was too heavy when I was five."

"You do weigh a pound or two," Mac agreed teasingly.

Not that he was showing any strain, Quin thought. He was awfully strong, and Cady really was a scrawny little creature. Besides, why not coddle her a little? Surely a broken arm,

Finally a Father

scraped knees and her first trip to the emergency room—to say nothing of her first major trauma with her father around to help—called for a little pampering.

They helped her into the back seat, where Quin fastened her seat belt for her before settling into the seat beside Mac.

"Now where?" Mac asked as he started the engine.

"Dinner." Cady spoke up from the back. "I'm hungry."

Weren't they all? Quin thought tiredly. This little ER visit had taken almost three hours out of their evening. The Naval Hospital was nothing if not slow.

"Why don't we get some hamburgers and take them home?" Mac suggested.

"That sounds wonderful," Quin said quickly before Cady could protest. Although the wonderful part, she admitted to herself, wasn't the food, but the other. *Home.* What a lovely fantasy, thinking of her cozy little house as home for the three of them.

But fantasies never came true. Then, remembering their infamous one evening together, she amended that to *almost* never. That night he had certainly fulfilled every fantasy her innocent mind had been able to conjure up. But surely such treasures were limited one to a person, and she'd already had hers. She wasn't entitled to another.

Was she?

Not unless Mac was the most understanding and forgiving man on the face of the earth, and when it came to Cady—to his daughter—to the daughter she had passed off as belonging to another man—she didn't imagine he would find much forgiveness within himself.

"All right," Cady agreed grudgingly. "I want a hot dog and tater tots. But as soon as I get my cast, I get to have real food. Restaurant food."

Quin gave Mac directions to the one drive-in in town where Cady could have her hot dog and tater tots. He ordered their dinner through the speaker, then removed his seat belt and shifted to face her. Automatically, though, his gaze drifted past her and became dark and unsettled.

She knew the cause without looking. The Beirut Memorial was located across the street. It had been built as a testament to the two hundred and forty-one troops—mostly marines, some sailors and a few soldiers—who had died in Lebanon. Another distant city, another terrorist's bomb, another marine battalion from Jacksonville decimated. Later the scope of the memorial had been expanded to include those who had died in the invasion of Grenada and the casualties from David and Mac's battalion.

"Have you ever been there?" she asked softly.

He shook his head.

"It's a nice memorial. There are a couple of plaques, and the names are engraved on the wall. There's a statue of a marine in the center, and there are dozens of azalea bushes that bloom in the spring. It's...nice."

Leaning forward, Cady said, "Just about every fall they do a memorial service, and we go for that. I have a rubbing of Daddy's name at home in my room. It says Ellis, David R., USMC. Sometimes when we go there, people have left flowers on the ground beneath someone's name. It's kind of sad."

But she found it sad in a distant, sort of unaffecting way, Quin thought gently. Bless her heart, she was far too young to be sad over people she'd never known.

"We could go over there after dinner," Cady suggested. "It's got lights and everything."

Mac gave her a weak smile. "Not tonight, kid. After we eat, you need to get home and prop your arm up, like the doctor said."

She settled back in the seat hard enough to shake the car. "That was no doctor. That was a physician's assistant. Matthew said *he's* been to the emergency room out there four times and has never seen a doctor. He says they don't really exist, that they call them on the intercom all the time just to fool the patients, but really it's the physician's assistants and the nurses and the corpsmen who are running the place."

"And Matthew's such an authority on the subject," Quin teased.

Cady's look was earnest. "He's been to the emergency room *four* times, Mom, and he's younger than me."

A pretty young carhop rolled out on in-line skates, coming to a graceful stop and balancing the tray while Mac raised the window a few inches. Cady was leaning to the left, watching with a glint in her eyes. Quin waited until she started to open her mouth, then said, "No skates, Cady."

"Aw, Mom—"

"You want a broken leg to go with that arm?"

"You're no fun," she muttered, slumping back in the seat.

"She's such a deprived child," Mac remarked as he began passing their food to Quin.

"You noticed." She unfolded the paper from her hamburger, then took a bite. "This wasn't quite the evening you had in mind when you invited us to dinner, was it?"

"Not exactly."

Not for her, either. She had imagined they would have a pleasant dinner, then return home. Cady would go out to play or watch TV, and sooner or later she would have to go to bed, and Quin would get the rest of the evening alone with Mac. She'd thought it would be almost like a date. Pleasurable. Sweet.

But there was nothing more pleasurable than having Mac to rely on when Cady was hurt.

There was nothing sweeter than seeing him soothe his daughter—*their* daughter—when she cried.

And there was still hope for the rest of the evening. They would still go home, and Cady would still have to go to bed sooner or later. There was still a chance for the kind of sweet pleasure she had been envisioning.

As soon as they finished eating, Mac got Cady a milk shake, then they headed home. There she limped from the car into the house—couldn't be carried when one of her friends might be outside to see—where she slumped down on the bottom step of the stairs. "Mom, my arm hurts," she said with a pout.

"I know it does, baby." Quin brushed her hair from her face. "Listen, let's go upstairs and get you ready for bed. You can take some of the pills the doctor gave you and lie down in my bed and watch TV for a while, all right?"

"All right." But before tackling the stairs, she turned to Mac. "Find a woman, fall in love, have plenty of kids and you, too, can have such joys," she said dryly.

Quin watched, her fingers clenching around the banister, as he slid his arm around Cady's waist and drew her closer. "Some of my marines whine more over a sprained wrist than you did with a broken arm. You're pretty tough."

"I know. I get it from my father."

Was that a hint of bewilderment in Mac's expression? Quin wondered. Probably, and with good reason. When she had told Cady she was tough like her father, she'd been referring to Mac. There hadn't been anything tough about David; in fact, he'd been just the opposite—teddy-bear soft and sweet.

But Mac didn't comment on her statement. "I know you try hard not to be, but you're a sweetheart, you know that, don't you?"

Finally she smiled. "Only for certain people. You're lucky to be one of the few."

"Modest child, isn't she?" Quin put in.

"'False modesty has no virtue,'" Cady parroted her grandmother. "I'm the light of your life, Mom, and you can't deny it." Switching her attention once more, she murmured, "Good night, Mac."

When she abruptly leaned forward and touched her lips to his cheek, Quin clumsily turned away, her eyes squeezed shut on the image. She couldn't stand this. God help her, she couldn't keep this secret much longer.

"All right, Mom," Cady said at last. "I'm ready for bed."

Upstairs, she helped her daughter dress in a nightshirt, then combed her hair with long, gentle strokes while Cady brushed her teeth. After a moment, talking around the toothbrush, Cady said, "I really am sorry about all this, Mom."

"Me, too, honey."

"I know it'll cost a fortune to go to the doctor."

"Don't worry about that, kiddo. We'll do all right."

Finally a Father

"Mom?"

"Hmm?" By now Quin had finished brushing and was admiring her daughter's hair, so dark and shiny and soft as silk. The color was a shade darker than Quin's and a shade lighter than Mac's, a rich dark brown that absolutely gleamed under the bright lights.

"Mom." Cady waited until her attention was on her, their gazes meeting in the mirror. "I really like Mac."

She felt a stab of pain in her chest. "I can tell."

"I mean I *really* like him."

"That's good, honey." Pulling her hands from her daughter's hair, Quin fished the medicine bottle from her pocket, shook out two tablets and offered them to her.

Cady took the pills, swallowing them with a cup of water, but refused to be distracted. "Do you like him?"

Quin straightened the counter, delaying, searching for courage. Then she caught a glimpse of Cady's dark eyes on her, watchful and waiting. All her life Quin had failed to be honest with her about the most important aspect of her life. The least she could do was answer this one question honestly. "Yes, honey, I really like him, too. Now…come on into my room. I'll tuck you in, turn on the television and get you the remote."

That took a few minutes more; then, with a kiss and a hug and a whispered good-night, she turned the bedside lamp to its lowest setting and slipped out of the room.

Mac was waiting in the hallway where they'd left him, his hands in his pockets. She slowed until she was standing on the last step, almost on eye level and just a few feet away from him, and for a long moment she simply looked at him.

"It's been a long day," he remarked at last.

"You must be tired." Tired and wanting to go home, she thought, her disappointment so strong, she could taste it.

"Not really. I figured you probably were."

"No. I don't usually go to bed for another couple of hours."

After another silence, he asked, "You want me to go?"

She shook her head.

"Can we go outside? Will Cady be all right…?"

"She'll be asleep soon." Coming down from the step, she led the way down the hall and through the laundry room to the narrow screened porch. It was quiet, peaceful and dark there. The sun had set, and no moon- or starlight could penetrate the heavily leaved trees in the yard. Only a soft, diffused light came from the kitchen window. It was a cozy, private spot that smelled of sweet flowers and old wood.

A cozy, intimate spot.

Bypassing the wicker rocker, she went straight to the hammock, but she didn't sit down there. Instead, she set it in motion and watched it swing, a ghostly white blur, before turning to look at Mac.

He moved so easily, so quietly. He was closer than she'd expected, but not nearly as close as she would like. He stopped a few feet away, facing the hammock as she had. "Is this the first serious injury Cady's had?"

"There have been plenty of scrapes and bruises, but nothing that ever required medical care. It was…"

"Frightening?"

"A little. I know a broken arm is no great tragedy—it won't even slow her down—but…" She sighed. "There, in the hospital, I kept having visions of how much worse it could have been."

"You were both lucky."

"I know." She hesitated. "Thank you for going with us to the hospital."

He didn't respond to that.

She smiled nervously. "What do you want to bet she'll be out there on her bike doing it again as soon as her arm's healed?"

"I thought you weren't much of a gambler."

"I'm talking about a sure thing. That's not gambling."

He turned toward her then. It was too dark to see his face, too dark to make out his expression, although chances were better than even that she wouldn't be able to read anything in it. "There's no such thing as a sure thing. Didn't your experience with David teach you that?"

Finally a Father 147

"You're wrong, Mac. There are a few things I can always count on."

"Such as?"

You. And my reaction to you. In ten years that hasn't changed.

But she wasn't ready for so risky an answer. Instead, with a shrug, she replied, "Cady living fast and dangerously."

"And her mother, barely living at all."

She went still for a moment, and in the silence the night sounds seemed magnified—a bird calling from the branches of the tallest gum tree, a car passing on the street out front, the rumble of artillery in the distance. "You think I'm afraid of life?"

"I think so. And I *know* you're afraid of me." His voice, low and smoky, wrapped itself around her there in the dark. She wanted to say something, anything, to make him speak again, and at the same time she wanted to remain silent, forever savoring its soft, challenging tones.

Answering that challenge, she moved a step closer, and his shadow gathered substance, became better defined—the breadth of his shoulders, the angle of his head, the thin line of his mouth. "Wrong again, Mac. I was never afraid of you."

He chuckled. Heavens, when had she ever found a chuckle sexy?

"Right, Quin."

"I wasn't," she insisted. "Not ever."

"Uh-huh. Anything you say."

She moved one step closer, near enough now to smell his after-shave, near enough to separate the slow, steady sound of his breathing from her own, almost near enough—or so she fancied—to hear his heartbeat. Stopping there, close enough to reach out, close enough to touch, she softly, provocatively issued a challenge of her own.

"Want me to prove it?"

Chapter 8

Mac's grin came slowly. On his way home from work this evening, he had considered the fact that Quin was older now, more mature. Damn straight. The girl he had fallen for ten years ago—despite her denials now—*had* been afraid of him. She would never have willingly gone into the dark with him, never would have come to him like this of her own volition. Trembling, she would have run to David for protection. To David, who had never made her feel like this.

As sweet as his memories of Quin at nineteen were—bittersweet—Quin at twenty-nine was a hundred times better. A hundred times sweeter.

"And how would you prove it?" he asked. "You can't change the past."

"No," she agreed. "But I can change your perception of the past."

"I'm not sure I want you tinkering with my perceptions."

"I was afraid back then—I don't deny that—but not of you." Her voice grew soft and thoughtful. "I was afraid of *us*. There wasn't even supposed to *be* an 'us.' I was supposed

Finally a Father

to be in love with David—everyone knew that. Everyone believed that. Everyone but you. And me."

"You certainly tried hard enough to convince yourself."

Her laughter sounded chagrined. "Why am I even telling you this? You *knew*."

Tentatively he touched his palm lightly to her hair. "I knew that you were absolutely the most innocent girl I had ever met. I knew that you had been sheltered and protected and cosseted all your life. I knew that you wanted desperately to be in love with David. I knew that you didn't want to risk everything with me."

"I was very young," she whispered.

"You were a child."

Again she laughed, a soft, sweet sound that he'd heard so rarely in the past. "Not that young," she chided.

"Sweetheart, I was older at ten than you were at twenty."

"Probably," she agreed. In the darkness her sigh seemed to shimmer. "I was naive."

"Hmm."

"And foolish. And innocent."

"Not after *I* touched you."

There was that sigh again. "I wish…"

"What?"

"That things had been different. That I had been wiser. That I hadn't been so blind, so stubborn." She reached for his hand, found it and clasped it tightly in hers. "I wish I hadn't hurt you."

He wished a futile wish of his own—that he could reassure her, that he could convince her that she hadn't hurt him, that she didn't need to feel guilty about that. But she *had* hurt him with her accusations and her blame, with her anger and her loathing. She had broken his heart.

After a moment of silence, she released his hand and took a few steps back. He missed her, God help him, more than the few feet between them accounted for.

Moving in the darkness, he circled to the opposite side of the hammock. There he leaned against the railing, the screen against his back, and with his knee put the hammock in motion again. "Is the hammock your place or Cady's?" he asked, trying to sound normal, not empty. Not lonely.

"Mine. The rocker belongs to Cady. She likes the way it squeaks every time she moves."

"Of course. And you like being lazy."

"Hey, it's a very comfortable place to be on a cool spring evening."

"How about on a warm summer night?"

Her voice was husky in the darkness. "Then, too."

He sat down, feeling the ropes give slightly beneath his weight, then swung his legs around and lay back. There was a pillow attached at the top that he positioned beneath his head. "I thought hammocks were supposed to be strung between two tall trees."

"Uh-huh. And the mosquitoes would carry you away. Without this screened porch, I wouldn't come outside at night."

"Honey, you haven't seen mosquitoes until you've been to Korea. While I was in Okinawa, we did some exercises with the Korean Marines. I thought the bugs were going to eat me alive."

She moved slowly, no more than a shadow identified by the slightly lighter colors of her clothes, around the foot of the hammock until she was standing beside him. "That must have been lonely, being on the other side of the world, so far from home."

"Not really. I don't have a home, Quin. I haven't had one since Chelsea died."

"Don't you ever talk to your mother? Don't you ever miss your brothers?"

He shook his head, even though she couldn't see him. "When my mother remarried, she had to make a choice between her husband and us. She chose him. She needed him more than she wanted us. She loved their children more than she loved us. When Chelsea died, our mother and her family had what they wanted. They were rid of both of us. They didn't care. They didn't miss her. They didn't grieve for her."

Finally a Father 151

"And so you don't miss them." She sounded confused. "But she's your mother."

Reaching out, he caught her hand and drew her over to sit on the edge of the hammock. "You are so innocent," he said with a grin that slowly faded. "Not everyone loves their kids, Quin. Not everyone cares about them. You're a schoolteacher. You have to be aware of that."

"Did they...neglect you?"

Neglect. She had wanted to say abuse, he knew, but couldn't bring herself to voice it. But *neglect* was a good enough word. It was accurate. "We had a place to live, food to eat and clothes to wear, but that's about it." There had been little affection, no love and a lot of anger. Their stepfather had had a hell of a temper, and Mac and Chelsea had been the easiest targets. For Chelsea's sake, he had made himself the easiest target of all.

Quin's fingers tightened around his. "He hit you, didn't he—your stepfather?"

"Not a lot."

"That was why you started running—to stay away from him."

"Yeah. For the most part, it worked."

"And that was why your sister was so miserable at home."

"He only hit her a couple of times—I put a stop to that—but...yeah, he was part of her problem. He constantly criticized her and put her down—made her feel stupid and unlovable and worthless. He tried the same stuff with me, but I was stubborn. It just made me hate him more. Chelsea wasn't as strong. She let him get to her."

"I'm sorry, Mac," she whispered.

They fell silent for a time, until an artillery shell, being used in training exercises on base, burst some fifteen miles away with sufficient force to rattle the screen door and the windowpanes. Quin stiffened, and he chuckled. "Don't you love nightfire exercises?"

"I used to think it was thunder, until I realized that thunder wasn't quite so regular in its cadence. It drove me nuts, but somewhere along the line, I got accustomed to it. These really loud ones, though, can still startle me. Cady doesn't even notice the artillery. It goes on at all hours of the day and night, but she's grown up with it. It's as normal to her as the birds singing or crickets chirping.''

Abruptly his brief amusement faded. "You still want to prove something, Quin?"

Her smile was slow and sultry. He *knew* it, felt it, even if he couldn't see it. "Hmm."

"Let me hold you." He didn't try to cajole her, didn't offer any promises that holding was all he would do, that he wouldn't kiss her or caress her or anything else. He simply made that one blunt request.

Did he hear, Quin wondered, the pleading that underlaid his request? Did he know that she had been wishing for just that—to be in his arms—ever since she'd come home this evening?

"I've never figured out how to gracefully maneuver in a hammock," she warned. "If I dump us both on the floor, I apologize in advance." But with his help, lying down was the easiest thing in the world. With her head pillowed on his shoulder, her hand resting on his chest, it was the sweetest. With his arms snug about her, it was the safest.

It was ironic that she felt so at home in a place she had only briefly been. She remembered lying like this, exactly like this, that hot August night. Except then they had both been naked. Their bodies had been slick with sweat. Their hearts had been pounding—hers more than his—and their breathing had been noisy and rushed.

That was before the shock had set in—for her, at least. When the satisfaction of their lovemaking had still been too intense to let her think. When all she could do was marvel at his gentleness, at his confidence, at his skill. He had known exactly what to do, where to touch her and how, to make her weak. To make her weep.

He had known exactly how to make her forget David, to forget the love she'd sworn she felt for David. He'd made her

Finally a Father 153

forget everything in the entire world except him and her and their sweet, sweet lovemaking.

"Mac?"

"Hmm?" The sound vibrated through his chest. She felt it in her fingers.

"Have you ever been in love?"

He was still for a moment. "So Cady gets her nosiness from you."

"Too personal, huh?"

After another quiet moment, he replied, "How can anything be too personal when we're lying like this?" But he didn't answer her original question.

"You've dated in the last ten years."

"Some."

"Why didn't you get married?"

"I believe you're supposed to be in love before you do that."

"I don't know," she whispered. "I married David out of loyalty. Obligation. Because everyone expected me to. Because I hoped it was what I wanted."

"Because you felt guilty for sleeping with me."

"That, too. Guilt can be a powerful motivator."

"That's why I didn't come to see you when the battalion came home," he admitted. "I felt guilty for seducing you, for trying to take you away from him, for wishing him out of the picture, for getting him killed. I knew I couldn't stay in Jacksonville and stay away from you, so before we even came home, I arranged a swap with a sergeant out at Camp Pendleton. I was only here a few days, then I left for California."

"You didn't seduce me." She was close enough now, intimately close, that when she raised her head, she could see his smile.

"Yes, I did."

"No, you didn't." There had been no seduction that night, at least not the first time. He had touched her, and she, heaven have mercy, had ignited. What had started as a simple touch had flared into uncontrollable fever. Passion. Desperation.

It had been sweet salvation.

"Mac?"

"Hmm?" He was stroking her hair now, had loosened it from its bow and was brushing his fingers over it. Strong hands, callused skin and gentle, gentle touches.

"Mac, I need to tell you…"

His caresses moved naturally down the length of her hair to her shoulder and over the soft skin exposed by the rounded neck of her blouse. Even so simple, so innocent, a touch made her breasts hurt, made her breath catch in her chest, made her words die unspoken.

They could wait just a little longer.

She couldn't.

"Oh, Mac," she whispered, pressing her face against his chest as his fingers skimmed lightly, too lightly, over the curve of her breast.

The back door creaked when it opened, and light flooded the porch. Quin stiffened, blinking against the sudden illumination. She tried to sit up, but Mac held her where she was.

"Why didn't you tell me you were coming outside?" Cady asked, her tone sour and her expression matching. "I've been looking for you."

He released her as he sat up, swinging his feet to the floor. Quin wasn't as graceful in getting up. "It's not a very big house," she said, her voice unsteady and a shade too hoarse. "You didn't have far to go. Are you having trouble sleeping?"

"I haven't been asleep," Cady denied, her tone just this side of a whine.

"Oh." Wisely Quin didn't point out her daughter's disturbed-sleep look, her puffy eyes, the indentations the covers had left on her skin or the fact that her hair was standing on end exactly as it did when she first awoke.

"My arm hurts. How am I supposed to sleep with a broken arm?"

"So what do you want to do, sweetie?"

Finally a Father

"I want you to come upstairs and lie down with me. You can read to me or something."

Given the choice, Quin thought wistfully, she would much rather share her bed with Mac than with her cranky daughter. But she was a mother. She didn't have a choice. "Okay. Why don't you go back up and I'll be there in a minute?"

"I want Mac to carry me."

"Honey—"

"It's okay," he interrupted. "I've got to get going anyway. I'll take her on the way." Careful of her splinted arm, he picked Cady up and headed inside. With a sigh, Quin followed along behind, locking up and shutting off all the lights Cady had turned on in her search. When she reached her bedroom, Mac had already settled Cady on the bed and tucked the covers—the grandmother's fan quilt—in around her.

"If I get my cast tomorrow, will you come see it?"

"I can't, kid. We'll be out in the field the rest of the week. But I'll see you Saturday if that's okay."

Cady didn't let him go that easily. "What do you do in the field?"

"Some training exercises, sleep on the ground, eat MREs."

"I know what those are—Meals Ready to Eat. I had one once. It was okay, and the cookie was pretty good. Matthew's dad gave it to us."

Quin felt a surge of pain as he told Cady good-night, then joined her in the hall. "Saturday's a long time away," she remarked as they made their way downstairs again.

"Not really. The artillery that bothers you the next few nights will probably be ours."

Stopping at the front door, she smiled dryly. "Something to remind me of you." At just that moment, the best reminder of all called from up above.

"Moth-er, I'm waiting!"

"She'll keep you busy. Saturday will be here before you know it."

"Hmm. By then, I'll be all out of coddling. I'll have to send her to her grandparents for the weekend for more."

He moved unnecessarily close to her as he opened the door, brushing his body against hers. He stood there for an instant, making her warm, making her tremble, and then he slipped outside. Before he was gone, though, he offered her three promising little words.

"Do that, Quin."

Mac was doing laundry Saturday morning when the doorbell rang. He knew it was Quin and Cady; he had stopped by their house on his morning run and talked to Quin for a few minutes. She had invited him to join them for lunch at the pizza place down the street, and after lunch... Well, she had made a point of informing him that her sister was in town and would be picking Cady up at the restaurant. The Ellises and the Austins were going to fuss over her for at least the next twenty-four hours.

Maybe while the families pampered Cady, he would do a little pampering of his own with her mother.

When he opened the door, Cady, with a backpack slung over her shoulder, walked right in, flashed him a grin and threw herself down on the sofa. Behind her, Quin gave him a smile and, as if it were the most natural thing in the world, touched his arm as she passed. "Hey," she greeted him.

"Look at my cast, Mac," Cady spoke up before he could respond, lifting her arm for inspection. Leaving her fingers free to wiggle, it extended from below her knuckles to her elbow. As casts went, it was typical—fiberglass, lightweight, strong. What pleased Cady so much, he suspected, was the color: a shade of neon green just bright enough to make you wince looking at it.

"The doctor had a nice red, and a pretty blue and orange and yellow and several other colors," Quin said dryly. "And look at what she chose."

"Don't worry. It'll get dirty." He sat down on the coffee table and examined the cast. "How are you feeling, kid?"

"My arm's all better. It doesn't hardly ever hurt at all."

Finally a Father

And her knees were scabbed over and her eyes were brighter and the cross little girl he'd last seen was gone.

"I'm going fishing tomorrow, Mac," she went on excitedly. "My grandfathers feel sorry for me 'cause I broke my arm, so they're taking me deep-sea fishing. We're taking the full-day trip, and we'll be gone all day tomorrow, and I'm gonna' catch a big one. Want to come?"

His idea of fun, Mac thought dryly—spending a full day on a fishing boat with Quin's and David's fathers. The only thing worse would be if Quin's mother went along. "Thanks, but I'm not big on fishing."

"Oh, come on, it's fun. My dad used to fish, and he caught one once that was bigger than I am now. My grandpa has pictures of it. And they catch sharks, too, although I never have." Bouncing up from the couch, she wandered around the room, looking without touching. When she reached the bookshelf, she paused. "Hey, there's my dad, Mac, and that's you. Who's the man?"

"My father."

"And who's the girl? Your sister?"

"Yes."

She strained on tiptoe to look closer at Chelsea's picture, then sank down again. "She's pretty. She looks like me. That must be an old picture. You're too old to have a sister that young. You ought to get a more recent picture of her."

Quin, looking startled and more than a little distressed, moved toward Cady, taking gentle hold of her ponytail and steering her toward the door. "Don't go snooping," she admonished. "We'd better get to the restaurant or you won't have time to eat before Aunt Lorna gets there."

Mac got his keys from the dresser, then followed them outside. "No car?" he asked as he locked the door.

Not surprisingly, it was Cady who answered. "We usually ride our bikes—it's the only exercise Mom gets all week—but since I can't do that just yet, we decided to walk. And you know what, Mac? It's harder to walk a mile than it is to ride a bike a mile."

"I think you'll survive it," he replied. The words were barely out of his mouth before she skipped off ahead of them. "I bet you're ready for a break. Has she had this much energy all week?"

"She's been not quite unbearable. She's playing this arm up for all it's worth. Jenny—the baby-sitter—told me that she's had the kids waiting on her hand and foot all week. But I think—I hope—the novelty's just about worn off. Things will get back to normal soon." Quin pushed her hands into the pockets of her shorts as they turned at the end of the sidewalk and glanced up at him. "How were your three days in the field?"

"Hot. Wet. Muddy."

"I thought of you every time it rained. I figured you would be pretty uncomfortable."

"I would have preferred cool and dry, but hot and wet beats cold and wet anytime." It was hot and muggy again today, and the clouds darkening the sky to the west, he acknowledged, didn't bode well for the afternoon. "So Cady's spending the night with your family."

"Mmm-hmm. I'll have to pick her up sometime after supper tomorrow evening." She gave him a smile that bordered on shy. "Would you like to come over once she's gone?"

It was an innocent enough invitation. Come over to the house and we'll visit. We'll talk. We'll discuss the past and maybe even venture into the future. But visiting, talking, innocence—those weren't exactly what Quin had in mind. He knew that as surely as he knew he would accept her invitation...and anything else she cared to offer.

"Yes." That was his only answer, simple and to the point.

Cady beat them to the restaurant; by the time they walked inside the door, she was already seated in a booth near the back. They joined her and ordered pizza, pasta and breadsticks, then let her dominate the conversation while they ate. She was finishing her last piece of pizza when a few fat raindrops hit the plate glass window.

"Oh, no," she moaned, searching for more and thankfully

Finally a Father

finding none. "It'd better not rain on my fishing trip tomorrow."

"Don't the fish come out in the rain?" Mac asked.

"Maybe they don't want to get wet," Quin suggested.

Cady rolled her eyes, then gave them both a disgusted look. "Grow up, you guys. Don't be so juvenile."

"My, my, child, I am glad you're going away for a day," Quin teased. "Don't worry about rain. Maybe it'll just sprinkle a little bit today and be hot and sunny tomorrow. Now... there's Lorna. Are you finished eating?"

"Yup." She scrambled out of the booth and grabbed her backpack from the floor. "I know. Be good, obey everyone—even Aunt Lorna—brush my teeth and don't get my cast wet." Climbing back onto the bench, she gave her mother a hug. "I love you, Mom. See you, Mac."

She raced out the door, greeting her aunt with a yell, tossing her bag into the back seat of Lorna's car and climbing into the front. When she was settled, Lorna gave Quin a wave, then drove away.

"Whenever Cady's in an exuberant mood and then she leaves, I feel almost stunned," Quin said, speaking slowly and softly. "I imagine it's the way a person caught in a tornado feels when it passes."

He knew the feeling, only he got it from the mother as well as the daughter. "Do you ever consider how much David would have loved her?"

A vaguely disturbed look crossed her face. "I don't know that he would have."

"Of course he would have. He loved everyone, and she's awfully easy to love."

"Maybe." She was only picking at her pasta now, using the fork to scoot the noodles from one end of the dish to the other. Was she nervous, he wondered, because they were finally alone? She hadn't been nervous Tuesday evening...but Tuesday evening Cady had been home. Today they truly were alone...and they each had ideas about how to make the best of it. He only hoped her ideas meshed with his, because if they didn't, he was going to be very disappointed.

But he'd been disappointed before, and he'd survived.

"Are you ready?"

Smiling tightly, she put her fork down and nodded. He took the bill to the cash register and paid, then followed her outside. Back out into the heat.

"It's going to rain before we get home," she remarked as they started across the parking lot. "I should have brought the car."

"Afraid of getting wet?" He reached for her hand, lacing his fingers loosely with hers. "You won't melt."

She gave him a look that was every bit as sultry as the weather. "Touch me in the right places and I just might."

Damned if he didn't want to prove her claim right there on the street. In an effort to distract himself, he asked, "What do you want to do this afternoon?"

Her laughter was delighted. "I make a statement like that, and you can follow it with that question? Oh, Mac, I may be lacking in finesse and skill, but—"

"You're not lacking in anything," he interrupted, feeling the heat of a flush gather in his face and spread down his neck in back.

"Yes, I am. Sophistication. Worldliness. Experience."

With his hold on her hand, he brought her to an abrupt stop and close to his body. Bending low, his lips brushing her mouth, he murmured, "Hallelujah for that."

The first raindrop landed on his neck, the next on his arm. Slowly raising his head, he looked up at the sky, the sun gone now behind a barrier of dark clouds, the raindrops picking up force, falling faster and harder until individual drops were lost in the flow. "How much do you care about not getting wet?"

Quin laughed. "If you mean do I want to make a run for your apartment, no, I don't care that much. You're right. I won't melt. What about you?"

"Hell, I've been wet the better part of the last three days. One more time won't hurt."

Finally a Father

The cloudburst ended as quickly as it started, leaving them a block from home and soaked. A nice excuse, he thought, for getting Quin out of her clothes when they reached the apartment.

But he didn't need an excuse. Her teasing remarks had left no doubt exactly what they were going to do when they got there, and clothing was definitely optional.

The rain was starting again, just a few drops, as he fished his keys from his pocket and unlocked the door. The air inside the apartment when he opened the door was cold against his skin, making him shiver...or was it Quin, close behind him, who was responsible for that?

"The bathroom's through there," he said, gesturing toward the bedroom. "There are towels under the sink. Help yourself to whatever you need."

The look in her eyes was as bright and lively as Cady's had been earlier. "Where are you going?"

"I've got some clothes in the laundry room. I'll change there."

With a small, secretive smile, she kicked her shoes off on the tile just inside the door, then went into his bedroom, leaving the door ajar. He watched until she was in the bathroom, her back to him, peeling her wet shirt off. Swallowing hard, he turned away, following her lead in removing his shoes, going barefoot down the carpeted hall to the laundry room.

It was warmer in there, the heat from the still-tumbling dryer raising the temperature in the small room by a good fifteen degrees. He took a pair of olive drab running shorts and a matching T-shirt from the basket on top, stripped, dried off and pulled them on.

Back out in the living room, he waited. No sound came from the bathroom. How long could it take her to undress, dry herself and find something in his closet to wear? he wondered edgily.

But maybe she wasn't looking for something to wear.

Maybe that odd little smile she'd given him and the open

door had been an invitation for him to follow. After all, they were going to make love, weren't they?

Finally, summoning his courage, he walked into the bedroom. Standing in front of the bathroom mirror, she saw him right away through the open door and smiled. She hadn't bothered looking for clothing. She wore a pale yellow towel wrapped underneath her arms and knotted, and she was combing her hair.

He went as far as the bathroom door, but stopped there, leaning against the jamb and watching her. She didn't pause but continued the long, slow strokes. Did she know, he wondered, that she was arousing him? That witnessing this simple act was making him hard and hungry and leaving him, damn, wanting her so badly that it hurt?

She knew. Her gaze, sweeping over his reflection in the mirror, pausing on his groin, told him that. Her satisfied smile confirmed it.

At last she finished with her hair and looked at the comb, big, wide-toothed, shaded in teal, hot pink and purple. "Why do you have this comb?"

Her voice sounded normal. His came out thick and husky. "I do have hair."

"Not enough for a comb like this. This is the sort of comb a woman would use. I have one like it at home."

Slowly he moved toward her. "The only other female who's been in this apartment since I moved in is Cady."

"Which means you brought it with you when you moved, which means it got left behind by some other woman in your life."

He stopped directly behind her, close enough to feel the thick terry cloth of her towel against his shirt, his thigh, his erection. "There's never been any other woman in my life, Quin. Just you."

She laughed softly. "Oh, you're sweet. You're a liar, but you're a sweet liar."

Then he touched her—brought his hands to her bare shoulders—and her laughter disappeared. Her gaze was locked on

Finally a Father 163

his, her lips slightly parted, her eyes soft and... Not startled. Not afraid. Aroused. She wanted him. Quin Ellis wanted *him*. He had waited ten years to be wanted by her. He had waited, wanted, obsessed over it for ten long, lonely years.

She watched in the mirror as he loosened the knotted fabric between her breasts, watched with only a slight catch in her breath as he peeled the towel away, as he laid his hands, dark and callused, on her stomach. Standing there, looking at her, looking at himself as he touched her, he uttered a soundless curse. He had thought he could handle this with more maturity, with at least some semblance of restraint. He'd thought he could seduce her, could kiss and caress and touch her in all the ways he'd always wanted. He'd thought he could take his time, building her desire and his need until they were unbearable, until they couldn't stand the waiting anymore. He'd thought he could delay the urgency, the desperation, the shuddering I'm-going-to-die-if-I-don't-get-inside-you-soon feeling.

Like hell he could.

She raised her hands. Lacing her fingers with his, she guided them slowly upward, over her stomach and across her ribs until they covered her breasts.

"Quin," he whispered, demanded, pleaded, and she leaned heavily against him, turning her head to the side for his hungry kiss. Welcoming his tongue into her mouth, she twisted around in his embrace, wrapped her arms tightly around his neck and returned his kiss with the same ardor, the same fever.

They were only ten feet from his bed, but they barely made it. They struggled with his clothing, discarded it and sank down together on the bed as he pushed inside her. Just that—being inside her, filling her, feeling her hot and tight around him—brought a moment's relief, allowed him to catch his breath and, for just one moment, enjoy the exquisite sensations as her body clenched, adjusted and stretched to accept him.

And then she moved.

He bit his lip, straining for control. It wasn't fair that one small movement, one simple thrust of her hips, should rip through him like that. His body's response was so intense that he groaned out loud and his fingers bit into her hips for strength. "No, Quin," he gritted out.

She softly, seductively insisted, "Yes, Mac. I need..."

She moved against him again, and his restraint broke. The hell with control. He pushed into her, harder and faster on each stroke, making her gasp and quiver and plead. She clung to him, moving with him, meeting him, drawing him deeper, and when she finished, she took him along, drawing him over the edge, taking his release, draining him. Emptying him.

Filling him.

He lay against her, still inside her, his breathing ragged in her ear. Quin, her own breathing none too steady, held him close and slowly, soothingly, stroked her palm along the length of his spine. Shudders still racked them as she tried with little success to uncurl her toes and relax the muscles in her legs, still intimately tangled with his.

After a moment, he drew in a deep breath, gave a wry laugh and muttered, "Hell, I feel like a damned overeager kid."

Holding him tighter, she shifted underneath him. "Not to me."

"I didn't even get to kiss you, not the way I wanted."

She offered him a promising smile. "We're not through yet, are we?"

He lifted himself enough so he could meet her gaze. His was so serious, so intense. "No. We won't be through for a long, long time...if ever."

That last part was a whisper nearly lost in his kiss. It made her warm inside, filled her with hope, let her believe. If he could want her this much, if he could kiss her this sweetly, then maybe someday he could love her, and if he could love her...

Maybe someday he could forgive her.

He kissed her slowly, leisurely slid his tongue inside her mouth, tasting her, soothing her, once again arousing her with lazy, exploring stabs. At the same time his hands were on her body, caressing her breasts, brushing across her nipples, sliding down between them to the damp heat where her body still

Finally a Father

sheltered him. When he touched her beneath the curls there, she gasped and bit his lip. Deep in his throat, he chuckled and continued the intimate caress, making her arch her hips, trapping his hand in place while she savored the small movements he was still able to make.

Breaking free of his mouth, she breathed deeply. "Oh, Mac, no…"

"Wrong words, sweetheart. You're supposed to say, 'Oh, Mac, yes…'" He deepened his touch, rubbing harder against her sensitive flesh, making her gasp again.

"Oh, Mac, please," she whispered helplessly, and he chuckled again.

"That's close enough."

She was dying, absolutely dying. The sensations building inside her were so intense, the pressure so strong, that she was simply going to burst into about a million pieces…but, oh, she would die happy. He knew exactly what he was doing, knew exactly how hard and how fast to do it. The muscles in her legs were trembling now, tight and hard, and her hips were moving, pushing against him, seeking more, that one little bit, that one last stroke that would allow her to…

Heat rushed over her, searing, blistering, stealing the air from her lungs. Whimpering, she clung to him, needing his strength to survive such pleasure, trusting him to hold her together when the quivering threatened to shake her apart. As the pleasure slowly abated, as the shuddering slowly eased, she pressed her face to his shoulder and softly, breathlessly murmured what he'd wanted to hear.

"Oh, Mac, yes…"

Chapter 9

Quin lay on her side, her head pillowed on her arm, listening to the rain outside and watching Mac sleep. Those night-training exercises had caught up with him; after they'd made love again, he'd drifted off to sleep as easily and naturally as a baby. He slept on his back and slept soundly, unmoving except for the steady rise and fall of his chest.

She didn't know how long she had lain there watching; she did know they had whiled away the entire afternoon in his bed. It had been... Her grin was self-deprecating. Here she was a schoolteacher, and she couldn't think of any words adequate to describe the past few hours.

The best time of her life.

Oh, yes, that was it.

Indulging herself, she slid her hand beneath the sheet to his chest. His skin was smooth and incredibly warm in spite of the frigid temperature in the apartment that had sent them both under the covers. Ten years ago, when he was younger and maybe a little bit more gung-ho, he had lifted weights as well as run endless miles daily. He'd been a little more muscular then, but she liked him fine now. She thought he was beautiful—truly, physically beautiful: broadchested and hard, lean and finely muscled. Such delicate grace and raw power. He was every woman's fantasy.

He was *definitely* her fantasy.

With a reluctant sigh, she raised up enough to see the clock on his nightstand. It was coming up on six o'clock. Time to see about getting home...and maybe getting him to go with her?

Leaving him asleep, she left the bed, shivering. Halfway to the bathroom, she stumbled across his T-shirt and gratefully pulled it on. It was too big, but not by much; he wore his shirts snug. It provided adequate covering while she hurried into the bathroom, where she hung up her towel and gathered her still-damp clothing before making her way through the quiet apartment to the laundry room.

The dryer had long since stopped running. They had heard its buzzer, signaling the end of the load, quite some time ago, but neither had cared enough to stop what they were doing. What they'd been doing, she remembered with a grin, had been far too enticing—far too enjoyable—to interrupt for anything so insignificant as a load of laundry.

There was a basket of clothes, dry and neatly folded, on top of the dryer—more T-shirts like the one she was wearing, running shorts, briefs and socks. On a bar overhead hung the camouflage uniforms Mac wore most of the time—five jackets and five pairs of trousers. When she had first moved to Jacksonville, she recalled—when she had still believed she loved David, when she had still been looking forward to marrying him—she had thought there would be a certain pleasure in having uniforms in the closet and combat boots by the door. It had never happened; when the battalion shipped out, he had left her with only a box of personal belongings and a few civilian clothes.

She still thought, now more than ever, that making room in her life for cammies and dress blues, for combat boots and dress shoes, held the promise of sweet pleasure.

Chilly, she filched a pair of Mac's uniform socks, olive drab wool and much too large but looking too warm to pass up, from the basket and tugged them on before she opened the dryer. She removed the towels inside one at a time, quickly shaking them out, neatly folding them atop the washer. The heavier ones near the bottom still held a little residual heat that warmed her fingers as she worked. When that task was completed, she tossed her own clothing into the dryer and started it.

For a moment she leaned against the machine, listening to it run, feeling its vibration through her hip. It would take at least fifteen or twenty minutes for her clothes to dry. She could spend them uncomfortably cool in here, shivering in the living room or sharing Mac's body heat back in bed.

With a grin, she flipped off the light switch and started down the hall.

Mac wasn't sure what awakened him—the fact that he'd napped long enough? The sound of the rain, blowing in sheets against the window? The distant boom of artillery?

Or the realization that Quin was no longer at his side?

For a moment he lay motionless, listening for her. The bathroom door was open, the light on, and there was no sign of her there. The bedroom door was open, too. No light shone through, no sound filtered in.

He tried to disregard the uneasy feeling in his stomach. She wouldn't have left without saying goodbye. Besides, how far could she get without her cloth— Abruptly, he raised up for a better look into the bathroom. Her clothes—the shorts, knit shirt, dainty bra and lacy little panties—that she'd left on the bathroom counter when she'd undressed were gone, and the towel he had dropped to the floor was hanging neatly over the shower curtain rod.

She hadn't left. She wouldn't have, couldn't have. She was just getting a drink from the kitchen or maybe using the phone in there. She was—

He heard her, humming softly, an instant before she appeared in the door. She was wearing his T-shirt and a pair of his socks, both well-worn, faded green and way too big, and her hair lay at odd angles—it had been wet when they'd come to bed—but she still managed to look utterly charming.

Utterly beautiful.

When she saw that he was awake, she came to a sudden stop. For a moment, she leaned there against the door frame, watching him. She folded her arms across her chest, pulling his shirt indecently taut and shortening its length by a few immodest inches, and slowly smiled. "Hey, Marine."

Already he was getting hard again. They'd made love twice this afternoon, taking their time the second time, seducing, playing, savoring, but with just one look, just that smile and that soft greeting, he wanted her again. He was ready to take her again.

"Nice outfit you're almost wearing," he said, his voice thick and hoarse. "I don't believe I've ever seen any marine who wore that uniform shirt as well as you do."

She shrugged, pulling taut fabric even tighter and making him swallow hard. "Olive drab's not my color."

"Oh, it looks fine." He pulled his gaze away for a glance at the clock, then immediately looked back at her. "I fell asleep, didn't I?"

"Mmm-hmm. I watched you. The whole time."

There was something disconcerting about that. A man was at his most vulnerable when he was asleep. He couldn't protect himself then. But there was also something endearing about the idea. She hadn't dozed off herself, hadn't left the bed in search of a book to read, music to listen to or a movie to watch. She had chosen instead to remain beside him and watch.

Sweet.

"So what are you doing out of bed?"

"I put my clothes in the dryer. I've got to go home soon. Whenever Cady spends the night away, she always calls me to say good-night. I have to be there."

"I had hoped you would stay here," he admitted.

She smiled. "I had hoped you would go with me. I have a comfortable bed."

"I know. I've seen it."

"Seen it?" she echoed with a laugh. "Honey, you changed my life in that bed."

"In what way?"

Her lighthearted mood seemed to slip away. Pushing herself away from the door, she started across the room. "You taught me things I never would have known."

"Such as?"

Now she was at the foot of the bed, the mattress giving underneath her knee. "You gave me passion and pleasure and wondrous satisfaction. You showed me how desperately I could want and how intensely I could feel." She crawled over him, as sleek and sensuous as any cat, rubbing against him, making him grit his teeth and groan. "I was naive before that night. I thought I knew what I wanted out of life, and you proved me wrong. I'm sorry I didn't have the courage to acknowledge it then. I'm sorry I said those things to you. I'm sorry I hurt you. I'm sorry I didn't grab hold of you with both hands and never let go."

She was hurting him now, rubbing so smoothly against him, so intimately that he could feel her heat through the sheet. She was creating a need so powerful that he ached with it, a hunger so raw that he wasn't sure he could bear it.

Sliding his hands to her hips, he gently pushed her into a sitting position astride his hips, pushing her hard against his arousal. "I hate to break this to you, sweetheart," he murmured, flinching as sensation burned through him, "but you were naive after that night, too. You learned a few things, but you didn't lose your innocence."

"Teach me a few more things, Mac," she suggested. "Teach me something new."

"How about a review of the passion and the pleasure and the wondrous satisfaction?"

Her smile took his breath away, as did her all-too-beguiling shrug. "I'm at your mercy."

Finally a Father

He moved his hands underneath her shirt. Her skin was cool, his hands hot. They warmed her, gliding across her belly and over her ribs, circling her breasts, teasing her nipples before covering both breasts in a light caress. Her eyes fluttered shut, and her head rolled back. "I want you inside me, Mac," she whispered.

"Soon." He rubbed her breasts, gently pinched her nipples, then feathered his fingers across them. "Do you remember the first thing I said to you after we finally made it to bed that night?"

"'You're a beautiful woman, Quin,'" she dutifully, dazedly repeated. "You were—" She caught her breath in a gasp as he abruptly pulled the T-shirt over her head, then lowered his mouth to her breast for a tingling kiss. "You were the first man to ever tell me I was beautiful."

He raised his head. "Surely David—" But no. Before David had introduced them, he'd had plenty to say about Quin—about what a great person she was, such fun, bright and friendly and nice as hell—but he had never called her beautiful. She was kind of pretty, he'd said. Cute. But never beautiful. "I thought you were the most beautiful woman I'd ever seen. You still are."

Holding onto her, he moved to sit up, propping the pillows behind his back, kicking away the sheet that was all that kept them apart. She knelt over him, wrapping cool fingers around his hardness, guiding him into place, then sinking down to take him fully inside her. He groaned, and she gave a deep shuddering sigh.

"Do you remember the first thing you said?" he asked, then nuzzled her breast, drawing his tongue slowly across her nipple.

She laughed throatily; he felt the sound vibrate through her. "I'd never seen a naked man before," she protested. "I was entitled to be surprised."

"And you expressed it quite well. 'Oh, my,'" he mimicked, matching her inflection perfectly.

"I was impressed. Awed. Amazed."

Drawing back, Mac drew his fingertips across her breasts in an airy caress and watched her skin ripple, watched her nipples quiver. Her breasts were lovely, just a shade less than large, full and comfortingly soft and delightfully responsive. They gave him great pleasure—looking at them, feeling their weight in his hands, suckling them.

"Oh, yes." The words escaped her in a sublimely satisfied sigh as he drew her nipple once more into his mouth, making it stiffen and swell. "Oh, my, yes…" Breaking off, she arched her back in a silent plea for more, and he obliged, teasing her nipple, suckling harder, tenderly biting and soothing and making her weak.

"Mac…" Her voice was breathy and tinged with pain. "Please…"

With his hands on her hips, he showed her how to move slowly back and forth along the length of him, nearly withdrawing, then taking him deep again. She found an easy rhythm that, at the same time, satisfied and intensified her hunger, that left him feeling edgy and sharp and too damned good for words.

As the sensations increased, so did her pace until everything collided—need, desire, desperate longing, completion, gratification and wondrous satisfaction. Yes, he thought hazily, groaning as he filled her, deep, hard and hot, once more.

Purely wondrous satisfaction.

"It's never gonna stop raining."

Plumping the pillow behind her back, Quin listened to her daughter's voice, plaintive and cross, on the phone. "Probably not," she agreed, grateful that she was here, snug and dry in her cozy little house with Mac, and Cady wasn't. "I imagine one day soon we'll just all float away, and you'll see far more of the deep, deep sea than you ever wanted."

"This isn't funny, Mother."

"It's also no great tragedy. If you don't get to go fishing tomorrow, babe, then you'll do it some other time. Come on, Cady, lighten up. Enjoy the time with your grandparents and

Finally a Father 173

your aunts and uncles, okay? Listen, I'll pick you up after dinner tomorrow evening, so have your stuff ready."

"Oh, Grandma said to tell you that we're eating dinner over at Grandma Ellis's house, and she wants you to come, too, and Grandma Ellis said bring Mac, too. Grandpa's going to cook out on the grill, and we'll eat about six-thirty, so be here, okay?"

Quin scowled fiercely, but kept all hint of it from her voice. "Okay, sweetie. You be good and have some fun."

Her daughter sighed heavily. "All right. I love you."

"I love you, too. Good night, babe." Hanging up the phone, she groaned out loud, then looked at Mac, leaning back against the footboard of her four-poster bed. "Have any plans for tomorrow evening?"

Immediately he looked wary. "Plans? Uh, yeah, I need to—"

Giving him a warning look, she stretched her foot out and made intimate contact with him. "I'm not going alone, sweetheart."

"I was just going to say that I need to finish the laundry, but it can wait. What's up?"

"We've been invited to dine at the Ellis home tomorrow, with both my family and David's in attendance. If I have to suffer, so do you." He didn't look overjoyed by the idea. What a surprise, she thought dryly.

"You just want me there because you think your mother is too polite to annoy you in front of me."

She picked up a pillow, a small heart-shaped one made from elegant antique lace, and hugged it to her chest. "She asked me last week if I was sleeping with you."

The wary look returned so quickly that she laughed. "Do you always discuss your affairs with your mother?"

"My 'affairs.' You make me sound promiscuous."

"I don't know how many men there have been."

"That's only fair. I don't know how many women you've been with."

"Do you want to?"

Biting her lower lip, she studied him for a moment. Sprawled across her bed, wearing a pair of button-fly jeans with the fly unbuttoned and nothing else, he looked handsome and sexy and downright disreputable. In spite of his sweet words back at his apartment—*There's never been any other woman in my life, Quin. Just you*—she knew there had been other women. Did she want details? Did she want to know how many? Did she want to know that he'd held other women the way he'd held her, that he'd made love to other women the way he'd made love to her?

Did she want to know that he'd loved some other woman?

"No," she replied decisively. "There's only room in this bed for the two of us."

"All right. So...do you always discuss such things with your mother?"

"Never."

"And what did you tell her this time?"

"That I was just waiting for the chance." She grinned at his expression. "I told her that it was none of her business. What's between you and me is strictly private."

Rising to his knees, he stretched over her, settling his hips snug against hers. "What's between you and me right now, sweetheart, is nothing more than a pair of jeans and a very flimsy nightgown." Pulling the heart pillow from between them, he tossed it aside, then gently kissed her.

"Will you go with me tomorrow?"

"I will. And, Quin?" He kissed her again. "For the record, there weren't as many women as you think...and not one of them ever measured up to you."

In spite of Cady's concerns, the rain stopped sometime during the night. Sunday was hot and muggy well into the evening—perfect weather for a cookout Mac didn't want to go to with people he didn't want to know. People who were important to Quin and Cady, he reminded himself. People he just might be seeing a lot of in the future, if things worked out with Quin.

Finally a Father

An elaborate patio extended from the back of the Ellis house halfway to the waterfront. Tables had been set up there, two shaded from the evening sun by umbrellas, the third placed in the shade of a nearby oak.

He sat beside Quin at the table under the tree, watching a sailboat on the sound, its sails flat and empty of air. Off to one side, Cady's grandfathers were grilling steaks and ribs; under one of the umbrellas, her grandmothers were chatting. Lorna and Greg, the youngest Ellis brother, were holding hands and entertaining Cady on the boat dock, and Rochelle and the other brother, Mike, were making plans on the other side of the patio.

It was a pleasant scene, one totally removed from anything in his experience.

"The boys look a lot like David, don't they?" Quin remarked.

Although he didn't need to—he'd been struck by the resemblance the moment they'd arrived—he looked for a moment at each of David's brothers. They had the same fair-haired, golden-boy looks that had drawn so much attention to David—blond hair, blue eyes, surfer tan. It was an uncomfortable feeling, having held David's lifeless body in his arms, to glance across the lawn and see his features on his brothers. "Yes," he admitted grimly. "They do."

"Thank you for coming," she said softly, laying her hand over his on the table. "I know this isn't your idea of fun, but…"

"It's not bad." And it really hadn't been. Cady had greeted him with the same enthusiasm she'd shown her mother—throwing her arms around his waist for a hug, grabbing his hand and dragging him into the Austin house to show him the fish she'd caught, now dressed and stored in her grandmother's freezer.

Quin's family had been friendly, although her mother's smile had slipped when she'd seen them holding hands, and David's family couldn't have been nicer.

But he still wished he was someplace else.

There were soft steps behind them, then David's mother sat down on the bench across from Mac. Call me Liz, she'd said when Cady had introduced them, but Quin, who had known her all her life, who had been her daughter-in-law for a third of her life, still called her Mrs. Ellis, and so he had done the same. "Dinner will be ready soon," she announced, folding her hands together on the cedar tabletop. "The men insisted we would be ready to eat at six, which is why I told everyone six-thirty. It looks as if we just might make it by seven."

"You can always count on Daddy and Mr. Ellis to be slow." Quin stood up, bracing her hand on Mac's shoulder as she stepped over the bench. "I think I'll give Lorna and Greg a break from Cady. I'll be right back."

Mac watched her go, then slowly shifted his gaze to Mrs. Ellis. Like her sons, like her husband, she was also blond, also had sharp blue eyes. But not like her granddaughter. There wasn't a hint of David's fairness in Cady's face, nothing to indicate that that child was a part of him.

"Don't worry," Mrs. Ellis said. "You don't need Quin to protect you from me. Janice, on the other hand..." She softened her implication with a smile. "I've heard a lot about you, Mac."

"From Cady?"

"Yes, but mostly from David. He used to write about you in his letters, used to bring your name into every conversation. He was very fond of you." She smiled sadly. "I think he wanted to *be* you when he grew up."

Mac stared hard at his hands, clenched together now, and concentrated on controlling the ache her words stirred. "I—I know I should have called when we got back, but..." He had tried to write a note, to send a card, but he could think of only thing to say: *Dear Mr. and Mrs. Ellis, your son is dead because of me.* And so he'd said nothing. He had ignored them as surely as he'd ignored Quin.

"That was a difficult time. We lost our eldest son, and I imagine you lost a lot of friends."

"All of them."

Finally a Father

She nodded sympathetically. "People are better equipped to deal with military deaths in a war-time situation, but when we're not fighting... I didn't worry about David joining the Marine Corps. I wasn't unduly concerned about that deployment. The U.S. was at peace. We weren't fighting anyone. He assured me the deployment was routine, and I believed him. I thought he would serve his six months, come home and finish his enlistment and live out the rest of his life, a better man for having been a marine. I never imagined he would die over there."

Mac could think of nothing to say. Her attitude was common and naive. He knew now that there was no such thing as a routine deployment—not as long as terrorists existed, ships caught fire and transport planes crashed. Something could always go wrong.

"So..." With a sigh, she smiled, putting the unhappiness behind her. "You knew Quin back then, didn't you, when she first moved to Jacksonville?"

"Yes, I did."

"Were you good friends?"

He shook his head. "We spent a lot of time together because of David, but we weren't..." His muscles tightening, he regretted the lie and told it anyway. "We weren't close."

The look Liz Ellis gave him was measuring and the slightest bit doubtful. She turned for a moment to watch Quin, standing at the water's edge with her arm around Cady's shoulders, then slowly turned back. "Yet you come back after ten years and meet her again and..." She laughed softly. "Don't try to tell me, young man, that you're not close now. I've been watching her watch you. You're the first man she's ever brought home, the only one she's ever allowed to have contact with Cady."

Again, there was nothing he could say. If Quin wanted to tell her in-laws that they were having an affair, that was up to her, but he wasn't doing it. He wasn't telling anyone exactly how close they were. He wasn't telling anyone exactly how close he wanted to be...not even Quin. Not yet.

"She's a lovely woman," Mrs. Ellis went on, looking at

her again. "I would like to see her fall in love and get married again. She's much too young to spend the rest of her life alone, and heaven knows, Cady could use a father." Then, with another of those delightful laughs, she turned back to him. "Don't feel that I'm putting any pressure on you, Mac. I'm speaking in generalities here. Just understand that most of us here would be happy to see Quin in love and married again." She rose gracefully from the bench and directed a cautionary look across the patio. "Most of us don't want to see her devote her life to being the keeper of David's memory."

He waited until she was gone, then glanced over his shoulder in the direction she had looked. Janice Austin sat there, her gaze on him. It held none of the friendliness, none of the welcome, the others had offered him. It held none of Mrs. Ellis's warmth.

Feeling suddenly edgy, he left the table and crossed the yard to join Quin and Cady, lying on her stomach now, watching crabs in the mud. Quin gave him a searching look that almost immediately dissolved into a smile. "That wasn't so bad, was it? Mrs. Ellis is a very nice woman."

"Yes, she is," he agreed, wrapping his fingers around hers, edging her slowly away from Cady.

"Did you talk about David?"

"Some. She wanted to tell me something."

"What?"

"That it's all right with them if I want to marry you and be Cady's father." He grinned, trying to treat it as a joke, but it cut too close to the bone to be funny. How long had he wanted just that—to claim Quin for his own, to marry her and have babies and live happily ever after? When had his obsession with her changed from short-term—*God, I want to make love to her*—to thoughts of permanence and marriage and forever?

Not the night they'd first made love. Not in the hurt-filled days that had followed. If he had to pin it down to a specific time, he would have to say the day David had told him that they were getting married. David had expected Mac to be happy for him, had expected congratulations and thumps on

Finally a Father 179

the back and best wishes. He'd gotten it from the other guys, but not from Mac, who'd been too stunned, too angry, too hurt. In that very instant, when he'd heard that Quin was marrying someone else, he had realized that that was what *he'd* wanted, what he'd been afraid to acknowledge because, deep in his heart, he'd known it would never happen. Quin would never have chosen him over David.

Ten years ago she hadn't.

But maybe now...

He had expected Quin to find her mother-in-law's maneuverings amusing or maybe a little embarrassing. He hadn't expected that distant, dark look in her eyes. He hadn't expected discomfort or dismay.

He hadn't expected her to turn and walk away from him.

"Where's Mom going?" Cady asked, rolling onto her side to face him.

"I don't know."

"I bet she's heading for the gazebo. That's her favorite place to sit. You ought to go over and see it, Mac. It's really neat." She turned back onto her stomach, then gave him one last look. "Unless you want to stay here and catch crabs with me?"

He smiled uneasily. "I think I'll skip the crabs this time, kid, okay?"

The gazebo was Quin's destination. It was on Austin property, located about halfway between the two houses, about the same distance between the street and the sound. It was octagonal, painted white to match the house, trimmed with gingerbread and lace, with wide steps sweeping up from two sides.

Inside there were benches, painted black. Quin was standing beside one, facing the water, her arms folded across her chest. He stopped at the top of the steps, a few feet in front of her.

"That wasn't a proposal, Quin," he said quietly.

Her smile was unsteady and unconvincing. "I know. It's not the marriage part. That's not..."

So what was it, then? he wondered, trying to remember what else he'd said. *It's all right with them if I want to marry you and be Cady's father.* Damn. He should have clarified that, should have said *step*father. "You know I would never try to take David's place in Cady's life," he said grimly. "She's all you have left of him—all his family has of him. She should always know him, should always believe in him as her father."

He wasn't having much success this evening. What he'd intended to amuse her had sent her running away. What he now intended to reassure her made her cry. He didn't know whether to hold her or leave her to mourn in private.

She made the decision for him, moving a step, reaching out. He drew her into his arms, pressing her face to his chest, and held her tightly. "Quin, I'm sorry," he murmured. "I didn't mean... I just thought you should know. I didn't mean to upset you."

At last she quieted, her tears fading to occasional shudders. "It's not you, Mac," she whispered, her voice muffled by his shirt. "It's my fault. I'm sorry, Mac. Everything...oh, God, everything is my fault."

"What?" He pushed her back, drying her cheeks, cupping her face in his hands. "What's your fault, honey? What have you done?"

Her mouth compressed in a thin line, she simply shook her head. After a moment, she asked, "Do I look awful?"

"Your eyes are red."

She rubbed at them. "My mother will know immediately that I've been crying and she'll think you're a horrible person."

He smiled gently. "She already thinks I'm a horrible person. If it doesn't bother you, it doesn't bother me."

"She doesn't think..." Her halfhearted protest faded, and she hugged him tighter. "Oh, Mac," she said with a sigh.

He liked the sound of that, soft and needy and sweet. One little sigh like that, and there wasn't anything he wouldn't do for her.

Stroking her hair, he remarked, "This must have been a great place to grow up."

"It was," she agreed. "We were very fortunate."

Finally a Father

"Too bad Cady doesn't have the same advantages." Advantages, he reminded himself, that David could have given her. Advantages that *he* could never afford.

"Oh, no. She loves visiting here, but she's perfectly happy where we are." She sniffed. "A few years ago I considered moving back home. Things were kind of tough—I was going through a very lonely period—and I was just a little tired of the demands of raising a child alone. So I suggested to Cady that we move in with my parents until I found a job up here and a place of our own. She didn't like the idea at all. Jacksonville was the only home she'd ever known. Her friends were there, and she loved our house and our neighborhood. Not even living in this big, beautiful house could entice her."

Her laughter ended in a hiccup. "She was just a little girl, but she was wiser than me. Jacksonville is our home. If I'd moved back here, even temporarily, I never would have gotten free again. I would have lived forever as Janice and Bradley's oldest girl, as David's widow. I never would have met you again." Her voice softened until it was barely audible. "I would have died."

After she finished, Mac moved to sit on one of the benches, then settled her close beside him. "Tell me about your sisters and David's brothers," he suggested. The more distracted she was from whatever had caused her tears, he reasoned, the less chance the families would notice anything wrong when they returned.

"Rochelle and Mike are just friends. They're the same age, and they grew up together. When neither of them is dating someone else—which is just about never—they go out sometimes, but there's nothing serious between them. Lorna and Greg..." She sighed forlornly. "Watching them is like seeing a replay of David and myself. He's a year older than her— David was two years older than me, you know—and they've been extraordinarily close since they were kids. They're planning to get married when she finishes college in two more years. She's never dated anyone else. She's never even looked at another guy."

"Are you sure about that?" he gently teased. "Does Greg have a best friend?"

She smiled at him. "Not one like you. If he did, I wouldn't worry. No, I tried talking to Lorna once about taking her time, maybe backing off a little and dating other guys, just to be sure. And she gave me this entirely too superior look and said, 'But I *am* sure, Quin. I love Greg. You, of all people, should understand that.'" She shook her head in dismay. "And what am I supposed to say to that? That I'd thought I was in love with David, too, but that I was wrong? That marrying him was the biggest mistake I'd ever made? That those tears I cried at our wedding were tears of regret instead of happiness? That, if he had survived the explosion, we would likely have been divorced before the first year was out?"

"What makes you so sure of that? David loved you, and even if you weren't in love with him, you cared a hell of a lot about him. Maybe you could have worked things out."

She gave him a wise look that left him feeling foolish without knowing why. "No, Mac, I don't think we could have. Those few hours I spent with you pretty much guaranteed that."

Quin watched him for a moment, then directed her gaze away. Let him find whatever meaning he wanted in that—that she'd been too attracted to him to work at her marriage to David; that she'd been too overwhelmed by him to find satisfaction with David. The simple truth was that she wasn't sure David could have accepted Mac's daughter as his own. He might have forgiven her for having a one-night fling with a stranger, but with his best friend? Some betrayals simply cut too deep to be forgiven.

It's all right with them if I want to marry you and be Cady's father. The echo of his words made her stiffen, but this time the tears didn't threaten. It was kind of David's mother to make such a statement. She couldn't possibly know that her approval wasn't necessary, that Mac *was* Cady's father.

And he couldn't possibly know why his assurances that he wouldn't try to replace David in Cady's life had made her cry.

Finally a Father

He was so sweet, so generous, and she was lying to him. Every day her silence damned her.

"Do you know what tomorrow is?" she asked softly, her head on his shoulder, his arm securely around her.

"Monday."

She poked him with her elbow.

He checked his watch. "August second."

"And?"

"And the beginning of another work week and..." His voice softened. "The tenth anniversary of our..."

Yes, of *our*... Ten years ago tomorrow, they had made love for the first time and—also for the first, but shamefully not the last—she had deliberately, selfishly struck out at him. She had hurt him. How she wished it was an anniversary of a different sort.

He didn't seem to share her wish. With an inviting grin, he asked, "Want to find a baby-sitter for Cady and do it again?"

"That would be nice," she agreed with a sigh. "Only this time we'll do it right."

Abruptly Mac got to his feet, throwing her off balance but catching her and drawing her up, too. "Honey, take my word for it," he said with a chuckle as he pulled her close against his body.

"It can't get any more right than it was then."

Chapter 10

Monday evening Quin hired a teenager down the street to watch Cady, and she and Mac went out to dinner. It was their first real date, she marveled. They'd been lovers, they'd shared a terrible shame, they'd had a daughter together and she, at least, had fallen in love, but they'd never been out on a date.

After dinner, without discussion, he took her back to his apartment. It was cool and dark, with only one small lamp in the bedroom turned on. There was no small talk, no pretense, no seduction. They walked in the front door, Quin tossed her purse on the coffee table, and they went straight into the bedroom.

"Cady was disappointed she couldn't come," she remarked, facing the dresser mirror as she let her hair down.

"We'll take her out this week, since our dinner last Tuesday got derailed by her accident."

She stepped out of her shoes, low-heeled and the color of cream with frothy grosgrain bows. Cady had teased her about the bows on her shoes and in her hair, but Mac had said she looked gorgeous, and the way he had looked at her—was look-

Finally a Father

ing at her now—made her feel gorgeous. "She's very fond of you."

"Good. I like her, too."

She began unbuttoning her dress, a pale linen with a deep V-neck and a gracefully curved collar edged with little bits of lace. After only a few buttons, though, she realized that Mac hadn't made a move. He was standing exactly where he'd stopped, leaning against the wall and watching her. "You're supposed to be undressing," she reminded him.

"I'm watching you."

Her cheeks flushed. "I see."

"I've never gotten to really watch you undress. We either wind up being in such a hurry or we're already naked from the time before."

Swallowing hard, she turned her attention back to her dress. It had only three buttons on the bodice, with another half dozen or so down the front to the hem. She unfastened each one, then shrugged out of it, first one arm, then the other. Looking around, she spotted a chair in the corner and laid it there.

When she had dressed earlier this evening, she had wished for pretty, sexy lingerie but had worn what she had: a simple camisole with ribbon straps and a tiny rosette sewn right between her breasts and a half-slip, both in a delicate shade of ivory. They were pretty enough—never sexy—but Mac didn't seem to mind.

Maneuvering beneath her slip, she removed her hose with a laugh. "There's no sexy way to take off panty hose," she declared, but the warm look in his eyes said he didn't mind that, either.

So now she was down to practically nothing—camisole, slip, panties—and he was still fully dressed. Moistening her lips with the tip of her tongue, she pulled the camisole over her head, letting it fall to the dresser top, then removed her earrings, her watch, her bracelet.

At last he moved away from the wall and approached her. "You've changed in the last ten years," he said, his voice husky.

"I've put on weight."

"But you needed it." He leaned against the dresser, facing her, and drew his fingers across her breast. "Your breasts are fuller, your hips a little more rounded. You were thin back then, a thin teenage girl. Now you're..."

Biting her lip as his caress reached her nipple, she waited to hear what he would say. None of the words she might have expected, though, came close to the pleasure his choice brought.

"Womanly," he finished. "Ah, hell, Quin, you're a beautiful woman."

She moved between his thighs and wrapped her arms around his neck. The soft weave of his shirt abraded her tender nipples, making them harder, increasing their ache, and his arousal was thick and hot through their clothes. "Did I ever tell you I thought you were beautiful, too?"

He grinned. "Never."

"I did. I do. The first time I met you, I thought you were the best-looking Marine—the best-looking man—I'd ever seen. And your eyes... The look in your eyes haunted me." He had interested her, had fascinated her, in a way no man ever had. She had lain in bed at night thinking about him. She had accepted the casual good-night kisses David had offered and wondered how much better such kisses from Mac would be. "If only I'd known then what I know now—"

Breaking away, she pressed a kiss to his jaw, then pulled his shirt free of his jeans, grasped the hem and tugged it up and over his head. His skin was hot and silky and invited her caresses over muscle and bone and soft, warm flesh. Below his ribs and across a flat expanse of stomach, she reached his jeans. Unbuckling his belt was easy, and each of the metal buttons slipped loose with the slightest pressure.

"There's something terribly sexy about a man in tight, faded jeans," she murmured, kissing his shoulder, then his chest and finally his nipple.

"Is there now?" He reached for her, but she avoided his hands and instead knelt before him. He was wearing his fa-

Finally a Father

vorite old running shoes again, and she loosened the laces, then removed his shoes and socks. Gazing up at him from this position, she had a tantalizing view of exactly what was so special about tight jeans on this man: the fabric, old and worn and faded almost white, stretched taut across his groin, leaving little to imagine about his arousal, long, hard and thick. It was an incredibly suggestive sight, provocative enough to make a woman's knees weak.

Fortunately, she wasn't going to be standing up anytime soon.

Sitting back, she stroked one hand along his leg. He had runner's legs, steely hard, muscular and strong—but even so hard and strong, she felt the muscles in his thigh quiver as her caress moved higher. Gently she stroked him, gliding her fingers with just a slight pressure along his length. When she slid her hand inside his clothing and repeated the long, slow caress, he sucked in his breath, and the muscles rippled across his belly. When she freed him from his clothes and intimately kissed him, he groaned out loud.

But he didn't stop her. He stood where he was, his legs wide apart, his hands clenched tightly around the edge of the dresser, his eyes shut. He let her explore, let her take all of him that she could, let her bite and tempt and savor, until he couldn't stand it any longer. "Quin," he gritted out.

She heard the warning in his voice, tasted it in her kiss, but still he made no move. He didn't push her away or hold her close. He let her decide how far she wanted to take this.

And she wanted it all, she decided.

Every bit.

Every experience.

Everything.

"What time is the baby-sitter expecting you?"

Quin raised Mac's wrist so she could see his watch and sighed. "I told her between ten-thirty and eleven."

When she let go, he looked at the watch himself. It was after ten-thirty now. "I wish you could spend the night."

She sat up, her hair disheveled, looking sleepy and lazy and thoroughly loved. "I'm sorry, Mac. I can't do that, and I can't ask you to stay at my house with Cady there."

"I know." It wouldn't be proper, and it would surely create more problems with Janice Austin if she realized her daughter was entertaining overnight guests around Cady. He never would have asked that she consider it. Still, it would be nice to have more than just one night together. To not have to get up after making love, get dressed and take her home.

But only one thing could make their sleeping together every night a possibility: marriage. If he and Quin got married. If he moved in with her and Cady. If they became a family.

Marriage. Wouldn't that be a hoot if he found the courage to ask and she had the love to accept? If, after ten years and such major changes in their lives, Quin Austin finally, and for all time, became *his* girl?

He tried to treat the idea lightly, but there was a part of him that refused. A long time ago he had wanted marriage to Quin with that same hopeless, helpless, desperate sort of craving that had characterized his life—wanting his father back alive, wanting a normal, loving family, wanting a chance to correct the mistakes he'd made with Chelsea, wanting to marry Quin. Wanting and never having. Needing and never getting.

If he had asked her to marry him then, she would have gone running to David. She would have married David so fast that his head would spin, just to keep herself from having to consider marriage to Mac.

But that was ten years ago. She wasn't a frightened, naive girl anymore. She wasn't trying to convince herself that she was in love with David.

But she wasn't offering any declarations of love to him, either.

She left the bed, gathering clothing as she made her way to the bathroom. Her panties were on the bed, her slip on the floor, her camisole on the dresser. While she was in there, he found his own clothes and quickly dressed, then went into the living room to wait.

Finally a Father

What if he asked her to marry him and she said no? What if she found him fine for spending time with, fine for sleeping with, but not suitable for a husband, not suitable to be stepfather to David's daughter? What if she preferred being keeper of David's memory over making new memories with him?

Restlessly he stopped in front of the shelf with its pictures. His father, the best family man he'd ever known. David, who had never had a chance to prove his devotion to his own family. And Chelsea. *She's pretty,* Cady had said. Then unselfconsciously adding, *She looks like me.* Indeed, Chelsea had been pretty, so delicate and feminine, so sweet and sad-eyed. And, yes, there was a resemblance to Cady. They both had the same coloring, the same older-than-their-years eyes—coincidence, of course. He knew such coincidences too well. The first months he'd lived in California at Camp Pendleton, he'd tensed up every time he'd seen a woman with short dark hair, dark eyes and dark skin, imagining for just one moment that it was Quin he'd seen.

Just coincidence.

"How do I look?"

Turning, he saw her coming out of the bedroom. Her question wasn't spurred by vanity, he knew, but rather necessity. Better phrased, it would have been, "Do I look the same as when we left? Do I look as if I've spent the last two hours in bed?"

Slowly he smiled. "You look as if you've been thoroughly made love to."

"So it shows, does it?" She tried to sound embarrassed, but just couldn't pull it off. The delight in her eyes gave her away. "I guess I'm ready."

He collected her purse from the coffee table and left the apartment with her. "You smell like me," he said as he helped her into his car.

"That's okay. *You* smell like *me*. No one will know the difference."

The drive to her house was too short. Once there, Quin paid

the baby-sitter, then waited outside on the porch until the girl was safely inside her own house down the street.

"I'd better get home."

She clasped his hand and drew him near. "Do you have to?"

"It's almost bedtime for both of us."

"Same time, different beds." She smiled ruefully. "Doesn't seem fair, doesn't it?"

No, it didn't.

"Come for dinner tomorrow night?"

"Let's take Cady out."

"Come and I'll cook. I don't mind. We can just stay home and be lazy."

Stay home and be lazy. With Quin. He liked that idea. "All right." He moved down one step, then lowered his head to kiss her. Sliding her arms around his neck, she welcomed his tongue and moved provocatively against him. She tasted of sex and hunger and desire, of everything he'd ever needed and everything he could ever want. It was with reluctance that he put her away and placed the rest of the porch steps between them. "Thanks for tonight, Quin. I'll see you tomorrow."

She let him get halfway across the yard before she spoke. "Mac? We did it better tonight, didn't we?"

Slowly he grinned. "Yeah. We did it just fine. Here's to the next ten years."

Only together this time.

For ten years, and ten years more and ten years more and more and more.

Tuesday night they had dinner at home. Wednesday night he took them out. Tonight they had eaten at home again, Cady's favorite meal of tacos and nachos and freshly made sopapillas. This was a routine, Mac decided lazily, that he could grow used to—hell, was *already* used to. He could live the rest of his life like this.

The night was unusually cool for August. The rain, steady since late afternoon, no doubt helped lower the temperature to a point that was truly comfortable for sitting on Quin's back porch—or lying, as the case may be. He was sprawled in the hammock, with Cady half sitting beside him, half lying against him. Once she went to bed, he was going to bring her mother out here, he decided. There was no telling what they would be able to do—definitely enough to send him home to an uncomfortable few hours in his empty bed.

Lately, merely looking at Quin was enough to guarantee that.

She was in the house now, cleaning up after dinner. He had offered his help, but Cady had wanted him to come out here, and Quin had shooed him away. She liked for him to spend time with her daughter, and, he had to admit, he found a great deal of pleasure in Cady's company.

"How long are you going to stay in the Marine Corps?" she asked, interrupting his thoughts.

So far this evening they had discussed the finer points of gambling, neighborhood bullies, which animal made the best pet and her career plans, which ranged from astronaut to Olympic athlete to mechanic. Now he got to talk about *his* career plans. "I'll stay in at least twenty years. After that, I don't know."

"Where will you go when you leave here?"

"No telling, kid. I'll find out when I get my orders."

"And when will that be?"

"A few months before my rotation here is up—nearly three years."

"Could they just send you to another battalion here at Lejeune so you wouldn't have to leave?"

"They could."

She offered him a quick smile. "Mom and I would like that. Then we could still see you."

"I'd like that, too," he admitted softly. He would like to stay here forever.

"Are you serious about Mom?"

He opened his mouth to answer, and abruptly she stopped him. "Don't tell me I'm being nosy this time, okay? I saw you kissing her last night, and you guys are always touching lately, and on TV when people do that, it means they're, you know, *serious.*"

He considered asking her just exactly what *serious* meant, certain that whatever answer her nine-year-old mind came up with would be interesting. But instead he seriously answered her question. "I like your mother a lot, Cady."

"Are you guys gonna get married?"

What was taking Quin so long? he wondered, wishing the creaky back door would open and she would come out and send Cady off to play or to take a bath or something. "I don't know. Maybe. And maybe you should ask your mother these questions."

She gave him a reproachful look. "My mother can only tell me how *she* feels. If I want to know how *you* feel, I have to ask you. Do you have your ID card with you?"

And that easily, the hard questions were over. Shifting so he could reach into his hip pocket, he pulled out his wallet and flipped it open to his military identification card. Sitting up, Cady studied it for a time. "Why do you look so tough?"

"Hey, I am tough."

"Yeah, right." she giggled. "Marines always try to look real mean and tough when they have their pictures taken. Like the picture of Daddy in my room. Like this picture."

"Have you ever considered that maybe marines look mean and tough because they *are* mean and tough?"

She giggled again and returned his wallet. "You're not—not mean, at least. Maybe you are a little tough. I get my ID on my next birthday. I think I'm gonna look like that. How's this?" She did her best imitation of a fierce scowl, but couldn't hold it.

"Pretty scary." He returned his wallet to his pocket, then lowered one foot to give the hammock a swing. "That's right—you get your first ID when you turn ten."

"Yup. Then if I have to go to the emergency room again, I have to use *my* ID instead of Mom's. That'll be neat."

"That's a long way away, though. Your birthday's in—"

Finally a Father 193

Pausing, he quickly added it up. "June, right? You just turned nine, Cady. You've got a long time to wait."

"Wrong. My birthday is in May." She leaned way to the side, checking the kitchen window, then, in a conspiratorially soft voice, she said, "I heard my aunts whispering about it once. They said I was born eight months after Mom and Daddy got married and that Grandma Austin was awfully upset, but Daddy died before I was born, you know, and everybody just sort of forgot about it. I really didn't understand what they were talking about. Matthew said I heard wrong because his mother told his big sister that women *can't* get pregnant before they get married, but Matthew's just a kid. He didn't turn nine until the middle of June. Do you know he thinks—"

She went on talking, but Mac had stopped listening. He had damned near stopped breathing. *My birthday is in May.* Eight months after Quin and David were married. Eight months after Quin and David made love for the first time.

Nine months after Quin and Mac made love.

It wasn't possible. She would have told him. At some point in the past month, she would have said *something*. It was just coincidence. Cady must have been a few weeks premature. Considering what Quin had been through, an early delivery wouldn't have surprised anyone, and that surely would have explained Janice Austin's distress. It was just coincidence.

Like the resemblance between Cady and Chelsea. Just coincidence.

Like the fact that there was nothing—absolutely *nothing*—of David in her features.

Just coincidence?

Right now he searched those features again. Granted, Quin's darker coloring was dominant over David's blond hair and blue eyes, but why wasn't there *something*, some hint—the shape of her face, her mouth, her nose or her jaw—of her father in her?

Her nose... Her nose was straight and strong, a little too strong for her delicate features. Like *his*. And her jaw was square, lacking the graceful lines of her mother's. Like *his*.

And her coloring not only lacked any hint of David's fairness, but was darker even than Quin's—her skin, her eyes, her hair. How was that possible if her father had had blond hair, light skin and blue eyes? Shouldn't the intensity of Cady's coloring have been tempered by the addition of David's genes instead of intensified?

"When exactly is your birthday?" he asked, carefully forming each word, unable to make his voice sound normal.

"I told you, in May. May second."

Do you know what tomorrow is? Quin had asked him Sunday. *August second. The tenth anniversary of our...* Ten years ago they had made love on the second of August, and nine months later—exactly, damn it—Cady had been born.

Coincidence? *Like hell.*

That explained the utter lack of resemblance between Cady and her so-called father.

David's genes weren't there.

David wasn't her father.

Quin had already been pregnant when she'd married David. *Pregnant.*

With *his* baby.

Abruptly he sat up, moving Cady aside so he could get to his feet. "I'm going to help your mother inside. Why don't you wait here?"

She stretched out in the hammock, dangling her head over the side. "Okay," she agreed. "Then when you guys are done, maybe we could go for a walk or to the ice cream store or something."

"Maybe." His movements carefully controlled, he let himself in and went straight to the kitchen. The smell of pine cleaner greeted him there; Quin was using it to clean the oil splatters from the stove and the surrounding counters. When she heard him, she glanced up, her smile ready. Something in his face chased it away.

Slowly she dropped the sponge into the bucket, then picked up a nearby towel to dry her hands. She took a few steps

Finally a Father

toward him and started to speak, but gave up the effort before the first word found voice.

He stopped a few feet away from her, wanting—needing—to see her eyes. He had always thought she was so transparent, so easily read, but for ten years she had kept the biggest secret of all from him. She had spent hours talking to him, had kissed him, had made love with him and had slept by his side, and she had never, not once, given any indication that she was lying to him.

"She's mine, isn't she?"

Tears formed immediately in her eyes, and she looked away, trying to blink them back. Swallowing hard, she met his gaze again. "Mac, let me—"

Angrily he raised his hand, signaling her to stop, and he quietly demanded, "Answer my question. Cady is my daughter, isn't she?"

She nodded.

"Say it, damn it!" he insisted, and the sound of his voice made her flinch.

"Yes," she whispered. "Cady is your daughter."

His daughter. Not David's.

A part of him, he realized, had wanted to be wrong, had wanted her to prove him wrong. He hadn't wanted to know she was capable of such deception. He hadn't wanted to believe that she could lie to him every day, every damned day of their daughter's life and longer.

He hadn't wanted to know that she thought so little of him that she wouldn't even tell him he was a father.

"Why?" He took a deep breath, hoping for restraint, for calm, but finding it impossible. "Why didn't you tell me? Why did you lie?"

Quin turned away, going to the sink to wash her hands. As soon as she was finished, she faced him again. "I'm glad you know," she said, her voice soft, her tone hopeless. "I wondered how you could look at her and not see, how you could spend so much time with her and not wonder."

He wasn't impressed by her words. With a heavy sigh, she

sought the ones that would answer his questions. "I didn't find out I was pregnant until a month after you and David deployed. I knew the baby was yours, but I was married to him. I was his wife, and I was determined to do everything I could to make our marriage work."

"That's why you never told him, isn't it? You never told anyone. What were you planning to do when he came home? Pass the baby off as premature? Lie to him, too?"

His sarcastic last words cut her. He could be a hard man, she reminded herself. Hard and unreachably cold. He was never going to forgive her for this. "I did tell him—in a letter I mailed three days before the explosion. I told him I was pregnant with another man's baby. I didn't tell him whose. I told him I was sorry and that I would understand if he wanted a divorce, that if he would forgive me and accept the baby, I would spend the rest of my life trying to make it up to him." A tear slipped free, sliding down her cheek, but she ignored it. "I got the letter back unopened a few weeks later. He was dead long before it got there."

"And you figured you would take the easy way out—let everyone believe you'd been a good and faithful wife, let everyone feel sorry for you and take care of you and fuss over you. You could have all the benefits of being David's widow, pass your baby off as his and never have to bother with me again."

She clasped her hands tightly together to keep from reaching for him. He wouldn't want her touching him now, she sorrowfully acknowledged. He would probably never want her to touch him again. "I was nineteen years old, Mac," she said, pleading with him to remember just how young that had been—how young he had told her she was. "My husband— my best friend all my life—had just died!"

"But *I* was alive!" he shouted, then, with a look toward the porch, he automatically lowered his voice. "I was alive, Quin, and I had a daughter, and you never told me."

"You never wrote," she whispered tearfully. "You never called. You never came to see me. David died, and you shut me completely out of your life. I was afraid, Mac. I was grieving for David, and I was pregnant and alone, and you wanted nothing to do with me."

"You knew how to find me." His tone was harsh and accusing. "All you had to do was call the legal office on base. They would have told you what to do. They would have located me."

Shamefully she bowed her head. Of course he was right; she knew that. If she had tried, if she had made the slightest effort... But she hadn't. She had taken the easy way out, and she had deprived him of nine years with his daughter. No words of apology could make that right. No explanations, no pleas, no excuses.

For a time he simply stood there, full of anger and hurt and sorrow. He had never looked so harsh. The expression in his eyes had never been so bleak. He was going to hate her for the rest of her life. She'd known that all along; still, somehow she wasn't prepared for it. She had hoped... Oh, God, she'd had such sweet hopes, but they were shattered now.

"Mac—"

"I want her to know."

"It's not that simple—"

"The hell it isn't!" he shouted. "You call her in and you tell her that you've lied to her every single day of her life! You tell her that her father isn't dead, that you simply chose to keep him away from her! You tell her that *you* decided she shouldn't be allowed to have a father! You tell her the truth!" He dragged in a deep, unsteady breath. "Just once in her life, Quin, tell her the truth."

"I will, Mac, I swear I will. But it's not just Cady. I have to tell my parents. I have to tell David's parents. They're going to be so hurt, Mac. They've loved her all her life. You said yourself, she's all his family has left of him. I can't just—"

He interrupted her again, his voice harsh, his words dark and threatening. "You can, Quin. Because if you don't tell them, I will, and I won't do it gently. I don't give a damn about David's parents. They're not her family. David *wasn't* her father."

Closing her eyes, she turned away. She had known for a month that this was coming, but she wasn't ready. How could she sit down with Cady and tell her the truth without earning her daughter's hatred? How could she survive knowing that, because of her own cowardice, she had lost her daughter's love and respect? And her parents' and the Ellises'…

Oh, God, wasn't losing Mac punishment enough? Did she have to lose everyone else, too?

Hugging her arms to her stomach, she shuddered. "I'll tell her, Mac. I'll tell all of them. Just give me some time."

With his silence, he granted that. After a moment, he started to leave—she heard his footsteps—but suddenly he stopped. "Tell me one thing, Quin. Are you just selfish as hell, or do you hate me that much?"

The little catch in his voice there at the end completed the breaking of her heart. Tears falling freely now, she hoarsely replied, "I've never hated you, Mac."

"You knew I would have come back. You knew I would have married you. You knew I would have loved Cady. I would have been a good father to her, and I would have—" His laughter was choked and desperately bitter. "Hell, Quin, I would have loved you, too. But you chose instead to raise her alone. To lie to her, to lie to everyone. To hide her from me. You chose to give her another man's name, another man's family." He broke off, then finished in a heartbreaking voice. "You thought a dead man would make a better father for her than I would."

"That's not true, Mac," she whispered.

"I wish I could believe you, Quin, but I can't," he said flatly. "I don't know if I'll ever be able to believe you again. Tell Cady…" Again, he stopped, then grimly repeated those two harsh words. "Tell Cady."

He left then, his footsteps echoing down the hall, the front door closing behind him. He left her alone and lonelier than she'd ever thought possible.

Finally a Father

It was her own fault. If she hadn't been so selfish, so stupid, so afraid... If she had taken the risk and told him the truth when David died... If she had been honest with him the day he'd come running past her house... If she had told him at any time in the past month, if she hadn't made him figure it out for himself...

So what if she felt as if she were dying inside? She had no one to blame but herself. She deserved all this hurt and much more.

And by Sunday, she was going to have so much more. Everyone was going to hate her. Everyone was going to despise her weakness and cowardice. Everyone was going to despise *her*.

"Is what he said true?"

Spinning around, she saw Cady standing just inside the kitchen door, her expression distressed, her eyes teary. Stunned that she had overheard even a portion of their conversation, Quin started toward her, arms outstretched, intending to hug and soothe her. But just as she reached her, Cady backed away. "Is it? Is it true that Daddy—that D-David isn't my father? That Mac is? Is it true that you've lied to me?"

"Honey, please—"

"It is, isn't it? It's true!" Cady was crying now, too, and Quin realized that Mac hadn't completely broken her heart; the job was finishing now. "You *lied* to me! All my life you told me it's wrong to lie, you punish me for it, and all my life you've been lying to me! Why?"

"Cady, sweetie, listen to me—" Again she reached for her, and again Cady shrank back.

"I don't want Mac to be my father!" she insisted. "I like him a lot, but I have a father already. Daddy—David—he's my father, isn't he? Mama, please, isn't he?"

Quin crouched in front of her, trembling so badly, she could barely keep her balance. She wished she could fall back on the comfort of another lie, but it was too late for that. She had to tell the truth. "No, baby," she replied gently. "Mac *is* your father, honey." She touched her then, grasping Cady's fingers where they extended beyond her cast. "I'm sorry, baby, I'm so sorry you had to find out like this. I wanted to tell you, I wanted to tell both of you, but I didn't—"

Cady struck out at her then, shoving her away, pushing her off balance. "No!" she screamed tearfully. "I don't believe you! You're lying to me! Mac said you lie all the time, and he was right! I hate you, I hate you!"

"Cady, please—"

Quin watched as her daughter ran down the hall, skidded around and raced up the stairs. A moment later she heard the bedroom door slam. Wearily, Quin sank into a small huddle on the floor, her knees to her chest, her arms tightly around them. If she could just contain the awful hurt inside, maybe it wouldn't destroy her, she reasoned. But in her heart she knew it was too late—it couldn't be contained. And this was only the beginning. It was only going to get worse.

God help her, what had she done?

Chapter 11

Mac couldn't remember ever being angrier than he was right then as he paced his apartment. Not the first time their stepfather had hit him. Not the first time he'd hit Chelsea. Not the time in Quin's kitchen when she'd shouted through her tears that she loved David and was going to marry him. Not the time he'd held David, the life crushed out of him by the weight of concrete and rubble.

Damn Quin.

She'd had no right. This secret wasn't hers alone to keep. Damn her. He'd had a right to know that he was a father, had had a right to see his baby girl, to watch her grow up, to know her and love her, to be there for her. He had every damn right in the world…and Quin had taken them from him.

Because she hadn't wanted to admit to her family that she'd been with a man other than David.

Because she hadn't wanted the shame of admitting that she was already pregnant before she made love with David.

Because she hadn't wanted to accept responsibility for what she'd done.

Because she hadn't wanted to give up her sympathetic place as David's widow.

Because she hadn't wanted to upset the balance of the cozy Austin-Ellis family friendship.

Because she hadn't wanted *him* to be her daughter's father.

That last acknowledgment sent a pain so sharp through him that his chest hurt with it. That was the part he could bear least of all. She had preferred a dead hero over a living, breathing, loving father for Cady. She had believed that David—who'd never known that Cady existed, who'd played no role in creating her, who very well might have hated her had he survived—was a better father dead than Mac ever could have been alive.

Even dead, David was still defeating him. Even dead, she thought he was the better man.

Restlessly, he went into the bedroom and changed into shorts, T-shirt and running shoes. It was stupid to run in the dark, stupid to run in the night rain, but he had to do something. If he stayed in the apartment, if he didn't get rid of some of this energy, the anger and the pain were going to kill him.

Sliding his key into his pocket, he left the apartment and turned away from Quin's house. In the past few weeks, he'd forgotten that there were streets to run that didn't go past her house. Right now he wasn't sure he would ever be going to her house again...except for Cady.

Except for his daughter.

The rain was cool and steady, hard enough to drench his clothes within a hundred yards but not enough to blind him. He ran steadily, making no effort to avoid the puddles in the street, uncaring that these were his good shoes, that the leather would never be the same again after this. Nothing was ever going to be the same again after tonight; why should his running shoes be spared?

Nothing would ever be the same again.

Nothing.

He had a daughter. A *daughter*. Sweet Cady, with her dark

Finally a Father

eyes and ready grin, with her charm and her sometimes-grown-up, sometimes-little-girl manner, was his daughter. He should be thrilled, overjoyed, amazed—and deep inside, he was.

But his daughter, his little girl, called another man Daddy—not him. She carried another man's name—not his. She loved this magical, mythical hero of a father that Quin and their families had created for her—not him. Oh, she liked him well enough—even more, it seemed, than anyone had expected—but, damn it, he deserved more from his daughter.

No matter what Quin thought, he deserved more.

Nothing would ever be the same. Not between Cady and the Ellises, maybe not between her and the Austins. God knew, Janice Austin already harbored a strong dislike for him for being what she perceived as a threat to Quin's status as David's widow. When she found out the truth, she would probably hate him for it, which was fine with him...as long as she didn't love Cady less for being his child instead of David's.

Things would change between Quin and the Ellises, too, between her and her own parents. Surely they would also be angry at her deception, would also be hurt. Surely they would also resent her lies.

Nothing would ever be the same between Quin and him.

He couldn't quit loving her, damn it. If he could, he would. Right now. Tonight. He would erase every kind thought and every sweet emotion he'd ever felt from his memory. He would quit wanting her, quit needing her, quit thinking about her. He wouldn't remember that odd expression on her face there in the kitchen, a mix of fear and apprehension and curious relief, as if she'd known it was going to hurt but the hurting had to be better than the dread. He wouldn't remember her tears or the anguish in her voice as she'd pleaded with him, wouldn't remember that some foolish part of him had wanted to hold her, to dry her tears and tell her that everything would be all right.

Brushing water from his face, he smiled sardonically. He had been angry with her for lying, and yet he'd been tempted to tell his own lie. Everything *wasn't* going to be all right.

They would find a relationship they could live with—for Cady's sake—for his own sake—but he couldn't imagine everything ever being all right again.

So what would happen now? Someday she would tell Cady. *Just give me some time,* she had asked, and he had agreed without asking how much time. How long would it take her to tell the truth? She hadn't managed it in the past ten years. She certainly hadn't managed it in the past four weeks. How much time did she need? A few weeks? A few months? A few years?

He couldn't wait that long. He couldn't stay on the sidelines while Quin gathered her courage. He couldn't wait until Cady was older, until she was grown, until Quin decided the time was right. He couldn't wait another ten years, playing his role as an old friend of Cady's father when, damn it, he *was* her father.

The road he was following led through a park, and impulsively he turned off, slowed his steps and walked the remaining few yards to the playground. He sat down on a swing, his feet wide apart, and leaned forward, letting his head drop while his breathing slowed.

He could wait.

No matter how much he hated the idea, no matter how much he hated thinking of David having any claim at all on his daughter, in the end she was the one who mattered. She was the one whose feelings had to be considered. She was the one who could be most hurt by this.

It wouldn't be easy for her finding out that her mother had lied. That the grandparents she had loved all her life weren't really her grandparents. That the only name she'd known wasn't really her name. That the only father she'd known wasn't really her father.

She would be hurt, too. Angry. Maybe rebellious. Maybe resentful. She might not want him for a father. She might blame him for upsetting her life. She might hate him and Quin both for turning her world upside down.

If it would be easier for her to find out when she was

Finally a Father

older—fifteen, maybe eighteen or even twenty—then he could wait.

But he wouldn't be cut out of her life again. He wouldn't lose the next nine years the way Quin had taken the last nine from him.

Whether as father or friend, damn it, he *would* be a part of Cady's life.

And of Quin's life, though not in the ways he'd wanted. In the past hour, marriage had become a distant dream. He wasn't sure he had any understanding left inside him, wasn't sure there was any trust to replace what had been damaged tonight. He could forgive lies and hurts, but he wasn't sure he could forgive her for choosing David over him once more. He wasn't sure he could forgive her for hiding his daughter from him, for cheating him out of those nine irreplaceable years of Cady's life.

He wasn't sure he could love her better than he hated her.

With a soul-weary sigh—a soul-weary sorrow—he stood up from the swing and started back toward the road. His first steps were halting and stiff, but gradually his pace increased, his muscles loosening so that his stride became fluid, transitioning easily from a walk to a jog to a hard run.

He was running away. Again.

The only problem, as he'd long ago learned, was that it didn't solve anything.

He always ended up right back where he started.

Friday morning Quin got up at her usual time, her face puffy from last night's tears and too little sleep. Tugging her robe on as she went, she went downstairs for breakfast and coffee, but she didn't have the energy for such effort. Instead she poured herself a glass of iced tea, then sat down at the kitchen table.

She had tried to check on Cady last night, sobbing in her room, but her daughter had locked her bedroom door. Quin knew how to unlock it—the locks were old, and all it took was a nail file to insert and twist—but she left her alone. Her daughter may be only nine, she had reasoned, but she had a right to privacy...at least until she'd fallen asleep. Then Quin had ventured inside, just to assure herself that she was all right. She had been lying atop the covers, her face tear-stained, her thin arms hugging her stuffed animals tightly to her chest, her even breathing disturbed by an occasional, hiccuping sob that had clutched at Quin's heart.

She had tried to check on Mac last night, too, had called his apartment a half hour after he'd left and again a half hour after that. There had been no answer. No doubt he'd known it was her and hadn't wanted to be bothered.

He would probably never want to be bothered by her again.

What was she going to do? How could she ever make right all the things she'd done wrong? How had she ever managed to hurt every single person she'd ever loved?

First, she decided, she was going to call in sick. It wouldn't be a lie—though Mac and Cady would undoubtedly see it differently; they had such faith in her ability to deceive and prevaricate—because she really was sick at heart.

Then...then she would deal with Cady. She would make her listen, would make her talk. She would explain things the best she could, would apologize, would plead, would...

Oh, God, the first thing she was going to do was cry again.

Shifting gears to hold off the tears, she turned her thoughts back to Mac. What would he do now? Would he be satisfied with seeing Cady on a regular basis, as he had been, or would he want more, and if so, how much more? Weekends? Vacations? Holidays? Still more?

What if he wanted her to live with him? What if he thought it only fair, since Quin had deprived him of the first half of their daughter's growing up, that he have her for the rest of it?

He wanted Cady to know the truth—he'd made that much clear—and now she did. That was only fair. He wanted her family to know the truth, too, and Quin also agreed that was necessary. But where would it stop? Would he want to change

Cady's name? Would he want custody of her? Would he want to take her with him when he transferred away?

Would he use her to punish Quin?

Slowly she rose from the table and went to the phone on the wall. Her boss always got to the office early; she answered on the second ring. After making her excuses, Quin hung up, gathered her robe around her and shuffled back upstairs, knocking at Cady's door.

After a long silence came a pitifully angry command. "Go away."

"Get up, honey, and get ready for breakfast." She tried to pretend that nothing was wrong, but her voice trembled anyway. "We'll talk, sweetie."

"I don't want to get up, and I don't want to have breakfast with you and I don't want to talk to you. I don't ever want to talk to you again!"

Quin bit her lip. Part of her wanted to gently tease her daughter out, to remind her that she never skipped a meal, no matter what the reason, to tell her that she couldn't stay in her room all day. But she could. She was just stubborn enough to do it. "Okay," she said sadly. "I'm going to get dressed, then, if you change your mind, I'll be in the kitchen."

She was sitting at the kitchen table again, wearing jeans and a T-shirt, when Cady finally wandered in. She had dressed in biking shorts and an oversize shirt, her hair was uncombed and sticking out at angles and her expression was definitely mutinous. If she got that lower lip out any farther, Quin thought, her amusement bittersweet, she would never be able to eat anything.

"I'm going over to Miss Jenny's," she announced sullenly, never making eye contact.

"No, honey, you're staying here today. I'm not going to work." Quin rose from the table and went to the cabinet. "Want some cereal?"

"I'm going over to Miss Jenny's anyway."

"No, Cady, you're not. I stayed home today because you and I need to talk. Sit down."

Muttering, she pulled a chair out, making a loud scraping sound, then dropped into it. After a moment's hesitation, Quin sat down opposite her. "I'm sorry about last night, Cady. I didn't know you had come in. I didn't know you overheard."

Her daughter sat there, scowling darkly, her chin on her chest, one foot swinging in the air.

Quin took a deep breath. "I know it was wrong of me to lie to you, and I apologize for that, sweetie. I never should have done it. I hope someday you can forgive me for it."

Maybe, but not, judging from her attitude, today.

"Mac is a good man, Cady. He'll be a good father—"

At last her daughter deigned to look at her. "I have a father," she said stubbornly. "I don't need another one."

"Honey..." Quin sighed, then forced herself to go on. "Mac is your father, Cady. He's your only father. I'm sorry I let you believe all these years that—that David was your father. That was my mistake, and I wish I had never done it. It wasn't fair to you or to Mac or anyone else."

"I suppose now you expect me to call *him* Daddy."

Her sarcasm made Quin wince, and her attitude concerned her for Mac's sake. Would he expect to be a father to Cady now that they both knew? Did he think he could come in and immediately fill David's place? After already being hurt by Quin, would he now have to endure whatever pain Cady might offer, too?

"No, honey," she said quietly. "The only thing I expect is that you continue to show Mac the friendship and respect that you've been giving him. None of this is his fault, Cady. It's all *my* fault. If you want to blame someone, if you want to be angry with someone, then be angry with me. Just be friends with Mac. Give him a chance. Give your new relationship with him a chance. You already know he's a good friend. I think you'll find out he can be a very good father."

"Am I gonna have to change my name?"

"No, not right away. That's something we would have to decide later—all three of us."

"Am I gonna go live with him part of the time?"

Finally a Father 209

"That's also something we'll have to decide later."

Cady gave her a calculating, malicious look. "That might not be so bad. Then neither one of us would have to see *you*."

Quin bit hard on the inside of her lip and looked away. At least Cady and her father agreed on one thing. That was a start.

With another loud scrape, she pushed her chair back and stood up. "I'll be nice to Mac," she said flatly. "But I'm not going to call him Daddy, and I'm not gonna use his name and I'm not *ever* going to like you again." Leaving, she made it as far as the door; then she doubled back to scoop a box of cereal off the counter. With the box tucked under her arm, she left the room in a huff. A moment later the TV in the living room came on, turned extra loud just to annoy her mother.

For whatever it was worth, she had talked to Cady. Tomorrow she would drive to Morehead City and have separate meetings with her parents and with Mr. and Mrs. Ellis. By tomorrow evening Mac would have the disclosure he wanted.

If only she'd done it last Saturday or the Saturday before or the one before that. She couldn't shake the feeling that if she'd broken the news to him herself, that if she'd done this voluntarily, he wouldn't hate her quite so much. He wouldn't be so unforgiving. He wouldn't be so bitter.

If only she had shown a little courage.

Just once in her life.

Mac sat at his desk, a stack of fitness reports on the company's noncommissioned officers in front of him. He was supposed to be reviewing the performance evaluations to be sure they were complete and accurate before passing them on to the first sergeant, but for the past hour he'd done little but stare into the distance. He was having difficulty concentrating on his job, difficulty thinking about anything at all except last night. He told himself it was because he hadn't slept well; last night's hour-and-a-half run had worn him out, but it hadn't helped him sleep. He had paced the apartment until early morning, then had tossed in bed until it was time to get up. But lack of sleep wasn't the problem.

Quin and Cady were.

The phone on his desk rang, but he ignored it. He'd gotten one of the few company phones in his cubicle by luck, but it was one of the company clerk's duties to answer it. Besides, it wasn't likely to be for him.

But damned if it wasn't.

"Phone call, Gunny."

Slowly he shifted his gaze to the clerk standing in the doorway. "Who is it?" he asked. As if it could possibly be anyone but the one person in the world he didn't want to speak to.

The lance corporal picked up the phone on Mac's desk, asked for the information, then, looking uncomfortable, held his hand over the receiver. "Quin Ellis."

"Tell her..."

Before he'd thought of a lie, the corporal interrupted. "She said if you didn't want to talk to her to give you a message—that Cady knows."

Grimly he reached for the phone, and after handing it over, the young man returned to his own desk. Mac didn't bother with greetings, but went straight to the point. "What do you mean, she knows?"

"She overheard us last night." She sounded hesitant. Subdued. Nervous. That same damned nervousness that he'd always hated was back. "As soon as you left, she came into the kitchen and asked if it was true, and—"

"And you didn't lie to her?" Her sudden silence made him regret his harsh interruption. Tempering his anger, he asked, "Is she okay?"

"She's very angry. She has a lot of questions, and she's not sure she wants another father, and—"

"Not another...Quin. I'm the only father she's ever had."

Again she became silent, and he found himself straining to hear something—the sound of her breathing, some background noise, anything—but except for the hum on the phone line, there was complete quiet until at last she sighed. "Could we meet somewhere at lunch time, Mac? I'd like to talk to you before you see her again."

His fingers wrapped tightly around the receiver, clenching until they hurt. "I don't think that's a good idea."

"Please, Mac…"

Relenting, he glanced at his watch. It was a quarter after eleven. "I don't have much time."

"I can come out there," she offered. "We can go someplace on base."

"All right. Meet me at the PX, over near the ice cream shop, in half an hour." There were several places to eat in that area, if either of them felt like eating. He sure as hell didn't.

She agreed, then hung up. Slowly, much more slowly, he did the same.

So Cady knew. Last night he had convinced himself he could wait a while—years, if necessary—before she found out the truth, and at that time she had already known. How had she managed to come in through that squeaky back door without either of them noticing? Because he had been yelling, he reminded himself, and Quin had been crying. Neither of them had been listening for their daughter.

Their daughter.

God, it still sounded so foreign. Most men got seven or eight months to prepare for becoming fathers; most men got to know their kids from the minute they were born. He'd been denied that chance to prepare himself. One minute he'd been utterly alone in this world, and the next—boom, he'd had a daughter. A lively, bright, daring, nine-year-old daughter.

And he shared her with Quin.

He couldn't quite get used to it.

For the first time since Chelsea's death, he had a family. He had responsibilities—and so damned many questions. He wanted to be a part of Cady's life, wanted all the obligations that other fathers had. He wanted to help support her. He wanted to have as large a place in her life as David had been given.

He wanted to add her as next of kin to the Record of Emergency Data in his service record, wanted to make her the beneficiary of his serviceman's life insurance, wanted her acknowledged by the Marine Corps as *his* dependent, not David's. And since legal problems might arise there, because everyone believed David to be her father, he wanted her birth certificate corrected.

He wanted David's name taken off.

He wanted his own put on.

He wanted David removed from her life.

Shuffling the fitness reports aside, he gave up on work, left the office and drove the few miles to the exchange. The ice-cream shop sat at one end, a tiny little building with a drive-through window and a few rickety picnic tables around the front. He got a soda from the walk-up window, then went to sit at the most distant table and wait.

Quin was a few minutes early. She parked beside his car, then got out, hesitating there a moment before approaching him. Damn, but she was beautiful. In her sleeveless dress with a yellow ribbon holding her hair back and dark glasses shading her eyes, she looked cool and untouched. He almost hated her for it. His and Cady's lives were in chaos, and she looked the same as ever.

Until she sat down across from him. Briefly she removed her sunglasses, using the tip of one finger to rub her eye, and he saw before she replaced the shades that her eyes were swollen and red from too many tears. There were tiny lines at the corners and around her mouth from too much stress, and the color in her lips wasn't from lipstick but because she kept biting them, first the lower one, then the upper one.

For a time they sat there, neither speaking, neither looking at the other. Finally he gestured toward the cup in front of him. "Want a Coke?"

"No, thank you." She folded her hands together on the tabletop. "I'm sorry about everything, Mac—about what I did and the way I handled it."

He didn't respond to that.

With a soft sigh that sounded full of defeat, she changed the

Finally a Father

subject. "I'd like for you to see Cady tonight. Just let her know that you're there and that you're not going to make any great demands."

"I have a whole list of demands, Quin," he said stiffly.

"You have to give her time, Mac. She's just a little girl. Granted, she never knew David, but he's the only...the only father she's ever known. Let her get used to the idea that he wasn't before you try to take his place."

"It's *my* place—my rightful place. You're the one who gave it away, who let someone else take it."

"Fine, then hate me for it, but be patient with her. She's upset. She doesn't know what to think. She doesn't know what you expect from her."

Fine, then hate me for it. Last night he had been positive that he did, that he hated her at least as much as he loved her. Even right now he felt an incredible anger toward her for doing such a thing to him, to Cady, to them. But the sad fact was he loved her, too. He might never forgive her, might never trust her or believe in her again, but he still loved her. He still wanted her. He still needed her.

"So what am I supposed to expect, Quin?" he asked sarcastically. "Is she still going to call me by my name? Is she still going to think of me as her mother's friend? Is she still going to treat me like the nice guy who lives down the street? She's my *daughter,* damn it."

Her voice trembled when she replied. So did her hands. "Just give her time to accept that. I don't know what you can expect from her. I don't know what kind of relationship the two of you can have, Mac. I don't have any answers. Just...be patient. Give her time. Don't pressure her."

He stared past her, watching the traffic. The parking lot got busy around lunchtime, with everyone making trips to the PX, the cashier's window around front, the bank or the restaurants at the opposite end. After a moment, still watching, he asked, "Will she go to dinner with me tonight?"

"I imagine she'll agree to just about anything that gets her away from me."

Part of him wanted to ask if she was having a hard time, if Cady was taking her anger out on her. The stronger part didn't care. It was no more than she deserved. "I'll pick her up around six."

"Thank you." She stood up from the bench but didn't walk away. "Mac? I know it doesn't matter much, but...I *am* sorry. If I could go back and do everything differently, I would."

Finally he met her gaze. The dark glasses hid her eyes, but he didn't need to see them. They had lied to him far too easily for far too long. "You're right, Quin. It doesn't matter."

With a sad little nod, she turned and walked away. Watching her go, he felt like a bastard for those last cold words. But, damn it, she deserved it. She was the one who had screwed up. She was the one who had lied. She was the one who had turned everyone's lives upside down. She was the one who had hurt everyone else.

So what if she was hurting, too? So what if she had obviously cried a great many tears and looked ready to cry some more? She had brought this on herself. She was responsible.

So why did he feel so damned guilty?

"I really like your car."

"Thanks." Mac waited until Cady's seat belt was fastened, then he started the engine. "Where do you want to go for dinner?"

She reached across to fiddle with the radio dial, then wiped a strand of hair from her face. "I don't care."

"Do you want fast food or a real restaurant?"

"I don't care."

"Are you hungry?"

She rolled the window down, then pressed the button and watched it glide up again. "Not really."

He pulled away from the curb, heading nowhere in particular. "Did you come because I asked, Cady, or because your mother made you?"

"She lied to me," she said flatly. "She always tells me to tell the truth, that no matter what I do, if I tell the truth, it'll

Finally a Father 215

be all right, and all the time she was lying to me. I hate her for it." She gave him a dark look. "I bet you hate her, too."

He swallowed hard, and color flooded his face. "I—I'm angry with her," he said cautiously.

"You hate her. I don't blame you." Abruptly she asked, "Can we stop here?"

Here was the same park he'd run past last night, the same place where he'd sat thinking about Cady. He pulled into the parking lot, and they got out, walking past kids playing and mothers watching them. She headed to a pair of empty swings, sat in one and began pushing herself back and forth. "You said the night I broke my arm that you wanted kids. So..." She gave him a sour look as he sat down in the second swing. "You're finally a father. What do you think of it so far?"

"It's not quite what I imagined."

"Were you in love with my mother? When she got pregnant with me? Is that why you never wanted to marry any of those other women?"

Feeling his face grow warm again, he unevenly replied, "You're an awfully nosy child."

She stopped swinging and gave him a truly obnoxious look. It matched her tone. "You're my *father*. I'm entitled to ask questions."

"And I'm entitled not to answer them."

"You must have been." Rising from the swing, she leaned over it, resting her stomach on the seat and swinging that way. "You were dumb enough to do it twice, weren't you?"

He ignored the insult and asked, "Do what twice?"

"Fall in love with her. Then and now. I bet you even wanted to marry her, didn't you?"

Clenching his jaw, he looked away without replying.

Abruptly she left her swing and came to him, touching his knee, drawing his attention to her. "Can I still call you Mac?"

"If you want."

"Do I have to use your last name?"

Two hopes down. There would be no sweet, soft voice calling him Daddy, no Cady McEwen to claim as his own. "Not unless you want to."

"Do I live with you or stay with Mom or live both places or what?"

"That's something we'll have to decide later. We're all kind of surprised and upset right now. We don't need to make any important decisions just yet."

"That's what Mom said. I told her it wouldn't be bad living with you 'cause then I wouldn't have to live with *her*."

He took her hand in his, gently twisting it side to side. "Did it make you feel better to hurt her?"

She jerked away. "I hate her. Do you understand? I'm always going to hate her for this—always!"

Mac watched her storm away, a lump in his throat and an uncomfortable ache in his chest. What in God's name had Quin been thinking when she'd started telling her lies? Had she believed she could keep telling them forever? Had she thought no one would ever find out? Had she even once considered the pain she would cause everyone involved?

After a moment, he left the swing and followed Cady. She was sitting on a rock, her knees drawn close, her chin resting on them. Her expression was dark and forbidding, but there was the gleam of tears in her eyes. He lifted her, sat down himself, then settled her on his lap.

"I like you, Mac," she said, her voice quavering. "I really do. But I want things to be the way they were. I want Daddy—David—to be my father again. I want you to be Mom's boyfriend and maybe my stepfather someday. I want Grandma and Grandpa Ellis and Uncle Mike and Uncle Greg to still be my family. I want Mom to quit crying, and I want you guys to get serious again, and I want it all to quit hurting, Mac!"

He held her close as she cried, stroking her hair. "I'm sorry, Cady," he murmured bleakly. "I wish I could tell you that everything's going to be all right, that everyone's going to end up happy, but I don't know. I don't know how things are going to turn out. I don't know what's going to happen between your mother and me or between you and me. I just know that I want

Finally a Father

to spend some time with you. I want to find out what it's like to be a father. I want to know what it's like to have a daughter.''

They sat there a long time, neither speaking. Her tears slowly dried, but she didn't move away. She seemed content to stay there in his arms forever. But finally she roused herself enough to speak in a wistfully soft voice. ''Even though Matthew says they're a pain, I always thought it would be neat to have a baby brother or maybe a sister if she was like me. I sure did hope that you and Mom would get married and maybe have one.''

Then, twisting, she moved right up into his face, practically nose to nose, her fierce gaze locked with his. She laid her hand on his cheek, her palm small and damp, and solemnly announced, ''I guess I'm going to find out what it's like to have a father.''

Chapter 12

Saturday evening was quiet, the unusual stillness that preceded a storm. The weather reports were calling for thunder and lightning and more rain, and Quin had been hearing rumbles in the distance—artillery or thunder, she didn't know. She didn't care. How could she concern herself with weather when her entire life had fallen apart?

Today was the first Saturday in as long as she could remember that she and Cady hadn't shared their ritual lunch at the pizza parlor. Instead, Mac had picked up their daughter around eleven o'clock for a trip to Wilmington. Quin had watched them drive away, then had climbed into her own car and headed northeast to Morehead City.

To her parents' house.

To the Ellises' house.

She turned onto her side in the hammock, watching the small patch of evening sky as lightning flashed. She loved thunderstorms, had watched plenty of them from right here with Cady curled up beside her. When she was younger, the thunder had frightened Cady and she had stuck close to Quin

Finally a Father 219

through every storm. She'd outgrown that fear, but she still liked snuggling close and watching nature's fury from the security of the porch and her mother's embrace.

Correction. She *used* to like snuggling close.

Last night she had come home from dinner with Mac and gone straight to her room without so much as a word for Quin. This morning she hadn't responded to Quin's efforts at conversation. She had eaten her breakfast of ice cream in front of the television, had then dressed and gone out to play with Matthew while waiting for Mac. She had even ignored Quin's goodbye as she climbed into Mac's car.

I'm not ever *going to like you again.*

How long could a little girl stay angry? she wondered unhappily. How long could Cady hate her? It had been only forty-eight hours, but it felt like a lifetime. Because there had been no one else to share their lives on a regular basis, they had always been extraordinarily close. That made this rift even harder to bear.

Another rumble sounded, this one going on and on. Definitely thunder. The storm was moving closer. It would provide just the right ending to one of the worst days of her life.

There was the sound of a car around front, a finely tuned engine abruptly shutting down, the thud of doors. Mac and Cady were home. She waited, knowing they would find her note on the front door directing them around back, knowing that Mac would see Cady safely inside, that *she* would see him at least for a minute. Part of her wanted to desperately. Part of her found the prospect too painful to bear.

Sure enough, Cady appeared around the corner first, and Mac was only a step behind her. She was wearing a ballcap bearing the name of the USS *North Carolina,* the decommissioned battleship that had been turned into a museum on the Cape Fear River in Wilmington, and carrying an armload of souvenirs. Apparently, her first father-daughter excursion with Mac had turned out well.

Quin wished she had been welcome to go along. She

wouldn't have—naval ships didn't interest her—but it would have been nice to be wanted.

Slowly she sat up in the hammock, pushing her hair from her face, offering a soft greeting. "Hey, Cady, Mac."

Her daughter pushed the screen door back for Mac to catch, then continued straight on through to the laundry room. She didn't spare so much as a glance for Quin. Inside, she paused and turned back. "Thanks for taking me down there, Mac, and for the stuff. I'll see you later."

"Okay." He let the screen door close quietly at the same time Cady shoved the back door shut. He stood there for a moment, looking uncomfortable. Of course. He didn't want to be alone with her any more than Cady did.

Quin lay down again, the hammock gently swaying from her movements. She wouldn't blame Mac if he made a quick escape, too, but he showed no signs of taking off just yet. Instead, hands in his pockets, he walked over to the wicker chair and pushed down on one of the curved rockers with his foot, making the chair tilt forward and creak noisily.

"We stopped and ate dinner on the way back," he said at last.

Even though he wasn't looking at her, she nodded. She had figured they would. Now she wouldn't have to fix a dinner that Cady wouldn't eat with her and that she wasn't hungry for herself.

"We toured the *North Carolina* and took a river cruise and went to the train museum."

"I'm sure she had a good time."

Finally he turned to look at her. Even in the dim light, she had a feeling he could see her better than she wanted to be seen. She wasn't looking her best these days. All-too-frequent tears and heartache saw to that.

"Are you okay?" he asked hesitantly, unwillingly.

"No." Her honesty just seemed to increase his discomfort. She was sorry for that. Today, yesterday and every tomorrow... She was going to be sorry for the rest of her life.

Finally a Father

At last he sat down in the rocker, turning it so he faced her. "Cady said you were going to Morehead City."

Her daughter must have eavesdropped when Quin had called to make sure her parents and David's would be free to see her this afternoon, because she certainly hadn't told her where she was going. She hadn't wanted her to know, not until after the fact. Not until she knew how her news was going to affect Cady's relationships with her grandparents.

"Did you tell them?"

"Yes."

"Did they— Are they...?"

"Yes." They were angry. Furious. Disillusioned. Disappointed. Upset. Dismayed, shocked, stunned, unforgiving, accusatory, condemning. Her mother had screamed at her. Her father had given her an enormously disappointed look before turning away from her, shrugging off her hand. Her father-in-law had sat in utter silence, had never spoken one single word. He had looked the way he did the day she told him that David was dead—dazed and hurt beyond belief. Her mother-in-law had cried, and Mike had called her a few choice names, harsh and obscene.

Shame. That had come up several times. You should be ashamed of yourself, Mike had said. Going to bed with that man was a shameful thing, her mother had shouted. And the one that had hurt worst of all, coming from her father, quiet and sad and oh, so disillusioned. *You've shamed us, Quin. You've dishonored your family, your husband, your marriage vows, yourself.*

"What did they say?"

She settled more comfortably on the hammock, lying on her side again, bending her knees. If she curled up any tighter, she was going to be in the fetal position, she realized. A common position for someone in great distress and so appropriate for her. "They weren't very pleased with me."

That was a fine understatement. Her mother had been so displeased that she had told Quin it would be best if she stayed away for a while. Until they had time to deal with her news.

Until they sorted through their feelings. Until they discovered whether they could ever forgive her appalling behavior. Until they decided whether they could forgive her deceit.

It was her fault. Everyone was hurt and upset, and it was all her fault. She deserved to be punished for causing such sorrow, but exactly how badly did it have to hurt? she wondered. How much pain did she have to endure until the scales were balanced? How much love did she have to lose?

"Why did you do it, Quin?"

She closed her eyes as a cool breeze blew from one end of the porch to the other, bringing the scent of rain with it. Now that Mac and Cady were home, she was ready for the thunderstorm. She wanted rain to match the tears she'd cried.

Feeling him watching her, she slowly opened her eyes again. The sun had set, and the storm clouds darkened the sky, hastening dusk. She could barely make out his features, but she knew as surely as if it were midday bright that his expression was hard. Unforgiving.

"It was the easy way out," she said with a sigh. "Everyone believed I was a good wife to David, that I'd been faithful to him, that Cady was his baby, and I let them. It was easy."

He recognized her version of the words he'd thrown at her Thursday night and muttered a curse. "Answer my question, damn it."

"I don't have any answers, Mac," she said wearily. "I was nineteen. I was stupid. Selfish. I made a mistake. It was a difficult time, and I wanted it made easier. I made a choice, and it was the wrong one. I'm paying for it now. And I'll pay for it for a very long time. If that doesn't satisfy you, I'm sorry, but that's the best I can do."

"Why didn't you tell me you were pregnant after David died?"

She gave a choked little laugh. "I could barely dress myself after David died. I couldn't plan ahead to what I should make myself eat for dinner. I stayed in bed for nearly a week just crying."

"Later," he said impatiently. "After the grief..."

Finally a Father 223

"After the grief?" she echoed. "Is that how it works for you, Mac? After your father died, after Chelsea and David died, did you mourn them for a few days, then go back to life as usual?"

He didn't answer. He didn't need to. Even now, years later, he still mourned each of those losses.

"After David's funeral, I stood there beside his grave, more than four months pregnant, holding the flag the honor guard had given me, and his mother came up and put her arms around me and said, 'At least we have his baby. As long as we have this baby, he'll never really be gone. He'll live on in his child forever.'"

She rolled to her feet on the side of the hammock away from him, leaned one shoulder against the corner support post and stared out into the night. "Through the rest of my pregnancy and the first few years of Cady's life, I had all the love and support that David's family could possibly offer—and not just from his parents. His brothers used to come down and help out around the house. When I was in school, his aunts took turns baby-sitting with Cady so I could go to class. His cousins included me in all their family activities so I wouldn't be lonely. They gave birthday parties for me and for Cady, they held Halloween and Easter and Fourth of July celebrations so we wouldn't have to spend even minor holidays alone. They celebrated Christmas from Thanksgiving on, held party after party, helped me shop and bake and decorate, because they were afraid the memory of David's death a few weeks before Christmas would make that time too difficult for me."

As the rain started, she raised her hand and laid it, palm flat, against the screen. A drop landing on the rail splashed through the wire to her finger. "Where were you, Mac?"

"I would have been here if I had known."

"You would have known if you had bothered to contact me," she whispered.

Mac left the rocker to stand at the opposite end of the screen. Five, maybe six feet, separated them—that and a lot of anger. A lot of hurt. A lot of mistakes.

She was right. If he had gone to see her when the battalion had returned home, he certainly would have noticed that she was seven months pregnant. He surely would have counted and known the baby was his. But would it have made a difference?

"Would you have found it possible to tell the truth if I'd been here? To tell David's mother that he wouldn't live on in the baby you carried because he'd played no part in giving it life? To tell her that the grandchild she was counting on wasn't hers?"

"I think so." She sighed softly. "I was alone, Mac. I was nineteen years old, my husband was dead and the father of my baby didn't want anything to do with me. I took what support I could get—from my family and from David's. If I had told them the truth, I would have lost most of that support. The Ellises would have turned their backs on me, and rightly so. My own family would have had a hard time dealing with me. For telling the truth, I would have been rewarded by losing the people I was relying on. It still wouldn't have brought you back. It wouldn't have made you want me. I would have been more alone than ever. But if you had been here, if I had known that I could count on you to take their place, if I had known that you wouldn't leave me alone, that you would be with me when Cady was born, that you would help me raise her and love her...I believe I could have told them."

And he knew that *he* could have. If her courage had failed her, he certainly could have broken the news to them. It wouldn't have bothered him to break their hearts, not if it meant getting to claim Quin for his own. Not if it meant claiming his daughter for his own.

If he had known.

If she had told him.

If he had gone to see her.

"I promised him I would stay away from you." He saw her head turn, felt her look his way. "I helped recover his body, and I felt so damned guilty, and...I promised him that I would stay away from you. It was my need for you that got him killed, and so I swore to him that I wouldn't come back, that I wouldn't contact you. That was my punishment for wishing him gone, for leaving him behind to die.''

"And you would have broken that promise for Cady."

"David was my best friend. Cady is my daughter. I owed him a great deal to make up for what we'd done, but I owe her more."

She turned back to the yard again, silent and still as she watched the rain. He watched her, wondering just how badly things had really gone with her family and the Ellises. What had they said to her? How had they hurt her? How would they treat her now that she had disillusioned them, now that she had failed to live up to their expectations of David's widow, as the keeper of his memory?

When she spoke again, her voice was tearfully unsteady, her question unexpected and wistful. "Are you going to take her away, Mac?"

"Take her..."

"Cady," she whispered. "Do you want her to live with you? Are you going to ask for custody? Are you going to take her away from me?"

He moved a few steps toward her, resting his hand beside hers where it was clenched around the railing. "Do you think I would do that, Quin? You're her mother. She loves you—"

"Not anymore," she interrupted, tears making her voice thick and quavery.

Hesitantly, wishing he didn't need to, wishing he hadn't waited this long, he touched her, gently turning her toward him, drawing her awkwardly against him. "She still loves you, Quin. She's just hurt. We're all hurt."

Her tears flowing as freely as the rain, she whispered, "I'm sorry, Mac. I made a mistake, and I'm so sorry."

He held her close, stroking her hair, and wished it didn't feel so damned right. He wished he could hold her like this forever. He wished he wouldn't ever need to hold her again.

Right. And maybe he would never need to breathe again, either.

After a time, her tears dried, and the delicate little shivers that rippled through her faded. Still, he held her. As angry as he was, as betrayed as he felt, he couldn't let go so easily. He couldn't give up the closeness.

But finally she pulled away from him. She put a few feet between them, then wiped her cheeks and breathed deeply. "Where do we go from here, Mac?"

He answered honestly. "I don't know."

"I had such hopes," she said softly, sadly. "Such dreams."

It was sheer lunacy to ask, but he did. "About what?"

"Us. Cady. Being a family. Falling in love."

Raw pain gripped him. It was one thing for him to think about marriage to Quin, about love and being a family. He'd had such dreams for a long, long time. But it hurt too much to hear *her* mention those same things. "You lied to me, Quin. You kept my daughter from me. I can never get back the time with her that you stole from me. I can't replace those years. I can't share that part of her life."

"I know." Her voice turned wistful again. "I don't blame you for hating me."

He approached her again, touched her again, laying his hand against her cheek. Her skin was cool and damp from her tears. "I wish it was that simple," he said regretfully.

"You don't have to see me," she offered. "I'll stay out of your way. You can see Cady whenever you want, and I'll— I'll—"

He brushed his lips across hers, silencing her. "Do you think not seeing you makes me forget you, Quin? Do you think it will make me stop wanting you? Do you think it'll make me stop—" Abruptly he broke off. *Loving you.* That was what he'd been about to say. She had to know he was in love with her; it wasn't as if it was anything he'd been able to hide. Still, he'd never said the words to her. He couldn't say them now, not like that.

"Mac, please..."

He touched his mouth to hers again, cutting off whatever

Finally a Father

she'd been about to say. Please don't do this? Please don't kiss me? Please don't leave me? Please don't hurt me?

He didn't know.

He didn't care.

All he cared about was *this*—being close to her. Touching her. Kissing her. He cared about having his tongue in her mouth and her body against his. He cared about feeling her heartbeat grow rapid and unsteady. He cared about the soft little sigh that passed between them, about the hunger and the desire and, God help him, the love he felt for her.

Those were the things he cared about, even if they were wrong. They couldn't make love, no matter how desperately he wanted to. Not with Cady in the house. Not when it wouldn't solve anything. Not when all their problems would still be there when their passion was gone. Not when it would only hurt them more.

Feeling as if he were destroying his own soul, he ended the kiss and walked to the screen door. There he paused and looked back at her. "I wish to hell it was that simple, Quin," he said, and then he left, stepping out into the rain, walking quickly around the house to his car. Quickly away from her.

If hatred was all he felt for her, he could walk away without looking back. Without pain. He could see her and not want her. He could deal with her without feeling so betrayed, so hurt and—worst of all—so hopelessly in love.

If hatred was all he felt, this misery would be gone. His bed wouldn't feel so lonely. His heart wouldn't feel so empty.

If hatred was all he felt, he would be untouched by this—seeing her. Hearing her cry. Knowing she was hurting. He wouldn't care. He wouldn't share her pain. He wouldn't want—wouldn't need—to make it better for her.

But she touched him. God help him, she touched him in ways no one else ever had. He wasn't sure he could live with her, wasn't sure he could forgive her for what she'd done, but he was damned sure of one thing.

He sure as hell couldn't live without her.

* * *

When Mac arrived to take Cady to dinner Wednesday evening, Quin breathed a sigh of relief—not because she was happy to see him, although of course she was, but because she needed a break from her daughter. Every day lately had been hard, but this afternoon Cady had been particularly difficult. Particularly angry.

It had started when Quin had come home early from work and interrupted Cady's games with the neighborhood kids. Cady hadn't been happy about having to leave her play, about having to go inside in the middle of the day and clean up for a stupid doctor's appointment. She had pouted all through the checkup, acting as if she couldn't possibly get away from Quin fast enough; then, perversely, when they'd gotten home, she had stayed close just to annoy her. When that had lost its appeal, she had called her grandmother.

Quin's patience had just about run out.

But Cady's anger had a long way to go.

"Hey, Mac," Quin greeted him when she answered the door. He looked handsome in jeans and a snug red T-shirt with USMC in gold block letters across the front. She wanted to reach out to him, wanted to just touch him or put her arms around him or something, so badly that she had to shove her hands into the pockets of her own jeans to keep from doing it. "Come on in. Cady's in the living room."

"She had her checkup today for her arm, didn't she?"

"Yes. They X-rayed it and said everything looks fine."

He studied her for a moment, then glanced through the wide door into the living room. Cady was sprawled across the couch and the coffee table, the USS *North Carolina* ball cap pulled low over her eyes, her attention stubbornly locked on the television. "She giving you a hard time?"

Quin tried to smile, but her mouth wouldn't cooperate. "She's adjusting."

"Slowly?"

"I figure she may get over some of that anger in about twenty years or so."

"I'll talk to her—"

Finally a Father

"No," she interrupted, touched that he'd offered but certain it would do more harm than good. Right now Cady was taking out all her resentment on Quin; if Mac interfered, she might easily turn some of it on him. "Take care of your own relationship with her. Don't worry about mine."

Looking away from her uncomfortably, he remembered the items he was carrying and offered them to her. "I got your mail and newspaper."

"Thanks." She accepted them, laying the paper on the hall table, sorting through the small stack of envelopes. There was a statement from the insurance company, no doubt regarding Cady's arm, one bill, three pieces of junk mail and a greeting card. For a long time she stared down at the cheery yellow envelope, looking a little ragged now after going to Morehead City and coming back again.

She hadn't cried in three days, had thought she was all cried out, but the tears that formed instantly proved her wrong. Her hands shaking, she laid the mail on the table, abruptly turned around and went down the hall to the kitchen. She was resting her hands on the counter, pushing hard against it, and biting her lower lip—anything to keep her emotions under control—when Mac, the offending card in hand, came to stand beside her.

He didn't say anything right away. He didn't have to ask for an explanation—he could read her parents' address, could read the note in her mother's neat hand: Return to Sender. He understood what it meant.

Before he found anything to say, she rushed in. "I have a favor to ask of you. Cady's been invited to spend a few days with my parents, and I think she should go, only I...I can't take her. Would you mind driving her up there after dinner this evening?"

"Why don't you come to dinner with us and ride along?"

As sweet as it was to be invited, she shook her head. "I can't do that." Cady would be angry if she went out with them, and her mother would be angry if she showed up at their house. She couldn't face any more anger tonight. She just couldn't bear it.

"What's in the card, Quin?"

She found a few dishes on the counter to rinse and started that, her movements graceless and uncoordinated. But after she dropped the same saucer three times, Mac shut off the water, dried her hands and turned her to face him. She tried to pull away, but he held her tighter. "It's a card for my parents," she said at last. "Friday is their thirty-second anniversary."

And her mother had sent it back unopened.

Oh, God, she couldn't stand this.

After a long still moment, he began pulling, drawing her nearer, folding her into his embrace. "I'm sorry," he murmured, stroking her hair. "Quin, I'm sorry."

"No, Mac," she whispered, pulling against him, even though in his arms was exactly where she wanted to be. She wanted to lean against him, wanted to rely on his strength for a while, wanted to forget everything that was wrong and, for just this moment, savor what was right. She wanted it so desperately that she ached.

But that was all she could have—*just this moment*—and that was why she resisted. It would be wonderful for just this moment to feel his arms around her, to feel his warmth, to be intimately close to him. But a moment didn't last, and then he would let her go, and she would be more alone than ever. She would feel emptier than ever.

But he held her in spite of her protest, held her close, one arm around her, his free hand stroking her hair. He held her and warmed her and soothed her and made her wonder how he could be so gentle and so unforgiving at the same time. How could he hate her and care that she was hurting? How could he be so angry with her and yet want to be so close to her?

After a time, just when she'd begun to relax, just when she'd begun to draw strength from him, he raised her chin so he could see her face. His gaze was so dark, so intense. What was he searching for? she wondered. Regret? Sorrow? Peni-

Finally a Father   231

tence? He would find all those things and more. Pain. Grief. Guilt.

Love.

"Quin..." His voice was low and husky, his expression mixed. After a moment, he lifted her hand from his chest, raised it to his mouth and pressed a kiss to her palm, then released her.

At least he did it reluctantly, she comforted herself. He let her go a little at a time, as if he couldn't quite bear doing it. God help her, she couldn't bear it.

"Get Cady's clothes together," he said softly as his hand slid away from hers. "I'll take her."

She wanted to protest again, wanted to throw herself into his arms and beg him to hold her just a little while longer. She wanted to sink to the floor in a huddle and cry until she couldn't cry—until she couldn't grieve—anymore.

Instead she gave him an unsteady smile, murmured, "Thank you, Mac," and started for the stairs.

"Why are you mad?"

Cady's question broke the silence of the last fifteen miles and drew Mac's attention her way. She was still wearing that cap, but finally it was pushed up on her forehead where he could see her eyes. Eyes more like Quin's than ever—dark, expressive, wounded. "What makes you think I'm mad?"

"You've hardly spoken all evening, and the closer we get to Grandma's, the faster you drive and the harder you hold the steering wheel. If you didn't want to bring me up here, we could've waited until after her date and Aunt Rochelle would've picked me up. Are you mad 'cause I wouldn't tell Mom goodbye?"

Quin had told him not to interfere, but damn it, Cady was his daughter. He had a right to interfere. "Are you going to hate her forever?"

"Maybe."

"Why do you want to hurt her, Cady?"

She turned to look out the side window. "She lied to me.

She's ruined everything. I used to have a great big family who loved me, and she took all that away."

"Everyone still loves you, kid."

"Grandma Ellis?" she demanded. "Grandpa Ellis? Uncle Mike and Uncle Greg and all the others? I'm not their granddaughter anymore. I'm not really an Ellis. I'm not related to them at all. I bet they never want to see me again. I know they hate Mom, and they're probably gonna hate me, too."

Slowing down, Mac turned off the road at the first available place, the parking lot of a small convenience store. There he twisted in his seat to face her. "No one's going to hate you, Cady," he said, removing her cap and brushing his hand over her hair. Such soft hair, so sleek and smooth. Like her mother's. "No one blames you for any of this. I don't know how things will change, honey. I guess maybe you'll get some idea while you're up here visiting. But no one's going to suddenly quit loving you."

"If they hate me, I'm never gonna quit hating *her*," she vowed darkly. "I'd rather have the rest of my family than Mom."

Her words increased the pain that had started deep inside when he'd seen Quin fight back her tears. "Would you really?" he asked, holding her hand, bending her fingers gently. "I'd rather have your mom than any of my family."

Pulling free, she wriggled out of her seat belt and rose onto her knees to face him. "No, Mac, don't say that. You're supposed to be mad at her, you're supposed to hate her, just like everyone else."

"Honey, it doesn't work that way. If I get angry with you, does that mean I have to hate you, too? Does it mean that right away, right then, because you did something wrong, I can't love you anymore?"

"But she *lied*, Mac!"

"She made a mistake, Cady. She was very young, younger than your aunt Lorna, and she made a mistake. She never meant for it to hurt so many people. She certainly never meant for it to hurt you." Or him, he silently acknowledged. She had

Finally a Father 233

been alone. She had thought he wasn't ever coming back. She had made what had seemed to be her best choice at the time, but it had been the wrong one. No matter how badly everyone involved was hurt, she hadn't meant for that to happen.

And even though she hadn't intended to hurt them all, it still had happened.

"Listen, sweetheart," he said, pulling Cady close. "I'm not asking you to forget all about it. I don't expect you to pretend that nothing happened. I understand that you're hurt and angry and confused. That's fine. I think we all are. Just remember that, no matter what she did, your mother loves you very much. Remember that she's hurt, too. Don't go out of your way to make things worse for her."

She held his gaze for a long time. There was such helpless anger in her eyes. Then abruptly she nodded, pulled back and plopped down in the seat again. After fastening her seat belt, she waited until he was ready to pull onto the highway again before she asked, "So do you?"

"Do I what?"

"You said if I do something wrong, does that mean you can't love me anymore. Do you?"

He looked at her, her gaze on her cast as if the dirty green fiberglass was the most interesting thing in the world right now, and he slowly smiled. He liked her a lot, he'd told Quin. He'd grown fond of her. He enjoyed her company. And, as far as they went, those declarations were true. But the more time he spent with Cady, the stronger the bond between them grew, the deeper the feelings got. Add the tie of family to that, and it became a lot more than fondness. A lot more permanent than liking.

After a moment's silence, she risked an uncertain glance his way, which immediately metamorphosed into a scowl. "Well?" she demanded.

"That's a difficult face to love," he teased, lifting her chin as she frowned harder.

"*Do* you?"

"Yes, Cady," he answered seriously. "I believe I do."

Her scowl slowly slid away, and for the first time all evening—for the first time, it seemed, in days—she grinned. "Of course you do. I'm your only child. You gotta love me."

Janice Austin came out of the house when she heard their arrival, and Cady went skipping off to meet her while Mac got her bags out of the back. She was staying here until Sunday evening, Quin had told him when she'd brought the suitcase and the smaller canvas bag downstairs. Maybe this break was what Cady needed to allow her to forgive her mother and get back on track. Maybe she would see that things hadn't really changed for her, that everyone did indeed still love and want her. Maybe she would realize that life could go on as normal if she only let it.

Maybe, after four days and four nights away from home, she would start to miss her mother.

After a hug and a kiss from her grandmother, Cady turned and yelled, "Thanks for the ride, Mac. See you Sunday." She went inside, and Janice came out to meet him and collect her things.

She had been polite the first time they'd met, cool and aloof the second time. This evening she made no attempt to disguise her dislike for him. "Thank you for bringing my granddaughter over," she said stiffly.

He set the bags down on the shell drive. "I brought her because Quin thought it would be best if she didn't come. She seems to have the impression that she's not welcome here."

Janice's cheeks turned a faint pink. "What's between Quin and us is family business, Mr. McEwen. It doesn't concern you."

"Cady's my daughter. Quin is my daughter's mother. What affects her concerns me."

She drew her shoulders back, the simple action making her seem taller and haughtier. "This is a difficult time for our family. I don't believe I care to discuss it with a stranger."

He almost smiled. If he'd been raised in one of these big houses, the way Quin was, instead of in a Philadelphia tene-

Finally a Father 235

ment, he would probably be too polite to force the conversation. But when it came to Quin and Cady, he didn't give a damn about being polite. "I'd think it would be a tough time for the Ellises, not you. They're the ones who have lost their granddaughter. They're the ones who found out that some part of their dead son isn't going to live on forever in Cady. You haven't lost anything."

"Oh, I see. We haven't lost anything. What about our pride, Mr. McEwen? What about trust? Liz Ellis has been my best friend all my life, and I can hardly look her in the eye. Quin lied to us. She shamed us in front of our best friends. She deceived our family and David's for ten years for her own convenience. She gave his parents a granddaughter to love and help raise, then callously took her away."

He found himself impatiently repeating the same thing he'd told Cady. "She made a mistake."

"She certainly did. Her mistake was in getting involved with you." She bent to pick up Cady's bags, then abruptly straightened to face him again. "Can you imagine how we felt, hearing her talk about being unfaithful to David? We couldn't have loved him more if he'd been our own son. They had been together all their lives. Everyone had always known they would one day be married. It was what they wanted, what we all wanted. They were perfect for each other. There was such joy in our families when they did finally marry, and such shock when he died. His death devastated both our families. It was only the news that Quin was pregnant with his baby that kept us going. And ten years later she waltzes in here and says, 'Gee, Mom, Dad, I lied. Cady isn't David's daughter. Her father is some—some *Marine* I had a one-night fling with. Sorry.' Do you have any idea how we felt? Can you even begin to imagine our shame?"

He wondered how she did that—turn marine into some sort of epithet. She made it sound as if Quin had gone to bed with some total stranger, someone she didn't know and would never see again. She made their one evening together sound cheap.

"Exactly what is it you're so ashamed of, Mrs. Austin?"

he asked quietly. "Cady's still the same person. The fact that she's my daughter instead of David's doesn't change who she is."

"I am ashamed of my daughter. She betrayed the man she loved," she said stiffly. "She betrayed our best friends who have loved her like a daughter. She made a mockery of her marriage vows. She made a mockery of our love for her."

"So your love for her was contingent upon her being faithful and true to David, to your idea of the perfect man for her." He shook his head in disgust. "Well, he wasn't perfect, Mrs. Austin, not for her. You say you couldn't have loved him more if he'd been your son. That's exactly how Quin loved him—like a brother. She wasn't in love with him, and she would have realized it before it was too late, before marrying him, if she'd been given a chance. If everyone hadn't *expected* her to marry him. If everyone hadn't made her feel as if she had to marry him, as if she didn't have the right to even look at another man."

The pale pink in her cheeks had turned darker as he spoke. Now it was mottled red, and it extended down her throat. She looked furious with him...and just a little guilty. Why? Because she did love her daughter less for not remaining faithful to David? Because she knew she had pressured Quin into a marriage she wasn't ready for to a man she didn't...

"You knew she wasn't in love with him, didn't you?"

The guilt increased.

"You knew, but you pushed her to marry him anyway. You were so anxious to see your family linked with your precious lifelong best friend's family that you didn't care whether they were happy. You didn't give a damn whether they were in love."

"They were best friends," she said, her voice tautly controlled, the words carefully enunciated. "They adored each other. That was far more important than the sort of love you're talking about."

"The sort of love I'm talking about is what marriages are made of. You achieved your goal, Mrs. Austin. You got Quin

Finally a Father

and David married. But you couldn't have kept them together. If David hadn't died, their marriage would have ended before Cady was born. If they'd been in love, maybe they could have dealt with it. But all the adoration in the world couldn't have saved them.''

''And are you and Quin 'in love,' Mr. McEwen?'' she asked snidely. ''She lied to you, too. She deprived you of your daughter's love for more than nine years. She preferred her husband's name for your baby over yours. She preferred to raise Cady without a father over letting you be her father. Are you going to deal with that? Or is your 'love' not strong enough to save you?''

Now it was Mac's face that was hot, and he felt more than a touch of the shame she'd mentioned earlier. Hearing the sound of voices, he glanced away to see Cady and her grandfather coming out of the house. They were holding hands, and he was listening intently to whatever she had to say.

Looking back at Janice, he met her gaze unflinchingly. ''That's a good question, Mrs. Austin. I think our conversation this evening has given me the answer.''

Breaking away from Quin's father, Cady raced along the driveway, skidding to a stop beside Mac, spraying bits of shell and dust over his shoes. ''You're still here,'' she announced unnecessarily. ''What're you guys talking about?''

''About what a nosy brat you are,'' he teased.

''Mac.'' Mr. Austin extended his hand, and Mac shook it. ''It's nice seeing you again. Thanks for bringing Cady up. I told her either Rochelle or I could drive down and get her after dinner, but she was too impatient.''

''It was no problem. I wanted to deliver something else, too.'' Walking back to the car, he reached in the open window and pulled out the yellow envelope he'd stashed on the dash. Her hand trembling, Janice Austin reached for it, but he gave it to her husband instead.

The older man's expression changed from curious to quizzical to angry. He gave his wife a sharp look, then quietly said, "Tell Quin I'll call her later. Tell her it would mean a lot to me if she would join us for the party Saturday."

Mac nodded, then crouched in front of Cady. He opened his mouth to speak, but with a giggle, she slid her arm around his neck and interrupted him. "I know. Be good, obey everyone, even Aunt Lorna, and don't get my cast wet."

"You forgot 'brush your teeth,'" he reminded her dryly. "Actually, I was going to say that I hope you have a good time. I hope things are better when you come home Sunday. I hope you find the answers to some of your questions."

Leaning forward, she laid her hand against his cheek. "That's a difficult face to love," she mimicked, then hugged him tight and whispered in his ear, "but I believe I do."

Chapter 13

Quin sat alone on the porch swing, one foot drawn onto the seat, the other on the floor for an occasional push. It was early Sunday evening, another still evening, but this time the stillness had nothing to do with an impending storm. This time it came from within.

These past four days had been the loneliest in her life. One moment Wednesday she had been eager for Mac to take Cady away and give her a little peace. The instant they'd left, though, she had wanted to call them back, to plead with their daughter to stay home where she belonged.

Mac had called her later that night. He told her about giving her card to her father, about her dad's invitation to yesterday's anniversary celebration, and he'd done it without apology. She didn't mind that he'd taken the card without asking—she was touched that he'd thought it important enough to bother with—although his actions had probably led to an argument between her parents. But she did mind the distant, impersonal manner in which he'd told her about it.

That was the last she'd heard from him—the last she'd heard

from anyone. In spite of her father's invitation, she had skipped yesterday's festivities. Her presence would only lead to problems, she had reasoned, and, after all, it was her mother's anniversary, too. She had the right to exclude whomever she wanted from the party.

There hadn't been a single goodnight call from Cady. That first night she had lain awake long past her daughter's bedtime, waiting and hoping. Thursday night she had waited, too. Friday she had stared at the phone, willing it to ring, and last night she'd given up all hope.

But Cady would be home soon. Mac was bringing her.

And even once they got here, she would probably still be alone and, oh, so lonely.

She picked up the book she'd been reading—trying to read—and opened it on her lap. It was uncomfortably warm out here, but she preferred that over the silence inside. Besides, chances were good that Mac would drop Cady off, then leave again. If that was the case, at least this way she would get to see him.

She hadn't read more than a page or two, and barely a word of that had registered in her mind, when she heard the sports car. Never mechanically inclined, she found it surprising that she could recognize its particular sound, that she could hear its engine and know before seeing the car that it was Mac's.

He pulled into the driveway and shut off the engine. Cady climbed out, leaving her bags, as usual, for someone else to carry. "Can I go over to Matthew's?" she asked, already heading in that direction.

"Ask your mother first," came Mac's reply.

"You know you can give me permission."

"And you know I'm not going to."

With a sigh, she came as far as the porch steps. Two weeks ago, Quin thought sadly, if Cady had been away for four days, she would have come racing up to the porch, taking the steps two at a time, and she would have thrown her arms around her mother, telling her, at the same time, what she'd done and how much she had missed her.

Finally a Father   241

This evening she simply stood ten feet away, looking awkward and ill at ease. "Can I go to Matthew's for a minute?" she asked.

"All right—but only for a minute."

Spinning around, she rushed off across the yard, skidded to a stop at the curb to look in both directions, then dashed across the street.

Mac came up the steps, set Cady's bags beside the door, then came on over and sat down at the other end of the swing. "If I had half her energy…"

Quin's smile was hesitant and unsteady. "I know. When she was little, I would pick her up after work and come home, and she'd have a list of six thousand things we needed to do before bedtime—everything from taking a walk to playing board games to reading books and playing catch. I kept her bedtime at seven-thirty long after she was old enough to stay up later just so I could have a little time to rest, grade papers and go over my lesson plans for the next day."

Fingering the chain that supported the swing, he asked, "So how were your four days of peace and quiet?"

"Too peaceful. Too quiet." She closed the book and, crossing her arms, hugged it to her chest. "What have you been up to?" She wanted details, wanted to know how he'd filled his time without her and Cady. She wanted to know what he found to do to make the emptiness more bearable.

She wanted to know if he missed her.

If he still wanted her.

If he might ever forgive her.

"Nothing much. Cady says you didn't show up for your parents' party yesterday."

"No," she murmured. "I decided I would rather stay home alone than go where I wasn't wanted."

"Your father wanted you there."

"But my mother didn't." She hesitated, hating this uneasiness between them, hating knowing that she was the cause of it. "Did Cady have a good time?"

"She said she had fun. She said David's parents didn't treat her any differently than before, that everyone still loves her and no one blames her." Finally he looked at her. "She said the Ellises told her she could still call them Grandma and Grandpa if it's all right with us. I told her it was. It's not as if she's getting any grandparents from me who might mind."

"I appreciate that. I know she's been worried about losing people she'd always known as family."

He shifted on the swing to face her. "Have you?"

"Been worried? Not really. I trust both the Austins and the Ellises to realize that Cady's the innocent one. They know it was my fault. They're not having any problem blaming me—"

"Have you been worried about losing your family?"

Smiling sadly, she answered with painful honesty. "I've been too busy worrying about losing you and Cady to give much thought to my family."

"Do you think that's going to happen?" He looked and sounded so serious, so hard. She wanted to relax the harsh set of his features, but she didn't know how. She didn't think there was anything she could do—short of going back ten years and changing their lives—that could take away that dark look.

Her sigh disturbing the heavy air, she replied, "I think eventually Cady will get over it. It might take a long time before she can like me again, and I'm sure it will be a very long time before she trusts me again, but someday she'll forgive me. She's stubborn, but she's fair. She doesn't generally hold grudges."

"And me?"

That little knot of pain that was always in her stomach lately started expanding. "I don't know, Mac," she whispered. "You're the only one who can answer that."

"You know we can't go on like this."

That sounded too grim. Too final. Too much like goodbye. *I can,* she thought, panic fluttering in her chest. It hurt—seeing him but not being with him, not being able to make him understand, not being able to love him. It hurt knowing that it was all her fault, that she had hurt him and destroyed what had been the sweetest relationship she'd ever known. It hurt

Finally a Father   243

like hell knowing there was nothing she could do to make it right again.

But it beat the alternative: having a cordial relationship for the sake of their daughter. Being polite and distant. Seeing him only when he picked Cady up and dropped her off. Passing messages through Cady. Never talking, never touching, never kissing.

"We've got some hard decisions to make, Quin," he continued. "We've got to—"

The sound of Cady's voice from the street interrupted him. "You did it on purpose, Jeffrey, just like always!" she shouted, her voice thick with tears. "One of these days I'm gonna hurt you, and you'll be sorry!" Spinning around, she came across the yard, her right arm held protectively close.

"Oh, no," Quin whispered, remembering the way she'd held her broken arm, starting to rise slowly from the swing.

Cady stomped to the top of the steps. "Look at my arm!" she demanded, holding it up for inspection.

Quin sank back down, her heart rate settling a bit. It was nothing as serious as a fracture this time, although Cady had lost a good deal of skin from her elbow to her wrist. "Did Jeffrey push you down on the rocks again?"

"Yes, and he did it on purpose." Defiance was slowly giving way to tears now. "I don't care if you said I can't, Mac, when it's time to get my cast off, I'm gonna break it over his head."

"Jeffrey... Isn't he the one who helped you break your arm?" Mac asked.

"Yes."

"And he's pushed you on the rocks before?"

"*Yes*. He's just a big bully, and I hate him!" She came closer, moving slowly so she could examine the blood gathering on her skin.

"Want me to have a talk with him?" The gentle teasing in his voice touched Quin, but it made Cady scowl harder.

"You can't. He's a tattletale. He'd go and tell his dad."

"Should I be afraid of his dad?"

Cady surprised Quin by giving her a conspiratorial look. "He's big, isn't he? He's a giant. He's seven feet tall—"

"Maybe six and a half," Quin corrected.

"And he's got muscles like this." Using both hands, she formed dinner-plate-sized circles in the air. "He'd probably squish you like a bug. Once he yelled at Mom. He could've picked her up in one hand like a rag doll and thrown her across the yard, but she yelled back anyway."

For once, Quin thought with a bittersweet smile, Cady wasn't exaggerating. Jeffrey's father *could* have done just that, but she'd stood up to him anyway—for all the good it had done. Jeffrey had continued doing whatever he wanted. Of course, Cady and the other kids in the neighborhood had continued playing with him.

She settled back against the swing again. "You need to get that washed up. You can show Mac where the antiseptic is."

There was a curious stillness that swallowed up the last of her words. Cady and Mac exchanged glances; then they both looked at her, and Cady, managing little more than a mumble, asked, "Can't you do it?" As an afterthought, in the voice of the little girl Quin so dearly loved, she added, "Please?"

The pain in her stomach began receding at the same time the lump grew in her throat. Who would have believed that one day she'd be thrilled to be asked to patch up her daughter's scrapes? It was definitely the best thing to happen to her in the past ten days. "Sure," she softly agreed. "Let's go into the kitchen."

There she washed her hands while Mac lifted Cady onto the counter. Her daughter voluntarily endured her touch for the first time in days, wincing as she washed the injury, twisting and exclaiming out loud when she applied antiseptic. When Quin was done, Cady sat there, blowing on the scrape in an attempt to ease the stinging. "I'm really going to get Jeffrey for this," she announced darkly. "I'll make him sorry he ever messed with me."

With a laugh, Mac lifted her down again. "Did you ever

consider that maybe Jeffrey likes you and just doesn't know how to show it?"

She gave him a dry look. "Oh, puh-leeze," she said sarcastically. "Do you wanna make me hurl?" Then, heading for the door, she said in her airiest voice, "I'm not gonna like boys until I'm at least Mom's age. It seems safer that way."

"It certainly does," Quin murmured as she gathered the washcloth and towel she'd used. She took them into the laundry room, then returned to put the antiseptic back in the cabinet.

She was delaying, Mac thought as he watched her. She didn't want to pick up the conversation Cady had interrupted. She didn't want to hear anything else he had to say on the subject.

Well, she had to hear it, because he'd meant what he said. They couldn't go on this way. He was miserable, she was miserable, and Cady... Bless her heart, Cady just might be starting to deal with her anger. But it would be easier for her if things were settled between him and Quin.

It would certainly be easier for *him*.

At last Quin had done all she could do. Stopping in the center of the room, her fingers laced together, she faced him. "I guess we can continue our talk now," she said softly, reluctantly.

He thought of different ways to say what he had to say. There were reasonable explanations, eloquent words to accurately describe his feelings, but he wasn't an eloquent man, and as for reasonable... When had that ever found a place in emotion?

Leaning back against the counter, he rested his hands there. His fingers automatically gripped the curved edge. "I've spent the last four days doing a lot of thinking, Quin, about Cady and about us, and I finally reached a decision."

Her eyes were shadowed with fear. "And what did you decide?"

He swallowed hard. It wasn't easy acting as if his future—hell, his entire *life*—wasn't on the line here. What if he told her and she said no? What if he was wrong in believing that she loved him? What if she believed there were too many strikes against them to guarantee any kind of a future?

And what if she didn't?

He hesitated, then cleared his throat. "I decided that I want to get married, Quin."

The color left her face, and the tension that knotted her fingers together spread all through her body. "Married?" she repeated in a near whisper.

He swallowed hard. This wasn't going exactly the way he'd intended. But they hadn't gotten to the important part yet. It would get better then. It had to. "I want to marry you, Quin. I want to live with you and Cady. I want to be a father to our daughter. I want to help raise her." His grin was nervous. "I want to prove your mother wrong."

She looked puzzled and anxious. Fluttery. "My mother? About what?"

"She thinks that finding out about Cady is going to end our relationship. She thinks we don't love each other enough to work through it. I want to prove to her that we do...at least, that I do...that we can..."

The tension drained from her body, and slowly, very slowly, she smiled. "Mac, are you saying that—"

He scowled at her. "I love you. I'm *in* love with you. I love you the way a man should love his wife, the way a father should love the mother of his child. I've always loved you, Quin, and I always will."

Just as slowly, her delighted smile faded. "But...what about me?"

His scowl intensifying, he reached out to catch hold of her, to pull her close. "I'm operating under the assumption here that you love me, too," he said gruffly.

She raised her hand to his face, stroking his cheek, his jaw, down his throat. "Of course I love you, Mac," she said softly, wistfully. "But I was referring to—to Cady. To my secret. To my lies."

Holding her close with one arm around her waist, he used

Finally a Father

his free hand to tilt her head back. "We can't change what happened in the past, Quin. It's done. All we can do is choose how to live with it—whether we're going to let it rule the rest of our lives or if we're going to put it behind us and move on. The way I see it, we don't really have a choice. We can all be hurt and angry, and we can all suffer, or we can deal with it. We can be alone and unhappy, or we can make a future for ourselves. We can make a home for Cady. We can make a family for Cady."

"A family for Cady," she echoed, her voice soft, her tone wondrous. "We can do that, can't we?"

Pulling her closer until their bodies were in intimate contact, he grinned. "We can start right now." Then, growing solemn again, he prompted her. "So?"

Her smile was the only answer he needed, but she offered the words, too, with a hug and a sweet, sweet kiss. "Yes, Mac, I'll marry you. I'll marry you and love you forever."

The Beirut Memorial was located in a shady grove within yards of a busy street. It was a solemn place, made more so this morning by the ongoing memorial service, the prayers, the color guard, the relatives of the men whose names were on the wall. Quin shifted, her low heels sinking in the soft ground, and let her thoughts wander from the speeches.

Mac stood beside her, more handsome than ever in his dress blues. The coat, with its long sleeves and standing collar, looked uncomfortably warm to her under the October sun, but he didn't seem to notice. He looked serious, stern—at least until he felt her gaze on him. His glance was sweet, gentle and loving—oh, so loving. Moving unobtrusively, he took her hand in his. His palm was rough, his fingers callused, the fourth one cool where his wedding band rested.

Standing in front of him was Cady, wearing a dress for only the second time since last year's memorial service. It was the same dress she'd worn to Quin and Mac's wedding six weeks ago, pale yellow and very simple. No frills for this tomboy. She was quiet this morning, behaving as well as a bored nine-year-old could in shoes that pinched her toes and surely, she had insisted, were invented as punishment. Her own toes starting to ache, Quin was close to sharing her opinion.

The past few months hadn't been easy ones for Cady, she thought regretfully. Things were improving—had been steadily improving since Mac had moved into the house following their wedding. There were still times when Cady turned against Quin, still times when Quin's word wasn't enough to satisfy her, and she still called her father by his name. Mac didn't pressure her, but Quin knew it hurt him. She knew he wanted to make Cady fully his own—wanted to be her daddy and not just her father, wanted her to have his name, wanted David completely out of her life—but he made no demands. He was willing to give her time.

Time. Everyone needed time. Her mother still hardly spoke to her and refused to accept Mac as part of the family. Janice had come to their small wedding at the chapel on base, but she'd found little cause for celebration.

Her sister Lorna was still resentful, too. Quin suspected it was because Lorna saw too clearly the similarities between Quin's relationship with David and her own relationship with Greg Ellis. She was afraid that the love she felt for Greg wasn't the happily-ever-after kind of love she wanted it to be. She was afraid that one day she would be tempted by another man, as Quin had been before her. Quin had considered talking to her frankly, openly, but had never followed through. Her sister would have to make her own mistakes, just as she had.

She would have to find a man who would forgive them. Just as Mac had.

A light breeze drifted across the crowd. She smelled aftershave and cologne and, nearly masked by them, the sweet woodsy fragrance of the pines overhead. The memorial was a lovely place to come and remember, but after today, she thought with a hint of bittersweetness, she didn't think she would be coming again. She had loved David, had loved him dearly, but he was her past.

Mac was her future.

Finally a Father

At last the service ended, and Mac turned to her. "Your family and the Ellises are over there," he said, gesturing toward the brick path. "Do you want to say hello?"

"Do I have to?"

He gave her a chiding look. "Go on. I'm going to look at the names."

Hello was about all she said to the small gathering. Mr. Ellis was cool, her mother rude. Neither Lorna nor Greg nor Mike spoke to her. Only her father and Mrs. Ellis seemed genuinely happy to see her.

She didn't care, she told herself as she headed toward the wall. Mac would rather have you, Cady had once told her, than any of his family. Well, she would rather have him and Cady than all of her family. She could give up anyone and everyone in the world, as long as she had her daughter and her husband.

When she joined him a few feet from the wall, Mac automatically wrapped his arm around her waist, drawing her close. He studied her for a moment, searching for some sign as to how those few brief moments with her family had gone. The same as ever, he saw. But he was a patient man. He believed in his heart that one day they would forgive her, that one day they would welcome her back into their close circle. Until then, though, he would do his damnedest to make sure she wasn't lacking for love.

Slowly he shifted his attention back to Cady as she traced one finger over the engraving of David's name. She seemed unusually solemn, touching the stone carefully as if it might break, outlining each letter as if she could imprint the memory of it in her skin, in her very pores. After a moment, she flattened her palm there, then sighed heavily before turning away.

When she saw them watching her, her eyes lit up, and she suddenly smiled. "Do I have to go to school? By the time I go home and change, it'll be lunchtime, and then I've already missed half the day, so I might as well stay home, right?"

"Wrong," Quin replied. "You have a math test this afternoon. You're not missing it."

The look in Cady's eyes grew calculating and sly as she turned her smile on him. "You know, you have an equal vote on this. Since you're not going to work, and Mom's not, it's really not fair for me to have to go to school. You can give me your permission to stay home."

He grinned. The fact that he and Quin had both taken the entire day off had at least as much to do with Cady's going to school as her math test did. It wasn't often they got an entire afternoon alone and uninterrupted. "Sorry, kid."

"Oh, please," she wheedled. "I can make up the test tomorrow. Please, Daddy?"

His grin slipped away as he stared down at her. *Daddy.* He had never asked her to call him that, had never pushed the issue, but it had hurt, damn it, every single time she had called him Mac. And now, out of the blue, she'd said it. Was that what the scene at the wall a moment ago had been about—saying goodbye to the father she'd grown up with so she could make room for the one she now lived with?

Releasing Quin, he bent and drew Cady into his arms, hugging her tightly. "You're a sweetheart, you know that?" he asked huskily. Then, standing up again, he went on. "But you still have to go to school."

"You're no fun," she said, her mouth curving down in a pout. But she clasped both his hand and Quin's as they started along the path toward the parking lot. After they'd gone only a few yards, she let go and skipped on ahead.

"Personally, Mac," Quin said with a delighted smile, "I think you're lots of fun."

"That's because you love me."

"Actually, I think it's because you love me, and you do it so very well." Moving closer, she murmured, "What do you say we make her wear that dress to school, take her there now and then go on home?"

It was a tempting proposition, but reluctantly he turned it down. Cady had never worn a dress to school in her life, and she wasn't about to start now. Trying to make her would be like trying to change the tides. "We'd better take her home

Finally a Father

and let her change. It'll only take—what? An hour and a half?—to do that, take her to lunch, take her to school and get back home. Then we'll have the rest of the day to ourselves.''

"Or at least what's left of it." Quin laughed. "Ah, the joys of parenthood."

Claiming her hand, he held her close as they walked along the grassy shoulder of the road to where Cady waited alongside their car. The joys of parenthood, he thought with more satisfaction than he would have believed possible. *So,* Cady had told him one summer night, *you're finally a father.*

But there was something even better, he'd discovered lately, something even more precious than merely being a father.

Now they were finally a family.

* * * * *

SILHOUETTE SPOTLIGHT

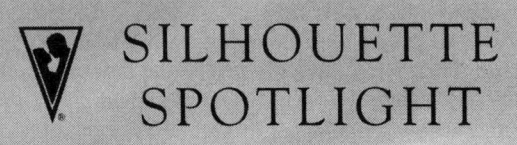

Two bestselling novels in one volume by favourite authors, back by popular demand!

The Millionaire Affair

Mystery Man *by Diana Palmer*
Mandy Meets a Millionaire *by Tracy Sinclair*

Handsome, powerful and wealthy. These sexy millionaire men had everything except true love – until now!

Available from 17th September 2004

Available at most branches of WHSmith, Tesco, ASDA, Martins, Borders, Eason, Sainsbury's and all good paperback bookshops.

2 FULL LENGTH BOOKS, FOR £5.99

NORA ROBERTS

No. 1 *New York Times* bestselling author

ENGAGING THE ENEMY

A Will and a Way & Boundary Lines

Available from 17th September 2004

Available at most branches of WHSmith, Tesco, Martins, Borders, Eason, Sainsbury's and most good paperback bookshops.

Available from 17th September 2004

Available at most branches of WHSmith, Tesco, Martins, Borders, Eason, Sainsbury's and most good paperback bookshops.

1004/055/SH84

Maitland Maternity Christmas

Where the luckiest babies are born!

Muriel Jensen, Judy Christenberry, Tina Leonard

Available from 15th October 2004

Available at most branches of WHSmith, Tesco, ASDA, Martins, Borders, Eason, Sainsbury's and most good paperback bookshops.

SILHOUETTE®

Desire™ 2 in 1

are proud to introduce

DYNASTIES:
THE BARONES

Meet the wealthy Barones—caught in a web of danger, deceit and...desire!

Twelve exciting stories in six 2-in-1 volumes:

January 2004	**The Playboy & Plain Jane** *by Leanne Banks* **Sleeping Beauty's Billionaire** *by Caroline Cross*
March 2004	**Sleeping with Her Rival** *by Sheri WhiteFeather* **Taming the Beastly MD** *by Elizabeth Bevarly*
May 2004	**Where There's Smoke...** *by Barbara McCauley* **Beauty & the Blue Angel** *by Maureen Child*
July 2004	**Cinderella's Millionaire** *by Katherine Garbera* **The Librarian's Passionate Knight** *by Cindy Gerard*
September 2004	**Expecting the Sheikh's Baby** *by Kristi Gold* **Born To Be Wild** *by Anne Marie Winston*
November 2004	**With Private Eyes** *by Eileen Wilks* **Passionately Ever After** *by Metsy Hingle*

▼ SILHOUETTE®

*Sensation™ and Desire™ 2-in-1
are proud to present the brand-new series by
bestselling author*

MERLINE LOVELACE

TO PROTECT AND DEFEND

*These heroes and heroines were trained
to put their lives on the line, but their
hearts were another matter…*

A Question of Intent
Silhouette Sensation
September 2004

Full Throttle
Silhouette Desire 2-in-1
November 2004

The Right Stuff
Silhouette Sensation
December 2004

For the sake of their child

The Country Club

Texas... Now And Forever

Merline Lovelace

The Country Club

Book 12 available from 20th August 2004

COUNTRY/RTL/12

SILHOUETTE

INTRIGUE™

GEN/46/RTE5

Breathtaking romantic suspense.

His mysterious ways

Amanda Stevens

THE TRUEBLOOD
Dynasty

Isabella Trueblood made history reuniting people torn apart by war and an epidemic. Now, generations later, Lily and Dylan Garrett carry on her work with their agency, Finders Keepers.

Book Two available from 17th September

Available at most branches of WH Smith, Tesco, ASDA, Martins, Borders, Eason, Sainsbury's and all good paperback bookshops.

SILHOUETTE

INTRIGUE

*proudly presents
a brand-new series from*

Dani Sinclair

HEARTSKEEP

Behind the old mansion's closed doors, dark secrets lurk—and deeper passions lie in wait.

The Firstborn
October 2004

The Second Sister
November 2004

The Third Twin
December 2004

SILHOUETTE® Sensation™

presents...

Cherokee Corners

by Carla Cassidy

Where one family fights crime with honour—and passion!

Last Seen...
(May 2004)

Dead Certain
(August 2004)

Trace Evidence
(November 2004)